VOYAGE OF
THE BASILISK

～✦～

BY MARIE BRENNAN

A Natural History of Dragons
The Tropic of Serpents
Voyage of the Basilisk

Midnight Never Come
In Ashes Lie
A Star Shall Fall
With Fate Conspire

Warrior
Witch

VOYAGE OF THE
BASILISK

A MEMOIR BY LADY TRENT

Marie Brennan

TOR ®

A TOM DOHERTY ASSOCIATES BOOK

NEW YORK

VOYAGE OF THE BASILISK

Copyright © 2015 by Bryn Neuenschwander

Interior illustrations by Todd Lockwood

Map by Rhys Davies

Designed by Greg Collins

A Tor Book
Published by Tom Doherty Associates, LLC
175 Fifth Avenue
New York, NY 10010

www.tor-forge.com

Tor® is a registered trademark of Tom Doherty Associates, LLC.

The Library of Congress Cataloging-in-Publication Data is available upon request.

ISBN 978-0-7653-3198-4 (hardcover)
ISBN 978-1-4299-5636-9 (e-book)

Tor books may be purchased for educational, business, or promotional use. For information on bulk purchases, please contact the Macmillan Corporate and Premium Sales Department at 1-800-221-7945, extension 5442, or write to specialmarkets@macmillan.com.

First Edition: March 2015

Printed in the United States of America

0 9 8 7 6 5 4 3 2 1

OTHOLÉ

DAJIN

Yelang

Atuko'a

Hona'apia

'Iosale

Keonga

Rahuahane

Lahana

Opunui

Keonga

Raengawi

Kapa Hou

Puian Islands

Seungdal

Arinevi

Melatan Islands

Copahuac

VOYAGE OF
THE BASILISK

PREFACE

Depending upon your temperament, you may be either pleased or puzzled to see that I have chosen to include my time upon the *Basilisk* in my memoirs. It was, of course, a lengthy period in my life, totaling nearly two years in duration, and the discoveries I made in that time were not insignificant, nor were the effects of that journey upon my personal life. Seen from that perspective, it would seem odd were I to pass it by.

But those of you who are puzzled have good cause. Those two years are, after all, the most thoroughly documented period in my life. My contract with the *Winfield Courier* to provide them with regular reports meant that a great many in Scirland were kept apprised of my doings—quite apart from the reports that were written *about* me by others. Furthermore, my travelogue was later collected and printed as *Around the World in Search of Dragons*, and that title is still readily available from the publisher. Why, then, should I trouble to tell a story which is already so widely known?

Apart from the oddity of glossing over so major a period in my life, I have several reasons. The first is that my essays in the *Winfield Courier* were heavily skewed toward matters of exotic novelty, which was, after all, what their readers wanted to hear, though not the most apt depiction of my own experiences. Another is that I said little there of my personal affairs, and as a memoir is *expected* to be more personal, this is the ideal place to provide those elements which I excluded before.

But above all, this volume is intended to set the record straight, for part of what I said in those essays is an outright lie.

When I wrote to the *Winfield Courier* that I swam to Lahana after my adventure with the sea-serpent, and that during the excitement which followed I took a knock to the head and had to be sent to Phetayong to convalesce, not a word of it was true. I wrote those lines because I had no choice: my lengthy silence (which had persuaded a great many people back home that I was dead at last) must be broken with *some* kind of tale, and I could not give the honest one. Even had I wished to make public everything I had done, a high-ranking officer in His Majesty's Royal Navy had forbidden me to do so. Indeed, it is only with some effort now that I have persuaded certain government officials to change their minds—now, so many years later, when a new dynasty rules in Yelang and the events in question are no longer of any particular political relevance.

But they have granted their permission, and so at last I may tell the truth. I will not attempt to recount every day of my journey aboard the *Basilisk*; two years will not fit into one slim volume without substantial abridgement, and there is no point in repeating what I have said elsewhere. I shall instead focus on those portions which are either personal (and therefore new) or necessary to understanding what occurred at the end of my island sojourn.

All in good time, of course. Before the truth comes out, you will hear of Jacob and Tom Wilker; Heali'i and Suhail; and Dione Aekinitos, the mad captain of the *Basilisk*. You will also hear of wonders terrestrial and aquatic, ancient ruins and modern innovations, mighty storms, near drownings, the rigors of life at sea, and more kinds of dragon than you can shake a wing at. Though there is a great deal I will omit here, I will endeavour to make my tale as complete and engaging as I may.

Isabella, Lady Trent
Casselthwaite, Linshire
3 Seminis, 5660

PART ONE

*In which the memoirist
embarks upon her voyage*

ONE

Life in Falchester—Abigail Carew—A meeting of the Flying University—M. Suderac—Galinke's messenger—Skin conditions

A t no point did I form the conscious intention of founding an *ad hoc* university in my sitting room. It happened, as it were, by accident.

The process began soon after Natalie Oscott became my live-in companion, having been disowned by her father for running away to Eriga. My finances could not long support the two of us in my accustomed style, especially not with my growing son to consider. I had to surrender some portion of my life as it had been until then, and since I was unwilling to surrender my scholarship, other things had to go.

What went was the house in Pasterway. Not without a pang; it had been my home for several years, even if I had spent a goodly percentage of that time in foreign countries, and I had fond memories of the place. Moreover, it was the only home little Jacob had known, and I did question for some time whether it was advisable to uproot so young a boy, much less to transplant him into the chaotic environment of a city. It was, however, far more economical for us to take up residence in Falchester, and so in the end we went.

Ordinarily, of course, city life is far more expensive than rural— even when the "rural" town in question is Pasterway, which nowadays has become a direct suburb of the capital. But much of this expense assumes that one is living in the city for the purpose of enjoying its glittering social life: concerts and operas, art exhibitions and fashion, balls and drums and sherry breakfasts. I had no interest in such matters. My concern was with intellectual commerce, and in that regard Falchester was not only superior but much cheaper.

There I could make use of the splendid Alcroft lending library, now better known as one of the foundational institutions of the Royal Libraries. This saved me a great deal of expense, as my research needs had grown immensely, and to purchase everything I required (or to send books back to helpful friends via the post) would have bankrupted me in short order. I could also attend what lectures would grant a woman entrance, without the trouble of several hours' drive; indeed, I no longer needed to maintain a carriage and all its associated equipment and personnel, but rather could hire one as necessary. The same held true for visits with friends, and here it is that the so-called "Flying University" began to take shape.

The early stages of it were driven by my need for a governess. Natalie Oscott, though a good companion to me, had no wish to take on the responsibility of raising and educating my son. I therefore cast my net for someone who would, taking pains to specify in advance that my household was not at all a usual one.

The lack of a husband was, for some applicants, a selling point. I imagine many of my readers are aware of the awkward position in which governesses often find themselves—or rather, the awkward position into which their male employers often put them, for it does no one any service to pretend this happens by some natural and inexorable process, devoid of connection with anyone's behaviour. My requirements for their qualifications, however, were off-putting to many. Mathematics were unnecessary, as Natalie was more than willing to tutor my son in arithmetic, algebra, and geometry (and would, by the time he was ready for calculus, have taught it to herself), but I insisted upon a solid grounding in literature, languages, and a variety of sciences, not to mention the history not only of Scirland but other countries as well. This made the process of reviewing applicants quite arduous. But it paid an interesting dividend: by the time I hired Abigail Carew, I had also made the acquaintance of a number of young ladies who lacked sufficient learning, yet possessed the *desire* for it in spades.

I will not pretend I founded the Flying University in order to educate unsatisfactory governess candidates. Indeed, most of those young ladies I never saw again, as they moved on in search of less stringent employers. But the experience heightened my awareness of that lack in our society, and so once I had my subscription to the Alcroft, I made the contents of my library (both owned and borrowed) available to anyone who wished to make use of it.

The result was that, by the time my sea expedition began, on any given Athemer evening you might find anywhere from two to twenty people occupying my sitting room and study. The former room was a place of quiet reading, where friends might educate themselves on any subject my library could supply. Indeed, by then its reach extended far beyond my own shelves and items borrowed from the Alcroft, as it became a trading center for those who wished to avail themselves of others' resources. Candles and lamps were one point upon which I did not scrimp, and so they could read in perfect comfort.

The study, by contrast, was a place of conversation. Here we might ask questions of one another, or debate issues on which we held differing views. Often these discussions became quite convivial, the lot of us raising one another up from the darkness of ignorance and into the light of, if not wisdom, then at least well-informed curiosity.

On other occasions, the discussions might better be termed "arguments."

"You know I love wings as much as the next woman," I said to

Miriam Farnswood—who, as a lady ornithologist, *was* the next woman, and very fond of wings. "But you are overstating their significance in this instance. Bats fly, and so do insects, and yet no one is suggesting that *they* are close relatives of birds."

"No one yet has found evidence of bats laying eggs," she said dryly. Miriam was nearly twenty years my senior, and it was only in the last six months that I had ventured to address her by her given name. Not coincidentally, the last six months had also seen the commencement of this particular debate, in which we were very much at odds. "It's your own work that persuades me, Isabella; I don't know why you resist so strenuously. The skeletal structure of dragons shows many resemblances to that of birds."

She was referring, of course, to the hollow structure of the bones. This was not often to be found in reptiles, which I championed as the nearest relation to dragons. I said impatiently, "Hollow bones may easily be evolved on separate occasions. After all, that is what seems to have happened with wings, is it not? Much *less* common to evolve a new set of forelegs, where none were before."

"You think it more plausible that reptiles suddenly evolved wings, where none had previously been?" Miriam snorted. It was not a very ladylike snort. She was the sort of woman one expected to find tramping the countryside in tweeds with a gun under her arm and a bulldog at her side, probably one of her own breeding. The delicacy with which she moved when out birding was nothing short of startling. "Please, Isabella. By that reasoning, you *should* be arguing for their relation to insects. At least those have more than four limbs."

The reference to insects diverted me from what I had been about to say. "Sparklings do complicate the picture," I admitted. "I really am persuaded that they are an extremely dwarfish breed of dragon—though I am at a loss to explain how such a reduction in size might come about. Even those tiny dogs they have in Coyahuac are not so much smaller than the largest breed of hound."

My comment brought a quiet chuckle from a few feet away. Tom Wilker had been in conversation with the suffragette Lucy Devere, discussing the politics of the Synedrion, but their talk had momentarily flagged, and he had overheard me. It was not the first time he had been subjected to my thoughts on sparklings, which were an endless conundrum to me in matters of taxonomy.

We could hardly avoid eavesdropping on one another's words. My Hart Square townhouse was not so large as to give us much in the way of elbow room. And indeed, I often preferred it that way, for it encouraged us to wander from topic to topic and group to group, rather than separating off into little clusters for the duration of the evening. Tabitha Small and Peter Landenbury had been sharing their thoughts on a recent work of history, but as usual, Lucy had drawn them into her orbit. With Elizabeth Hardy rounding out their set, there were seven of us in my study, which more or less filled it to capacity.

Miriam's eyebrows had gone up at my digression from the point. I shook my head to clear it and said, "Be that as it may. I think you are reading too much into the fact that the quetzalcoatls of Coyahuac have feathers. They are not true dragons, by Edgeworth's definition—"

"Oh, come now, Isabella," she said. "You can hardly use Edgeworth as your defense, when you yourself have led the charge in questioning his entire theory."

"I have not yet reached any conclusions," I said firmly. "Ask me again when this expedition is done. With any luck, I will observe a feathered serpent with my own eyes, and then I will be able to say with more certainty where they fit in the draconic family."

The door opened quietly, and Abby Carew slipped through. She looked tired, even in the forgiving candlelight. Jake had been

running her ragged lately. The prospect of going on a sea voyage
had so fired his imagination that he could hardly be made to sit at
his lessons.

The notion of bringing my son along had come to me about two
years previously. When I first conceived the notion of a trip around
the world, to study dragons in all the places they might be found,
Jake had been a mere toddler—far too young to accompany me.
But such a expedition is not organized overnight, nor even in a
single year. By the time I was certain the expedition would happen, let alone had prepared myself for it, Jake was already seven.
Boys have gone to war at sea that young. Why should one not go
in the name of science?

I had not forgotten the opprobrium I faced when I went to Eriga, leaving my son behind. It seemed to me that the clear solu-
tion to this problem was not to stay forever at home, but rather to
bring him with me the next time. I saw it as a splendid educational
opportunity for a boy of nine. Others, of course, saw it as more of
my characteristic madness.

I excused myself to Miriam Farnswood and crossed the room
to meet Abby. She said, "Natalie sent me to tell you—"

"Oh dear," I sighed, before she could finish. A guilty look at the
clock confirmed my suspicion. "It has gotten late, hasn't it?"

Abby was kind enough not to belabor the point. The truth was,
I did not want to show my guests to the door. This was to be our
last gathering before I left—or rather I should say *my* last gathering, since Natalie would continue to host them in my absence. As
much as the upcoming voyage excited me, I would miss these evenings, where I could expand my mind and test its strengths against
people whose intelligence dwarfed mine. Thanks to them, my understanding of the world had grown far beyond its early, naive be-
ginnings. And I, for my part, had done what I could to share my

knowledge in return, especially with those individuals, male or female, whose opportunities had not been as great as mine.

I write in the past tense now; I caught myself *thinking* in the past tense then, and shook myself. I was going on a voyage, not relocating to the other side of the world forever. What had started in my sitting room was not ending tonight. My part in it was merely pausing.

They went without a fuss, though with a great many good wishes for safe travels and great discoveries. The farewells took more than a half hour in all. The last to depart was Tom Wilker, who had no need to say farewell; we would be going on the voyage together, for I could not imagine trying to conduct research without his assistance.

"Did I overhear you promising specimens to Mrs. Farnswood?" he asked, when it was just him, myself, and Natalie in the foyer.

"Yes, of birds," I said. "She will pay for them, or sell those she does not wish to keep for herself. It will be another source of funds, and a welcome one."

He nodded, though his smile was rueful. "I don't know when we'll find the time to sleep. Or rather, when *you* will find the time. I'm not the one who has promised regular reports to the *Winfield Courier*."

"I will sleep at night," I said, very reasonably. "Writing by lamplight is a terrible waste of oil, and there are not so many species of nocturnal birds as to keep me busy *every* night."

It got a laugh from him, as I had intended. "Sleep well, Isabella. You'll need your rest."

Natalie came out into the hall in time to bid him goodnight. When the door was shut behind him, she turned to face me. "Are you very tired, or can you spare a few moments?"

I was far too awake to sleep just yet, and would only read if I tried to go to bed. "Does it have to do with the arrangements for my absence?"

Natalie shook her head. We had been over those matters enough times already: my will, in case I should die; the transfer of my town-house to her temporary stewardship; how to contact me once I was abroad; all the logistical hedges that must be leapt before I could depart. She said, "I spoke with Mr. Kemble again today."

I sighed. "Come to my study. I shall want to sit for this, I think."

My worn old chair was some comfort to me while pondering a topic that was not comfortable at all. Once ensconced in its em-brace, I said to Natalie, "He wants me to make a deal with the Thiessois."

"He is at a standstill," Natalie said. "He has been for more than a year. The fine structure of dragonbone continues to elude him, and so long as it does, you do not have synthesis. M. Suderac's aer-ation process may be what we need."

The mere mention of this topic made me want to beat my head against my desk. Only the knowledge that Frederick Kemble had been beating his head against something far less yielding for nearly a decade now restrained me. Tom and I had hired him to create a synthetic replacement for preserved dragonbone, so that human society might enjoy the benefits of that substance without having to slaughter dragons to obtain it. Kemble had re-created its chem-ical composition, but the airy lattice of its structure, which reduced the already-slight weight without sacrificing strength, had proven less tractable.

Natalie was correct: the aeration process devised by M. Suderac might indeed help. I, however, could not abide the man—to the point where the mere thought of partnering with him for such a venture made me ill. He was a handsome Thiessois fellow, and clearly thought his good looks ought to earn him more than mere friendliness from me. After all, I was a widow, and if not as young as I had once been, I had not gathered so very much dust on the shelf yet. It was not marriage M. Suderac wanted from me; he had a wife, and even if he did not, I offered very little in the way of property to tempt him. He merely wanted unfettered access to my person. To say that I was disinclined to grant it to him is a howling understatement.

And yet, if financial partnership would save the lives of countless dragons . . .

The secret of preserving dragonbone was out in the world. That particular cat had escaped its bag before I went to Eriga, when thieves employed by the Marquess of Canlan broke into Kemble's laboratory and stole his notes, and Canlan subsequently sold them to a Yelangese company, the Va Ren Shipping Association. The fellows there seemed to have kept a relatively tight lid on their information, for it had not become common knowledge yet, but I knew it was spreading. Which meant the need for a synthetic substitute was urgent.

I weighed these factors, until my heart sat like lead in my chest. "I do not trust him," I said at last to Natalie. "I *cannot*. He is the sort of man who sees a thing and wants it, and thinks that alone entitles him to have it. I truly would not put it past him to crack the problem at last, but then keep the results for his own profit. And while I might forego my own stake if it meant having the answer, I cannot allow Kemble and the others to be robbed in such fashion."

Natalie dropped her head against the back of the chair, staring in resignation at the ceiling. "Well, I tried. You are not wrong about Suderac, I think—but I do not know how else we will make it happen."

"Perhaps *I* should try hiring thieves. They could break in and steal the secrets of the aeration process."

"Thank God you're about to get on board a ship," Natalie said. "Otherwise, I think you might honestly follow through."

She exaggerated—but not by much. For the sake of dragons, there was very little I would not do.

The next morning's post brought a number of letters, some of them from people who had not noticed that I was about to be gone from home for an extended period of time and would not have much chance to answer them. One, however, caught my eye.

The handwriting on the outside of the envelope was unfamiliar to me. It was not merely that I did not recognize the hand; the entire style of it was strange, as if written by a foreigner. And yet it reminded me of something, but I could not say what.

Curious, I slit the flap with my knife. The note inside was written on excellent paper, again in that strange hand. It was an invitation to join one Wademi n Oforiro Dara for lunch at the Salburn that day, if I was not already engaged.

Now I knew what the handwriting had evoked. I was still in occasional contact with Galinke n Oforiro Dara, the half-sister of the oba of Bayembe. This man's script showed traces of the same style, though in his case much fainter. From this I deduced that he was more accustomed to writing in Scirling than Galinke was.

Oforiro Dara. He was of the same lineage as Galinke. A brother? No, I was fairly certain she had no brothers born to the same mother, and the Yembe inherit their lineage names through the maternal line. He might be anything from Galinke's mother's sister's son to a far more distant cousin than that. But the connection was enough to make me dash off a quick acceptance and send it to the man's hotel. My alternative plans for lunch involved a quick meal gulped down while packing; this promised to be far more interesting.

In those days, I did not often dine at the Salburn—which is my polite way of saying that I could not really afford it. I minded very little; I have never been a gourmand. But it meant that Wademi n Oforiro Dara was either a wealthy man or well-funded by someone else, as lunch for two there was not a thing to undertake lightly.

I had no difficulty spotting him in the lobby. He was Yembe and dark, and dressed after their fashion in a wrapped and folded cloth, though he made concession to Scirland's cooler climate and stricter sense of propriety with a mantle over his upper body. The coloration was almost Scirling-sober, too: black and gold in a simple geometric pattern. He was already on his feet when I entered, and approached me immediately.

We exchanged Yembe greetings, which served to show me just how badly my accent and grammar had deteriorated. When he shifted to my native tongue, I apologized to him for it. "I'm afraid my command of Yembe has atrophied terribly for lack of use—and it was not good to begin with. Galinke and I correspond in Scirling."

His own Scirling was accented but fluent. "You should come for a visit! I hear that you are about to set off on a journey. Will you be stopping in Bayembe?"

"Would that I could go *everywhere*," I said. "But I'm afraid that my research requires me to expand my knowledge in breadth, rather than depth. I must devote my time to new areas and new species."

This was true, but not the entire story. I could not tell this man about my conversation with a certain member of the Synedrion (who shall remain nameless, though he is dead now and cannot be harmed by the gossip), wherein he made it clear to me that the government would not look kindly on my ever returning to Bayembe. What precisely they feared, I cannot say; I only ever knew the one state secret about our affairs there, and it was long since out of the bag. But having thus erred once, I could not be trusted not to err again.

To my surprise, Wademi and I did not dine in the main room. He had acquired one of the private rooms for us—perhaps because that way we attracted less attention, the Yembe man and the woman once accused of betraying her country for his. The mystery of how he could afford such a thing was soon cleared up, for it transpired that he was indeed the son of Galinke's mother's sister. Anyone so closely linked with the oba of Bayembe, even through a lesser wife, could easily purchase me and my entire household without so much as a blink.

We passed the starter course with pleasantries, but after the main course arrived, I discovered that he had another reason for arranging this private room.

"What have you heard of the dragons?" he asked, once the waiter was gone.

"The dragons?" I echoed. My mind was so full of various draconic species that it took me longer than it should have to see his meaning. "Do you mean the ones the Moulish have given to Bayembe?"

It was not that I had forgotten them. One does not easily forget about deals one has helped broker between two foreign peoples, especially when that assistance has caused one to be accused of treason. But my interest in dragons was biological, not political; the fact that there were now Moulish swamp-wyrms in Bayembe rivers was not at the forefront of my thoughts.

Wademi nodded, and I spread my hands. "I have heard very little, really. Galinke mentioned that the eggs had been brought as promised, and then had hatched—I believe she said the total was somewhat poor, though. There were arrangements to make sure the fangfish were sufficiently fed. But nothing since then." Which, now that I thought of it, was peculiar. Granted, the dragons in the rivers of Bayembe were intended as a defense for that country's border, and as such might be a protected secret. But Galinke would know very well that I wanted to hear more of their progress, and could have found some way to tell me *something*. Instead, her infrequent letters had diverted me with other matters.

It seemed that she had indeed found a way to tell me something, and his name was Wademi n Oforiro Dara. "The situation has become . . . odd," he said, "and we are hoping you can make sense of it."

This, of course, piqued my curiosity like nothing else. "What do you mean, 'odd'?"

He spoke slowly, in between bites of his food. I reminded myself to eat my own, though I fear the best efforts of the Salburn chefs were entirely wasted on me that day.

Wademi said, "At first it was the eggs, which did not hatch in the quantities hoped. But the Moulish brought more the next year, so we have enough now. The fangfish ate one another, and those who survived grew—some of them. Many were runts. But even those which grew are not like the dragons in the swamp. They are more slender."

"Juveniles," I said. "Have you asked the Moulish? They would know how long it takes to reach full maturation."

He shook his head. "They should be fully grown now. And their hide is different; their scales are more fine."

I could not stop myself from asking, "Are you certain it is not a skin condition?"

By way of reply, he reached beneath his mantle and brought out a small box, which he laid on the table between us. When I opened it, a strong smell of formaldehyde marred the air. The box contained a scrap of skin, which I pinched gently between my fingernails and lifted for a better view.

It was not a skin condition. I had often observed the rough, crocodilian hides of swamp-wyrms, and while they were vulner-able to disease, what illness would *refine* their integument? What I held in my hand was more like the skin of a fish.

Or a savannah snake. "They cannot have bred with the drag-ons of Bayembe," I said. Although some of that species ventured into the fringes of the Moulish jungle, they did not go far enough in to encounter swamp-wyrms. And even if they did—and suc-ceeded in producing viable eggs—the Moulish would not have given those eggs to the oba. They had a very rigorous process for breeding their dragons, which involved taking the males of the swamp proper to the lake where the queens swam.

My fingernails pinched tighter on the skin. The queens . . .

I had not learned as much about swamp-wyrm biology as I would have liked. I knew that the Moulish took the eggs after their laying and distributed them about the swamp, and I knew that the different incubation of the eggs encouraged some to develop into queens, while the rest remained male. (At the time I suspected, but had not had a chance to prove, that some of the "males" were either neuter or infertile females. Neuter sex was known in other draconic types, and I had a sense that only some of the wyrms in the swamp were eligible to breed with the queens. But I had not gotten to examine enough dragons at sufficiently close range to be certain.)

My head was awhirl with these thoughts and others, various the-ories and observations colliding in untidy ways. What emerged from the scrum was this: what if the transplantation of the eggs to the rivers of Bayembe had produced queens instead of males?

My observations of the queen dragons had all been at *quite* a dis-tance, so I was only speculating that their hides featured such fine, overlapping scales. It made sense, though. They swam in the tur-bulent waters of the lake below the Great Cataract, where they would benefit from a more streamlined surface.

But if that were the case, why had the Moulish not said anything to the Yembe?

Because they did not want the existence of the queens known. The oba would certainly try to trade for one, and if that failed, he might well try to take one by stealth or force. Or, if he learned enough of the incubation procedures, try to mimic them so that he might breed his own dragons, without needing to rely on the Moulish.

Which left me in rather a pickle. If my theory could be correct, then I desperately wanted confirmation. Moreover, Wademi—and through him, Galinke and all her people, half-brother included— were looking to me for aid. But it would not very well repay my Moulish friends if I spilled a secret they were trying to keep.

I laid the skin back in its box. "I am not certain what to say. It may be a response to the cleaner, fresher environment of the rivers; swamp water is very full of silt and organic matter, which I imagine is quite an irritant to the skin of the young dragons." Certainly it had been an irritant to my own hide. "Do your dragons seem healthy?"

"For the most part," Wademi said.

"I should like to know if they keep growing," I said. "Some fishes change size according to their environment; it is possible that your dragons will grow larger than those in the swamp, because of the more open waters." If they grew to more than four meters in length, that would tell me a great deal. The queens, from what I had seen of them, were much larger than the males.

Wademi made the humming noise that, among the Yembe, stood in for the refusal it would be rude to state directly. I thought about our private room, and Galinke's reticence in her letters. He had invited me to lunch so as to convey information they did not want committed to paper. (It did not occur to me until some months later that someone in Scirland might even be reading my mail. If they did not want me going to Bayembe, they might have an interest in the letters I sent to and received from there. To this day, I do not know if it was so.)

My thoughts were not on such matters that day, but even then I knew it might be difficult to keep me informed. I sighed, saying, "It will be difficult to write to me regardless, as I shall be rather peripatetic for a while."

"But what of the dragons?"

Even had I possessed the courage to defy that unnamed gentleman of the Synedrion, I could not change our itinerary now. Although there was room for diversion in it—as this account will demonstrate—we could not divert all the way to Bayembe, just so I could look in on the dragons in the rivers. "I'm afraid there is very little I can do from where I am, sir. If they are healthy, then surely that is enough."

He looked dissatisfied. Had I given the Yembe such a high opinion of my knowledge that they believed I could resolve this question over lunch in a distant country? Or had they expected me to come to their aid in person? If so, it pained me to disappoint them. But there was nothing for it: too many things prevented me from going.

As a sop to Wademi, I said, "I anticipate a great expansion in my knowledge of dragons, thanks to this expedition. It is possible I will learn something of use to you."

Which, as it happened, was true—albeit in a roundabout way. But that was no comfort to him at the time, and so we both left our meeting in less than good spirits.

TWO

This was my third time departing from Scirland, and by now the process was beginning to feel familiar. I had put my affairs in order and packed everything I anticipated needing to the point where I could not do without—as packing for shipboard life requires great thriftiness when it comes to volume. I had bid farewell to the family members with whom I was still on good terms, which is to say my father and my brother Andrew, and (less warmly) my brother-in-law Matthew Camherst. Leaving Natalie in Falchester, Tom, Abby, Jake, and I went down to Sennsmouth, where our vessel awaited the start of our great adventure.

For the sake of the maritime enthusiasts among my readership, and also so that my story may be more clearly understood, I will take a moment to acquaint you with the Royal Survey Ship *Basilisk,* which was to be my home for most (though not quite all) of my voyage.

It had, during the Nine Years' War, been constructed as what they call a "brig sloop," which is to say it had two masts, both of them rigged with square sails. Following the conclusion of the war, some enterprising shipwright transformed it into a bark by refitting it with a third or mizzen mast, lying astern of the first two, with a sail rigged fore and aft—for what reason, I am not sailor enough to say. The captain tried to explain the addition to me on more than one occasion, but my head was full of dragons and other such matters, leaving not much room for the finer points of nautical engineering. (And nowadays, I fear, my memory is not what it once was. Whatever understanding I once had is long gone, as I did not see fit to record it in my journals.)

She was a pretty thing, the *Basilisk* was, though perhaps my opinion is coloured by the memories of my experiences there— which, though not without their dark spots, are still on the whole pleasant. She had seen little action during the war, and therefore had taken little damage, so her railings and hull were bravely painted in white and green. Her measurements were seven or eight meters from one side to the other, and nearly thirty from stem to stern.

This sounds impressive, and when I first approached the vessel, I indeed found her enormous. Of course, what is spacious when seen from the dock or on a first tour rapidly becomes much smaller when it is your entire world. Before the first month was out, I felt I knew every last inch of that boat, at least from the deck on down. The rigging I left to others, except when my observations could not be made without a higher vantage point.

Her captain was Dione Aekinitos, and it takes some restraint on my part not to refer to him as "the mad Dione Aekinitos" every time I write his name. He certainly had that reputation before we came aboard, and did nothing to persuade me it was undeserved during my time there.

At first he seemed perfectly ordinary. To begin with, he lacked both peg-leg and parrot, which certain childhood stories had convinced me were the necessary accoutrements of any dashing captain. He kept, or attempted to keep, his dark, curly hair confined in a tail at the nape of his neck, but strands were forever escaping to blow in the wind. How they did not drive him mad, I cannot say, for I was more than once minded to cut my own hair off entirely

RSS *Basilisk*

and save myself the irritation. (Though in the end, the choice was not mine to make.) He was tall enough that he could stand fully upright only in the open air—the interior of a ship being rather a cramped place—and he had both a laugh and a bellow that could and did carry from the stern to the very tip of the figurehead's nose.

His madness lay not in outward appearances, nor even in daily behaviour, but simply in the fact that he considered the sea a *challenge*. Like all sailors who survive for longer than a year, he had a healthy respect for the dangers the ocean poses . . . but "respect for" and "fear of" are not quite the same thing. One had no sooner to tell him a thing was difficult than he would immediately begin formulating plans to test himself against it.

As you may imagine, this gave him certain troubles in the keeping of crew. But over the years since the war, he had, by a cycle of attrition and recruitment, driven away all those who were not willing to tolerate his eccentricity and put together an assortment of men who did not mind overmuch. Very few of them were married, though most if not all availed themselves of the hospitality to be found in ports the world over, and I have no doubt that between them they could crew another ship with the natural children they had sired. The notion that their captain might get them killed in some doomed attempt to navigate an unnavigable channel or outrace a lethal storm was one they accepted with philosophical resignation. So long as they were paid on time, all was well.

These souls—some sixty-five in number—were to be my companions for the next two years. To that list I added Tom Wilker, Abby Carew, and my son, plus others encountered along the way. My social world had been restricted before, but through solitary hermitage, not confinement among a group of people whom I could not escape. I had my cabin, but I shared it with Abby and Jake, and furthermore I—who had enjoyed so much of the natural world in my past—could not endure being cooped up in it for long. I had no desire to escape into the rigging, however, as Jake habitually did (my son having taken to the ropes with the ease and confidence of the monkey he sometimes resembled). The best I could do, when the company became too much, was to seat myself in the bow of the ship, as far forward as I could go, and pretend there was nothing in the world but myself and the sea.

But I get ahead of myself. It was a bright Graminis morning when we arrived on the dock in Sennsmouth, baggage in tow, to get ourselves situated aboard the *Basilisk*. The captain had sent the jolly-boat to collect us, while a larger tender waited to take our gear; the ship's draught was too great for it to come right up to the docks. We therefore had what seemed like all the time in the world to survey our new home as the sailors rowed us out.

Tom and I had both seen the *Basilisk* more than once before, when making the arrangements for this journey. For both Abby and Jake, however, this was their first sight. Abby studied it in silence; I knew her well enough by then to recognize it as a cover for nerves. Jake, by contrast, would have dived over the side if he thought he could swim there faster. I had to call him back rather sharply, for he was getting in the way of the oarsmen.

Abby was in skirts, as was I, for we had not yet left Scirland. Because of this, they lowered the bosun's chair for the two of us, while Tom and Jake climbed the ladder. Tom, thank heaven, had the good sense to delay Jake as long as he could, such that by the time my son reached the deck, I was almost there myself.

Almost, but not quite. I could not reach out to restrain him as Jake attained the boards, took one wide-eyed look around, and bolted off to explore.

He did not get more than ten steps before a voice bellowed, "*Halt!*"

It was not a voice one could disobey. Even the sailors checked briefly in their movements, and they had long practice in determining who was the target of any given order. Jake skidded to so quick a stop, I almost laughed.

The voice had come from the raised quarterdeck. The sun stood just behind, so I had to squint against the light as I looked up, and saw only a looming figure at first. I do not put it past him to have been aware of that, and to have used it a-purpose.

It was, of course, the mad Dione Aekinitos. He descended to the main deck with a heavy tread, the ladder creaking beneath his boots. He was not so large of a man as all that, but he had a knack for making himself sound weighty when he chose; I think he knew where every board on his vessel groaned the most heavily. As he went, he said, "There is no running on this ship unless I command it. And I have not commanded you to run. What is your name, boy?"

My son licked his lips, staring up at him. "Jake. Jacob Camherst. Um. Sir."

By then I was on deck. Maternal instinct—which I do possess, despite rumours to the contrary—urged me to go forward and intervene, for Aekinitos was looming over Jake in a menacing fashion. But I knew enough of shipboard etiquette to know that it would be the height of bad form to get in the captain's way on a matter of discipline. We were not sailors under his command . . . but in the absence of a very good reason, it was better to behave as if we were. To do otherwise was to undermine his authority, create ill will, and generally get our voyage off to a very unfortunate start.

"Have you ever been on board a ship before, boy?" Aekinitos asked.

"No, sir."

"Then here is your first lesson. You do not touch anything. Boys who have never been on ships before create problems. They play with ropes, and do not put them back properly. Then the rope does not uncoil smoothly when it is needed. Perhaps we are in a storm when the tangled rope is found. The items that need to be lashed down are not secured in time, and they go overboard. Perhaps it is a man who goes overboard. Perhaps he dies. Or a sail is not adjusted quickly enough, and the mast breaks, or we run aground. Perhaps we all die. All because a boy did not know to keep his hands off that which he does not understand." Aekinitos paused in this impressive recitation. "Do *you* understand, boy?"

"Yes, sir."

Aekinitos bent ever so slightly over him. "*What* do you understand?"

To his credit, Jake stood his ground, instead of backing up. Or he might have simply been rooted to the spot. "That I shouldn't touch anything, sir."

"Good." Aekinitos straightened and, without the slightest pause, turned to me with a broad smile upon his face. "Mrs. Camherst. Welcome aboard."

"Thank you, captain," I said. Now I did go to Jake's side. I did not put my arm around him; the chastisement had been a necessary one, for without it he would have gotten into everything before the day was out. But I did not want him to feel wholly abandoned. "The lady behind you is Jake's governess, Abigail Carew. Tom, of course, you know already."

When the introductions were finished, Aekinitos sent his first mate, Mr. Dolin, to show us our living quarters. Tom bunked with the officers—we always used that word, "bunked," even though he slept in a hammock, as we all did—but Abby, Jake, and I had been given the luxury of our own cabin in the stern, beneath the poop deck.

If I tell you that it was cramped, you will not truly catch my meaning, unless you have lived on board a ship yourself. Throughout most of the room, Abby could not stand fully upright; my own head almost brushed the beams. The exception was beneath the raised skylight, which gave us our only natural illumination. We had to learn to sleep through anything, for the officers carried out their work directly above our heads, and although Aekinitos could step quietly when he wished to, the same could not be said for a few of the others. The room as a whole was less than three meters on a side, and we shared it with the mizzenmast; I often had occasion to curse the fellow who decided to add it to the ship's design, driving the thick post directly through our cabin.

Into this space we crammed ourselves, our trunks, our books (as well as every other book aboard the ship, not that there were many), and a table on which to work. And so we lived for two years.

To Jake, of course, it seemed at first like a great adventure. Every novelty is enjoyable, when you are nine. Too, he spent much less time in that cabin than I did, for while Abby, Tom, and I did keep up his lessons, he was not directly engaged in the work of the expedition. For my own part, I found my quarters at first shockingly small, then acceptable, then unbearable, and finally as unworthy of comment as the water in which a fish swims.

The reason for the cramped quarters was that I would have needed to be the richest woman in Scirland to hire a ship and crew for two years, solely for the purpose of looking at dragons. No amount of household economy could prepare me for such an expense. The voyage of the *Basilisk* was a joint venture, its burden shared with the Scirling Geographical Association, the Ornithological Society, and a Nichaean trading company, the Twelve Seas Fleet, which has since gone out of business. The first two meant I had obligations not only to the *Winfield Courier* and to my own research, but also to those intellectual bodies. The third meant that what space on the *Basilisk* was not taken up with people and supplies must be devoted to cargo—and those people and supplies must take up as little space as possible.

I had tried, of course, to interest the Philosophers' Colloquium in our endeavour. Some of their members had spoken in praise of my research, and Tom had made inroads with that body, such that I fully expected him to be offered a fellowship upon our return. Despite pressure from our patron, however—Lord Hilford, now sadly ailing—they had declined to lend us any material assistance, or indeed anything beyond vague and halfhearted good wishes. The woman and the lower-class man from Niddey had yet to earn their respect.

At the time I resented it, but the sting has long since worn off. Besides: had they granted us financial support, we might not have been forced to take certain measures so as to keep the expedition funded. And had we not done *that*, how different might my life have been?

Many people assume that an expedition which would later become so famous must have departed with great fanfare, but nothing could be further from the truth.

Back then, all eyes were on the diplomatic voyage upon which the king's niece Princess Miriam was soon to embark. It was a gesture of goodwill to a variety of countries with whom we were not on the best of terms at the time: Haggad, Yelang, Kehliyo, Thiessin, and others I have forgotten. The more political news-sheets were busy speculating as to whether her mission would result in conciliation, and if so, at what cost; the more frivolous ones filled their pages with gossip about whom Her Royal Highness would meet and what she would wear. Either way, they had very little attention to spare for a mere scientific survey.

I had been to sea before, but never for the purpose of being *at* sea. My previous voyages had been a means of arriving at my destination, nothing more. While that was true to some extent now—I

did have an itinerary of places we intended to visit—the ship was
to be my home for the duration, rather than merely a conveyance.
I must confess there was a feeling of excitement to it, as if I were
a child achieving something magical, though sailing had never
been a girlhood dream of mine. That first evening, as we rode the
tide out to sea, I stood with Jake in the bow and laughed into the
wind. Perhaps it is hindsight only that says I knew this was the beginning of something significant. Perhaps not.

We headed first into northern waters, the seas around Svaltan
and Siaure, taking advantage of what little summer that latitude
could afford. Much of the region becomes icebound for the better
part of the year, the sea freezing solid or nearly so for miles
around. Nowadays, of course, we have icebreakers—vessels whose
engines can force them through the pack—and owing to this, much
polar exploration has become possible. At the time, however, we
lacked such ships. The *Basilisk* was not even fitted with the kinds
of reinforcement that could protect her against ice. But it hardly
mattered, for what we came there to observe was only ever seen
in the summer months, regardless.

The debate over the migration of sea-serpents was an old one.
Sailors had reported them in latitudes ranging from the tropics to
the far north, and some claimed the great beasts moved with the
seasons. Others disputed this, citing various facts to support their
position. Tendrils above the eyes and around the snout, for example, were often reported on tropical beasts, but rarely if ever
on arctic ones. In the mid-latitudes, serpents were often seen
year-round; those in the north were generally larger than those
in the south, suggesting that perhaps they were different species.
Round and round the points had gone, but most of those engaged
in the debate were arguing from data that amounted to little
more than anecdote and hearsay. I aimed to change that.

"There's no easy way to prove it in one direction or another," Tom said our first night at sea. He and I were dining in the wardroom with the captain and his officers, which is a courtesy sometimes extended to passengers. The table had low railings around the edge, which helped prevent our dishes from sliding into our laps when the seas were rough. That night, however, there was only a mild swell: enough to serve as a reminder that one was at sea, but not enough to inconvenience. (Unless one happened to be Abby, who struggled greatly with seasickness at first.)

I said, "If it were possible to mark the serpents, as they do with cattle or His Majesty's swans, we could know for certain. Simply brand them with something to indicate the latitude at which they are found, and the date, and then see if you find them far distant in a different season. But even supposing we could persuade them to hold still for such an operation, how would we ever find them again? Needles in haystacks do not enter into it."

Aekinitos nodded. He did not need me to tell him how vast the sea was, and how dangerous its creatures.

Curious, Tom asked, "What is your opinion, sir? Do you think they migrate?"

The captain gazed meditatively at the beams supporting the deck above. "They do not behave the same, those in the north and the south. You know of this?"

"Do you mean their method of defense?" I asked. "Yes, of course. It is one of the key points in my broader consideration of taxonomy. How much does extraordinary breath matter, in terming something a 'dragon' or a mere 'cousin'? In the tropics, sea-serpents suck in water and then expel it in a great jet."

"It can kill a whale," Aekinitos said. "Or crack the hull of a ship."

He sounded entirely delighted with this, as if admiring another man's strength, and nevermind that said strength could mean the end of him and all his crew. I said, "If they expel the water from their stomachs, rather than as a form of breath—and the observations generally agree that this is the case—then it is not extraordinary breath, and traditional taxonomy says they are not dragons. Regardless, this is not seen in the north. The serpents there constrict their prey instead."

"It is not breath," he agreed. "We have killed sea-serpents before, and in their stomachs, we find water. But only in the south. Is this because they are different?" He shrugged. "Perhaps it is only because the water in the north is colder."

This was precisely my theory: that the variation in behaviour was due to environment, not species difference. Filling one's stomach with icy arctic water would be a tremendous shock to the system. But that did not prove migration one way or another; for that, we would need better observation of the creatures themselves.

Achieving this was no easy matter. We had no difficulty finding the serpents; among our equipment was a set of very good telescopes, and during those first weeks Tom and I spent hours staring through them, our hands going cold inside our gloves, watching the great coils rise and fall through the chill blue waters of those northern waves. The men in the rigging soon developed a habit of bellowing down to us any time they spotted one—which became tedious when we were engaged in other, more pressing work. But that was in movement, at a distance, and we only ever saw bits at a time. This was the sort of data upon which the current theories had been founded, and it was not enough. To establish anything for certain, we needed to do as we had done before: hunt one of the creatures, like mariners out of a tale.

THREE

Luring serpents—Sharks—The battle is joined—Seaborne dissection—Jake and the head—Pronouns—I consider taxonomy

Much like sharks, sea-serpents can be attracted with chum. To do so is a risky business, however, if there is more than one serpent in the neighbourhood.

We had to choose our spot carefully, in waters that, according to the Svaltansk sailors we questioned, were less haunted by the beasts. This meant it took us several attempts to attract our prey, but it was a sacrifice all were willing to make, if it meant not attracting four at once.

The sailors took in fish, chopped them up, and filled a tarpaulin with the stinking results, which the jolly-boat carried some distance away before tipping it over the side. Then those aboard rowed with all haste back to the *Basilisk*, for the entire purpose of that part of the exercise was to make sure the bait was not too close to the ship. This having been done, several lookouts were posted in the rigging to scan the waves for coils, telltale wakes, or dark shadows moving beneath the surface.

The first three times we did this, our watch was fruitless. Countless other predators and scavengers came to enjoy the bounty—and in fact they, not the fish, were our true bait, for while sea-serpents will swallow any meat they can get, no matter how small, they prefer to eat larger creatures such as arctic sharks. Despite the lure, however, we saw nothing draconic in the water.

Our effort was not entirely wasted, for the hides or meat or teeth of various predators will fetch a good price in the right places. We had a good hunt of our own. I keenly felt the need for our expedition to turn a profit whenever possible, though. Much discouraged, I told the captain we should abandon the effort and move on; but he was not a man who abandoned anything without great cause. He insisted on trying once more.

The day was a bright one, the sky an intense blue that only seems possible at sea. The air for once was warm enough that I was prepared to call it "bracing," instead of complaining that I could not feel my fingers. We caught and butchered our fish, cast our bait, and waited.

A few sharks became embroiled in a conflict over the bounty. One was enormous—surely at least six meters in length—but even slower than most of his breed, and two others were attempting to take advantage of that fact. Their quarrel drifted toward the port side of the *Basilisk*, and many of us were engaged in watching the fight. Jake, who had permission to remain topside until a serpent was sighted, was standing on a crate with one hand wrapped tight around the rigging, observing the whole thing with eyes so wide, you half-expected his eyeballs to fall right out of their sockets. "Mama," he called out to me, "is that the biggest shark in the world?"

Even when one wishes to foster intellectual curiosity in one's offspring, it can be vexing to be asked a question to which one hasn't the faintest clue of an answer. I was racking my brains for what I knew of shark breeds when a frantic bellow came from above: "*Port beam!*"

Perhaps the lookouts had been distracted by the fight. They later claimed, and I believed them, that the fault was not with their vigilance, but with the serpent, who came up from deep waters completely without warning. Directly off to our left—which is what "port beam" means—a shadow came surging upward. The sharks attempted to scatter, but they are not quick beasts; an instant later, one was in the serpent's jaws.

This was entirely too close to the ship for comfort. The men had their guns and harpoons ready, and began to fire. "Jake, get down," I said, reaching up for him. "You must go below, *now*." I did not fear him toppling overboard, for his grip upon the ropes was firm; but with that many firearms about, it was much too easy to imagine a bullet going astray.

Abby joined me, and together we got him down (though not without many protests) and headed for safety. I was climbing to the poop deck for a better view when the guns fell silent, and I turned to see what had happened.

The waves off our port beam were sloshing restlessly, but there was no sign of the serpent.

Aekinitos was a few feet away, standing next to the helmsman, Mr. Forde. "Has it fled?" I asked him—and then I had my answer.

The ship *staggered* to one side. I have no better word for it; the entire frame lurched, quite out of its usual motion. The men shouted, and a few more fired shots. Aekinitos bellowed for them to hold fire. The serpent had struck us below the waterline; on the lower decks, men raced to stop the leaks that began spraying water into the hold. Silence fell again, ragged and broken by the occasional call. Guns in hand, the crew scattered to the railings on both sides, looking for their target.

"Two points off the starboard bow!" came the cry, and Aekinitos bellowed again for his men to hold. He knew the behaviour of sea-serpents well; an instant later the creature was curving around our bow and back to port, and had the men all rushed to shoot at where it had been, they would have missed where it was. More gunfire, but no one had yet gotten a clear shot with the harpoons, and only those can be trusted to penetrate a sea-serpent's tough hide deeply enough to do it any true harm.

All bullets generally do is anger the creature.

Sailors tell exaggerated tales. So far as I have seen, this is true the world over; and so one easily grows into the habit of discounting anything one hears from a sailor as being more than the reality. A four-meter shark becomes six, or eight. A bad storm becomes a hurricane. A narwhal sunning itself on a rock becomes a beautiful maiden combing her hair.

I am not a sailor, and I tell you with utter and scientific honesty: a sea-serpent can and will come hurtling up out of the sea like a geyser, just as the stories say, a column of grey-blue scales five, ten, fifteen meters high, streaming water from its length—and then curve itself midair so that when it falls, its head enters the water on the far side of its prey.

The lighter ropes of the rigging snapped like twine. The great stays that held the masts, cables as thick around as my arm, gave it more trouble. The serpent's head dove between two of these and splashed into the sea once more—but stays are meant to withstand the worst storms the ocean can devise. The shining coil of body was suspended from the mainstay, sliding forward as it tightened, until halted by the foremast.

The serpent did not know what transpired above. It knew only that there was a great beast in the water, as big as the largest whale, and that the beast was the source of its wounds. Had we been hunting in southern waters, our mark might have struck us with a jet of water, and the *Basilisk* might have taken a wound from which she could not recover. But this was the icy northern sea, and the serpent therefore aimed to crush us to death.

Men rushed forward, howling. One fellow at the starboard rail put the barrel of his gun right against the serpent's scales and pulled the trigger; gore exploded outward from the wound. Others followed Aekinitos' shouts and concentrated their fire together, chewing ragged holes in the creature's side. These then became targets for the men with harpoons, who hurled their spears with all the force they could muster, hoping to strike something vital within.

But all the while, the coil was tightening. The mainstay groaned in protest; then, with a dreadful tearing sound, it snapped. The serpent's body crashed into the deck, splintering the railings on both sides. With the *Basilisk* now properly in its grip, the beast settled in to crush us.

The one advantage was that the serpent's body was now within better reach. With cutlasses, a few of the men hacked away enough scales to make a good opening. Then, roaring, a knot of sailors threw their weight behind a harpoon, driving the point deep into the creature's side.

It reached vital organs, and the serpent spasmed. The movement nearly threw Tom off its back, for he, along with two others, was climbing atop the coil. They too had cutlasses, and began chopping with desperate ferocity at the scales. Blood and bits of scale flew, while the decking below creaked and bent. Their blades finally exposed their target: the creature's spine.

By then the beast was trying to escape. Its length slithered across the deck, doing more damage as it went; two of the men atop it lost their balance and fell. Tom, the last of the three, followed a moment later—but his cutlass did not. It remained lodged in between the vertebrae, and when the serpent slipped free of the *Basilisk*, it was apparent that the front half was dragging the dead weight of the back.

Though it still moved, the serpent was finished. Half-paralyzed, a harpoon in its vitals, and bleeding from the great rents in its sides, it tried to swim away, but soon it floated lifeless atop the waves.

* * *

And what did I do, while this epic battle raged?

I crouched in front of the helm and took notes. Not on the fighting, you understand, but the creature itself: its movement, its behaviour. It is exceedingly difficult to observe a sea-serpent at close range, and as this might be my only opportunity, I did not want to squander it. I would not have been any use in the fight regardless, as my last (and only) experience with a gun had been when I was fourteen.

In some ways I think it might have been easier had I thrown my lot in with the men after all. When one is in a fight, the hot blood of the moment overwhelms many other considerations. Watching from a slight distance as I did, with my mind set to record every detail, I could not help but be sickened by the butchery. We had dissected dragons before, but that was clinical, conducted after the beasts were dead. As for the killing itself, it had always been done neatly, with a few shots fired from a rifle. Never had it been this sort of mêlée, with swords and spears and men howling to give themselves courage. Nor, for that matter, had the lives of my companions ever been in such direct danger—as I had no doubt that, given a little time more, the serpent might have broken the *Basilisk*'s back.

All things considered, we escaped rather less scathed than we might have been. A few men had been injured by falling debris and the recoil of snapped ropes, but none of the rest suffered more than scrapes. The burst stay was a serious concern, but our mast had not been broken, nor our hull too badly ruptured. We could afford to stay for a time and enjoy the fruits of our victory.

I could also release my pent-up feelings by chastising my son. Fixed as I was upon the battle against the serpent, I did not realize until afterward that Jake had not gone below with Abby as instructed. He had instead climbed the rigging up to the "top"—the platform where the lower section of the mast met the one above. He had taken with him a knife concealed inside his shirt, which he intended to use against the serpent by diving heroically on it from above. Fortunately for both his safety and my own sanity, common sense had prevented him from following through with this plan when he saw the bloody reality below him.

He was not as much daunted by this as I should have liked, though, nor did my reprimand leave much more of a mark. Mine was not the only tongue-lashing he received, though—Abby had already delivered one, as did the sailors in the top, several of the ship's officers, Aekinitos himself, and Tom—and in the aggregate, they did have the effect of making him promise to be more obedient in the future.

In the meanwhile, we had other tasks to which we must attend. The crew lowered the ship's boats and used them to tow the beast back to our side, as they do with whales. We had to work quickly; already the carcass was drawing attention. Gulls flapped down to consider it, but disdained the meat after a few pecks; as with terrestrial dragons, the flesh of a sea-serpent is rather foul, owing to the chemical composition of the blood. There are scavengers in the sea, however, who do not mind its taste, and many of these came to investigate as we conducted our studies.

This at least was familiar work, although I had never before carried it out while straddling the carcass with my feet turning to ice in the sea. (I was, of course, wearing trousers, and had been since we left Sennsmouth.) I had to sit atop a piece of tough sailcloth, for the edges of the scales are viciously sharp; their serration had contributed to the destruction of the mainstay. Tom and his two allies had suffered numerous cuts, though that did not prevent him from joining me in the dissection once bandaged.

Those scales were the first focus of our interest. We had studied a few specimens donated to museums, for they are sometimes kept as items of curiosity by the sailors who kill the beasts. Without detailed information on their collection, however, those scales told us little. We hoped that by examining these closely and then comparing them against scales taken from a serpent in the tropics, we might establish more about the relation between the two. We also had the chemical equipment to try preserving a bit of bone, and extracted a vertebra for the purpose.

Then it was the basics, as we had practiced them before: we took a variety of measurements, and then Tom (whose tolerance for the cold water was much greater than my own) cut open the body to survey the internal organs. I meanwhile had the sailors remove the head and bring it on board, where I could study it in peace and relative warmth.

Jake knew I was a naturalist, of course. He had looked through my scholarly works, more for the plates that illustrated them than out of any deep interest in the text. Enough of the plates depicted anatomical drawings that he knew perfectly well what his mother did in her work. Knowing, however, was quite a different matter from seeing her in communion with a severed head.

He made an awed noise and laid his hand on one of its fangs. "Pray do not block my view," I said, sketching rapidly. I wanted to finish quickly, so that I could deflesh the head and draw the skull. There appeared to be faint scars above its eyes, which suggested it might have once possessed the tendrils seen on its tropical kin.

"Is this bigger than the other dragons you've killed?" Jake asked.

"I have not killed any dragons myself," I said. "Can you open its mouth? Or call one of the sailors to do it."

Jake pried the head open, giving me a look when I warned him not to cut himself on the teeth. It is a look I think all children master at about his age—the one that insists the looker needs no warning while, by its very confidence, convincing the one looked at that the warning was very necessary indeed.

Open, the jaws could easily have swallowed my son. That gave me an idea. I said, "Stay where you are; I want to use you for scale."

He mimed being eaten by the serpent, which would have been less unnerving had I not just been reminded of precisely how much danger I was placing him in by bringing him on this voyage. I had underestimated the hazards of hunting a sea-serpent. But I would not do so a second time; I vowed to put him ashore before we went after one in the tropics.

Jake soon tired of pretending to be a victim and so began mock-wrestling with the head, pretending to be its mighty slayer. "I'm going to kill one of these someday," he proclaimed.

"I should prefer you didn't," I said, rather sharply. "I did this for science, but it having now been done, I hope it needn't be done again. Only the fangs have any real value on the market, and those only as curiosities and raw material for carving; should an entire animal die, just so we might take four of its teeth? I almost feel sorry for it. At the end, it was trying to swim away. It only wanted to live."

"She," Tom said, climbing over the railing. He was dripping with bloody water. "No eggs in her abdomen, but the ovipositor marks her very clearly as female. I wonder where they lay them?"

My chastisement had made little mark on my son, but Tom's revelation silenced him. Much later, he admitted to me that the pronoun was what struck him so forcefully: the pronoun, and the possibility of eggs. With those two words, the sea-serpent changed from a terrible beast to a simple animal, not entirely different from the broken-winged sparrow we had once nursed back to health together. A dangerous beast, true, and one that could have sent the *Basilisk* to the bottom of the ocean. But she had been alive, and had wanted to go on living; now she was dead, and any progeny she might have borne with her. Jake was very quiet after that, and remained so for several days.

Tom set to work defleshing the skull, and talked with me while he did. "The lungs are much like those we've seen in other

JAKE FOR SCALE

dragons—more avian in structure than mammalian." I sighed, thinking of my debate with Miriam Farnswood. I feared I was likely to lose that particular argument. "The musculature around the stomach and oesophagus is interesting, too. I'll have to look at one of the tropical serpents to compare, but I think the purpose is to allow the creature to suck in water very swiftly, without having to swallow, and then vomit it back up again."

"The jet of water," I said, excited. "Yes, we'll have to compare. If they do not migrate, perhaps their life cycle leads them further north as they age? A creature this large might have a difficult time keeping itself cool in tropical waters. That would explain why those in the north are generally larger, if their growth continues throughout their lives."

We debated this point until the skull was clear of the bulk of its flesh. As I began sketching again, he asked me, "What do you think? Taxonomically."

"It's difficult," I admitted. By then my hand was capable of going about its work without demanding all of my attention; I could ponder issues of classification at the same time. "The dentition bears some similarities to those reported or observed in other breeds, at least in number and disposition of teeth . . . though of course baleen plates are not a usual feature. The vertebrae certainly pose a problem. This creature has quite a lot of them, and we do not usually consider animals to be close cousins who differ so greatly in such a fundamental characteristic."

Tom nodded, wiping his hands clean—or at least less filthy— with a cloth. "Not to mention the utter lack of hind limbs. I saw nothing in the dissection, not even anything vestigial. The closest thing it has to forelimbs are some rather inadequate fins."

"And yet there *are* similarities. The generally reptilian appearance, and more significantly, the degradation of the bones." I thought of the six criteria customarily used to distinguish "true dragons" from draconic creatures: quadripedalism, flight-capable wings, a ruff or fan behind the skull, bones frangible after death, oviparity, and extraordinary breath. We might, if we were *very* generous, count the serpent's supraorbital tendrils (presuming it had once possessed them) as the ruff, and Tom had just confirmed that the creatures laid eggs. Together with the bones—which decayed more slowly than those of terrestrial dragons, but *did* become frangible quite rapidly—that made three of six. But was there any significance to the distinction between "true dragons" and their mere cousins? What if there was only one characteristic that mattered?

Yet there were problems as well with declaring osteological degradation the true determinant of draconic nature. We had established a fair degree of variation in the exact chemical makeup of different breeds, ranging from the rock-wyrms on whom the process had originally been developed to the simple sparklings who could be preserved in vinegar. There was every chance that it would prove to be a spectrum rather than a simple binary. Where, then, would we draw our boundary?

I could not answer those questions that day—nor, indeed, for years to come. But that dead sea-serpent, for whom I had conceived a belated sympathy, brought me one step closer to understanding.

FOUR

Wyverns in Bulskevo—Protégés—Jake's disinterest—
In the doldrums—Jake's promise

I had not forgotten the message Wademi brought to me regarding the peculiar appearance of the dragons in Bayembe's rivers. I had, however, put my thoughts on the matter to one side for a time.

There had been enough to do in preparing for our departure that I told myself I would discuss the matter with Tom after we had gotten settled on the *Basilisk*. Once on board, however, I found the flaw in my reasoning: there was simply *no* privacy on such a ship.

The sailors attended very little to our scientific discussions, caring naught for such matters. I could not trust, however, that they would continue to ignore us if phrases like "queen dragons" caught their attention. There were opportunists among them who might pursue such a prize—or at least sell word of it to an interested buyer. Even if they did not, they might reference it in their dockside gossip. Whether this might rebound ill upon Bayembe and Mouleen, I could not say for certain; but I did not like to risk it.

I therefore had to wait. Fortunately, we were not always ship-bound, and in time I had my chance.

The *Basilisk* stopped in Svaltan to replace the broken stay and repair the other damage inflicted by the sea-serpent, then rounded the northern edge of Anthiope and dropped anchor off the shore of Lezhnema at the mouth of the Olovtun River, some distance north of Kupelyi. We had the goodwill of the tsar; he had not forgotten that we were instrumental in the discovery of a firestone deposit in Vystrana, from which he had profited handsomely. Because of this, not only had we been granted visas, but he had arranged for a guide to take us inland, where we might observe wyverns.

These haunt the mountains of eastern Bulskevo and up into Siaure. A part of me wished that scientific rigor did not require me to carry out research in such places; even in late Caloris and early Fructis, and even confining ourselves to the foothills rather than going up into the mountains proper, what passed for their "summer" was decidedly on the chill side. The long days gave us ample opportunity to chase our prey, though, while the *Basilisk* continued down to Kupelyi and the markets there before returning to retrieve us from Lezhnema.

I will not say much of the wyvern-hunting itself, for it has little bearing on the key aspects of this narrative, and its scientific significance has been recorded elsewhere. Suffice it to say that the limb configuration of a wyvern—wings and two legs, instead of four—was of interest to us, chiefly as a possible link between the near-limbless serpents of the ocean and the quadripedal winged dragons.

This terrestrial detour gave me ample time to speak with Tom, particularly when we lay in interminable wait for a wyvern to happen past. I recounted what Wademi had said to me, and my speculations as to its possible import.

He frowned, laying one hand over the stock of his rifle. "I have a hard time believing the Moulish would make such an error."

"We must consider the possibility," I said. "Their usual treatment of the eggs is traditional, handed down to them through who knows how many generations. Things become habit, done because that is how one's father and grandfather did them, rather than because their import is fully understood." I paused, dissatisfied, and then was distracted by movement that proved to be some farmer's errant goat.

When it was gone, I returned to the point. "But I must consider other possibilities, too. For example: what if the Moulish *want* queens in the rivers?"

Tom blew out his breath in a quick huff. "To what end? Do they mean to conquer Bayembe for themselves?"

We both knew that was ludicrous. The Moulish loved their swampy forest, even when it was trying to kill them; to them, the arid savannah of Bayembe was a wasteland. And they had no government at a scale larger than the elders who happened to be in camp at any given time, no warfare beyond small gangs of young men scuffling over personal insults. They had no desire to conquer Bayembe, nor the means to do so if they did. Not even with dragons.

"I wish I could go see them for myself," I murmured—not least because an icy wind chose to blow through at that precise moment, reminding me of how much warmer it was in Eriga.

Tom knew why I could not. He was no more free to travel there than I. "What you need," he mused, "is a protégé you can send in your stead."

This made me sigh. "I am not likely to ever have one of those."

He said nothing. After a moment, I became aware of his gaze on me. When I turned my head to look, he was staring. "What?" I asked.

"What of all those people who flock to your house every Athemer?"

"None of them are dragon naturalists."

"Well, no—but gather enough bright young things about you, and sooner or later one of them will be. Likely sooner, if you go on a speaking tour after this expedition."

I wanted to protest that the speaking tour, if it even happened, would simply be a means of raising money (which I expected to be in short supply by the time I returned home). My talks would be popular, not scholarly. But if I could be inspired to my career by something as trivial as a sparkling preserved in vinegar, was it so ludicrous to think that someone else might be inspired by hearing my tales? I thought of protégés as the sort of thing a man like Lord Hilford had: a respected peer, a Colloquium Fellow. Yet I might someday have one, too.

It even crossed my mind that Jake might go, though of course he might have been refused on the grounds that he was my son, and in any event it would have been at least six or seven years before he was old enough to send to Eriga on his own. By then, the matter was likely to be resolved in one way or another. But as I soon discovered, he seemed unlikely to follow that path regardless.

While Tom and I were lying in wait for wyverns (and occasionally venturing into their dens, which did lead to Tom getting poisoned, wyverns having no extraordinary breath but more than adequate venom to take its place), I had left Jake in the keeping of Abby Carew and Feodor Lukovich Gavrilenko, the guide the tsar had provided. This was, to my way of thinking, a splendid example of the sort of education Jake could receive by travelling the world: Feodor Lukovich was a hardy man, very familiar with the environs of the Olovtun Mountains, and could teach my son a great deal about the environment and the creatures to be found there. After more than a month cooped up aboard the *Basilisk*, I expected Jake would welcome the opportunity to tear about the countryside.

Upon my return, however, I learned that such was not the case. "It's cold up here," Jake complained, huddling inside his coat.

I might not have been closely involved with his early rearing, but it seemed that some things were transmitted *in utero*. I had, after all, been shivering in Vystrana when he was conceived. "Yes, it is," I agreed. "But did you not want to go hiking? Feodor Lukovich told me he would show you how his falcon hunts."

Jake shrugged, in the way that only nine-year-old children can manage—and usually male children at that, girls not being permitted the same kind of insouciance. "It would only kill rabbits and such. I want to go back to the ship."

Whatever kindred feeling had been engendered by his complaint of cold, it vanished in the face of this inconceivable prospect: that any son of mine might not be interested in *something with wings*. "At your age, I would have been mad to see a falcon hunt, only no one will take a girl for such outings."

This did not sway him. He wanted to go back to the ship; Haward, one of the sailors, had promised to teach him knots. "I am sure Feodor Lukovich could teach you some," I said, whereupon Jake informed me (with no little scorn) that he already knew all of *those*.

Cruel mother that I am, I forced him to stay there a while longer. Tom and I were not done with our work, and I was not about to send Jake down the Olovtun with nobody but his governess for company. If he would not learn about northern Bulskevo, then he could sit and drill Spureni verbs with Abby.

When I spoke with her privately about his behaviour, she spread her hands in a helpless gesture. "He likes it on board the ship. He'll settle down once we get back."

"I hope you're right," I said. "If he is this contrary for the entire expedition, there will be no living with him. And I do not want to shackle you to the *Basilisk* simply because that is where Jake would rather be."

"I don't mind at all," Abby demurred.

This was exceedingly kind of her to say, but I knew it was not true. "Ah, well," I said with a philosophical sigh. "He is only nine. I imagine he will tire of it soon enough, and long for some variety."

Which just goes to show how little I understood my son.

From Bulskevo we could have continued down the eastern coast of Anthiope, for there were certainly dragons to be found in places like Zmayet and Uhwase and Akhia. But Tom and I, after assembling the most complete list we could of dragons and draconic cousins, had agreed that it would be better if we focused our efforts elsewhere. For one thing, the existing literature on such creatures was heavily biased toward Anthiopean observations, with much less known about them elsewhere. For another, there was relatively little taxonomic variation to be found in Anthiope, apart from cousins like sparklings, wyverns, and wolf-drakes. To truly question the nature of dragons, I needed to look farther afield.

The *Basilisk* therefore provisioned herself in Kupelyi, then struck out across the ocean toward the continent of Otholé. On this passage—a journey of nearly two months, during which the cramped conditions ceased to be awkward and started to become intolerable—I began to grasp the truth of what was happening with Jake.

As related in the first volume of my memoirs, a tipping point in my life came early on, when at the age of seven I first learned how to preserve a sparkling and then dissected a dove to study what the wishbone was for. From those two events I formed an obsession with all things winged, which eventually settled more firmly upon dragons (though I still retain a great fondness for birds and some insects).

Jake's tipping point was the *Basilisk*. From the moment he set foot on her decks, he knew—though he did not articulate it this way until years later—that he was home. He loved the great and complex array of rigging and sails that brought the ship to life. He loved the clever way the necessities of life were miniaturized and tucked into every available corner. He loved the tang of salt water and the whip of the sea wind and above all, the sheer feeling of *freedom* that came from being in flight across the waves.

I did not understand this at first. While I enjoyed being at sea, it was not an unmitigated delight. And Tamshire, my childhood home, is a landlocked county, so I had no personal familiarity with the way in which the ocean calls to some hearts. It was inexplicable to me that Jake, who had grown up in the quiet suburb of Pasterway and the busy streets of Falchester, would take so instinctively to the sea. But so it seemed to be; and if indeed it was a passing infatuation, as I had at first assumed, then it was exhibiting a notable failure to pass on schedule.

Of course, Jake being nine, he did not take to shipboard life in anything like a dignified fashion. Despite that early admonition from the captain and his experience with the sea-serpent, he went where he should not, touched things he should not. And one day when we were in the middle of the ocean, with the *Basilisk* standing almost motionless on a glassy plate, Aekinitos hauled my son before me by the scruff of his neck.

We were then in the region sailors call "the doldrums," near the equator. Here the winds sometimes fail altogether, leaving sailing ships utterly becalmed. The sky was hot copper above us, the water flat gold below. I was on deck, taking advantage of the stillness to produce more finished drawings of the sea-serpents and wyverns. I did hear the commotion down below, but I disregarded it, as I had learned to disregard many of the noises and activities that periodically roiled the crew.

I did not even look up when a clump of people began moving toward me across the deck. Not until they stopped before me did I pause in my pencil work. Then, to my dismay, I saw Aekinitos standing with one hand clenched around the collar of my son's shirt, and Jake looking both sullen and guilty. Sweat plastered his hair to the edges of his face in damp swags that could not muster the will to be curls.

"What is going on?" I asked.

Aekinitos gave a quick shake of his hand, making my son twitch. "Mr. Dolin caught him playing with *this*."

The first mate handed him an object, which Aekinitos then thrust toward me. A sextant, I saw. "Whose is that?"

"Mine," the captain rumbled. "Your boy stole it, and was using it as a *toy*."

I had no doubt that Jake had borrowed rather than stolen it; what would he do with a sextant of his own? But such a distinction would not mean much to the captain, nor should it. "Jake," I said, my own voice hardening, "is this true?"

Shame-faced, my son nodded.

We were gathering more of a crowd: not just the sailors who had followed Aekinitos and Dolin and Jake from belowdecks, but others who were up above, and Tom and Abby besides. The captain raised his voice slightly, no doubt for their benefit. "I cannot have such disobedience aboard my ship. For theft, the penalty is flogging."

"Now see *here*," I said, shooting to my feet. My drawing board and pencil clattered to the deck. I knew enough of sea life to know there was a world of difference between the switching a disobedient boy might get at school and the sort of flogging practiced on board ships. Aekinitos could not be serious.

Nor was he. But neither was he speaking in jest. I met his gaze, and saw that while he did not intend to flog my son like a common sailor, he *did* intend to leave an impression Jake would not soon forget.

And I had a notion of how to accomplish that.

"You will *not* flog my son," I said, the words as firm as I could make them. Then I allowed myself to wilt, sighing. "But you are right. You cannot have such behaviour on the *Basilisk*. This is not the first time Jake has been disobedient, and it will not be the last. Our next port of call is, what—Axohuilli? Not ideal, but it can't be helped, I suppose. If the winds will cooperate and take us there, then I will make arrangements for Jake and Miss Carew to sail back to Scirland."

"Mama, no!" Jake cried, jerking in the captain's grip.

I met his gaze, letting my sorrow show. "I am sorry, Jake. I said too much of the adventure to be had here, and not enough of the responsibilities that would come with it. I did not prepare you adequately for this, and perhaps you are simply too young."

"I'm not," he said desperately. "I won't do it again, I promise. I'll behave—don't send me home!"

"And when you grow tired of behaving? I cannot leave you in a situation where you might be flogged. It would be very irresponsible of me."

Reckless, he said, "I won't get tired of behaving. I'll prove it! If I don't, you can beat me, just like he said."

To Jake, who had never suffered anything worse than a spanking, a flogging probably sounded very romantic. (I had overheard him talking gleefully to Tom about keelhauling not three days prior.) I sighed again, putting my head in my hand, then lifted it and addressed the captain once more. "Surely there can be some sort of allowance made for first offenses—provided there is not a second. What else would you do to punish a sailor who had erred so grievously?"

"I would break an officer," Aekinitos said. "But this boy has no rank to strip from him."

I opened my hands, half in pleading, half a shrug. "Then treat him as if he did. Demote him to—oh, I do not know my sailing terms well enough. Some lowly position, from which he might learn proper naval conduct."

Jake's face, which had fallen like a mudslide when I spoke of sending him home, began to light up. To him, this would sound less like punishment, more like a wondrous treat. But I trusted Aekinitos to disabuse him of that notion. "*Boy*," Aekinitos rumbled. "That is the lowest position he could have, and if there were a lower, I would give it to him."

"What sort of tasks does a ship's boy do?" I asked.

Although his fate hung in the balance, Jake could not resist saying, "Swabbing the decks?"

Aekinitos' heavy brows drew inward and down. I imagine his glare must have looked very fierce from below, for Jake quailed. "*The bilges*," the captain said.

He was as good as his word. Aekinitos could guess as well as I could that Jake adored the notion of learning to be a proper sailor; accordingly, the captain at first did not let him do anything that seemed sailorly in the least. Jake spent that first day down in the filth of the bilge, about which the only good thing one could say was that it was out of the blistering sun. After that he assisted the cook in the galley or helped drag stores about in some arcane maneuver designed to improve the balance of the ship—always supposing its sole purpose was not to keep a disobedient boy busy.

It would have broken the spirit of any child staying on a whim. Had Jake come to me and begged for mercy, I would have told the captain to desist . . . and then, as I had said before, put him on a ship for home. I could neither torment my son nor ask Aekinitos to tolerate his misbehaviour. But Jake's desire to stay was no whim, and so he persevered, though he be up to his eyebrows in muck. And so, one step at a time, Aekinitos began to teach him more.

Not directly, of course. The captain of the *Basilisk* had better things to do with his time than train a single boy. But he put Jake into the care of his bosun, a fellow of mixed Anthiopean and Erigan ancestry named Cranby, and that fellow undertook to make my son a sailor. Jake learned the parts of the ship, the points of the compass, how to tie more knots than I knew were geometrically possible. He did tedious work like picking oakum out of old ropes, scraping barnacles off the hull, and (yes) swabbing the decks. Eventually he did more interesting things like holding the reel when someone else threw out the log-line to measure our speed. Much, much later, Aekinitos let him hold the sextant again, and learn how to take a sighting so as to chart our position.

And Jake loved it. Sailing is exhausting, back-breaking work, but the complaint I heard most often from my son was that he was neither large enough nor strong enough to do more. A boy his age was no use in handling sails or hauling on ropes; he would only get in the way. But Jake vowed that he would someday be like those men, and after seeing the labor he was willing to endure so long as it was on a ship, I believed him.

The bulk of that, however, lay in the future. In the immediate term, we finally escaped the doldrums, and when we came to port at Axohuilli in Coyahuac, I did not send Jake home. We reprovisioned and asked some questions, then set sail for Namiquitlan . . . where, we were told, there were feathered serpents to be found.

FIVE

Coyahuac reminded me a great deal of Mouleen, the only other tropical country of which I had personal experience. Here the vegetation was equally thick, the trees towering giants laced together with vines and ferns. Beneath the canopy, I sweltered almost as much as I had in that swampy land. But there were differences: rather than being half-drowned by muddy rivers, Coyahuac had no surface water, all rainfall soaking through the porous ground to gather in underground streams and wells. The verdant life that rose above it was a thin skin over rocky bones, and here and there the bones showed through.

Such was the case with Namiquitlan, where we went in search of feathered serpents—*quetzalcoatls*, as they are known in the local tongue. The waters in the region of that town are an intense, deep blue, even close to shore, for the ground there drops off precipitously; even the harbour of Namiquitlan is a mere pause in the sheer face the land presents to the sea. We passed close to one of these sea cliffs as we came into port, and those of us not occupied in the task of keeping the *Basilisk* safely clear of that peril crowded to the rail for a good look.

Twenty meters of stone gleamed gold in the westering sun, an emerald cap of thick vegetation spilling from its edge. I looked at that cap and sighed. I knew from experience that finding dragons in such an environment was not easily done; and here, unlike in Bulskevo, we had no guide arranged in advance.

I was about to say something on this matter to Tom when Jake tugged at my sleeve. "Mama, look! There are men on the cliff!"

My son had good eyes. The movement was well hidden in the vegetation, and not easily identified. After a moment, however, three men came up to the edge. Two hung back; the third, dressed only in loose slops, went to the very brink. A local, I presumed: his skin was rich brown against the pale fabric. "What is he doing?" Jake asked.

The man had peered over the edge briefly; now he retreated some distance, almost to the trees. I opened my mouth to say, "Perhaps something blew into the sea," when the man turned and, sweeping his arms in a great arc for momentum, sprinted forward and leapt from the cliff.

It was no suicide. His body gathered itself in a graceful line as he plummeted downward. Despite his care, the sound when he struck the water reached us clearly, and Abby flinched back. My own breathing stopped. I could not draw air again until his dark head and gleaming shoulders broke the surface once more, followed shortly by a shout of delight.

"He is *mad*," I said, staring.

Next to me, Tom snorted. "So says the woman who once threw *herself* off a cliff."

"I had a glider," I reminded him.

Tom forbore to mention that it had been of untested design. (We had long since agreed that we should be cautious as to which of my various deeds we allowed my son to hear of at what age, lest Jake get Ideas.) I returned my attention to the top of the cliff. The men there chose not to follow their friend, but clapped one another on the shoulders and vanished back into the trees. Before I could ask whether we should send the longboat after the fellow in the water, he set off with a powerful stroke, heading, I thought, for the harbour.

The wind was carrying us onward regardless, and it would likely have been dangerous to veer so close to shore, lest we be blown onto the rocks. I watched the swimmer recede in our wake, wondering if he begrudged us leaving him behind, or was enjoying his time in the water. I did not know whether to call the season autumn or spring—we were south of the equator, though not by much—but the air was warm and the seas mild enough to make for a pleasant swim.

Soon enough I had to turn my attention elsewhere, for we were coming into port. The swift descent of the land meant the harbour, though small, was deep enough that we could approach quite close to shore. Had Namiquitlan been a great city, they might have built piers alongside which we could dock, and then we could have disembarked directly. But it was merely a small town, noteworthy only because several of the local trading routes converged there for the monthly market, and so we had to use the ship's boats—a procedure that had been exotic five months previously, but was now almost routine.

There was a small hotel in Namiquitlan. I immediately sent Tom to book a pair of rooms there, so grateful for the chance to escape the confines of the *Basilisk* that I nearly wept. While he did that, I oversaw the gathering of our luggage and equipment. We intended to stay in Namiquitlan for at least a month, during which time the ship would go elsewhere for trade; we could not leave behind anything we might need.

Partway through this process, shouts drew my attention down to the beach, where a small knot of men had gathered. Someone had just come out of the surf, and those around him were slapping his back and shaking his hand. They eddied our way, and I understood—not from their words, which were a polyglot salad, but from their tone—that they were taking the fellow for a drink.

As they drew closer, I recognized the man at the center as the cliff diver we had seen. He was not, as I had assumed, a local. His skin was nearly as dark as theirs and his nose aquiline, but his face was not so broad nor his lips as full, and his dripping hair was loosely curled. Akhian, perhaps—especially now that I could see his slops were the loose trousers they call *sirwal.*

They were also rather torn from the force of his dive. I looked away, my cheeks heating. I had seen men in far less clothing than that on my Erigan expedition . . . but I had still been grieving then, for all I had thought myself recovered. I was not nearly an old woman yet, though, and my long solitude itched.

The knot of men passed, seeking one of the dockside establishments where they could celebrate the diver's deed. I put him from my mind, and prepared to hunt for dragons.

I knew better than to blunder about aimlessly in the forest, hoping to find my quarry. The region was unfamiliar to us all and prone to sinkholes, which (thanks to the vegetation) we might not see until we fell into them. Tom put it about that we were looking for a guide who could show us where the beasts might be found, and in the meanwhile we turned our thoughts to birds. I had promised Miriam Farnswood and the Ornithological Society that we would collect new species wherever we could and ship them home for further study.

Namiquitlan was a splendid place for acquiring bird specimens, though not an inexpensive one. The people of Coyahuac make great use of feathers in their art and clothing, which means there are many sellers but their prices are steep. The monthly market, which convened two days after our arrival, was a raucous plaza filled with people in triangular mantles of patterned cotton, dickering over everything from coffee beans to coral. After so long at sea, with no one but my companions and sailors for company, I found it almost overwhelming.

I was therefore glad, when the market ended, to retreat to the verandah of our hotel. It was not the most comfortable of refuges; the boards creaked alarmingly when trod upon, and were so weathered by the elements that one could peel strips up with a fingernail. It did, however, have the virtue of being quiet. I retired there and paged through the birding book Miriam had given me, comparing its plates against the sketches I had drawn in the market.

From behind me, a man said in Scirling, "I hear you're looking for feathered serpents."

I turned in my seat and found the voice belonged to the cliff diver. He was properly dressed now, with jacket and sash over his mended sirwal, his hair dry and curling about his face. The garb and his light accent both confirmed him as Akhian. "I am, sir," I said guardedly. "But not to hunt them."

He waved this away, as if the very notion were absurd. "No, of course not. I've seen several out near my site, though. Or one, several times; it's hard to say which."

"Your site? Do you mean the cliff?"

His delighted expression transformed his face. Grave in thought, it lit up like the sun when he smiled. "You saw that? Please, tell everyone who will listen. Half the men don't believe I did it."

"I hardly believe it myself," I said dryly. "Why ever did you?"

"To see if I could," he said, in the tone of one who needs no better reason. "And because it's exhilarating—the flight through the air, and then the slap of the sea. I have never felt more alive. But that isn't what I meant by my site, no. There's a ruin a few miles southeast of here where I've been doing my work."

Belatedly recalling my manners, I invited him to sit in the verandah's sole remaining chair, the battered twin of my own. I hoped it would not break beneath him. "I am Isabella Camherst," I said.

He touched his heart. "Peace be upon you. I am Suhail."

I waited, but he said no more. The pause grew long enough to be awkward, and he cocked his head in inquiry. "Forgive me," I said, colouring. "You are Akhian, are you not? I was given to understand there is usually more to an Akhian name than that."

His elegant mouth twisted in a rueful line. "There is, but my father would not thank me for using it. So I am only Suhail."

"Mr. Suhail, then," I said, making the best of an odd situation. (With little success. I am not certain I ever addressed him formally apart from that one time. It is difficult to be formal with someone you first saw half-naked and hurling himself from a cliff.) "What work is it that you do?"

The chair creaked ominously behind him as he leaned back. "I'm an archaeologist."

I might have guessed that without asking. Coyahuac is rife with ruins, half of them the remnants of a great empire that had dominated the place some hundreds of years prior, before its collapse broke the region into its current array of city-states and Anthiopean protectorates. The other half . . . "Are you studying the Draconeans?"

Suhail's grin came easily, I discovered. "What they left behind, at least."

They had left a great deal behind in Akhia. Many believed the center of that ancient civilization, if indeed it had possessed a center, had been in the deserts of southern Anthiope. It was no surprise that Suhail might take an interest in them.

He dismissed the Draconeans with a wave of one hand. "I imagine you want living dragons, though."

"I do," I conceded. "In fact, my companions and I are on a voyage around the world to study them."

"Your companions," Suhail said. "Even the little boy?"

Less than a week off the ship, and already Jake was complaining about the absence. "He is my son."

Suhail made a gesture I interpreted as apologetic. "I did not realize the other Scirling man was your husband."

"He isn't." I sighed and laid the birding book down. I suspected—and was not wrong—that I would be explaining our arrangement from one side of the world to the other. "I am a widow. Tom Wilker is my colleague. Our fourth, Miss Carew, is my son's governess. Tom and I are the ones looking for dragons. Could you direct us to your site?"

"I can do better than that," Suhail said. "If you wish, I will lead you there tomorrow."

For a moment, my mind's eye was filled with visions of feathered serpents. Then common sense and basic self-preservation asserted themselves. "I will have to consult with Tom," I said. "We have several other obligations here, and I am not certain what arrangements he has made."

Suhail nodded. "By which you mean, all you know of me is that I dive off cliffs and claim to be an archaeologist. Speak with your colleague, and if, when tomorrow morning comes, you have decided that I can be trusted, meet me at the town market's eastern end."

This was blunt, but accurate. "Thank you," I said. He rose gingerly from his chair, eyebrows twitching in relief when it bore this process without disintegrating, then touched his hand to his heart and was gone.

"They didn't use the word 'archaeologist,'" Tom said, "but that seems accurate enough. He's been here for the better part of a month. Started out combing the area for ruins, and eventually settled on the place he mentioned to you. No one can understand why; it's too close to Namiquitlan. Antiquarians and treasure-hunters have already picked the place clean."

"Then he is either incompetent, or better than the rest of them." I shrugged. "Regardless, he doesn't sound like the sort to crack our skulls and leave us in the forest." I caught Tom's expression and sighed in exasperation. "What? Are you shocked that I have, after nearly thirty years of life, learned a degree of caution at last?"

Tom laughed. "Something like that."

We met Suhail outside the market plaza the next morning. He was rising from his prayers as we approached; when he saw us, the serene stillness of his body gave way to sudden energy. From this I surmised that he had not been certain of our coming. I made the introductions, after which he said, "I forgot to warn you, the way is not easy."

I gestured to my attire: a practical shirt, men's trousers, and sturdy boots. "As you can see, I am prepared. And I have been in rough territory before."

Too late, I realized that my gesture had not been what one could call modest—certainly not when I was in trousers. I had grown accustomed to the company of Tom, who saw me only as a colleague. Now I was abruptly aware of my own body, to which I had just drawn a stranger's attention.

Fortunately, Suhail's concern lay in more practical directions. He led us out of Namiquitlan and into the forest, where the close, humid air soon drenched us all in sweat. He had not exaggerated: the way was quite strenuous, and would have been worse had he not cut a path with a machete. "I cut this every time I come," he said ruefully, hacking away. "It grows over again as soon as I turn my back."

A trek that should have taken perhaps an hour therefore took more than two, and I was quite blown by the time we arrived. But the result . . . it was more than worth the effort.

I had never truly understood the fascination Draconean ruins held for so many. I had seen a few in Scirland, which were sadly decayed and had never been all that grand to begin with; I had seen the remains near Drustanev in Vystrana. I had glanced at any number of woodcuts and engravings in books.

None of that prepared me for the experience of seeing a Draconean *city*.

Half a dozen pyramids rose from the jungle, their stepped sides festooned with greenery like oversized *jardinières*. In between the tree trunks and vines, I could glimpse the weathered outlines of carved murals. Birds flitted between these ruinous perches, calling to one another, and sunlight made golden the air through which they flew.

It was, in short, the sort of place I had heretofore thought existed only in tales. I stared at it for a time, my mouth agape, while Suhail spread his hands in the manner of a conjurer who has just revealed his crowning trick.

"The entire place has been thoroughly looted," he said when I had collected my wits. "More's the pity. But there is still a great deal to learn here."

Incompetent, I had said to Tom—or better than the rest of them. "Such as what?"

He led us up one of the pyramids, but not to investigate the place itself. Ignoring what remained of the temple at the top, he began sketching in the air, overlaying our surroundings with imaginary lines. "The pyramids are obvious, but not the interesting part. There used to be streets—see? And if you walk over the ground there, or there, it is not even. Little hillocks beneath you. Even the Draconeans could not all have lived in great pyramids and halls; there must have been ordinary residences, workshops, marketplaces. The ruins of those are here, too. I've dug about a bit to see. The wood has all rotted away, but there are little things. Nothing that's much of interest to antiquarians, the sort of people who only want gold and firestones and terrible statues of ancient deities. Broken pottery and the like. But it tells its own tale."

Suhail's tone was one I recognized in my marrow: the passionate intensity of someone who has found his intellectual calling and will pursue it to the ends of the earth. "What do you think of their relationship with dragons?" I asked—for that point of connection had generally been my only real interest in the ancient civilization.

"You will not laugh?" he said. I thought this time his grin was a shield: pre-emptive self-mockery. I shook my head, promising solemnity, and he said, "I think they tamed them."

The legends claimed it was so, and yet— "People have tried, many times. The Yelangese supposedly have had success with breeding them in captivity; that is something I should like to look into. I have seen dragons chained to act as guards. But actually taming them? Domesticating them, as we have done with horses? We have no evidence of it."

"Unless you have found some," Tom said.

Suhail turned to look out over the ruined city. "These aren't the first ruins I've studied. In Akhia, there are enclosures, large ones, with high walls and little areas inside, like cells. Everyone has a different interpretation for what those places were. Markets, prisons, storehouses for valuable goods. Most of the interpretations assume there used to be a ceiling, now gone. But we find no broken tiles, no holes in the walls for support beams. If they were open to the sky—and I think they were—they would not be good storehouses."

"But they could be dragon pens," I said, understanding. "Presuming, of course, that they either tethered the dragons, or trained them sufficiently to keep them from flying away. It's a possibility, I'll grant you . . . but not proof."

"Of course not. That's why I'm here. I'm looking for proof." Then Suhail shrugged, his expression lightening. "Of that, and many other things. Come—I promised you feathered serpents. I hope they cooperate."

He led us down from our vantage point and across the tangled ground of the city. It was treacherous going, with roots and stones always ready to turn the ankle and trap the foot, and made no easier by the need for stealth. "They often sun themselves at this hour," Suhail told me, "but any close approach and they flee. Or it—I'm not sure if it's always the same one. Perhaps you will be able to tell."

"Few of the large ones are gregarious," I said. "But I am surprised to find even one this close to Namiquitlan. I knew there were some in the region, but with the demand for their feathers being what it is, I expected I would have to go much farther afield."

Suhail nodded. "I had not told anyone about this, until you. I do not want hunters tramping through here trying to kill it."

He stopped us then and pointed at the last pyramid, lying some distance out from the others. "Near the peak—two tiers down—do you see?"

At first I did not. We were too far away, and the thick vegetation acted as both cover and camouflage. But I followed Suhail's pointing finger, and then, indeed, I saw.

The quetzalcoatl lay along the stone tier of the pyramid as if it were a great bed, its body curling through and around the surrounding growth. Its feathers gleamed iridescent green in the sun, the same shade as the quetzal bird from which it took its name. I estimated it to be at least five meters in length, quite possibly more.

Could the creature hear us at this range? I had read what was

QUETZALCOATL

known about quetzalcoatls, but there had been no mention of the quality of their hearing. In a low voice, I asked Suhail, "How close can you get before it flees?"

He shook his head. "I haven't really tried. The first time, I stumbled on it by accident. I was at the base of the pyramid."

Then I could get closer. I spent a few moments studying the beast through my field glasses, then picked my way with care across the rough ground, not wanting to trip and startle him off. To my chagrin, I discovered that approaching closer was of very little use; I could hardly see anything at all through the bushes and trees that had taken root along the pyramid's sides. If I wanted to see more, I would have to climb—and surely that would provoke it into fleeing.

I considered what I knew of them. Crepuscular hunters (as many dragons were), and flightless. If I contrived to be atop the pyramid before it came for its midday nap, could I observe it from above?

I could indeed, though Suhail was astonished when he heard I wanted to try, and Tom insisted on standing ready with a gun in case the creature noticed our presence and took offense. It required a dreadfully early start the next morning, not to mention a trip through the forest in the dim light of dawn, but the climb was the worst part. We identified the path by which the quetzalcoatl usually ascended, then made our way up on the far side, so as not to leave a scent trail that might alarm it. Since our quarry had chosen the *easy* route for its ascent, that perforce left us with a more difficult one. But once atop the pyramid, we were able to build a blind, and from there observe the thing to our heart's content.

Thanks to these efforts, which continued over the next fortnight, I was able to tell Suhail that his site had only the one draconic visitor, and that she was female. (Males possess a patch of red feathers on the throat beneath the head, which this one lacked.)

I never did discover where she spent her nights; it was not at the ruin, and we could not track her well enough to find the location. But she was atop that pyramid more days than not, and I came to know her rather well.

This, perhaps, is why we did not shoot her. At the time I named other reasons, chief among them the fact that her return to an area from which her kind had been driven was a good thing, one I did not wish to undo. We also knew the skeletal details moderately well, for while the bones of a quetzalcoatl are delicate, they do not decay as those of true dragons do—this being one of the chief arguments against classifying them as dragons.

And yet I was not sure. We gathered feathers she had molted where she lay, and haggled with a local hunter for samples from the quetzal bird. At the hotel one evening, I sat fingering them both. "They are so alike," I said to Tom. "I look at these and think that Miriam must be right—that dragons must be related to birds. And yet, if that were true, why should there be only one breed that exhibits feathers? Unless we count the kukulkan as a second—but by all accounts, it is as like the quetzalcoatl as a crested quetzal is to a resplendent one. And drakeflies, I suppose, if we stretch the family tree to include them. Conversely, if dragons are *not* related to birds, why is there a feathered breed at all? Why should they not all have scales?"

Tom was conducting repairs on one of his boots. Indistinctly, because of the needle clamped in his mouth, he said, "Perhaps they aren't dragons at all."

It was the simplest answer. After all, what grounds did I have for calling them dragons? A serpentine body and a draconic head, the latter quite unlike the head of either a snake or a bird. But they had no extraordinary breath, their bones did not decay, and they lacked limbs entirely, let alone wings. Yet sea-serpents had only fins as forelimbs, and wyverns had only hind limbs and wings.

Which created the possibility of a continuum, with the feathered serpents at the far end from, say, a desert drake.

At which point I had to ask myself how such a continuum came to *be*. It made no sense. Primates might encompass everything from human beings to lemurs, but there were no ocean monkeys, no feathered gorillas. The very notion was absurd.

Suhail mostly worked at the far end of the site, tramping across the rough ground with a methodical regularity that refused to let anything short of an entire tree divert him from his path. He was, he explained to us, attempting to map the old city—not merely the pyramids, which everybody knew about, but the smaller bits that were of interest only to him. Periodically he would stop and dig, and then on the trek home we would listen to his grandiose plans of hiring a hundred workers to excavate the entire site. "I'll never do it, though," he admitted. "Not for many years, at least. I am like you—I aim to circle the world and see it all. Only then will I know where to focus my effort."

When that day came, I was certain his effort would be formidable. He seemed incapable of exhaustion: he would labor all day at the ruin, pausing only to pray, then come back to Namiquitlan and teach Jake to swim. My son was already able to keep himself afloat, but Suhail taught him how to use his movements more effectively, how to protect his ears when he dove. This did much to reconcile Jake to being shore-bound; he spent half his day in the water, collecting shells and other marine life to show to Abby. "He isn't learning what he's supposed to," she confided wearily to me, "but I can't say he isn't learning."

I shrugged, accepting it with philosophical resignation. "He already has a better education than I did when I married. The history and such he can acquire later."

He certainly had more than enough opportunity to pick up odds and ends of knowledge, for he was present in the evenings when

Tom and I argued points of natural history, sometimes with Suhail in attendance. On those nights, our conversations often turned to the question I had raised before: the relationship between the Draconeans and the creatures they had worshipped, from which we derived their name.

"They never *domesticated* dragons," I said very firmly, early on in this debate. "Not as we have done with dogs or cattle. Domestication does not simply mean that you keep such animals around; it implies a host of changes, from the behavioural to the physical. Think of the differences between your average hound and a wolf. If anything similar had ever taken place, we would know, because domesticated dragons would still be around today."

The chairs in our rooms were sturdier than those on the verandah. Suhail had a habit of leaning back in his, the front legs slightly off the floor, while he alternately steepled and interlaced his fingers. I had seen him teasing delicate remains out of the ground with those fingers, and knew he could be very still and slow when he wished—but without something to excavate, he very rarely wished. Now he tapped his forefingers together, thinking. "They could have gone feral."

"But that is not the same as returning to their wild form. Besides, they would make dreadful candidates for domestication. Have you not noticed that most of the creatures we alter in such fashion are social? It is easier to domesticate a species that is accustomed to co-existing with others. They understand the concept of hierarchy and will follow humans as their leaders. But most of the bigger draconic breeds are solitary—or near to it."

Tom grinned. "And I have yet to hear anyone claim the Draconeans rode into battle on the backs of fire-lizards."

Since fire-lizards are the size of small cats, the mere thought was laughable. Suhail grinned, too, but it was brief; he lapsed back into thoughtfulness. "Men have tamed cheetahs, though. Even to the point of sending the cats to hunt for them."

I was rapidly learning that he relished a good debate and was not afraid to throw himself fully into one, armed with whatever information he had to hand—and his memory was encyclopedic. Fortunately, he was equally unafraid of conceding the point when faced with superior knowledge. I said, "Yes, but taming is a different matter. A tame animal has merely been socialized to tolerate human contact, and perhaps a modicum of control. But the change is individual: its offspring will need taming all over again."

"Is it possible the Draconeans did that?" He waved a hand before I could respond, dismissing one interpretation of his question. "I mean from a biological perspective. The practical considerations are another matter. *Can* dragons be tamed?"

"It isn't as simple as that," I said. "I can't answer yes or no. Much depends on which breed you mean, and what degree of effect you require before you would call the creature 'tamed.' In Bayembe, the oba keeps savannah snakes on chains. The Moulish have ways of shepherding a swamp-wyrm where they want it to go. But none of that is comparable to, say, a falcon on your wrist, hunting at your command."

The conversation devolved then into a discussion of the different draconic breeds and their characteristics, which might make them more or less suitable for taming; and this topic we revisited many times over subsequent days, interrupted by digressions onto matters ranging from Draconean architecture to survival tactics while out in the jungle.

Suhail was a fascinating man to converse with. His intellectual curiosity matched my own, but his field of knowledge stretched in different directions, intersecting with mine in just enough places to give us common ground on which to range. I have written before about my growing sense of myself as a scholar; those conversations in Namiquitlan were an affirmation of that truth and, in a small way, consolation for the temporary loss of the Flying University. It is a wonderful feeling to have one's brain stretched and tested, to know both that one *has* knowledge, and that one is gaining more.

So congenial were those days that I felt quite regretful when the time came to bid Suhail farewell. I could have stayed for six months in Namiquitlan, studying the local quetzalcoatl and searching the region for others, but the rest of our journey beckoned, along with our obligations to our various financial backers. "If you should find yourself in Scirland," I said, "then do not hesitate to seek me out. I am easily found."

Suhail wrinkled his nose. "Scirland's Draconean ruins are not very interesting."

"True," I said, and chided myself inwardly for feeling so crestfallen. I knew from my previous expeditions, and especially from the peripatetic nature of this voyage, that I would form friendships and then leave them behind. From the start, I had known that this one would not persist beyond our association in Namiquitlan. Yet knowing did not prevent me from wishing.

At the time, I thought I concealed that desire well. As later gossip would prove, however, I did not succeed half so well as I might have hoped.

PART TWO

In which we encounter
a wide variety of dragons
and an even wider variety
of problems

SIX

The perils of bureaucracy—Sabotage—My illiteracy—Dragon turtles—A matter of propriety—Jake goes for a ride

There is a great deal I am glossing over in this account, of course. Some of it is documented elsewhere (such as in *Around the World in Search of Dragons*), but some of it is simply of no interest to anyone.

Into this latter category I place the finer points of the difficulties we faced upon arrival in Va Hing, one of the great conquered cities of Yelang. Contrary to popular assumption, going on an expedition around the world is not merely a matter of obtaining a ship and charting a course. There are visas to be considered, and bureaucracy to navigate when those visas fail to arrive in time, expire too soon, or meet with blank stares on the receiving end. The politics of nations and their economic markets may interfere with your journey. In short, you may spend an appalling amount of time mired in stuffy little offices, trying to get permission to be where you are.

I was fortunate in that the dragon's share of this burden fell on Tom, not me. He had greater patience for such things than I did; but more to the point, he was male, and therefore more to be respected in matters of bureaucratic deadlock. I am not often grateful for the way in which my sex has historically been dismissed, but in this instance I must admit I was glad to leave the task of arguing to him.

Tom was also more capable than I of reading the gentlemen on the other side of the argument. He spotted, as I would not have, an oddity in their conduct.

"I think they know who we are," he said, after another fruitless afternoon ashore.

My afternoon had been spent in study; my head was full of dragons. I blinked owlishly at him. "What do you mean? Our papers give our names, quite clearly."

Tom shook his head, mouth opening to answer me. Then he glanced around. We were on deck; I was not about to closet myself in the coffin that passed for my cabin when I did not have to. All around us were sailors who might overhear. Tom put his hand on my elbow and nudged me toward the bow, where we might speak in something more like private.

Once there, he said in a low voice, "I think they *recognize* our names."

Various scandal-sheets had made me notorious at home, but it was absurd to think anyone cared about such matters here, on the other side of the world. "There is no reason they should know us."

"Isn't there?" Tom said. "We are in Va Hing, Isabella. And we are here to study dragons."

My jaw sagged loose as I caught his meaning. Several years previously, just before our departure for Eriga, the Marquess of Canlan had stolen our research on the preservation of dragonbone, and possible methods for synthesizing the material. We had never acquired proof—not enough to risk accusing him—but it would have brought little good if we had; the damage was already done. Needing ready money, that nobleman had sold the information to the Va Ren Shipping Association, based here in this city.

"What should it matter if we are here?" I said, my bitterness no less for the wound being so many years old. "They have what they wanted. Let us conduct our research in peace."

"If they believed that was all we were here for, they might. But put yourself in their shoes. We might be using this expedition as cover for something else."

"Such as what? Espionage on behalf of Her Royal Highness?" The princess' diplomatic mission had not yet arrived in Yelang, nor was she due to visit Va Hing, but that would not prevent excitable minds from spinning tales. More likely, though, what they feared was specific to us. "Do they think we will steal the notebooks back? There's no point; by now they'll have made any number of copies."

Tom's eyes were grim and hard in his weathered face. "Sabotage."

I could not help myself; I let out a bark of laughter that attracted curious looks from the nearest sailors. "Would that I could! They greatly overestimate me, if they think I can do such damage."

"I believe the phrase is 'better safe than sorry,'" Tom said, so dry it burned. "Even if we are innocent of such schemes, there's no benefit to them in allowing us to wander about Yelang, looking at dragons. So they've taken steps to block us." Then he stopped, sighing, and ran both hands over his hair, smoothing it back into place against the constant lifting of the harbour wind. "At least, I *think* they have. This seems like too much of a bureaucratic—"

He caught himself before he could use whatever term he intended; I expect it was very foul. "Too much so for chance," I said, with a sigh of my own. "Very well. How do we circumvent it?"

Tom's mouth twisted. "Money. Isn't that the way of bureaucrats everywhere? Either they've only been told to refuse us—not paid to do so—or they weren't paid that much. One of them was distinctly hinting that he'd be amenable to a bribe."

If they had indeed been paid, then apparently the going rate for keeping Scirlings out of Yelang was higher than it had any right to be, for our bid had to be even higher. The sum was enough to make me quail. "This . . . will not do anything good to our finances," I said in my cabin, staring down at the ledger.

"It's that," Tom said, "or give up on visiting Yelang entirely. Or ask Aekinitos to put us ashore in a longboat along some uninhabited stretch of coastline, and hope no one asks for our papers."

Aekinitos would have done it, I had no doubt. I had no desire to risk arrest in a foreign country, though. Among other things, it would cause great embarrassment for Princess Miriam's diplomatic mission, which should soon be arriving in Yelang—and I was already in bad enough odor with His Majesty's government. "Then we pay," I said. We would worry about the consequences later. I could try selling my art in the market square, perhaps.

Tom conveyed the bribe to the necessary officials, and we received our stamps. After all that trouble, I had half a mind to seek out the Va Ren Shipping Association and see if I *could* interfere with them somehow. Common sense asserted itself, however—the aforementioned lack of desire to be arrested, not to mention that I had no idea where in the city they were—and so, as always, we turned our attention to dragons instead.

One of the first things I did was scour the bookshops of Va Hing until I found a volume on the Yelangese taxonomy of dragons, which is quite different from our own. At least, that was what I hoped it was: there were very fine woodcuts of dragons in it, and I had brought along one of the sailors from the *Basilisk*, who could read a little Yelangese. As I have said before, I am not much of a linguist, and Yelangese characters had defeated me entirely. I could learn their shapes well enough, but my mind persistently failed to link those shapes to sound and sense.

(Why, you ask, did I bother to acquire the book if I could not read it? Because I intended to have it translated when I returned home. Which, it is true, would have been rather late in the day for my consideration of taxonomy—but as it happened, I was able to have it translated much sooner. That, however, comes later in this tale.)

I had no hope of studying all the dragons to be found in Yelang. There are simply too many, from the subterranean *hok tsung lêng* to the aquatic *kau lêng* to the winged *bê lêng*, not to mention the various draconic cousins: the *lêng ma* or dragon horse; the *hung*, said to have two heads; the *pa siah*, which will hunt even elephants. One could spend a lifetime simply attempting to understand them all—as indeed several naturalists have done, from Kwan Jan Siong in the forty-ninth century to Khalid ibn Aabir in recent years.

My chief aim was a simple one: to lay eyes on one or more Dajin dragons. The specimens of that continent constitute a major branch of the draconic family tree, quite distinct from the Anthiopean one, and no amount of reading about them would give me the same understanding that observation could. I knew that many Dajin dragons were not winged (which led Edgeworth to dismiss them as not 'true' dragons), and that a number of them were waterloving; I knew they had often been revered in Yelang, though not in the same manner as the Draconeans were thought to have done. With the quetzalcoatls of Coyahuac so fresh in my mind, I wanted to study the creatures to be found here, and see if I could derive any insight regarding possible relationships between them.

To do that, of course, we had to *find* them first, which has always been the most vexatious hurdle encountered in my work. Lacking a friendly tsar who might provide us with a guide, we had to hire one ourselves; and this task, too, belonged to Tom, while I scoured the bookshops for that text.

The day after I returned victorious, Jake came running down the deck toward me, with Abby in hot pursuit. I would have liked to take a hotel room in Va Hing, as we had done in Namiquitlan, but the expense of the bribe meant I had to practice economy and stay on board the *Basilisk*. I was therefore ensconced near the bow, perusing the woodcuts in my new acquisition, when Jake skidded to a halt beside me. "Mama! Mama! Can we go to see the dragon turtles?"

"The *what*?" I said, which I fear did not make me sound very clever.

"The dragon turtles! The man said there are lots just down the coast. He said I could go swimming with them. Please, can we go? Please?"

My son seemed liable to vibrate right out of his skin with excitement. Abby puffed to a halt behind him, one hand on her stays, and said between gasps, "He ran all the way from the other end of the docks."

How could I say no? It was the first time Jake had shown much interest in anything draconic. I suspected his interest would have snuffed right out had they been dragon *tortoises* instead of turtles, and therefore land-bound—but I was not one to look a gift drake in the mouth.

Presuming, of course, that there were any such things as dragon turtles. I could not read my book, but paging through it, I found a woodcut of something that indeed appeared to be a swimming dragon with a turtle's shell. That did not guarantee that the beast existed; the book also had a woodcut of a *hung* that showed it with two heads, which is arrant nonsense. (It has a club at the end of its tail, which can be mistaken for another head in poor light or stressful conditions.) But it was enough to merit investigation.

Asking questions around the docks, I learned that there was indeed a region just down the coast where dragon turtles or *lêng kuh* were known to be found; unsurprisingly, the place was generally called Dragon Turtle Bay. I also learned that the fat of the creature's body is considered a great delicacy, and that the poor beasts are rather easily slaughtered, being on the slow and trusting side. The only reason that any of them survived in the area was because the local villagers take pains to cultivate good conditions for them, ensuring that the breed does not go locally extinct.

Tom was still engaged in the hunt for a guide to the interior, and Aekinitos was busy trading, to keep our expedition in hard-tack and potable water. I therefore bought passage on a small junk for myself, Abby, and Jake, as well as Elizalde, the Curxia sailor who had helped me with the book. He served as our interpreter, and I must note for the record that without him, we would have been entirely adrift.

The *Basilisk* would not have been able to sail in close regardless. The region of Dragon Turtle Bay is breathtaking; the coastline there curves in for a small bay, which is dotted with countless steep-sided islands, their rocky slopes thick with greenery. The waters are treacherous for any ship with a draught deeper than two meters or so, especially if her helmsman does not know his way about.

Through Elizalde I heard the legend of the bay, which holds that those islands are all the bodies of dragon turtles, variously said to be either sleeping or dead and petrified. Even in the latter case, however, the fishermen assure you that if not kept happy with offerings of incense and charms, the *lêng kuh* will rise from their places and swim away into the sea, taking the wealth of the bay with them.

This last point was particularly stressed to us, for the locals insisted on our making suitable offerings before we could be permitted to go swimming with the dragon turtles. When I nudged Jake to cooperate, he looked at me with wide eyes. "Aren't you coming with me?"

"I am sure you can report to me very well," I said.

"But—they're *dragons*!"

"They *may* be dragons. Or they may simply be turtles with peculiar-looking heads."

Jake nodded firmly, as if I had proved his point. "Exactly. You have to come and see!"

I sighed and knelt, lowering my voice. Of all the people around us, I think only Abby and Elizalde spoke any Scirling, but I still did not want to advertise my thoughts to the world. "Jake, I cannot go swimming. I haven't brought the costume for it."

He stared at me, a puzzled line creasing his brows. "What do you mean? What costume?"

My son had grown up in Pasterway and Falchester, at a time when we could not spare the money for seaside holidays. "When ladies go sea-bathing, they wear special clothing. So as not to be . . . indecent when the fabric gets wet."

You may doubt that I delivered this explanation with a straight face, given that I was kneeling on the shore in men's trousers at the time. But I meant it quite sincerely: trousers were an eminently practical choice—even the local women wore them, with long tunics over—but getting sopping wet in them was another matter entirely. It had happened from time to time in Eriga, but only by accident or when I had no choice. And besides, when those around you are wearing only loincloths, immodesty becomes a relative thing.

"Who cares?" Jake said, with the careless shrug of the young. "There's nobody here to see. Only Abby."

"And Elizalde," I pointed out. "And all the people of Dragon Turtle Bay." I might never see them again, but that did not mean I wanted them telling stories for years to come about the scandalous foreign woman who went swimming in men's attire.

Jake did not see my reasoning. "So? There's dragon turtles! Isn't this what you came here for? Isn't this the whole point of us going around the world?"

It was. And as much as I hoped to encourage my son to follow in my footsteps as a naturalist, sending him to observe dragon turtles in my place was not the best way to conduct my research. Why, then, was I so reluctant to go into the water?

Again, readers may disbelieve me when I say this, but the reason was right in front of me: my son. Jake knew I was a naturalist, and knew this involved me doing a variety of things that were not considered socially acceptable at home. He had heard some percentage of the rumours about me, I was sure, because it is impossible to quash such matters entirely. But if I had been outrageous on previous expeditions, I found myself surprisingly reluctant to behave in such ways in front of my son. The nobler part of me said I did not want to set a bad example for him. The more selfish part said that I did not want him to think less of me.

But which sort of mother would I rather be? The sort who did not go swimming without a proper costume—which in those days consisted of voluminous pantaloons and a knee-length overdress, all in a stiff fabric which would not cling when wet—or the sort who did what she had sailed halfway around the world to do?

"Very well," I said. "Let us go swimming with dragons."

We paid two local women for the use of their goggles, which they employed in pearl-diving. With the glass lenses protecting my eyes, I was able to see clearly beneath the water—and found myself in a different world entirely.

The ocean floor spread out below me, plunging steeply downward in narrow gulches between the islands. Kelp forested the sides of these gulches, and fish swam through them in glittering schools. The sunlight here became a visible thing, bars of radiance slicing through the water. Floating above it all, I felt as if I were flying—and my readers, I trust, understand what joy that brought me.

Jake became my instructor, passing on what he had learned from Suhail: how to pike my body and dive, how to pinch my nose and blow to relieve the pressure in my ears. I was not as agile in the water as Jake, for he was young, had more (and more recent) experience, and was less burdened by fabric besides; he swam in his drawers, while I swam fully clothed. But I did not need to be a champion swimmer to see the dragon turtles, for they are both huge and relatively fearless of human company.

In shape they are more like enormous turtles than anything else. Their shell alone is often two meters or more in length, and when they extend their flippers, a swimmer feels positively tiny in comparison. The name "dragon turtle," however, derives from the shape of the head, which is indeed like that of a Dajin dragon: a thrusting, squarish muzzle; flaps of skin depending from the jaw; long whiskers which dance in the current as the turtle swims.

They come on land to lay their eggs, and I am told they are pathetically clumsy then, hauling themselves along the ground with their flippers. In the water, though, they are serene and graceful, propelling themselves with easy strokes, changing direction with the casual turn of one limb. I floated above one, watching as he steered a course between two up-thrusting rocks, and scarcely remembered to lift my head for air. (There are hollow tubes one may use for breathing without having to lift the head. They were not employed in that region of Yelang, however, and I lacked the experience to know in advance that such a thing might be of assistance.)

When I had seen all I could for the moment, Jake swam over to me. "May I? Please?"

"By all means," I said, and my son dove.

We had delayed this maneuver because of the risk that the *lêng kuh* would startle and swim off. As indeed it did—but not before Jake had laid hold of its shell.

DRAGON TURTLE

Then its slow drift turned much more business-like, moving off at what I estimated to be two or three meters per second. Which is not so very fast when compared with a galloping horse, but in the water it is impressive—and all the more so when your son is not moving under his own power, but rather is being pulled along by an enormous dragon turtle.

I swam after them in some alarm, fearing to lose my son out among the islands, but did not have to go far before Jake released the creature and kicked for the surface. He broke into the air with a shout of joy. "Mama! Did you see?"

"I did," I said, and then did not get another word in edgewise for several minutes, as Jake told me every detail several times over. I had never seen him so exhilarated. His only regret was that he had not been able to go farther, but it transpired that when the *lêng kuh* began swimming away, the sudden acceleration had startled Jake into releasing some of his air. He wanted to try again, but by then the creature was gone, and despite the tropical waters I was beginning to feel a chill. We returned to our fisherman's boat, and thence to the shore, where Abby had bargained for blankets to wrap us in. I was grateful for both the warmth and the conceal-ment of my bedraggled state.

Once I was something more like dry, we ventured among the tile-roofed huts of the village to one where some men were butch-ering a dragon turtle. Much of its substance was already gone, but I was able to study the flippers and the shell, and (through the good assistance of Elizalde) confirm with the men that neither the bones nor the carapace disintegrated after death. Indeed, the people of that region make use of almost every part of the *lêng kuh*, even carv-ing the bones into needles—though not fish-hooks, for they be-lieve it would be deeply offensive to the creatures of the sea if they put the bones to such use. The scutes of the shell, once separated, boiled, and polished, are used in the same manner as ordinary tortoiseshell, and are much prized for ladies' hair ornaments throughout Yelang, for their distinctive blue-and-green mottling.

I would very much have liked to see a carcass that had been less thoroughly interfered with, but the people of the bay do not take a dragon turtle every day, and we could not afford to spend too long there. We therefore bid them farewell, with many thanks, and returned to Va Hing.

SEVEN

Tom's new contact—The gold rush—Into Yelang—A mated pair—Soldiers in the mountains—Return to Va Hing

The city of Va Hing has long been a cosmopolitan port. It drew trade from all over Dajin well before Yelang seized it as one of their possessions, and although that seizure still draws resentment from the native Hingese (who dislike being forced to exchange their own ways for the pigtail and other Yelangese habits), no one can deny that the local economy has thrived under Yelangese control. From the deck of the *Basilisk* I could see the streets and buildings of the city spreading out through the shallow bowl of the valley in which it sat: a sea of orange roof tiles packed closely together around small courtyards and narrow lanes, more densely populated than any city in the world. Va Hing is not large in terms of geography, but it boasts wealthy merchants and great temples, industrial companies and busy markets, two separate universities and a strong navy.

It also, like all great cities, has an underclass of people who engage in work that skirts the line of legality, where it does not cross that line entirely. During my absence, one fellow of this sort approached Tom with a peculiar offer.

"He thought I was here to hunt dragons," Tom said upon my return, quite late that night.

I was caught between exhaustion and elation for what I had seen that day, and did not quite follow him. "I would not object to studying a carcass—although I thought there were laws restricting the

hunting of dragons?" (Their status as a symbol of imperial authority means that the emperors of Yelang do not much like having
the common folk shoot them. It strikes a little too close to home.)

Tom nodded. "This wasn't what you would call a *legal* offer. But
it seems there's a lot of money to be had in hunting dragons right
now, laws or no laws."

"What?" This penetrated the fog that had enveloped my brain,
making me sit upright on the barrel where I had perched. "For
sport?" I had not forgotten M. Velloin, the big-game hunter we
had clashed with in Eriga.

"With the kind of money apparently on offer, I don't think so.
And it seems to be more of a local phenomenon—Yelangese doing the hunting, rather than foreign visitors. But it's been going
on for long enough that this fellow assumed I had heard about the
business and wanted my share."

If people were thinking to profit . . . I let out a soft but heartfelt curse. "Dragonbone."

Even in the scant light of the moon and the distant docks, I could
see the grim set of Tom's mouth. "I think so. I didn't pursue it,
though—didn't want to make any promises to this fellow before
telling you."

I forced myself to think it through, ignoring the cold knot that
had formed in my stomach. "We already know who has the formula for preservation, but it would be of value to know for certain whether that is where the remains are going." I snapped my
fingers as a thought came to me. "If this *is* for preservation, they
must be sending chemists with the hunters; the bones would
be too badly decayed otherwise. Did the man who approached
you sound like he was working *with* the Va Ren Shipping Association?"

"No, he sounded like an opportunist. But that's entirely plausible: if there's a gold rush on for dragonbone, there will be all sorts

of fellows jumping on board, without really knowing what they're doing."

As much as I wished for Tom to be wrong, I knew he wasn't. Which meant this could be the start of what I had feared when we first discovered what Gaetano Rossi had done: the wholesale slaughter of dragons for their bones, with potentially disastrous consequences.

I rubbed my hands over my tired eyes, willing my thoughts to stop racing ahead. We didn't know for certain that there was a rush, only that one man in Va Hing thought he could turn a profit by taking Scirlings to hunt dragons. But it merited investigation.

Tom said in a low, cynical voice, "I wonder if they even bothered to *try* synthesis."

"It has been years since they obtained the formula," I pointed out, trying to be optimistic. "If they had been harvesting bone so energetically all that time, we would have heard about it before now. They may have spent some time trying, at first."

Neither of us said what we both must have been thinking: if they *did* try, then it seemed they had failed. Just as Frederick Kemble had, thus far. If so much effort could not produce an answer—if synthesis was ultimately impossible . . .

I was not doing a very good job of improving the mood, and I was too tired to do better. "I think you should follow up with this man," I told Tom. "If nothing else, we need someone who knows how to find dragons. The rest . . . we will deal with it later."

Tom's contact reminded me of nothing so much as a squirrel: small and full of seemingly inexhaustible energy. He was not entirely trustworthy; no man who offered to take another on an illegal hunt for dragons could be given such a recommendation. But his untrustworthiness was, as Tom said wryly, "within allowance"—a phrase we had both acquired from Natalie and her engineer friends. It meant that working with the fellow was unlikely to harm us, or at least unlikely enough that we could risk it.

The risk was minimized in part because we were not, in fact, going to hunt a dragon. Tom and I suspected that the spate of men doing so would bring on an equal (if not larger) spate of government officials or soldiers trying to put a stop to the practice; and our desire to avoid prison, which I have already mentioned, argued in favor of keeping our noses clean of anything worse than ink.

We therefore set out armed only with field glasses and notebooks. We did not carry a single gun between ourselves, nor any knife longer than a hand's span. If accosted, we could say with perfect honesty that we had not the *means* to kill a dragon, much less the desire.

For this side expedition, our company consisted only of myself, Tom, Elizalde, and Khüen, our guide. I was not entirely convinced of our safety, and if arrest should happen, I did not want it to catch my son or his long-suffering governess in its net. We intended to be gone for approximately three weeks, during which time the *Basilisk* would go about its other duties, meeting us back in Va Hing in mid-Ventis.

Those of you who have read the earlier volumes of my memoirs may notice an oddity here. Of the four in our group, I was the only woman. The same had been true in Vystrana, but my husband was with me then; in Eriga, I had Natalie as my companion, excepting only when I was separated from her by the events at the Great Cataract. Never before had I deliberately gone gallivanting off without any kind of chaperon for my virtue.

It was not my wisest decision. Though I could not know it at the time (our mail being most irregular; it had to await us where we might arrive soon, or else chase us from port to port), the letters and reports I had written about our time in Namiquitlan had excited comment back home.

Ever since I went to Bayembe, rumours of loose behaviour had dogged my steps, particularly where my interactions with Tom were concerned. I was, after all, on a first-name basis with the man, and there were some who could not conceive that we might simply be friends and professional colleagues. (Or, I think, that *any* woman might be in such a relationship with *any* man.) I had learned to shrug off these whispers, largely because I lacked any viable alternative: insisting on their groundless absurdity only encouraged those who wished to think the worst of me.

But meat loses its savour after it has been chewed for long enough, and so various gossips had begun to link me with every man who crossed my path for more than five minutes. At home, that had been the assorted gentlemen who attended my Athemer gatherings; now that I was on this expedition, Dione Aekinitos had been drawn into the net. And so, it transpired, had Suhail.

I had written too effusively of him in my reports to the *Winfield Courier*—though perhaps any effusiveness was too much, where a strange man was concerned. That, in combination with some of my letters to various correspondents, had planted the notion that our interactions in Namiquitlan were something less than innocent. When I wrote to the *Winfield Courier* about my trip to the interior of Yelang, I did not think to conceal the fact that my companions consisted of Tom (my supposed long-term lover), Elizalde (a sailor and therefore salacious), and Khüen (who, as a foreigner, provided an exotic spice to the whole *ménage*). Primed by tales of my supposed fling with a handsome Akhian traveller, the scandal-sheets back home were quick to declare me now fallen beyond all hope of redemption.

I knew nothing of this as we journeyed away from the coast. We were not headed into wilderness; where Yelang extends its control, it also extends its highways, which are excellently maintained. We stayed in roadside inns or, when those ran out, the houses of hospitable locals. At all times I had a room of my own, or else shared with other women. Not once did I share with Tom or the others, whatever the rumours later claimed. But I was unmarried and unchaperoned, and that was more than enough.

We did not originally intend to travel so far into the interior. Khüen meant to bring us to a place much closer, where we could spend two weeks or so in observation before returning to Va Hing and the *Basilisk*. But when we came there, the village headman told us, with much regret, that there were no dragons to be found in the vicinity. He recommended a neighbouring town, a day's journey farther inland. There we met with much the same story, and so onward, until we were nearly at the end of our rope: if we went any deeper into Yelang, we would not return to Va Hing in time.

Tom and I could guess the cause of our difficulty. We assured Khüen, over and over, that we did not blame him for the failure to find dragons; it was not his fault that others had already denuded the countryside. Each time we heard yet again that there were no dragons there, however, I grew more sick at heart. I felt terribly adrift, more than a week's journey into a land where I spoke scarcely two dozen words of the language, with evidence all around me that dragons were being exterminated for their bones. If I could have wished myself back home in Falchester, the entire expedition of the *Basilisk* canceled, I might have done it.

But I could not, and so I pressed onward. We were at the foot of the An Kang mountains, and on their slopes, the locals assured us, dragons could be found. "Two more days," I said to Tom.

He inhaled, looking apprehensive. "We'll be late coming back."

"Aekinitos might be late himself," I said. "Winds and weather are not fully predictable. And he will not begrudge us a few days, not when the alternative is to have wasted this entire effort." So I hoped, at least; but I did not let my doubts show.

Tom did not want our side trip to end in failure any more than I did. "Two more days," he said, and we went on.

I am grateful we travelled two days farther into the interior, not only for what I learned of Yelangese dragons, but for the other things I learned along the way—though at the time I was not grateful at all.

First I should speak of the dragons. What we found there in the mountains were two of the broad type the Yelangese call *ti lêng* or "earth dragons" (as contrasted with the *tien lêng* or "celestial dragons," which can fly). There is debate even now about the precise classification of that breed; I will not delve into the specifics of that debate here, but merely note that the locals termed these particular creatures *tê lêng*, which in Yelangese writing includes a component that likens them to mountain demons. If I were to call them "mountain demon dragons," though, it would give you entirely the wrong impression of their nature. I shall therefore leave it at *tê lêng*, on the grounds that those of you who know enough of Yelangese writing to know the reference also know not to read too much into the term.

They are not demonic in the slightest, save insofar as they are majestic and dangerous creatures, which gives them a supernatural aura in the eyes of the humans who encounter them. Their scales shade beautifully from grey to black in wavering stripes, which makes for excellent camouflage in the mountain rivers where they spend much of their time. (Many Yelangese dragons are either aquatic or amphibious.) Like most of their kind, they possess long, whisker-like tendrils on the snout, not unlike those found on sea-serpents, and a shorter fringe beneath the jaw; but unlike most, they have no horns—those being a particular characteristic of the Dajin branch of the draconic tree.

One other thing distinguished them from the rest of their kind: the two we found were a mated pair. I can say this with certainty because we came upon them mating—a rare sight, as they are long-lived creatures and do not breed frequently. I was perhaps more elated by this good fortune than is proper to admit; once again, I fear I shall give my editor the vapors by discussing such matters outside a purely scholarly context (where the more distant phrasing can lend a veneer of respectability to the otherwise prurient-seeming habit of a naturalist spying on other creatures' intimate lives). But it was a tremendous sight: they danced in the midst of a river, twining about one another's bodies, occasionally rising into the air in a manner not unlike that of the sea-serpent which had attacked us. Upon being asked, the locals confirmed that the two shared the river and had mated together before, with their successful offpsring migrating elsewhere in search of homes. Dragons are often solitary; when they are not, they most often form sibling bands, or juveniles stay for a time with one parent after they are mature enough to survive on their own. *Tê lêng* are one of the few breeds known to mate for life.

That discovery first elated me, but as we observed the dragons afterward, it made me melancholy. In part this is because I was thinking of the absence of dragons we had encountered on the way here. I cannot pretend, however, that my mood was entirely scientific in origin.

The mating put my mind on offspring, which caused me to miss my son. We had made great strides since those early days in which I could hardly bear to look at Jake, let alone take an interest in his upbringing; and as I had hoped, this journey was bringing us closer still (albeit not without some difficulties along the way). I hoped he was enjoying himself in Va Hing, and not disobeying Abby *too* much.

But more than that, I found myself *envying* the dragons before me.

The words look absurd as I write them out. I admire dragons and have made them my life's work, but I have never wanted to *be* one. (These were not even flying dragons, whom I might have envied for their wings.) Watching the two *tê lêng* sunning themselves on the riverbank to dry, though, I was struck by the companionship they shared—or rather that I imagined them sharing. It is not as if they were reading the latest scholarly journal together, or doing anything else I associated with the domestic harmony of marriage. But they were mated, and according to the villagers had been so for many years. I had that briefly, and then I had lost it. Whether I would ever have it again . . . at the time, I could not say.

Perhaps it is just as well that we could not stay for long. Tom and I had already pressed too far in coming here; we could not risk angering the captain by going completely off the leash. Even if we had allocated weeks in which to study the *tê lêng*, however, we would not have gotten the chance.

"Someone's coming," Tom said, as I searched for a good path up a rocky face.

"Elizalde?" I asked, for we had left him behind in the village with Khüen while we gallivanted about after dragons.

Tom did not answer immediately. When he did, the tension in his voice stopped me mid-search. "Yes. But he isn't alone."

It took me a moment to turn myself about, lest my precarious footing slip out from under me. Once that maneuver was complete, however, I saw why Tom's voice had gone tight. There was a group

of nearly a dozen men headed our way, and while our sailor-
interpreter was among them, the rest wore the high-collared uni-
forms of Yelangese soldiers.

"We haven't done anything wrong," I said to Tom, but it came
out apprehensive. We had not done anything wrong—that we *knew*
of. In a foreign country, though, it is easy to step awry, simply out
of ignorance. And pleading innocence on those grounds does
not always find a sympathetic ear.

Whatever conversation we were about to have, it would not be
helped by being conducted atop a slope of scree that threatened
to go out from underfoot if one inhaled too vigorously. Tom and
I picked our way to flatter ground, and by the time we got there,
Elizalde and the soldiers had reached us. "What's going on?"
Tom asked.

Elizalde's answer was simultaneous with the soldiers' actions:
two of them came forward and dragged our packs from our backs,
unceremoniously emptying them onto the ground. "They want
to know what we're doing here. They haven't said it, but I think
they think you're here to hunt dragons."

In a way, it was almost a relief. This was a difficulty I had imagined before, rather than one which took me by surprise. "They can
see for themselves," I said, trying not to sound too bitter as the
soldiers picked through our notebooks and other gear. "We have
no weapons of any sort."

They saw, but it did not seem to impress them. One of them
snapped a command at Elizalde, who translated. "He wants to see
your papers."

These we carried in our pockets. Tom and I produced the visas we had bought at such expense and handed them to one of the
soldiers, who gave them to the man I supposed was his captain.
This fellow looked them over, then tossed them to the ground in
annoyance. A second command to Elizalde produced confusion;

our interpreter engaged in brief discourse with him. Then he said, "He wants to see your papers for the dragons."

I frowned in puzzlement. "Our notebooks? There, on the ground."

Even as I said it, I suspected that was not what he meant. There was a delay, however, when Tom—not wanting to see our investment go blowing off into mountainous oblivion—moved to collect the visas; this provoked some shouting, and only when that was done was Elizalde able to say, "I think he means a permit."

"A permit to study dragons? No one told me we needed such a thing." Under other circumstances, it might have occurred to me to wonder whether this was the sort of trick used in bureaucracies the world over, telling the ignorant visitor that he needs to pay for some document the bureaucrat has just made up. These circumstances were specific, though, and my thoughts went elsewhere. I straightened and looked the captain in the eye. "He means a permit to *kill* them. Doesn't he."

The man did not like me staring him down. Or perhaps he spoke some Scirling; I have done it myself, pretending to know nothing of a language so as to eavesdrop on the conversation of others. (It is not polite, but at times it is necessary.) He began a rapid battery of questions, filtered through Elizalde, probing into our purpose and our past; it was all we could do not to inadvertently admit that we had to bribe a functionary in order to enter the country at all.

It might not have made any difference if we *had* admitted it. The end result was much the same: we were permitted to collect our belongings, then marched downslope to the village, where we gathered Khüen and our remaining gear. We were, the captain made it clear, to return immediately to Va Hing, not pausing or detouring along the way.

And we might have gone quietly, were it not for one thing.

As we prepared to leave, I saw three of the soldiers talking to

the village elder who had originally directed us toward the dragons. His gestures now were the same: pointing up the slope, then
his hand curving to indicate a bend in the river. The three men
nodded and shouldered their rifles, then set out with purposeful
strides.

"Isabella," Tom said in warning, but by then I had already
launched myself toward the captain.

It did not matter to me that the man likely did not speak Scirling;
the words burst out of me regardless. "That's what you came here
for, isn't it? To kill those dragons! Are you the ones who laid waste
to the countryside below? Now you will come up here and slaughter this pair—"

At this point Tom caught up with me. Eschewing propriety, he
flung one arm around my waist and stopped my forward charge,
catching my wrist with his free hand when I fought against his grip.
I think he tried to say calming words, too, but I did not hear them
over my own shouts. "They just *mated*, you fool! The female is likely
pregnant. If you kill her, there won't be any new generation;
you're burning the forest down just to get a few logs. You *can't* shoot
them, you *can't*!"

I will not relate the rest of my words. Few of them were polite;
some were the unfortunate byproduct of months spent in the company of sailors, whose language can be as colourful as advertised.
Tom dragged me away bodily while Elizalde and Khüen fell over
themselves with apologies; no doubt they had visions of my tirade
ending in the lot of us being shot. What the captain said to them,
I do not know, for Tom quick-marched me out of the village, not
even bringing our packs with us, trusting the other pair to collect
what we had left behind.

Which they did, and then we went back to Va Hing.

I would like to tell you that I came up with some clever plan
for protecting the *tê lêng* against the soldiers who had come to kill

them. I would not kill the soldiers myself, and my attempts to per-suade them (if I may use the verb loosely) had failed—but perhaps I might have found a way to scare the dragons off, at least for long enough that their hunters would give up the hunt.

But I did not. I tried; I racked my brains for any method that might suffice. Unfortunately, this was not Vystrana or Mouleen. I had not spent long enough in this locale to know the terrain, nor even the habits of the dragons themselves in any great detail. None of the information that might have given me a chance of success was in my possession. I was a stranger here and a foreigner; and I had a son waiting for me in Va Hing, who needed me to come back to him, rather than being arrested in a foreign country—or shot.

Some of you reading this memoir may think me a hypocrite for my rage. After all, had Tom and I not killed dragons in the course of our research? It was not long since I had sat astride the corpse of a sea-serpent, wet to the knee in water bloodied by its death. But I thought then, as I do now, that there is a great deal of differ-ence between shooting one or two animals for the purpose of better understanding their live cousins, and hunting many for profit. The one makes it more possible for humans and dragons to live in harmony. The other . . . I had seen the first fruits of that already.

We went in silence for the rest of that day. When we stopped for the evening, Tom said, "Soldiers. Are they doing this on their own time, for money? Or is this something the Yelangese govern-ment is backing?"

"I thought dragons were supposed to be *protected* by the government," I said.

He shook his head, baffled. "So did I."

Against my better judgment, I turned to look back in the di-rection of the mountains—where, I feared, one or both *tê lêng* already lay dead. "Give me the jungles of Mouleen again," I said.

"I had rather face wild beasts and diseases than the perils of civilization."

There is a proverb, which Tom was kind enough not to voice: *be careful what you wish for.* Unfortunately, not only did I get it, but so did those around me.

EIGHT

In our absence, Jake had assembled a monumental collection of starfish and miscellaneous shells, which he showed to me with great pride. I praised it, wondered where we would put it aboard the *Basilisk*, and decided it did not matter; I remembered my own childhood collection of oddments and how it had pained me to lose them. I would not subject my son to the same.

Aekinitos might have complained, had he not been distracted by the delay in our return, which had left the *Basilisk* sitting for several unproductive days in port. Fortunately—for suitably broad values of that word—he was almost immediately distracted by yet another matter, which was our impending deportation from Yelang.

"What did you *do?*" he demanded of me, after a visit from a very stern-faced official.

It says something about Dione Aekinitos that he sounded less angry than impressed. Because I do not wish to defame the man, I will not say here what suspicions I had about his past and the activities he engaged in then . . . but he had a tendency to admire trouble with the law, provided the cause was either good or entertaining enough.

Tom and I had already related to him what occurred during our overland sojourn, but we had not given him the background: dragonbone, the Va Ren Shipping Association, and the apparent trade in dragon poaching. Now we exchanged glances, for we had not planned in advance what to say on that topic if queried.

(And why, I ask you, did Aekinitos look at *me* when asking what we had done? I did not think I had done anything while aboard the *Basilisk* to make him assume that between Tom and myself, I would be the troublemaker. Perhaps the stern-faced official had said something of my behaviour during the incident in the mountains.)

Now, choosing my words very carefully, I said, "There may be an . . . organization here in Va Hing that has a grievance against the two of us. It is a long story, and involves some research being stolen from an associate of ours in Falchester several years ago. We did not expect it to cause trouble."

Aekinitos was standing in front of the windows that formed one wall of his cabin. He linked his hands behind his back and paced the short distance available to him, side to side before the windows, the light briefly limning his profile from each angle in turn. "Research. On dragons? I have never yet heard of dragons causing someone to be barred from entering a country."

"It happens, I assure you," I said dryly. "This is not even the first time it has happened to *me*."

The novelty of that statement halted him in his pacing, with a tilt of his head I interpreted to mean curiosity. I waved it away, saying, "That is a story for another day. In the interim—are we truly barred from Yelang?"

"You are." Aekinitos sighed and pulled out the chair behind his desk, then dropped onto it with a complete lack of grace. "We are permitted to go into Yelangese ports, but you may not leave the ship. Either of you."

Tom made an inarticulate noise of frustration. "But that makes complete hash of our plans. We were going to the Phăn Shân river to look at the *kau lêng*, so we could compare it to Moulish swamp-wyrms. The *hung*, the *yin lêng—*"

Aekinitos cut him off with a growl. "And if you had kept to your schedule, coming back here rather than pressing on ahead, you might have had a chance to do those things. But now? You have a choice. Sit aboard the *Basilisk* with your specimens and your notebooks while we trade through Yelang, or make different plans."

The galling part, of course, was that he was right. Going up into the mountains had been a mistake—one that had cost us more than we knew at the time. Our fleeting observations of the dragons there did not counterbalance all the work we might have done elsewhere, which was now barred to us. It is possible the Shipping Association might have caused us difficulty elsewhere; I did not know if the hunt for dragons was confined to the lands around Va Hing. But they were a Hingese company, and I had to believe their reach did not extend clear across the Yelangese Empire. We might have been able to work in peace. But Tom and I had chosen wrong, and this was the price.

We were not the sort to sit idle, so it will surprise no one when I say we chose to make different plans.

We had promised to do various bits of surveying for the Scirling Geographical Association, and one of the places they showed an interest in was the Melatan island chain of Arinevi. After our Yelangese debacle, we backtracked to spend more than a month in this region, tramping about doing the meticulous (not to say tedious) work that surveying requires. It felt like penance: our zeal for dragons had led us to err, and so we separated ourselves from dragons for a time, putting our efforts into repaying those whose support had made this voyage possible at all.

With all due respect to the organizations that funded my expedition, our time in Arinevi was sheer drudgery of a sort I did not enjoy at all. Furthermore, hindsight proved it to be an unwise choice—though in all fairness, the same misfortune could have befallen us elsewhere in the tropics, whether we were studying dragons or not.

The islands of Arinevi are tropical, with all the perils that implies. Several of the sailors fell ill with malaria, which is a common enough occurrence. (Several others fell ill with diseases endemic to ports the world over, or rather to certain establishments within those ports.) We thought very little of this, and upon completion of our survey work, set sail with the intention of resuming our draconic research.

Not long after we departed, however, I was struck by a fever. I choose the word "struck" quite deliberately, for it seemed to come out of nowhere; one moment I felt fine, and then before the hour was out I was shivering in my hammock. "It can't be yellow fever," I said to Tom, through my shudders. "I've had it already."

The hammock was soon an agony to me, for all my muscles and joints ached, while my skin flushed and became quite sensitive. The ship's doctor, who had been through the tropics before, diagnosed my affliction as dengue fever. As the more colloquial name of "breakbone fever" implies, the aches can become quite painful, and my flushed skin soon developed into a rash not unlike the measles.

Upon hearing I was ill, Aekinitos promptly locked Jake and Abby into his cabin, allowing no one other than himself in to see them; he even brought them their meals. (It did little good; we know now that dengue is transmitted by mosquitos, of which there were none at sea. But at the time that was not certain, and so I am grateful to him for the precaution.) Jake, I am told, objected strenuously to confinement, and spent an entire afternoon shouting imprecations through the door at the man who would not let him go tend to his mother, until his voice quite gave out.

Three of the sailors who had assisted us similarly fell ill with dengue. Like myself, they were fortunate enough to escape with a mild case of the disease—mild meaning that we suffered a few days of nauseating, painful fever, during which we bled from the nose and the mouth, but after that we recovered. Partway through this ordeal, I was shifted from my hammock to a proper bed; I did not understand until my fever broke that Aekinitos had brought us to Seungdal, which was the nearest port of any real size. When I woke free of pain for the first time in days, Abby told me where we were—and why Aekinitos had diverted from his course.

Weak as I was, I insisted on rising from my bed. With Abby's aid, I limped from my room to Tom's.

When I had fallen to yellow fever in Eriga, I had been one of the unlucky few who pass from the first, milder stage of the disease to a more serious secondary one. For Tom, it was the same with dengue. His breathing was rapid and shallow, as if he could not get enough air, and he was shockingly pale. Someone—I later learned it was the ship's doctor—had shaved his head to bring down his fever. Bereft of that cap, his face seemed raw and unfamiliar, as if it belonged to a different man, and the alienation unnerved me greatly.

I will not pretend that what I suffered then in any way compares to Tom's own trials. His life was in great danger; we were exceedingly lucky that he recovered not long after. But I was weak with my own recovery, and it had not been long since I was forced to abandon those mated dragons to the soldiers who were trying to kill them. Now it seemed I might lose the man who had been my friend and comrade for the better part of my adult life. My knees gave out beneath me; Abby very nearly had to carry me back to my bed, where I wept into my pillow and wondered if this entire journey had been a mistake.

The storm of my emotional outburst soon passed, leaving in its wake a terrible itching and the realization that my head, like Tom's, had been shaved. I scarcely recognized my own drawn, mottled face in the mirror, bereft of the hair which had been its frame since I was a child. When I recovered enough to go out, I wrapped my stubbled head in a kerchief before putting on my bonnet, and still felt terribly self-conscious.

It did not help that our location was completely unfamiliar to me, and unwelcoming. Seungdal only allows travellers from their favoured allies to roam freely about the city and countryside; all others are confined to an islet in the harbour. Scirland not being one of those favoured allies, we were on that islet, and further-more lodged in a rather dreary hotel used for quarantine. I could not blame the authorities for their caution, but it meant my im-mediate surroundings were dingy and the streets beyond them dedicated to little other than trade.

I had some cause to be grateful for the menagerie of foreign-ers, at least, in that among them I could find a few with whom I shared a language. On a voyage of this sort, visiting so many dif-ferent parts of the world, I could not hope to do as I had done in Vystrana and Eriga, attempting to learn the native tongue: there were simply too many. I had until now gotten by mostly on what I possessed of Chiavoran, Thiessois, and Eiversch, and the mercy of those who spoke some Scirling. I had also studied the simpli-fied pidgin known as Atau, a Puian language spoken by traders throughout much of the Broken Sea—but that did me no good in Seungdal, where the locals (who are of Dajin stock, not Puian) frown on that tongue as a degenerate interloper. As a result, I was unable to engage with much beyond my own door, and between that and my exhaustion, I stayed largely in the hotel.

There my mind worried incessantly at the problems that beset me. Aekinitos, Abby told me, had taken the *Basilisk* out for trad-ing; he would return in a few weeks and see where matters stood. Although I initially cursed him roundly for abandoning Tom at such a critical time, I had to accede to his logic; they could do nothing for Tom that they had not done already—the hotel had a doctor who was probably superior to the *Basilisk*'s in any case—and Aekinitos could not afford to sit in harbour doing nothing. I mean that quite literally: it takes a great deal of money to keep so many men fed, to say nothing of the pay they are owed, and had he kept the *Basilisk* in Seungdal the entire time, our expedition would have ended in bankruptcy. So long as Aekinitos was earning money *somewhere*, he could give both us and himself a financial reprieve.

But this did not solve the underlying problem, which was that we were growing alarmingly short of money. The bribe in Yelang had gone almost entirely to waste, the changes to our itinerary had thoroughly mangled our budget, and doctors do not come cheaply. I sat on my sickbed, staring at maps, and thought with bleak resignation that we would have to abbreviate our journey. I did not know what sorts of trading opportunities Aekinitos might find in the Broken Sea, but it was not a region we could sweep through in a week—not even if we ignored both the sea-serpents and the fire-lizards that dwelt on the volcanic islands. If we bypassed it entirely, however, the remainder of our voyage might yet be saved.

These were not thoughts I enjoyed having. It felt like admitting defeat, in a way I had not done since the beginning of my grey years, when I attempted to forswear my true interests in favour of more ladylike behaviour. But it was no virtue to forge ahead and deepen our difficulties; better to salvage what I might from the situation, while I still could.

I owe Jake a great deal for his actions during that time: first because he kept me company even when I was not good company to keep, and second because, once I regained a modicum of strength, he insisted on dragging me from the hotel into the streets of Seungdal. Without his determination, my voyage might have been far shorter and less interesting, and my own life less complete.

Abby had of necessity allowed Jake to run about on his own while she looked after Tom and myself, but Jake had taken his freedom with surprising maturity. He showed me about the place, indicating which merchants he had dealt with in obtaining food and other necessities; he spoke none of their language and they spoke none of his, but gestures will go a surprisingly long way in bargaining. Even that small grounding, orienting me in the crowded and unfamiliar maze of the harbour islet, did a great deal to make me believe that this problem, too, could be surmounted.

My optimism did not long outlast my strength, and the latter flagged with alarming rapidity. Jake, carefully solicitous, was about to lead me back to the hotel when he gave a sudden yelp of recognition and dove into the waterfront crowd.

His abrupt departure left me off-balance and grasping for the nearest wall. I could not spot him in the press, and called out his name with growing alarm. Then my searching gaze lit upon a face that I, too, recognized.

"Mrs. Camherst!" Suhail said, his familiar grin spreading across his face. It faltered, though, when he took in my state. "Are you well?"

I let go of the wall, intending to tell him that I was fine, but gave the lie to those words before I could even speak them. As Jake said later, I turned an alarming shade of paper-white and swayed like a reed. Suhail was there in an instant, one hand on my elbow, the other on my waist, first catching and then guiding me to a seat on the nearest crate.

When I was sure of my stability, I said, "I have been ill."

"I can see that," Suhail murmured. "Please forgive me. I would not ordinarily touch a woman outside my family, but—"

I waved away his apology before he could finish it. "I had rather you catch me than let me fall down in the street. If propriety takes issue with that, it can go hang." I drew in a steadying breath. "Forgive *me*. I was clearly too ambitious in coming out today."

"Are you in the quarantine hotel?" Suhail asked, and I nodded. "Let me help you back."

A minor comedy ensued, in which his sense of good behaviour, my own determination not to be a complete milksop, and Jake's eager gallantry all collided in their rush to determine whether I could get home without leaning on Suhail again. Jake ended up being my support, for all that he was less than half my size, and I could not decide whether I was relieved at not needing a grown man to keep me on my feet, or humiliated that I needed to lean on my own son.

Once back at the hotel, Suhail offered to leave and come back when I was feeling better, but I said, "No, no. I only need to sit for a little while, and perhaps drink something. It gave me quite a turn, seeing you—not that it was unpleasant! Just a surprise."

Suhail nodded, glancing about the unimpressive lobby as he took his seat. "And your companion? Is he here as well?"

"He is recovering," I said, and gave him the briefest outline of our recent misfortunes.

Suhail listened with a grave expression, and shook his head when I was done. "Truly, you have both been very lucky. I have had dengue myself, some years ago, and although I survived, others with me were not so fortunate."

"Did they shave your head, too?" Jake asked.

I could have quite cheerfully strangled my son in that moment, for his question caused Suhail to look first at him, then at me; and after a moment he realized that the kerchief beneath my hat was not covering a very large volume of hair. To his credit, however, he did nothing more than nod in silent acknowledgment of my loss.

To Jake he said, "They did not. But they did tie me to the bed, to keep me from scratching myself bloody."

As I had frequently been tempted to do the same to myself, I could sympathize. "How long did it take you to recover?" I asked.

"To be on my feet, only a few days. But I was tired for a fortnight after. Your companion . . ." Suhail paused, the tip of his tongue resting against his lip as he thought. Then he shook his head. "I cannot remember the name of it. There is an herbal concoction, common in this region, which will restore his strength more quickly."

I sighed. "I already asked the doctor here, and he had no suggestions."

Suhail waved this away. "Any herbalist here should know it. If you ask them, they can tell you."

"If I *could* ask them," I said, too tired to hide my frustration.

"Then I will do it for you. If you would like."

He said it so matter-of-factly, apart from the belated realization that perhaps he was overstepping his bounds. That was not at all what put me aback, though. I knew from our interactions in Namiquitlan that he spoke the Coyahuac tongue quite well. His Scirling was accented but grammatically impeccable, and one could presume a mastery of his native tongue of Akhian. "How many languages do you *speak*?"

Suhail cocked his head to one side, eyes fixed on a high corner of the room, as if counting silently. "Speak? Or should I also include the ones I can only read?"

"Good heavens," I said, marveling. "I have never learned any language as well as you speak mine, let alone so many beyond it. I haven't the head for such things."

He shrugged, seeming unimpressed by his own ability. "I have always enjoyed languages. They are like ciphers. When I was a boy, my father—" Upon that word, Suhail stopped. For the first time in our acquaintance, I saw a hint of bitterness cloud his normally bright disposition.

Jake rescued us both from that awkward moment. "Can I go with you?"

Suhail blinked, momentarily confused. Then he recalled the offer he had made, before we embarked upon our tangent. "You should perhaps stay with your mother."

My words overlaid my son's, both of us assuring him that I was perfectly capable of sitting quietly in a hotel without supervision. "Besides," I said when I was done, "Abby is upstairs with Tom." (She had proved a patient nursemaid, having worked for a family with sickly children before coming to mine. Such labors are often unappreciated—especially with patients as grumpy in their recovery as Tom became—and so I want to express my gratitude toward Jake's governess here, for all posterity.)

I think Suhail had exaggerated in saying that "any herbalist" should know the concoction, for he and Jake were gone quite some time. They returned victorious, however, and whether Tom's subsequent improvement was due to the medicine or his own stout constitution (which had shrugged off wyvern poison with remarkable ease), I was nevertheless grateful to Suhail for his aid.

He returned the following day, and found me well enough to feel that I could not bear facing the quarantine hotel's dreadful food yet again. They had, during my illness, fed me a broth made with pig meat in it. In Dajin lands, where few people are Segulist or Amaneen, pigs are quite commonly used for food, and Abby had been too distracted with her duties to realize. When I heard about it afterward, I was nearly ill in a new way, and scrubbed my mouth thoroughly before I consumed anything else. After that, I insisted on pig-free meals, but what I was given in its place was scarcely more appetizing.

We went therefore to Suhail's hotel—myself and Jake; Tom was not yet recovered enough to leave his bed, and Abby would not leave him unattended—and found it, unsurprisingly, to be much better than our own. I would gladly have shifted there as soon as Tom was judged no longer a risk, but our strained finances weighed heavily upon me. The quarantine hotel at least had the virtue of being cheap.

The server at this establishment greeted Suhail with familiarity and seated us right away. Once settled, I asked, "How long have you been here? He seems to know you quite well."

Suhail thought it over. "A month? No, not quite so much."

My brow furrowed. "Are there ruins here of particular interest? I do not recall hearing of any." Akhia was no more a favoured ally of Seungdal than Scirland was, but I knew it was possible for individuals to gain permission to move about more freely. Perhaps he was attempting to obtain such a permit.

But he shook his head. "There is only record of one ruin here, and it is long since gone. The Jeonhan Dynasty had it dismantled, stone by stone, for being idolatrous. No, I am . . . not exactly here by choice."

"Were you shipwrecked?" Jake asked.

Suhail laughed. "Only in a manner of speaking. I had a disagreement with the captain of the ship I was on. The end of the disagreement was that he put me ashore here, to find new passage as I might."

"That's not like a shipwreck at all," Jake complained, as the server arrived with bowls of soup Suhail assured us were entirely free of pig.

The beef stock and cabbage were very welcome after my illness, even if the quantity of pepper was rather more than I liked. My eyes watered a little as I said, "But surely it should not take a month to find passage off this island—not with the number of ships that come in to port. Where are you trying to go?"

Suhail had no apparent problem with the pepper; Akhians like their food well spiced. He ate quick, tidy spoonfuls in between bits of his answer. "It isn't my destination that poses the problem. It's my baggage."

When I gave him a mystified look, he elaborated. "A device I had made for me by an artificer in Tuantêng. It was the source of my disagreement with the captain, for the size and weight of it made him very unhappy. Have you ever heard of a diving bell?"

"I have!" Jake said, before I could admit my ignorance. "It's a big dome of metal. You sink it down into the water and it keeps the air inside, so you can go swimming out and come back for air."

"That is the general idea, yes, although the details are more complex—especially with the diving bell I had made. A friend of mine designed it, and—" Suhail caught himself and waved the rest away. "You would not be interested in the technical details. The heart of the issue is that with the addition of this bell, my baggage became rather more substantial than it had been, much to the displeasure of the captain. And although I offered to pay him well for his trouble, he chose rather to seek new employment."

Jake looked very much as if he wanted to argue the assertion that he would not care about the technical details, but I had something else on my mind. "Why burden yourself with such a thing, though? I thought your interest was in archaeology."

Suhail's grin spread across his face, as if he could not hold it in. "How else am I to study the ruins underwater?"

"Draconean ruins?" I asked dubiously. "Whyever should they—oh. Of course they would not *build* underwater. You mean that the ruins have been drowned since their day, like the lost city of Cyfrinwr." Despite my usual disinterest in ancient civilizations, the notion intrigued me. "*Are* there such ruins? Or are you hoping to find some?"

"I know there are several," Suhail said. "Scattered throughout the Broken Sea."

Jake was bouncing in his seat at the thought of this. Draconean ruins on land held only moderate savour for him, but underwater? He could imagine nothing finer. For my own part, I was arrested by a sudden thought.

The Broken Sea. To which I very much wished to go . . . assuming our finances could support it. In the meanwhile, here was Suhail: with money, but no ship.

I almost asked him there, in the middle of our luncheon, without pause for consideration or consultation with my fellows. But it was not the issue of what Tom would say, nor Aekinitos, that stopped me that day. Rather I found myself questioning my own impulse. I had enjoyed Suhail's company in Namiquitlan, and certainly he had been good to us here in Seungdal—but I knew from personal experience that a ship is not a spacious home to share with a near stranger. We had our share of tiffs with the crew, and they fell under Aekinitos' authority, which meant he could punish them when necessary. How would we handle it if we came into conflict with Suhail?

(Furthermore, I was by then self-aware enough to consider a different question, which was how pure my motives were in desiring his company. The irregular packets of mail that awaited us in different ports had not yet included any of the rumours back home, but I knew such things start easily enough, even when they are entirely baseless. Any supposition of attraction to Suhail would *not* have been baseless, and so I had to be doubly careful of my behaviour.)

But he might rescue us from our current straits, and I did not want to lose that chance.

I fear that what I said then was an utter fabrication. "Our captain knows the routes through here quite well, and many of the ships that sail them. Do talk to us before you make any decisions. We may be able to point you toward a better option."

"Thank you," Suhail said, and I felt like a terrible bounder for lying. But I could hardly take it back now—and, in the end, it hardly mattered.

I put the matter to Tom once he was strong enough to consider it. He was propped up against one of our packs, with a pillow over it, for the hotel would not give us enough pillows to support him sitting upright in his bed. I had never seen Tom like this, with the hair on his jaw almost longer than that on his head; the next day he begged until Abby entrusted him a razor, so that he might at least remove the former, while he waited for the latter to grow back.

He shrugged wearily. "I'm used to close quarters. If our paths lie together, why not take advantage of it?"

"If we can find a place that serves both our interests at once, it could work very well," I said. "Many of the Puian islands are volcanic, though of course not all of the peaks are active. There are sure to be fire-lizards in abundance, and sea-serpents. Though we cannot be certain of their relation to the ones near Siaure, given how far we've come around the world."

"Observing them there doesn't stop us from looking elsewhere. But we'd need to find a place with interesting ruins, too. And unless Suhail can fund this entire byway out of pocket, we'll need to make an arrangement with Aekinitos."

That, of course, required our erstwhile captain to return. Which he did near the end of Graminis: somewhat after he had intended, but I suspected he knew enough of dengue to guess that if Tom lived, he would not be up and about any sooner than this.

(This makes Aekinitos sound heartless, which I do not intend.

Indeed, I feel for the man, at least in this regard. His line of work made him accustomed to facing off against forces beyond his control, but he relished those cases because there was something for him to *do*. Where illness was concerned, there were no sails to reef, no items of ballast to rearrange. He could do nothing, and so it was no loss for him to at least go where he could distract himself.)

We met in his cabin, and I put the matter to him thusly. "I may have found a way to resolve, or at least lessen, our financial difficulties. But it will require your approval, for it involves an additional passenger aboard your ship—one whose research would likewise shape our itinerary." Then, realizing that sounded ominous, I hastened to add, "I do not expect the disruption to be much, or I would not suggest it."

Aekinitos made a low, thoughtful rumble. "Who is this mystery passenger?"

"A fellow we met in Namiquitlan; you may recall me mentioning him. It is Suhail, the gentleman who took us to the ruins."

The captain's black brows drew together as if pulled by a magnet. I should like to blame my recent illness for the erroneous thought I had then—but the truth is, I was simply foolish, and thinking too much of propriety, not enough of politics. I thought Aekinitos' frown was due to my terming Suhail a gentleman, when we had no evidence of his family one way or another. In his defense, I would have pointed out that anyone who could afford to commission a special design of diving bell was at the very least *wealthy*, and in Akhia as in Scirland, I imagined that wealth could go a long way toward purchasing the right to claim good breeding.

Fortunately, Aekinitos spoke before I could embarrass myself with such protests. "An Akhian," he said, and it was almost a growl.

Then, at last, I understood. I was from northern Anthiope, and while I was moderately well acquainted with the politics of the continent's southern reaches, they were not often my first thought. The Nichaean Islands, off the southwestern coast, have fought more than one war against Akhia. (Now that I pause to look it up, I count at least seventeen distinct conflicts throughout history, and possibly more; it depends on whether one considers matters like the Atelephaso Schism to have been one war or several, all sliding into one another.) Relations between their two peoples are like those between Thiessois and Eiversch, with the added provocation of religious difference—which is to say, they are not good at all.

"He does not seem to be very close to his people," I said, feeling it was quite an inadequate response. "At least, I do not think he is on speaking terms with his family."

Aekinitos' snort told me this might recommend the gentleman, but not very far. "What kind of research does *he* do?"

"Archaeology. His particular interest is in underwater ruins. He is not a treasure-hunter, though—he is a scholar."

The captain almost looked disappointed at my last comment. Treasure-hunting would have been far more lucrative for our expedition, and I already knew Aekinitos cared relatively little for respectability.

"It will soon be the season of storms," he warned me. "They are powerful things in this part of the world, and the Broken Sea is not easy to sail in the best of times."

Had our plans not been overturned by deportation from Yelang and dengue from Arinevi, we would have been safely inland somewhere in Dajin about now, with Aekinitos free to sail the safer coastal waters. "Is it too dangerous to attempt?" I asked.

Aekinitos chuckled. It was not a reassuring sound. "The storm has not blown that can sink me." I had enough time to reflect that this only meant he had not been sunk *yet* before he asked, "Where is it you intend to go?"

At my request, he brought out a map. It was not as complete as I might have liked: the Broken Sea was in those days very imperfectly charted by Scirlings, and more accurate maps were jealously guarded by the Heuvaarse, who dominated trade through the region. Still, it was clear enough for me to indicate the general area I considered our best prospect.

The captain barked with laughter when he saw it. "Of course. I should have known that you, with all the Broken Sea to choose from, would want to sail into the dragon's mouth."

You may laugh to read this, but after a year travelling about studying dragons, my first interpretation of his words was anatomical rather than metaphorical. "What makes it so perilous?" I asked, once I understood his meaning.

"Pirates or Yelangese—take your pick." He saw my perplexity and explained, jabbing one finger down at a cluster of islands. The name his fingertip obscured was *Raengaui*. "The king of this place is a man named Waikango."

"I know that name!" I exclaimed. "At least, I read it in one of the news-sheets that was discussing Her Highness' diplomatic voyage. He is one of the pirates, yes?"

Aekinitos snorted derisively. "That is what the Yelangese call him. They'd rather say they're hunting a pirate than admit they're trying to stop a king from unifying part of the Broken Sea against them. The Puians do their share of piracy, though—ambushing Yelangese vessels, that sort of thing. Keeping the empire out while Waikango marries his female relatives off to the kings of other islands in exchange for support."

I bit my lip, studying the map. "Do they ambush ships that are not Yelangese?"

"They might," Aekinitos said. "Or they might not."

The smile lurking in his beard suggested he relished the thought of sailing into trouble. I did not; I had seen battle in Mouleen, albeit on a small scale as such things go, and did not like it at all. And although the *Basilisk* carried guns (as most deep-sea vessels did back then), and her crew practiced briefly with them every Helimer afternoon, none of us had signed on for a naval battle.

And yet that was one of the more volcanically active regions of the Broken Sea. If I wanted to study fire-lizards, it was a good place to look for them.

"We can head in that direction, and change our plans if it seems too dangerous to proceed," I said. "I have no wish to involve myself with either pirates or Yelangese. But what of Suhail?"

Aekinitos' face pulled into graver lines, and for a moment I doubted my chances. Then the smile returned, fierce and showing teeth. "Tell the Akhian he may board."

NINE

The Broken Sea—Hunting komodos—Rostam's arm—Suhail and the parang—Aftereffects—The bell

Jake was utterly delighted by this addition to the *Basilisk*'s complement. Quite apart from the fact that he liked Suhail, he could not wait to see the equipment our new companion was bringing on board.

Suhail's personal effects were extremely sparse, scarcely filling a large rucksack. In addition to that, however, he brought with him not only the diving bell but several large crates of equipment and books. The volume these occupied had been a point of contention when Aekinitos learned the full extent of it, but he had been mollified by the price Suhail offered for his passage. (Later on, their arguments would revolve around the effect that equipment had on the *Basilisk*'s sailing efficiency. I do not pretend to understand the details, but the diving bell was exceedingly heavy, which caused difficulty. It could not be lashed into place on deck, as that put the weight too high; but maneuvering it through the main hatch and into a better position below was not so easily done, given the lack of elbow room down there. Eventually Aekinitos got it stowed to his satisfaction, though—not long before we had to take it out again, of course.)

"I can't say I'm eager to get back on board," Tom said with a sigh, looking out at the *Basilisk* while we waited on the dock. His colour had improved, but he could not yet stand for long without becoming fatigued.

I admitted, "Nor I. But if we find a good location for research, we may settle ourselves there while Aekinitos seeks out opportunities for profit. And the Broken Sea is not reputed to be as plagued with fevers as some other regions." After the places he and I had been, it sounded positively idyllic.

For the price he had paid, Suhail was put with Tom and the officers of the ship, rather than with the common sailors. It was for the best: not only because to do otherwise would have been an insult, but because although the *Basilisk*'s crew was a motley assemblage, a goodly number of the men were Nichaean or Haggadi. Only one of them ever showed outright hostility to Suhail, but I think that if he had been living in their midst, an ugly situation might have resulted.

My son, by contrast, was over the moon to have him with us. He babbled incessantly from the moment Suhail came on board, telling the man everything he had done in Yelang and elsewhere since leaving Namiquitlan. (The tale of the dragon turtle must have been recounted a dozen times in the next week, for Jake never tired of it.) Suhail took this in stride, and deflected Jake's insistence that the diving bell be demonstrated that very minute. "Soon enough," he said, grinning at my son's impatience. "There is nothing of interest to show you here—too much debris and filth from the ships. The bell needs a place worthy of its use."

We set out for such places not long after. As I had discussed with Aekinitos, we directed ourselves toward Raengaui and the other archipelagos making up that cluster within the Broken Sea, but did not rush; there were opportunities for us along the way, and if political trouble lay ahead of us, we preferred to hear of it before diving in headfirst.

As is my wont, I shall take a moment here to describe the region. To many of my Anthiopean readers, the Broken Sea has the status of a legend: a beautiful and exotic realm on the far side of the world, whose reality seems dubious at best. Indeed, four hundred years ago there were Anthiopeans writing of the Broken Sea as the abode of men with three heads and islands that floated in the air.

But it is a real place, if not so fantastical as our literature has sometimes painted. Its boundaries are indistinct, owing to the fact that geographers divide the islands into different groupings, some of which do not lie wholly within the area customarily referred to as the Broken Sea. But in general terms, it is the sea between Dajin and Otholé, which is pocked with more islands than even the geographers can count. (They have tried, but some of the islands vanish at high tide, or become divided into smaller islands as the sea rushes through the channels between them. Meanwhile, volcanic activity in the region can raise up new land with very little warning. Add to this confusion some general disagreement over what size a rock must be before one can term it an island, plus the sheer scale of the endeavour, and it is no wonder that the numbers vary so widely.)

This complex array lies between the Tropic of Serpents and the Tropic of Storms, but its climate is made extremely pleasant by the mitigating influence of the sea. Oh, it can become airless and despicably hot where the vegetation grows thick—but compared with what we had endured in Eriga, I could find very little to complain about here. Fruit trees grow in abundance, and fish swim the warm, shallow waters in even greater abundance, so that in many places dinner requires little more than pulling a breadfruit from the nearest tree and roasting it over a fire, alongside the fish you have scooped from a lagoon. It may not offer the comforts of what we term civilized life, such as padded armchairs and running water . . . but for those who idealize a return to nature, it is easy to imagine those islands as close kin to the world described in the very first lines of Scripture, before the Fall of Man.

The social world of the Broken Sea is not so easily described. The geographers group the islands according to one scheme; ethnologists have different groupings entirely, following the divisions of culture. The peoples in the southwestern portion of the sea are generally Melatan, except where other countries have laid claim to territory, while those in the northeast are Puian. Neither group is a unified state, but like neighbouring peoples the world over, they have warred against one another (when they have not been warring against themselves), and in the zone between them a creole strain prevails, mixing the physical and cultural qualities of the two.

The lack of a unified state meant that we could not be certain of our welcome anywhere we went. At each port of call we would have to negotiate with the inhabitants anew; a local king might rule as many as three dozen islands, but that is a mere pebble in the great expanse of the Broken Sea. I could not recall whether the princess' diplomatic voyage included any ports of call in the region, but I doubted it; Scirland did not have a large presence there. We were therefore strangers in strange waters, even more than was usually true.

We began our efforts in Melatan territory, for I wanted to see the beasts referred to as "komodo dragons." Their claim to that term was not under debate by dragon naturalists for the simple reason that nobody had yet taken a good look at them and ventured an opinion one way or the other. They were said to be wingless and reptilian, perhaps three meters in length; beyond that and the name, I knew little.

There were no ruins for Suhail to study on the island we chose, for which I apologized. He shrugged and said, "I have already seen what remains of the great complex at Kota Cangkukan." (This he had done before visiting Tuantêng.) "After that, I am not certain anything in the Melatan region could compare."

He offered his services as a linguist, though. Tom and I had both studied the simplified Atau pidgin, which would suffice for basic requirements throughout much of the Broken Sea (and give us a solid base for learning any related Puian language), but Suhail's gift for such things meant he spoke far more fluently than either of us. With his aid, we obtained a guide—and a warning.

"They're dangerous," the guide (a swarthy fellow named Pembi) told us bluntly.

"Do they have extraordinary breath?" I asked in Scirling, for I could not think how to render the concept in Atau. Suhail found a way, and got a shake of the head in return. "Not wind. Bite." Pembi peeled his lips back from his teeth to illustrate, mime being the closest thing humans have to a universal language.

Tom snorted. He was not going with me; his strength was not yet sufficient to face a journey through the island's interior. He refused to lie quietly on deck, though, "as if an invalid"—never mind that he *was* an invalid, or at least a very tired convalescent. Thus he was with us at the teahouse where Suhail had found Pembi. "Sharp teeth, eh? That makes an improvement over most dragons. They'll have to get close enough to bite you."

"After facing things that can breathe at you from meters away, it does seem almost tame," I agreed. "Tell the man we shall take all due care."

Pembi, upon hearing this, shrugged with the philosophical air of a man who is willing to leave fools to their fate. We made arrangements to depart the next day, and returned to the *Basilisk* to prepare.

Jake and Abby came with us, as did Aekinitos himself and two of the sailors, for there were apes on the island whose pelts were considered valuable. (Whether Aekinitos wanted to keep an eye on Suhail, since Tom could not be there to do it, I cannot say, though in light of what transpired I think it may be so.) We departed from the leeward side of the island, where the terrain is drier and the vegetation scrubbier; Pembi assured us the greater number of komodos were to be found there.

I will not bore you with a full account of our days out there. We forced our way through tangled undergrowth that often required the assistance of a parang, a machete-like blade. Aekinitos and the sailors, two fellows named Rostam and Petros, shot various things for food and profit; Jake got lessons in wilderness survival from Pembi; and I stalked creatures that, I was increasingly sure, were not dragons at all.

My suspicions began with my very first sighting. Apart from the fact that most dragon breeds are scaled, a komodo has very little in common with them. Its head is serpentine in shape, entirely lacking the ruff or other cranial characteristics that tend to mark the draconic from the merely reptilian. It has no extraordinary breath, and when Aekinitos shot one for me to dissect, I found no sign that it had ever possessed anything like a wing.

The final test was to wait for the bones to dry, to see if they would decay. Pembi did not know; his people do not eat them (for good reason), and although they are shot as predators, no one particularly cares to do more with them than sling the carcass into the forest. We therefore defleshed a few and set them in the sun, then prepared to make camp a little distance away.

It happened with very little warning. There was a rustling in the undergrowth, not far from where Rostam was pitching his tent. He turned to look—and then screamed, as a komodo charged at him.

I would not have believed the squat creatures could move so quickly, had I not seen it with my own eyes. Rostam had only enough time to fling his arm up in a warding gesture; because of that, the komodo's jaws closed on his hand and forearm instead of his shoulder. He shrieked, and then it was chaos everywhere as the men lunged for their guns and blades.

I ran for Rostam as he fell. In hindsight, it was not a wise thing to do; I risked being shot by one of the others, or at least fouling their aim. But he needed aid, and in any event by the time I reached him, the komodo was dead.

Rostam's arm was a horror, blood soaking his sleeve up to the elbow. I knocked my hat aside and tore the kerchief from my head, pressing it to one part of the wound, shouting for someone to bring other bandages. Then Suhail was at my side, his own neckerchief in his hands, and his eyes met mine. They were wide with horror.

"The bite," he said. "I don't know if it's venom or infection— Pembi wasn't clear—but it will kill him."

Aekinitos was close enough to hear this. He stood over us, gun dangling from his hand, and stared down at Rostam. "He needs a doctor."

"There isn't time for that," Suhail said violently. He cast about, as if looking for something, then shot to his feet, leaving me to try and stanch the bleeding. "*Help* me," I snarled at Aekinitos.

Before the captain could move, Suhail was back. In his hand was Pembi's parang.

Aekinitos growled something in Nichaean and tried to seize Suhail, who evaded him with a swift step. "It's the only chance he has," Suhail said. "Damn it—the longer you wait, the worse his chances are!"

"That could kill him!" Aekinitos shouted.

"And if I don't, he *will* die."

Even now, I can hear Suhail's voice at that moment. Most men, when facing an ugly decision in a time of crisis, become harsh. Their voices grow hard and cold. His did not: it was soft, compassionate. He regretted the necessity—but did not flinch from it.

Aekinitos said nothing. But he stood without moving as Suhail stepped past him and took Rostam from me.

I think I screamed when the parang came down, severing Rostam's arm above the elbow. Certainly Rostam did, just before he fainted. The world went dark around the edges for a few moments, and I stayed sitting in the dirt, because I knew that if I tried to rise I would find myself on the ground in a heap.

When my vision cleared, Suhail had finished tying a tourniquet around the stump, to keep Rostam from bleeding out. I gathered my wits and went to fetch Petros' bottle of arrack. I had no idea whether the alcohol would help, but we had nothing else with which to disinfect the wound. Suhail poured it over the stump before bandaging it in the cleanest fabrics we had. Then he stopped, looking helpless, for the terrain was entirely unsuited to beasts of burden, and so we had come out on foot.

Aekinitos solved the issue by carrying Rostam on his own shoulders. He set out in the direction of the port without a word, leaving the rest of us to scramble in gathering our gear. I found Jake standing white-faced by my tent, and had to shake him gently before his eyes focused on me. "You have to help," I said. "We cannot tarry."

He did help, as did Abby. Aekinitos outpaced us in any event, even burdened as he was; Jake could not endure a forced march of that speed for long, and it was vital that Rostam be taken care of as soon as possible. Not that anyone could do much for him, beyond washing the wound and putting him in a bed to rest. By the time we reached town, those things had been done, and Suhail, who had gone with the captain, was nowhere to be found.

I weighed my options. Exhausted as I was, Aekinitos had to be even more tired, and heartsore to boot. He was not the sort of captain who behaved as a father to his crew, but their well-being was his responsibility. And yet . . . I could not allow this to go unremarked, for my sake or Suhail's.

Aekinitos was sitting in the shade of the house where they had put Rostam, a pipe in his hand. I do not think he had drawn on it other than to light it, for it dangled unused from his fingers the entire time I conversed with him.

"I am so very sorry," I said to him. Inadequate words, but all I had.

The captain shook his head, a slow movement that soon halted. "We face enough dangers. Sooner or later, luck runs out."

"In this case, it ran out because of me. I was warned that the komodos were perilous, but I pursued them anyway." I hesitated, then added, "I also brought Suhail. Please—I do not know if what he did was right, but I *do* know that his only thought was to give Rostam a chance of living."

The concealing mass of his beard made it hard to see, but I thought Aekinitos' jaw tightened at Suhail's name.

The silence stretched out, like a ship's cable pulled tighter and tighter. Finally, my voice very quiet, I asked, "Did you send him away?"

"Yes."

My heart sank within me.

Then Aekinitos said, "He wanted to remain until Rostam woke—or did not. But if he stayed here, I would have taken that parang and cut off *his* arm. He is on the ship."

On the *Basilisk*. At first I envisioned him packing, making arrangements for the diving bell to be extricated from the hold. But Aekinitos said nothing more, and then I understood: Suhail had not been sent away for good. Only evicted from the captain's presence for the time being.

"Thank you," I said quietly. "Would you like me to remain?"

Aekinitos shook his head. "You have your son to see to. Go."

I think he wanted solitude, and Jake was the first reason he could think of for occupying me elsewhere, but it was a good one. Up until now, this had all been a grand adventure for my son. Seeing a man's arm cut off was shocking beyond words for a boy of ten. He had nightmares for some time afterward, and was much subdued.

As were we all. We remained there long enough to know that Rostam would not die; infection did set in, but it was of a mild sort, not the horrific and lethal fever the islanders told us was the hallmark of a komodo bite. Suhail's quick work with the parang had indeed done some good. But we could not stay there forever, and so Aekinitos left Rostam with the pay he was owed and the price of passage home, and I gave him more besides. Then we put to sea once more, but we were not the excited band we had been before.

I sat at the table in our snuff-box of a cabin, with a vertebra in front of me as I wrote. Abby had retrieved it while we were packing up and given it to me after our return. My feelings on the thing were quite mixed: it was for this that Rostam had lost an arm and very nearly his life, and all it did was prove that komodos were not dragons. The lack of any visible decay was the final nail. No decay, no wings, no extraordinary breath; even with my doubts about Edgeworth's criteria, I could find no grounds to call the beasts anything other than very large lizards. It was a useful discovery—but when one's subject of study is dragons, it is upsetting to think a man was so badly maimed in order to prove something about mere lizards.

The air in that little cabin was stifling, even with the tiny windows of the skylight open to catch what breeze they could. I put down my pen and went out on deck.

Suhail was in the bow. The crew's opinion of him had grown even more dubious once they heard what happened to Rostam, even though the captain placed no opprobrium on him (and showed tacit approval by allowing him to remain). I did not blame him for trying to keep apart.

His expression as I approached was a sad half-smile, and I realized with a start that Suhail had not been the only one practicing avoidance. I had hardly spoken with him since our return. The smile said that he had noticed, and did not blame me, but he mourned the loss.

I straightened my shoulders. I had not been thinking about that matter when I came in search of him, but now it must be addressed before anything else. "Please forgive me," I said, once I was close enough to speak in normal tones. "It must look like condemnation, that I have been avoiding you. It is not."

He nodded, waiting as I searched for a way to explain. "I have been close to violence," I said at last. "My husband was murdered—stabbed in front of me, though he did not die until some days later. I have also seen men savaged by animals. But it is still shocking to be within arm's reach when a man—" I realized the terrible irony in my choice of words, and winced. "You understand. And it is all the more shocking, I think, because you did not wish him ill. You were doing the best you could for him."

Suhail's hands knotted about one another. I followed their motion, and remembered once more the way they had gripped the parang. "I have hunted," he said, "and I have given aid when men have been injured. But I have never done that before."

I stilled. It had not occurred to me that the event might have left its mark on Suhail as well. Now that I looked, however, I saw shadows around his eyes, a slackness that spoke of poor sleep. I remembered the dove I had dissected when I was a small girl, and the way the visceral memory of it had stayed with me. The dove had not been screaming.

"Are *you* all right?" I asked him, so quietly the wind almost stole my words away.

He glanced away, shrugging. "I will be. I am not the one who lost an arm."

"If you would like, I can leave you in peace," I said, half-turning. "I quite understand if you would prefer not to think about research just now."

A ghost of Suhail's usual smile returned. "I would be grateful for it. Research, that is—not you leaving. I could benefit from distraction."

As that was much how I would have reacted, I needed no persuasion. I went to lean against the rail; Suhail rose and offered me the coil of rope upon which he had been sitting, and after a brief argument of polite gestures, I gave in. He leaned against the rail in my place. When this was done, I said, "I thought you might be able to assist me. One of the reasons I shoot the subjects of my research—or rather, ask others to shoot them for me—is because there is no easier way for me to observe them closely, except when they are dead. Few dragons will tolerate a human measuring them and poking at their joints."

Suhail nodded. "How may I be of service?"

"Your diving bell," I said. "It has windows in its sides, does it not?"

"Small ones." He cocked his head to one side. "Are you after sea-serpents?"

I gave him a seated bow, acknowledging the point. "I know I would not be able to observe much from within the bell, but it would be a substantial improvement compared with leaning over the rail. And it would let me see them while they are alive."

It was our swim with the dragon turtles that had put the notion into my mind—or rather the desire, for at the time I did not know it was possible to observe from underwater for any longer than one could hold one's breath. The notion seemed to have fired Suhail's mind, too, for he came off his slouch against the rail in a burst of energy. "You could see much more than that! There is a suit—a waterproof one, with a bell that fits over the head and locks into place. A hose supplies air. It allows you to move about as you please, so long as you do not go too far." He stopped, thinking, looking out across the channel we were currently threading be-tween islands. "Though you would not be very safe if a serpent chose to bite you. We could construct a cage, though, with steel bars, large enough that you could float in the middle—"

"And be blasted through the holes on the far side if a serpent took offense at my presence."

He had clearly forgotten about the jet of water a serpent can ex-pel. I almost found myself apologizing as his face fell. But he re-covered soon enough, saying, "I see now why you thought the bell would serve. It might do. But I would not call it safe."

"Do you think a serpent could crush it?" I asked. The thing had seemed very sturdy to me when it was loaded onto the ship— its sides were solid steel—but he would know its limitations better than I.

Suhail shook his head. "Perhaps, but that is not my concern. The diving bell is open at the base. There are reasons for this, but chief among them is that I intend to use it for excavation: if I sink it into the ocean floor in shallow waters, I can pump the water out and then dig in the silt for artifacts." He dismissed this with a wave of his hand, for it was a digression from his true point. "An attack from the serpent, whether a blast or simply a strike of its tail, could turn the bell on its side. If that happens, the air will escape."

And I would be left floating in the water, easy prey for the ser-pent. "Oh," I said. Now it was my turn for my face to fall. It had seemed like such a very good idea.

When I looked up, I found Suhail standing with one hand hovering in front of his mouth, fingers poised as if to catch something. His eyes were wide. "You have had an idea," I said, smiling. "Should I be afraid?"

"If we were to close off the bell," he said, still gazing into the distance. "It would not be able to go as deep—there are issues of pressure. But ten meters should be safe. Do sea-serpents swim in water that shallow?"

I rose to my feet, feeling suddenly alive again. "We shall find out."

TEN

Searching for a site—Differences of scale—Scripture and history—My new theory—Draconean writing—An impudent thief—Two tongues

We did not find out immediately, for it was some while before we had the chance to put our theory to the test. As chronicled in *Around the World in Search of Dragons*, we did not have much luck in locating a place where both the draconic and archaeological halves of the expedition could further their efforts.

Modern-day dragon naturalists are much more organized about this than I was. They correspond with colleagues in their intended region, or at least with people who know the place, and make plans in advance for where they will go and how long they will stay. At the time, however, the Broken Sea was too unfamiliar to Scirlings, and my sense of what I needed to do too vague. I could only flit about, chasing rumours of possibility. For a while we were largely a trading expedition, Aekinitos choosing where we went, the rest of us asking questions in every port, seeking fire-lizards, sea-serpents, and ruins.

Jake grew bored, and annoyed Abby in equal proportion to his boredom. I sent them through the markets to hunt scales and fangs from the serpents, so that I could try to make a comparative collection. Tom occupied himself with a careful regimen of exercise to regain his strength. I pored over the book I had acquired in Va Hing, which Suhail had been kind enough to translate for me; it sparked a great many thoughts on evolution and taxonomy. (Also no small amount of frustration that I had so little gift for languages. I would have liked to compare that book against others, for of course with only one author to draw from, I could hardly be certain that the facts were rigorous to begin with.)

Suhail fared better than the rest of us, at least initially. At our first Puian port of call, the island of Olo'ea, he discovered that the locals used bits of carved stone as charms for good fortune—stones which were retrieved from beaches or found by pearl divers in the course of their work. He traded for one of these and brought it to me in great excitement. "Look!" he said.

I looked, but shook my head, for I did not see the significance. "These are found around Draconean ruins," he said. "Very common—too common to fetch any great price among treasure-hunters. I think there is a ruin offshore."

"Will you use the bell?" Jake asked, almost bouncing in his excitement.

Suhail grinned at him. "Not to begin with. I will use something else."

The "something else" proved to be the contents of one of the crates he had brought on board. I had never before seen anything like it: a suit of bulky, waterproof canvas twill over rubber with a metal collar, and a copper globe I initially thought was a pot of some kind. It had a glass window in one side, however, and proved to be a helmet, which could be affixed to the collar in a perfect seal. A hose entered the helmet at the back.

It was what we now call a standard diving dress, though Suhail referred to it by an Akhian term. As he had described to me, it allowed him to range underwater for an extended period of time, thanks to a pump supplying fresh air to him via the hose. "For excavation, it is not the best," he said ruefully, showing me how stiff his fingers were in the canvas gloves. "That needs the bell. But I can use this to find the site."

Jake, of course, would not hear of being left behind. We went out in a canoe paddled by men from Olo'ea, and Jake splashed around on the surface while I oversaw the operation of the pump.

It was not very interesting to watch from above. Through the waves, I could just make out Suhail below, drifting across the shallow seafloor. Clouds arose wherever he poked into the sand, and fish startled away in a quick rush. Jake called out reports to me: "He just tucked something into the bag! Now it looks like he's found a wall!"

I scarcely listened, content to wait for the more detailed account after Suhail was done. Instead I sat in the canoe and contemplated taxonomy. In my pocket I had a set of three sea-serpent scales—one from our specimen in arctic waters, the other two acquired locally—which I laid along the bench in front of me.

Examined under the microscope we had on board the *Basilisk*, they did show differences. All sea-serpents possess ctenoid scales, meaning that they have a toothed outer edge, but certain structural features are more similar to the placoid scales of sharks. This created an interesting puzzle for the taxonomist: are the serpents more closely related to bony fish (and evolved to acquire characteristics of cartilaginous fish); are their nearest cousins cartilaginous fish (while the serpents evolved to in some ways resemble bony fish); or was the answer some third thing entirely? But while the basic structure was the same in all three instances, the arctic one was substantially thicker, and the features of its exterior surface less prominent. Small differences—but in the field of natural history, such minor discrepancies can herald a large enough separation to merit distinguishing two different species.

Or it could simply be age. I knew from my reading prior to the voyage that ctenoid scales grow outward in rings, like trees. The

enameloid dentin pulp epidermis

bone dermis

pseudocycloid
scales

LOCKWOOD

Scale Detail

arctic sample, in addition to being thicker and less textured, had many more rings. Very well, so far as it went: our arctic serpent was older. Did that explain all the differences? Or was it simply a bias in my (admittedly small) sample, that the tropical scales came from younger specimens? Perhaps there was a scale somewhere in the Broken Sea that would show as great an age. Or perhaps the Puians and Melatans hunted their serpents too energetically for them to ever become so elderly.

It is a very good thing that the canoes we had hired were out-riggers, with a stabilizing lateral float on the port side. Had I been in an ordinary canoe, I might well have tipped myself into the water when Suhail broke the surface. I had been too caught up in my contemplation of scale anatomy to notice him rising from below.

Jake swam over to help me fumble the weighty brass helmet off. Suhail could not assist us; all his effort went into staying afloat. (Ordinarily this was no challenge for him, but diving dress includes lead weights all over the body to keep the air within the suit from constantly dragging it upward.) Once the helmet was off, Suhail and Jake removed the weights, and then he easily hoisted himself over the gunwale into the canoe.

I retrieved the scales just before he would have sat on them. "Did you find anything interesting?"

"Of artifacts, very little," he said, turning out the string bag he had taken down with him. A few pieces of stone fell free. "The waves have washed most of the small pieces ashore, I think—I will not find more without excavation. But there is definitely a site there. Likely a peasant village."

"A peasant village?" I said, startled.

Suhail laughed. "Did you think the Draconeans lived only in great cities and temples? There must have been many villages, but most of them are gone now. Plowed under by later peoples. This is why I'm looking underwater: because *those* sites are untouched, except by the sea."

Jake hung off the side of the canoe, kicking his legs idly in the water. "Why are they underwater now? Did the islands sink?"

"Quite the reverse," Suhail told him. "A geologist I know thinks the seas have risen since the glory days of the Draconeans."

I laughed. "Like the tale in the Book of Tyrants? I do not know if you have that one in your Scriptures."

"We do," Suhail said. "And if you read through the metaphors, there might be truth hidden there. What if the great beasts that ruled over mankind were in fact the Draconean kings?"

"Great beasts?" The canoe rocked slightly as Jake pulled on it in excitement. "What great beasts?"

Readers of these memoirs know that I have never been very religious. I am not ashamed of this fact; I have endeavoured to be a good woman nonetheless, and to do good for those around me. Still, it was embarrassing to have it revealed that my son was a little heathen, ignorant of even the most basic stories in Scripture. Flushing, I said, "I thought that most scholars agree the beasts are symbolic of the state of sin into which mankind had fallen."

Suhail shrugged. "There is no reason they cannot be both. The Draconeans worshipped dragons as gods; surely their civilization would count as greatly degenerate because of it."

"Does your geologist friend also think the other calamities described in that book took place? The plague of vermin, the skies falling dark for a year and a day, the slaughter of the children?"

Jake was listening in openmouthed fascination. The islanders were sitting idle, enjoying their leisure, as we were speaking in Scirling (and they might not have cared a fig for our conversation even had they understood it). For my own part, I had never thought to discuss theology while sitting in a canoe in the middle of the Broken Sea; but here I was. Suhail said, "The writer of the Book of Tyrants surely exaggerated to make his point. But why should there be sunken villages, if the waters did not truly rise? And archaeologists have found remnants of things—trees, plants, animals—far south of where they should be. Creatures of cold weather, in areas that are too warm for them."

"Too warm *now*," I said, following him. "But why should warmth—oh. Seas cannot rise without water to swell them. He truly thinks it changed enough to melt such a volume of ice?"

The notion seemed outrageous to me, but Suhail nodded. "It would not take as large a change as you think. Or at least, he does not think so."

It was hardly my field of expertise. Still—"I cannot imagine the temperature rose overnight, however small of a change it might be."

"No," Suhail agreed. "And so we are back to metaphor: the oceans swamped the coastal settlements under, but it happened over a long period of time. Not in three days, as Scripture would have it."

"A fascinating theory," I murmured. It will surprise no one, I think, that I was less interested in its implications for Draconean civilization (or theology, for that matter) than in the consequences for draconic species. They are so well adapted to their circumstances that such a change in the environment would necessitate migration or further change—or else it would drive them to extinction. I cursed again the peculiar quirk of their osteology that robbed me of any fossil record to study . . . even though I knew that without it, I likely would not have any dragons larger than ponies to study, and those almost certainly flightless.

This speculation put new thoughts into my head, though, which stayed with me long after we returned to shore, and kept me up quite late that night. Suppose (I said to myself) the world had indeed changed in that fashion, many thousands of years ago. It had—according to Suhail—driven many cold-weather creatures toward the poles, allowing residents of warmer climates to expand their ranges. Might this have some bearing on the question of the sea-serpents? I could imagine the changing world inspiring a great deal of movement and turmoil, as the beasts went in search of waters whose temperature was more congenial. But because there is variation in all species, some tended toward higher latitudes, while others preferred to remain closer to the tropics.

If that were the case, then it put a new wrinkle in my taxonomical questions. What if they had been a single species, back in the days of the Draconeans . . . but were in the process of differentiating into two?

I did not know if the hypothetical progenitors had been tropical or arctic to begin with, but I suspected the former. Our globes, after all, featured the *Tropic* of Serpents, not the *Arctic Circle* of Serpents. They were more common in tropical latitudes than temperate ones, let alone the far north. Which made sense if they had gotten their start here, and had expanded as the world changed around them.

Some of you may read the preceding paragraphs and shrug at them. I had an idea; very good for me. The scientists among you, however, may understand why this was a matter of sufficient excitement to keep me awake well into the night. I had studied dragons before, and contributed something to our stock of knowledge about them. I had even made a few discoveries of note, among them the natural preservation of dragonbone, the mourning behaviour of Vystrani rock-wyrms, and the peculiar life cycle of the dragons of Mouleen.

But never before had I devised a *theory*. Even my purpose on this voyage—to reconsider draconic taxonomy—did not have the same glamour as this new idea. The former was merely (I thought) a revision of other people's ideas. It might win me acclaim in some quarters, but others would resent me for it, as an upstart woman arguing that a respected authority like Sir Richard Edgeworth was wrong. My theory regarding sea-serpents, however, was entirely new. It brought natural history together with observations from archaeology and geology to craft something never before considered. It was a fresh contribution to the field—and, I thought, the one that would make my name.

I said in the first volume of my memoirs that one must be cautious of imagining patterns in data, especially when that data is scant. Alas, on this occasion I did not take my own advice.

That night I rose from my hammock, crept out onto deck, and by the light of the moon penned an explanation of my ideas. This was the first draft of an article later published as "On the Differentiation of Sea-Serpents," which I, in a state of great excitement, sent off to the *Journal of Maritime Studies* not one week later, when we came into port at Moakuru and had an opportunity to send mail. Tom, to his credit, cautioned me to wait; although he found great merit in my idea, he felt it would be better to submit a more substantial work after the expedition was done. I, however, wanted this to be the first volley in a series of publications that would astonish the scientific community.

In a way, it was. "On the Differentiation of Sea-Serpents" garnered quite a bit of attention while I was still abroad, and while a portion of that was negative (for the aforementioned reason of my being an upstart woman with little scholarly standing), many found merit in my ideas. And certainly I have followed that article with many later works that have indeed made my name.

Unfortunately—as many of you know—my theory was entirely wrong.

I did not know it when I posted my article back to Scirland. I did not even suspect until some months later, and confirmation had to wait until M. Esdras de Crérat published the definitive work to date on sea-serpents, years after my expedition ended. But had I delayed and allowed my ideas to mature, I might have escaped a great deal of embarrassment later.

I suffered a scholarly frustration of a different sort soon afterward, when we had left Olo'ea for a more volcanically active archipelago—one that might be home to fire-lizards.

On that day Suhail had asked to have the use of our cabin, because it was out of the wind. When I returned some time later (intending to retrieve one of my sketching pads), I found him ensconced with a stack of three books, one small notebook, and an array of little boxes, which seemed to be filled with cards. "What on earth are you doing?" I asked, peering shamelessly at the notebook. Suhail was doing mathematics; that much and no more was apparent to me.

"Oh," he said, looking up with the distracted air of one who had not noticed his interlocutor approaching. Given the minuscule size of the cabin, that meant he had been concentrating very hard indeed. "I am working on Draconean."

Given his talent for languages, I was not surprised. Good manners warred with curiosity, and lost. "Very well; I concede my ignorance. What use are mathematics in deciphering an ancient language?"

He stretched the kinks from his neck and gestured at the little boxes full of cards. "An analysis of the frequency of each character—that is the simplest part of it. Sadeghi thinks he has found a mark that indicates separation between words, so if he is correct, it is also possible to record how often a character is found at the beginning of a word, or the end, or in its middle. After that, it becomes more complex: the likelihood that two characters will be found in conjunction, or three."

When I described this to Natalie much later, she saw very quickly what Suhail was about, but between my difficulty with languages and my limited grasp of mathematics, I did not. "Very well—that would give you a sense of the patterns in the language. But it cannot tell you what the words mean . . . can it?"

"Not yet," Suhail said. "It tells me, though—or rather it told ibn Khattusi, who was the first to observe this—that the Draconean script is likely a syllabary, with many characters representing groups of sounds."

"How can you be sure of that?" I asked, fascinated.

"Because of the number of characters. There are only so many individual sounds in a language; even the largest has no more than a few dozen. Your alphabet has twenty-six letters, while mine has twenty-eight, with marks sometimes employed for vowels. The largest have fifty or sixty. But even a small syllabary usually has at least eighty characters—more often hundreds." He nodded once more at the cards. "Draconean has two hundred forty-one— perhaps. It is not easy to count. If an inscription carved in clay adds a downward serif on one symbol, is that a different character, or was the scribe simply careless in making his mark? If three marks overlap one another, is that significant, or is it just an artifact of the small size of the writing?"

My eyebrows went up, and he dismissed his own rambling with a wave of his hand. "The point is this: knowing the script is a syllabary tells me something of how it must have sounded. And calculating the frequency of different arrangements helps me find patterns—"

"And where there are patterns, there are words," I said, understanding at last. "You can find the shape of them, at least."

"That is the hope." Suhail stretched in his seat, and his back popped alarmingly. "It will be a great deal of work, though, and I have only just started."

Getting from the shapes of words to their meaning seemed like another hurdle entirely, but Suhail did not need me to point that out. Instead I reached my hand toward one of his boxes, and when he nodded permission, browsed through the cards. I could read nothing of his notes, which were all in a tidy (and microscopic) Akhian hand, but the Draconean characters in the upper left were vaguely familiar to me. "I have found a few inscriptions myself," I admitted.

"Oh?"

"Most of them from a ruin in Vystrana—near a village called Drustanev."

Suhail made a sound of recognition and picked up one of his books, flipping through it with practiced fingers. "These, yes?"

The book, I later learned, was the most recent supplement in a series begun by the Akhian scholar Suleiman ibn Khattusi, who had made it his mission to collate all the Draconean inscriptions then known and to encourage people to gather more. At the time, all I knew was that I was looking at two pages of unintelligible Akhian script, captioning a pair of line drawings I knew *quite* well.

My voice was much too loud for the small cabin. "Where did you get these?"

"The books? I—"

"Not the books, *these*." I stabbed one finger down on the Draconean inscriptions.

Suhail took the volume from me, perhaps as much to rescue it from my violence as to read what was on the page. "It says these were gathered and submitted by Simon Arcott of Enwith-on-Tye."

The first sound to emerge from my throat was an outraged squawk. It was shortly followed by a string of epithets, the kindest of which was, "That *sneak*! I sent him those drawings myself, made from the rubbings I took in Vystrana. And he has the *gall* to pass them off as his own work?" I snatched the book from Suhail once more, studying the images to make certain there was no error. Indeed there was not; I had painstakingly copied them for Mr. Arcott, and knew every line.

Suhail did not question my certainty. He said, "If you wish, I can send in a correction."

I did my best to moderate my tone. "That is very good of you. 'Correction'—pah. That is the word, but it makes the attribution here sound like a regrettable error, rather than a damnable lie. Oh, when I get back to Scirland . . . or really, why wait? There is such a thing as mail service."

"Having been in a similar dispute once myself," Suhail offered, with the wary air of a man who is hoping a cat will not bite him, "I would advise waiting. If you write to him now, he will have months in which to prepare a defense."

What defense could protect Mr. Arcott, when I had the original rubbings in my study and he had never been to Vystrana in his life, I could not imagine. Still, Suhail's advice was good, and I nodded in reluctant agreement.

(When I finally did confront Mr. Arcott, after my return to Falchester, he had the cheek to try and argue that his intellectual thievery had been a compliment and a favor. After all, it meant my work was good enough to be accepted into ibn Khattusi's series—but of course they never would have taken a submission from a woman, so he submitted it on my behalf. What I said in reply is not fit to be printed here, as by then I had spent a good deal of time in the company of sailors, and had at my disposal a vocabulary not commonly available to ladies of quality. But I had greater satisfaction in due course: he was drummed out of the Society of Draconean Scholars, and subsequent editions of ibn Khattusi's series had not only my name but a note explaining the discrepancy in thoroughly condemnatory terms.)

I returned the book, restraining my uncharitable urge to throw it across the cabin. It would not have gone far, but the impact might have satisfied my sudden need for violence. "Well. I may take comfort that he cannot possibly have stolen the other inscription I found, as I never took a rubbing of it."

Suhail gave me a sharp look. He knew well enough by then that I was not often the sort to pass up a chance to record knowledge. "Why not?"

I laughed, my ill humour not gone, but receding to where I could think of other things. "I had very little paper with me at the time, and nothing fit for a rubbing. Nor could I stay long enough to try and draw it—I had other tasks to address." (To wit, getting off an island in the middle of a waterfall without breaking my neck.) "Besides, I am not certain it would be useful to anyone. The Draconean part of the inscription looked very odd—quite primitive."

My dismissive words might as well have been the scent of prey, for Suhail perked up like a hound that has caught the trail of a rabbit. "Primitive? How so? Where was this? And what do you mean, the Draconean *part* of the inscription?"

"Which question do you wish me to answer first?" I asked with asperity, for he seemed likely to go on pestering me without pause for reply.

He apologized, and I said, "It looked . . . well, let me show you." I fetched out my own notebook and sketched a few shapes as best as I could remember them: awkward scratches at bad angles.

Suhail frowned at the images. "Were they arranged precisely like this? No vertical stroke here?" One brown finger traced a line through what I had drawn.

"My dear fellow, this was six years ago, and I have already said I kept no record of them. This is me trying to recall the general

style. I have no idea if there were any characters that even looked
like this."

He conceded this with a nod. "And the rest of the inscription?"

"You mean the part that wasn't Draconean? I have no idea *what*
it was. Rounded little blocks; they might not even have been writing at all." I sketched another few shapes. These were decidedly
more fanciful, as I had not even my vague familiarity with Draconean to aid recollection.

Suhail seemed to recognize them nonetheless. "Like this?" He
took my notebook from me and wrote a quick line.

"Yes!" I exclaimed, hands flying up. "What *is* it?"

"Ngaru," he said slowly, looking at the page. "A very old script—
logosyllabic—ancestral to the writing systems now used throughout eastern Eriga."

"Well, that makes sense. I was in eastern Eriga at the time."

Suhail pushed the notebook back at me. His movements had
gone suddenly cautious, as if too quick a gesture might cause the
mirage in his mind to dissipate. "Draw the whole thing, if you will.
Not the inscriptions themselves—I know you do not have them
recorded—but what it was that you saw."

I obligingly laid out the general shape of it: the slab of granite,
divided roughly in half, with the chicken scratches of Draconean
at the top and the Ngaru script below. When I showed it to Suhail, his expression gradually lit up, until he was glowing as if
every birthday gift for the rest of his life had arrived all at once.

"Truly God has sent you!" he cried. I think that, had I been a
man, he would have embraced me on the spot. "Do you realize
what this is?"

Laughing despite myself, I said, "Clearly I do not."

"If my guess is right—if I am the most fortunate man in all of
creation—then this is a bilingual!" He saw my incomprehension.
"The same text, written in two languages. Draconean above,

Ngaru below. We cannot read the former, but the latter . . ." His hands flapped with his excitement. "That has been known for years!"

During my childhood education, I had labored through various works of foreign literature in facing translations, with Scirling on one side and the original on the other. The idea had been that my native tongue would aid me in learning the other language—and so it would have done, I imagine, had I been inclined to effort, instead of reading only the Scirling side.

I mentioned this to Suhail, and he crowed with delight. "Better than that! It is the key to the code. Find names in the Ngaru, or some other element that will not change much between languages—count them. Count the Draconean, and find the words with the same frequency. Likely they will even write the same sounds, or close to it. This is the key!"

He *did* almost seize me then, so caught up was he in his joy. I startled at the movement, and that recalled him to his manners; he clasped his own hands instead, shaking them with his eyes to the heavens.

His good cheer was infectious. I came down to earth a moment later, though, when he asked me, "Where is this stone?"

"In Eriga," I said, drawing out the words while I thought. "But the stone—it is not very accessible."

"I do not care," Suhail vowed. "God willing, I will climb the highest mountain to reach it, cross the deepest gorge. Is it in a desert? I grew up in one. I do not fear the heat of the sun."

His grandiose declarations made me smile, but my heart was heavy. "It is not that. Well, it *is* that to some degree—the way is indeed dangerous. But the greater problem is not the land; it is the people. The stone sits in a place that is . . . sacred. I was permitted to go there as part of a trial, a rite of passage. But I do not know if they would let you do the same."

This checked him in his headlong dreams of success. "Is the stone itself sacred to them?"

"Not that I know of. I am not even certain they know it is there; I only found it because I went searching."

"Then I could buy it from them."

I opened my mouth to tell him how little the Moulish cared for money, but stopped myself. I had not yet said the stone was in the Green Hell, and thought it better to leave that unspecified. Everything I knew of Suhail said he was a good man, but the dual inscriptions dangled before him the possibility of the kind of achievement most scholars can only dream of. I did not think he would go after the stone without permission . . . but without certainty, I could not risk it. The Moulish had shown trust in sending me to that island, and I did not want to betray it.

"I do not know," I said at last. "But I can tell you who to contact. There is a woman in Atuyem, the half-sister of the oba—Galinke n Oforiro Dara. She knows the people who keep the stone, and can ask them on your behalf."

This roundabout path made Suhail sigh with impatience, but he nodded. After all, we were halfway around the world from Bayembe and Mouleen; he could hardly go racing off there right now. I fear I quite destroyed his concentration, though, for soon after that he packed up his notebooks and cards and took to pacing the deck instead—dreaming, I suspect, of what secrets the Draconean inscriptions might hold.

PART THREE

*In which the expedition
makes substantial progress
by running aground*

ELEVEN

The storm—Encounter with a reef—An island welcome—
The needs of the Basilisk*—Our new home—Hostile responses*

One consequence of my eventful life is that it has given me an utter horror of helplessness.

Put me in peril, and so long as it is something I may struggle against, I will be well. Not *happy*—for despite what others say about me, peril is not a thing I enjoy—but I will keep my equilibrium, diverting all my fears into the effort to find safety once more. This tendency has preserved my life in a variety of circumstances and places, from the skies above the Green Hell to the lethal slopes of the Mrtyahaima peaks.

What I do not handle half so well are situations in which I may do nothing. This is why disease is one of my especial nemeses: when I am ill, I am capable of little more than refusing to die, and when others are ill, I cannot even do that. I was helpless when my husband died in Vystrana—and perhaps that incident, even more than the general tenor of my life, has instilled this horror in me, for I have never forgotten the fact that I could do nothing to save him.

All of which is by way of explaining that when the great storm arose on the Broken Sea, it began what may well have been the most wretched span of time in my entire voyage. I suffered other misfortunes that were arguably worse, but in those cases I could *do* something. On this occasion, however, I was rendered totally helpless.

Ackinitos had warned me of the storms, but thus far I had only seen rain showers, blowing past so regularly you might set your pocket-watch by them. When I saw clouds on the horizon that day, I felt no particular apprehension. Aekinitos, however, spent a minute and a half contemplating them in silence. Then, nodding once, he turned and ordered all his passengers below.

"How long are we expected to stay there?" I asked him—for I lacked the captain's weather sense, and did not understand what the shadow in the distance portended.

"Until it is safe," Aekinitos said.

This was not a reassuring answer. First, because it advertised danger; second, because it was so very unspecific; and third, because Aekinitos delivered those words with a mad gleam in his eye. As I have said before, he was of my mind in preferring perils against which he could pit all of his strength. He was not quite so mad as to *seek out* such things, at needless risk to the lives of his men; but if such incidents presented themselves, then he did not hesitate to throw himself into the fray.

I tempered my frustration and asked, "Is there nothing we can do?"

Aekinitos said, "Stay out of the way."

It was the worst possible instruction he could have given me. Unfortunately, I had no choice but to obey. My time aboard the *Basilisk* had given me a very rudimentary understanding of which bits were which, but not enough to be useful even in calm weather. In a storm, I would be a positive liability, as conditions required the men to do precisely the right thing at precisely the right time—without any landlubber standing in the way.

Jake protested when he heard he was to be sent below. "I'm not a passenger!" he insisted. I privately cursed the arrangement that treated him as a "ship's boy," which now gave him notions. (Though

I cannot fault Jake for wanting to help. My impulse had, after all, been the same.)

Aekinitos settled the matter quite tidily. "You are not a passenger, and so you obey my orders. Which are to go into my cabin and stay there with the others."

It is a mark of how much our voyage and that arrangement had transformed my son that Jake did not continue his protest. He looked mulish and set his jaw, but he did not argue against Aekinitos' logic. Instead he turned to me and proferred his arm, saying, "Ma'am, if you'll come below with me?" Abby muffled a laugh.

There was no laughter an hour later, when the first edges of the storm reached us. We had been in tempests before, this past year and more. On those occasions Tom had been permitted to help, and Jake as well; Abby and I had not so much been ordered out of the way as advised to step aside, and we had occupied ourselves with tasks such as making certain food and drink were distributed when conditions allowed. Now, however, the lot of us were packed into the captain's cabin, Suhail included—that being the only space where we could all fit and be out of the way.

Nearly everything on a ship is "stowed," meaning that there are measures in place to make certain things will not fall out or down or over when the ship pitches or rolls. In our own tiny cabin, for example, thick straps held the books on the shelves. In the captain's own quarters, everything was as neatly stowed as could be, and yet soon after we had a demonstration of the limitations of such measures.

It began with an ominous creaking and swaying as the winds rose. The lights had been extinguished, but in the grey gloom that came through the stern windows, we could see the hammock and hanging sacks swing in ever-wider arcs. This lasted until a sailor hurried in and closed the shutters, to protect us against the possibility of broken glass; in exchange he left us one meager lantern. The latter risked fire, but I am glad we had that one allowance, for otherwise we would have spent the next two days in utter darkness.

Yes, we were two days in the grip of that storm—or perhaps it was a whole series of them, striking us one after the other. I cannot tell you the details of what transpired outside the cabin, for I was not there to see them, and what explanation we got afterward was both incomplete and somewhat incomprehensible to me. It was not a hurricane; had it been that severe, the *Basilisk* should certainly have been sunk. But a whole ocean of rain came thundering down upon us, drowning the decks and half-drowning the men, and the wind whipped the seas into waves that must have made the ship look like a toy lost in the bath. Against this, Aekinitos and his men struggled not to sail to safety—we were caught too far from land to have any chance of that—but simply to keep our bow turned into the waves. If at any point the ship turned broadside to the waves, the next one would have swamped us, sending the *Basilisk*'s masts into the water and dooming us all.

Had there been a harbour available nearby, we might have tried to run for it and take refuge there. This would certainly have doomed the *Basilisk*—we would have found her wreckage scattered across the Broken Sea—but we ourselves might have been safer. Lacking such an option, however, the open waters in which we found ourselves became a blessing, for they meant we could run as the winds and waves directed us . . . to a point. But I get ahead of myself.

For those two days, the five of us huddled in Aekinitos' cabin, safe from the battle on the decks but suffering in our own way. Every one of us was most miserably sick at some point, even those who had not previously had any trouble at sea. We had only hard-tack and water to sustain us, for there was no hope of hot food in such a storm, and the cook was busy elsewhere regardless. The smell soon mounted to dreadful levels, from illness and sweat and the chamber pot in its little closet; the latter got emptied only once, when Jake defied the captain and crept out to fling its contents through a porthole. None of us got a wink of sleep, and if you have ever gone two days without rest, you will understand the kind of madness that overcomes you when you pass through exhaustion to another realm entirely.

I was terrified, and nauseated, and furious with my utter inability to do anything. I almost wished Jake would collapse in tears; then at least I could busy myself with comforting him, which would give me the illusion of use. But my son, though afraid, was made of stuff too stern to oblige me. He said at intervals that the captain was a brilliant man who could overcome any storm, and occupied himself with comforting Abby, who was the most ill of us all. I take pride in his conduct, but it left me with nothing to do but endure.

I could scarcely even converse with Tom and Suhail, the clamour of the storm was so great. Besides, what was there for us to speak of? We could not take refuge in discussing dragons or archaeology; it was impossible to maintain coherent thought for long in the chaos. We spoke in brief, elliptical turns about the conditions and what we might do to better them, but little more. After a time, Suhail began to sing quietly, I think to give himself something to focus on besides our circumstances. He had not much range, and the Akhian songs he sang (lullabies and children's songs, I think) were unfamiliar to me, but the sound was comforting nonetheless.

So for two days there was neither night nor day, but only the continual gloom, relieved by that single lantern, whose refilling provided brief moments of painstaking terror. Then, just as we began to tell ourselves that the winds were slackening, there came a dreadful, grinding shudder from below—and the *Basilisk* ceased to move.

"What was that?" Abby cried.

I met Tom's eyes, and Suhail's, and Jake's. All four of us were thinking it, I believe, but I was the one who gave it voice. "We have run aground."

In a storm, this can be a death sentence. So long as the *Basilisk* ran freely, she could mitigate the force of the winds by giving in to them. Trapped against a sandbar or reef, however, she had no such defense. The storm would force her farther into the obstacle, until one or more things gave way: the masts, perhaps, or the hull.

The loss of our masts would cripple us, but the shattering of the hull could kill us.

"The bilge," Tom said, and Suhail nodded. Then they were out the door, and I only just caught Jake when he tried to follow. He fought against me, but ship's boy or no, he would not be of much use now. If the hull had cracked, the men would need to bail against our sinking, and Jake was not strong enough for that.

(In fact the men had been bailing the whole time, taking shifts at the hand-cranked pumps that siphoned water from the bilge and disposed of it outside once more. I did not know then that the planking of a ship flexes quite a bit even when intact, and a storm may cause it to spring any number of leaks. But the point still stands that running aground increased the danger.)

Jake, Abby, and I waited in the cabin, listening to the *Basilisk* groan. I understand why men speak of ships as if they are alive; we could feel her pain in the vibration of her boards. But the winds *were* slackening, and I was just beginning to hope that we might yet survive this when I heard a great crack from above, and then a crash that shook the whole stern.

It was the mizzenmast: the very same pole whose presence I had cursed for consuming so much space where it ran through our tiny cabin. Weakened by two days of the storm, it had broken at last, slamming down across the decks with all its rigging in tow. It knocked one man overboard and broke the captain's leg. But as wounds go, the *Basilisk* could have suffered much worse.

At the time we did not know that. All the three of us knew was that something dreadful had happened, and more such things might follow. We stayed huddled in the cabin until Tom came to the door and said, "The storm is passing. You can come out now."

Emerging from that dark little room after so long was like being born again. The wind, still stiff, was flogging the tail ends of the clouds into the distance; the clearing sky was pink with dawn light. We came on deck through a hatch amidships, for the one closest to the cabin had been blocked by the wreckage of the mizzenmast. Around us was choppy, white-capped sea—and islands.

They reared up from the waves like solid shadows, broad shapes furred with trees. As the light grew stronger, the darkness turned to emerald green, and the edges gleamed like pearls: sandy beaches, much spotted with seaweed and fallen palm branches after the storm, but radiant in the dawn. They were not so very far away, either. Suhail and some of the others could swim to shore, if it proved necessary.

We did not need to abandon ship, though. The *Basilisk* was sorely damaged by her encounter with the reef, but not sinking, at least not at present. Aekinitos was soon on deck once more; he could not walk, but the doctor had set his leg, and from a throne of crates the captain directed the efforts of his men. Their first concern was to cut away the wreckage of the mizzenmast, which was dragging in the surf and causing the *Basilisk* to shift uneasily; then they took stock of our losses.

At least, they began to. Not long after the mast splashed free, Jake tugged at my sleeve and pointed outward. "Mama, look."

I was already looking, but too high. One promontory above the sea had an oddly regular shape; there were no trees there, and the corner looked suspiciously square, as if someone had built a platform of stone. Jake directed my attention lower, to the water. Two canoes—no, three—were rounding the base of the promontory and making all speed toward us.

So these islands were inhabited. It was no particular surprise; whether it would be a blessing or a curse remained to be seen. We certainly needed assistance, but would these people be inclined to give it?

I hastened to notify Aekinitos. He called his men away from all but the most vital of tasks, and they surreptitiously brought out their guns and cutlasses. The captain did not want to present a hostile face, but he did wish to be ready in case it was needed. I recalled Jake to my side, and waited to see what would happen.

Two of the canoes stopped at a little distance, their rowers occasionally dipping oars into the water to maintain their position against the waves. The third circled the *Basilisk*, no doubt taking stock of our condition. Then it returned to its companions, and the men aboard conferred.

They were of course Puian, clad in loincloths, with tattoos marking their faces in patterns whose significance I could not decipher. None of them were small. Puians in general are a large people, tall of stature and generous of flesh, but these fellows were robust even by the standards of the region. From the crow's nest of the mainmast, one of the sailors called down in a hushed voice, "They have weapons. Slings, spears—looks like clubs, too, with stones or teeth or summat in them." He did not say, though, that they held the weapons in hand.

One of the two canoes that had waited now came forward a

bit, the oarsmen steering it with expert skill. In the bow, a man stood up and called out in a strong voice.

I caught only some of what followed. He was not speaking simplified trade Atau, but rather the dialect common to those islands. Two of the sailors and Suhail spoke in low voices to sort out their translations, then conveyed the result to Aekinitos. To begin with, the man in the canoe had said, "I wish to speak with your chief."

Aekinitos gestured for Mr. Dolin and Cranby to help him. The rest of the crew crowded to the rail, obscuring the view from the water; they did not clear away until Aekinitos had been carried forward and propped against a barrel, so that his crippled condition would not immediately show. Then he nodded to one of the interpreters, who called an introduction down.

In many fits and starts, through confusions of dialect and the elaborately flowery speech Puians affect when they need to be formal, Aekinitos told them that we were survivors of the great storm, and our ship was trapped on the reef.

Their answer, when it came, was startling. "You are not Yelangese. Are you Scirling?"

The captain was exhausted from the storm and in no small amount of pain, with his leg only recently splinted, but he did not betray surprise by so much as a blink. "Some of my crew are Scirling," he answered in even tones. "But I am Nichaean. We hail from all over."

I was glad not to be standing where the men in the canoes could see me. My confusion was mirrored in Tom's eyes. "That didn't sound friendly," I whispered to him.

He shook his head. "Trouble with the Yelangese—that I can see," he murmured back. "Raengaui and some of the other islands are in conflict with them, after all. But what has Scirland done to offend the people here?"

There were possibilities. A belligerent trading expedition; she-luhim come to proselytize the Magisterial faith; even a hunter like Velloin, though the Puian region as a rule boasts little in the way of large game. Someone might have come poaching sea-serpent teeth, though.

Aekinitos was not being entirely truthful with the islanders. He might be Nichaean, but the *Basilisk* was commissioned as a Royal Survey Ship, under the authority of the Scirling crown. I cast a sur-reptitious glance upward and saw that the Scirling flag no longer flew from the masthead; I later learned it had been carried away in the storm. There was nothing to identify us as hailing from that country, then, in more than an individual sense.

The conversation had continued while I pursued these thoughts. Aekinitos assured the men below of our peaceful intent, and begged for assistance in repairing and resupplying the *Basilisk*.

It pained him to beg, I could see. A captain is a king aboard his vessel, but the simple fact of the matter was that we had only two options here: to ask for what we needed, or to take it by force. He was not innately inclined to the latter, and furthermore pragma-tism constrained him. We did not know how many people were in this island chain, but they were sure to outnumber us, even with the advantage of our guns.

Fortunately the islanders, once assured of our neutral origin, were willing to let us come ashore and speak with their chief. They had knowledge of guns, and told us to leave ours on the ship, which Aekinitos agreed to with reluctance. Then they stood their canoes clear while we lowered one of the ship's boats, into which we loaded a slew of other people: Aekinitos, Mr. Dolin, four other sailors, myself, Tom, Suhail, Abby—and Jake.

You may question the decision to bring Jake along. To be quite blunt, it was a calculated defense on our part. In most parts of the world, the Broken Sea not excepted, a group composed entirely of grown men gives a different impression than one that includes two women and a child. I even thought—too late to change my attire—that I should have put on a dress, to reinforce my harmless civilian qualities. But in any event, I calculated that my son would be safer in the long run if I brought him with me than if I left him on the ship.

And so, escorted by the trio of canoes, we came ashore at Keonga.

The beach opposite the *Basilisk* had seemed all but deserted, apart from the rock platform I glimpsed on the promontory. It turned out this was because we had run aground on the wrong part of the island.

Just on the other side of the promontory was a thriving little village. At least, I thought of it in those terms; not until later did I understand this was the largest settlement on the island, most of the population being scattered in farms connected by footpaths. Here stood the chiefly residence and those of the priests, who carried out their ceremonies on the platform I had seen, which was a great temple.

Their position on the far side of the promontory had given them a degree of shelter from the storm, but not enough to escape damage. We saw many huts without roofs, their thatch having been torn off and strewn across the beach. Some of the weaker trees had been downed, and one of those had crushed a storehouse. There were some injuries among the common folk, for although they know these storms well and take what precautions they can, few structures can stand against such force. (The chief and his priests, I later heard, had sheltered in an old lava tube some distance up the slopes, which I would visit in due course.)

We landed on the beach and were taken toward an open space

before a large building. The space was marked with stones along its edge, and the posts and boards of the building were splendidly carved. We were made to wait outside that stone border, while a crowd gathered to gawk at us. I took some comfort in seeing women and children among this group as well, though it seemed virtually every man was armed in some fashion, even if only with a knife.

"Do we have any notion where we are?" I asked Aekinitos. He had been given a large bundle to sit on; any attempt to hide his injured state became impossible the moment he left the *Basilisk*.

He snorted. "Do you think I ceased to pay attention, simply because of a storm? If I do not miss my guess, we are in Keonga."

I had seen that name on his charts. This was not a place we had intended to go; it lay on the fringes of the Raengaui island cluster, and was therefore judged too far out of our way to be worth visiting, especially as the waters around it were said to be especially treacherous. Before I could ask Aekinitos more, however, someone began to chant in a loud voice, taking my attention away from the captain entirely.

The first greeters we saw did not look welcoming in the least. Three men, their loincloth-clad bodies magnificently tattooed, stamped toward us brandishing weapons. I think the only thing that prevented us from misreading their intention was the obviously stylized nature of their movements: they hammered their feet against the ground, slapped their chests and legs, and contorted their faces in terrifying expressions. "Hold your ground," Aekinitos growled. "It is only a test."

I had cause to be glad of the discipline with which his sailors followed him, for he seemed to be right. Although the men threatened us for at least a full minute, they made no move to attack—and then, just as suddenly as they had begun, it was done. They set leaves on the ground before us and retreated, their expressions now watchful. The chant shifted tone, and we were beckoned forward, into the marked space of the courtyard.

Others came out of the building then. It was not difficult to pick the chief out from among them. He was flanked by two men carrying great plumy things on sticks—overgrown cousins of fly-whisks, which seemed to be symbols of the chief's status—and wore a splendid feather cape that would have been the envy of any Coyahuac lord. Moreover, like rulers the world over, he was accompanied by an entourage of other resplendent people, whose presence announced very clearly his importance.

He walked with measured steps and halted some distance from us. Then, in a fashion that reminded me strongly of the oba of Bayembe, he spoke through one of his heralds. "Who are you, that have come to the shores of my island?"

We made a sorry lot in comparison. No member of our delegation had changed their clothes in days, and the only wash-water anyone had seen was the rain that sluiced down on the sailors. Furthermore, the man who spoke for us was exercising all his will to remain upright on a barkcloth-wrapped bundle, with his splinted leg obvious for all to see. But we could not leave Aekinitos behind; what we knew of Puian customs said it was vital to bring the most important person among us to converse with the chief, no matter what state he might be in.

It was a mark of the improved relations between Aekinitos and Suhail that the latter was permitted to speak for us—though not, of course, without direction. Suhail was unquestionably the best linguist among us, but that would not necessarily have swayed Aekinitos two months ago.

He introduced our group, and received the entire recitation of the chief's lineage in return. This, of course, was designed to impress upon us the mighty nature of the man we faced, and our own insignificance in return. I could not repeat the whole thing for you if I tried; his given name seemed to be Pa'oarakiki, and that is what we called him amongst ourselves. We later learned that he headed one of the greatest chiefly lineages in the archipelago, second only to that of the king, who ruled the neighbouring island of Aluko'o. Indeed, his mother's sister had been wife to the current king's uncle, which make Pa'oarakiki a great man indeed.

Undoubtedly he had already been told about our troubles, but Suhail repeated them now for his benefit. I could not follow half of what he said; not only was he endeavouring to describe the situation of the *Basilisk*, which involved a great deal of technical terminology I did not recognize even before Suhail found a way to express it in the Atau pidgin, but my exhausted brain simply lacked the will to struggle with a foreign language in the first place. My wandering gaze took in the battered state of the village, then studied the green slopes of the volcano above us, in which I could begin to pick out the signs of farms and the occasional hut.

And, in the air above the trees, a flock of shapes whose recognizable outlines immediately woke me from my stupor.

I did not realize I had made a little exclamation of pleasure until everyone turned to stare at me. Then I flushed hot and stammered out an apology. "I did not mean to interrupt. It is only that I saw a flight of fire-lizards up there."

I said this in Scirling, which meant of course that it had to be translated for the islanders. Then someone else spoke up, in a clear enough tone that I could understand. "What is your interest in them?"

The speaker was a large, deep-voiced woman in the king's entourage. She seemed to be about my age, perhaps a little older, and she was looking at me with a sharp expression. I surmised that she had some special position in his court, for her appearance was odd: the tattoos on her face exaggerated her eyes and her mouth, the barkcloth draped over one shoulder was thick and bulky, and the

skirt wrapped about her lower half was extravagantly padded at
the hips.

I attempted an explanation, but soon foundered on my tired-
ness and lack of fluency. Suhail raised his eyebrows, and when I
nodded in gratitude, he explained on my behalf. To them he said,
"She seeks to know all there is to be known about creatures like
the fire-lizards."

The woman's dark brows rose at his words. Much too late, I
found myself wishing I had held my tongue. Our experiences in
the Puian regions of the Broken Sea had introduced me to the word
tapu, which indicates the restrictions and prohibitions that mark
a thing off as sacred. I had not yet encountered any *tapu* which interfered with my studies, but such things vary from place to place,
and it was entirely possible that my interest violated one here. I
hastened to say, "Please, do not let that stand in the way of our ne-
gotiations. I do not wish to give offense. What matters is that we
repair the ship."

I do not think the Keongans would have ever refused us outright. Their archipelago is rather isolated—a fact which served us
well during the storm, for it meant the *Basilisk* could run freely before the wind. That isolation causes them to be an insular folk indeed (if I may be forgiven the etymological pun). But they are not
so xenophobic as to kill outsiders who are careful to offer them
no violence. Indeed, like many people in societies without cities,
they place a great deal of importance on hospitality. But Puians
are also a trading people, and they recognized that in this instance,
they held all the advantage—for we could not leave without their
help.

We might have done without the mizzenmast. Alert readers may
recall that it was a later addition to the vessel's structure anyway;
she could sail without it. But she could not sail as well: the captain and crew knew her as a bark, not as a brig sloop, and would

need to change their arrangements of sail and ballast and all the rest if they wished to do anything more than limp clumsily along.

With a mizzenmast or without, however, we could go nowhere while the *Basilisk* was pinned atop that reef; and likely not for some time after, as the coral had assuredly done sufficient damage to her structure as to warrant repair. We would at a minimum require the hospitality of the Keongans while those repairs were done, and likely some assistance besides. It was for this that Suhail had to bargain, translating the demands of Pa'oarakiki for Aekinitos, and the captain's counteroffers in return.

The barriers of language and exhaustion meant I followed very little of this. I can only marvel at both Suhail's linguistic agility and Aekinitos' strength of focus, for I doubted the captain had slept more than two winks at a stretch through the storm; and yet he sat there on his bundle with his broken leg before him and haggled like a Monnashire housewife on market day. The result was a payment of cargo and various other oddments in exchange for a beach to live on, some assistance with the ship—and a promise.

"They are insisting that we remain on Keonga until the repairs are done," Suhail said to the captain. "Neither you nor anyone else from the ship may travel to the other islands, without his express permission. As soon as the *Basilisk* is seaworthy once more, we are to sail away and not return."

It was an oddly cold demand, for a people who seemed otherwise friendly. (I had the impression Pa'oarakiki could have mulcted us for a good deal more than he did.) Aekinitos said, "What if we need timber or such that cannot be found on this island?"

"I inquired about that. He said it could be fetched for us, but we may not seek it ourselves."

Aekinitos grunted and shifted his injured leg. With so many eyes upon him, he did not permit himself the luxury of a wince. "As restrictions go, that one is easy enough, I suppose. I will make certain my men know."

He did not ask after the reason then, nor any time later—at least not directly. I know Pa'oarakiki's demand roused his curiosity, though, as it did mine. The prohibition might have been a matter of *tapu*, and in any event we had no desire to pry into the private affairs of the islanders. But it did raise questions, even if we kept them to ourselves.

Although it will put my narrative somewhat out of order, I must first relate what transpired with the *Basilisk*, for it is the framework that shapes everything else which happened during our stay. We could not leave until the ship was repaired; we could not go anywhere else in the islands while the repairs were conducted; and so we found ways to fill the time. Had we been able to leave sooner, a great deal of what follows would never have occurred.

The receding flood of the storm had left the *Basilisk* stranded atop the reef, in a kind of saddle between two higher bits of rock. This was a dangerous position to be in, for every wave that came in shifted her on her perch, and coral is not forgiving. Given sufficient time, the sea would have pounded our ship to pieces.

Unfortunately, she could not be retrieved at once. Discussion with the Keongans established that the next high tide would not be at all sufficient to float the *Basilisk* free. Aekinitos would have to wait for the "spring tide," a higher surge which comes on the new and full moons; and the new moon was not for more than a week.

For the men still on board the ship, this was dreadful news. By working the pumps they could keep the hold from filling with water—but to man them for a week and more could not be borne. Fortunately, they were able to devise a "fother," a patch of sail filled with oakum and tar, which is sucked into the breaches by the in-rushing water and thus seals them, at least partially, against their doom. Inspired by this, Aekinitos had more such patches made, buying barkcloth and fiber in great quantities from the islanders, which his men then lashed in place where the coral ground worst against the hull. These had to be replaced on a frequent basis, but they preserved the ship against some of the damage she might otherwise have taken.

Dragging her free of the reef required tremendous effort from not only the sailors but also the Keongans, who tied cables to their canoes and paddled mightily to haul the *Basilisk* clear. At that point we faced new problems, for deprived of that support, however destructive it may have been, the *Basilisk* promptly began to sink in earnest. It was a race between the sea on one side and the rowers on the other (not to mention the fellows manning the pumps belowdecks) as to whether they could get the ship to safety before she foundered irretrievably. This meant bringing her along the fore reef until there was a gap through which she could enter the lagoon, and then drawing her as far onto shore as Aekinitos dared, without beaching her so thoroughly she could never be removed again. This is called careening, and in the absence of a dry-dock, it was the best we could do.

His carpenter and other skilled men dove into the water to investigate the damage; the rest of us had to wait until the tide went out to see it. When the ship's hull was exposed, I shuddered at the sight. I had not known before that the *Basilisk*, like many ships, bears a "false keel" and a sheathing of thin boards over the keel and hull proper; these protect the structural fabric of the vessel from shipworms and other troubles, collisions with the seafloor included. The reef had torn away much of the false keel and a good deal of the sheathing, cracking the planks beneath. Aekinitos swore for a full ten minutes after he heard the report, in a medley

On the Beach

of languages that impressed even Suhail. Even for a linguistically
inept landlubber such as myself, the message was clear: we would
not be going anywhere any time soon.

That simple fact dominated our thoughts throughout our enforced stay on Keonga. It could hardly do otherwise; the immense
hull and tilted masts of the *Basilisk* towered over our encampment,
heaved first to one side, then to the other, while the men worked
to make her seaworthy once more. It was an inescapable reminder
of our misfortune, and our hope of returning home.

We knew that we were in the Keongan Islands; we knew very
little more.

That part of the Broken Sea was but very poorly charted by Anthiopean sailors; indeed, few other than Puians knew the secret
of reaching it, for doing so required a vessel to thread a maze of
shoals and reefs and underwater mounts whose treacherous currents could easily sink the unwary—unless the unwary happened
to be riding the surge of a storm. Aekinitos' charts, rescued from
his cabin, showed the type of vague markings that said the draughts-
man had no idea how many islands were in the chain, much less
their size and individual coastlines.

The Scirling Geographical Association would have given several left arms for accurate charts of the archipelago and its surrounding waters; alas, Pa'oarakiki's interdiction meant we could
not oblige them. Judicious questioning of the islanders taught us
there were eleven islands that merited settlement, and several more
that were barren volcanic rocks, waterless atolls, or otherwise un-
fit for human habitation. The largest of these was the neighbouring Aluko'o, which lies to the northeast of Keonga, and is the direct
domain of the archipelago's king.

The island upon which we had wrecked ourselves is the one

known properly as Keonga. It gives its name to the chain courtesy of a mythology that attributes great religious significance to
the two volcanoes that make up its bulk. These stand a little distance apart, and must originally have been two separate islands,
but their ejecta have run together in the middle, leaving a saddle
of lower-lying terrain in between. Owing to the orientation of this
saddle, which lies parallel to the prevailing winds, the area receives
a great deal of rain and wind, and is the breadbasket of the archipelago (so to speak—Keongans cultivate no grains, but only
tubers, fruit, sugarcane, and some vegetables).

In ancient times the island chain was divided between a number of chieftains who amounted to petty kings, but for the last few
generations they have been under the rule of a single man. We had
no direct dealings with the king until shortly before our departure; we could not go to Aluko'o to present ourselves, and we were
not important enough for so august a personage to greet. "Bigger
fish to fry," Tom said to me, during the days before the *Basilisk* was
freed and then careened. "Do you remember that Raengaui pirate-
king Aekinitos mentioned? Waikango? It seems he's been captured
by the Yelangese."

"He does not rule here, does he?" I asked. I knew he had been
extending his reach, but I did not think it had yet encompassed
this outlying archipelago.

"No," Tom said, "but the king's wife is a cousin of Waikango."

Then it was easy to guess why the people here did not like the
Yelangese. But what had my countrymen done to offend them?
I thought of Princess Miriam's embassy, which ought to have arrived in Yelang some time after I was deported. The news-sheets
had blown a lot of hot air about how her visit was to "deepen
the bonds of amity between our two great nations," but everyone knew that was a polite way of saying she was there to see if
Scirland and Yelang could be induced to get along. If they had,

perhaps the Puians of the Broken Sea had taken it as a hostile sign. But I could hardly imagine the princess had worked so quickly in establishing rapport; was it merely the fact of her visit that had offended them?

I could not ask. The people we dealt with had no reason to follow such matters, and the chief and his close retainers avoided us as much as they could. In the meanwhile, of course, we had our own affairs to address.

Much of the work in dealing with the *Basilisk*, first on the reef and then careened on the shore, was carried out under the supervision of Mr. Dolin, for the breaking of Aekinitos' leg greatly hampered his movements; but the captain was up and about before we were ready to leave. He took *very* badly to the limitations of his injury, and was a tyrant in the beach camp. All of his supernumerary passengers were pressed into service on such tasks as we were fit for—even Jake.

"He is crew," Aekinitos growled when I protested. (Virtually everything he said in that time came out as a growl, for enforced sedentism had made him a bear.) "If he wishes to sail from here on the *Basilisk*, he will work. As for you, Mrs. Camherst—there is no time to chase after dragons when my ship is wrecked. Much less ancient ruins."

That last, of course, was directed at Suhail, who had not protested at all. I resented the captain a great deal for his declaration, but he had the right of it: restoring our ability to travel took precedence over anything else. I was not much use in anything ship-related, nor things that required physical strength, but I sighed and joined Abby in making our beach camp a habitable place. If we were to be there for as long as it seemed, I had rather our quarters be something other than makeshift.

I cannot pretend our situation was entirely comfortable. (For one accustomed to the life of a Scirling gentlewoman, anything that does not involve padded armchairs cannot be termed "comfortable.") But the climate of Keonga is exceedingly agreeable, and after more than a year cooped up in that snuff-box of a cabin, the freedom to stretch out my limbs was a positive delight. I acquired a particular fondness for the ceaseless rush of the waves upon the shore, which I believe to be the most soothing sound in the world. It is because of my time on Keonga that I have made a habit of spending time on Prania in my later years—now that I can afford to do so.

We attracted a great deal of interest from the Keongans, of course. Much of our official cargo had gone in the bargain for supplies and assistance, but all the sailors had possessions of their own, and there was soon a brisk market between them and the islanders, each craving what they saw as exotic from the other. Tobacco pipes, penny whistles, and broken pocket watches were soon to be found in the proud keeping of the locals, while the sailors competed with one another to see who could obtain the most splendid flower wreath or shark-tooth club.

I took little part in this, as most of what I had with me was either scientific equipment I needed or specimens I had collected for my work. I did, however, converse with the islanders as much as I could, cudgeling my brain into accepting the sound changes and subtleties of grammar that differentiated their tongue from the trade pidgin I had previously learned. And, as you may imagine, I asked them about dragons.

My interest was divided between the sea-serpents I knew must be in the region and the fire-lizards I had seen with my own eyes. At first the locals could not understand my words; then, once the words became comprehensible, they did not understand my purpose; then, the more I questioned them, the more they retreated from me, their friendliness draining away.

"Am I giving offense?" I asked Suhail, knowing his command

of the language far outstripped my own. "I know they have many customs I am not familiar with, and I may have violated one. Is it wrong for me to ask about dragons?"

He shook his head, brows knitting in thought. "Not that I have heard. There are things that *are* forbidden to talk about, at least for the likes of me—but they make it clear when that is the case. I can try to find out, though."

"Please do." I did not like the thought that I might, out of sheer ignorance, close the doors that needed to be open for me. I could not heed *tapu* if I did not know where its boundaries lay.

Out of habit, I glanced up the slope of the nearby mountain. Once again, small figures were circling in the air: a flight of fire-lizards. I wanted to observe them, but until I cleared this matter up, it would be better for me to pretend they were not there . . . however much of a wrench it might be.

Turning away from the fire-lizards, I saw someone partway up the path that led to the village. It was the woman from the chief's entourage; I had learned her name was Heali'i. She had been lurking about our camp for some time now, watching us.

Or rather, watching *me*. I was sure of it now. Her eyes remained on me as Suhail went down to the water's edge. I nodded to her, reflexively polite, and she laughed—I could see the motion, though she was too far for me to hear the sound. Then she turned and began climbing the path, vanishing into the growing dusk.

TWELVE

Heali'i—The hostility grows—Keongan etiquette—Ke'anaka'i—
Matters of marriage—Bowing to necessity

Heali'i was a point of great gossip among the sailors. As I noted before, her appearance was not quite like that of other Keongan women, with her tattoos and her exaggerated clothing. She was said to live with her husband partway up the slopes of Homa'apia—the volcano at whose base we crouched—but somewhere in the course of things, a rumour started that her marriage was in some fashion peculiar. The men took this in predictable directions, and so whenever they encountered Heali'i (which they did often, on account of her tendency to lurk about camp and watch me), they greeted her with increasingly unsubtle propositions, all of which she laughed off with a flirtatious but unyielding refusal.

She did not seem to engage in the routine life of Keongan women. They spend some time in garden cultivation, and a great deal more making textiles: rope, twine, and above all barkcloth, which among them is a high art. (Larger-scale agriculture, hunting and fishing, canoe-making, and most aspects of warfare are the province of men—along with cooking, which I initially found to be a charming reversal, as I have never learned to love the task.) She did not quite seem to be a priestess either, though. As in many societies, the clergy of Keonga are drawn from particular bloodlines closely allied with those of the chieftains and the king, and they spend their time in activities such as the interpretation of omens and the conduct of rituals. They also dwell close by their leaders, in houses whose support posts and ridge beams were grandly carved with images of great significance. None of this described Heali'i, either.

Indeed, had I been forced to choose a single word to describe her status, it might have been "outcast." Her husband—a fellow named Mokoane—was a bit solitary, but seemed to be accepted well enough by Keongan society. Heali'i, by contrast, fit in nowhere. And yet she was not shunned, either. When islanders encountered her, they always greeted her with careful respect—unlike our own sailors. I could not make sense of it, and I could find no graceful way to ask why she was watching me.

Being who I am, when the graceful way failed, I decided to be more direct.

If this seems unwise, you must understand the circumstances I found myself in. Even though I had curtailed my questions about dragons, turning my eyes from the high peak where the fire-lizards flew, I found myself hedged about with growing hostility. Suhail had attempted to discover whether I had somehow violated *tapu*, but with no real success. "They all say no," he reported to me. "But it is the sort of no that means, 'you are asking the wrong question.' And yet no one will tell me what I *should* ask."

On the theory that perhaps it was not the question but the questioner that was wrong, I tried asking them myself. I say "tried" because no one even allowed me to finish, let alone answered. They all backed away, making signs I presumed were wards against evil. My frustration began to take on the cast of fear. I had once earned the hostility of Vystrani peasants by trespassing in ignorance, and it had almost resulted in us being chased out of town. Here we had no means of fleeing. If the current shunning turned to violence, I could destroy much more than simply my hopes of conducting research.

In all of this, Heali'i stood out as an exception. She did not approach me or speak to me, but where others turned their eyes away and abandoned my presence at the first opportunity, she was constantly there, watching. "I know it is not on your list of tasks to be performed," I told Aekinitos, "but I should like to try and talk to her."

He knew as well as I how the local mood was turning. "Go," he said. "Try not to get yourself killed." (I told you his mood was foul.)

I did take some precautions before approaching her. *Tapu*, you see, extends not only to certain subjects, but also to people and how one interacts with them. And while the common people observe a few forms of *tapu*—men and women, for example, may not eat together, which fortunately we discovered before we appalled the locals with our degenerate ways—individuals of importance observe many more. Thus far I had not been able to determine Heali'i's exact position in society, but I did inquire as to whether I would commit any unforgivable offense by trying to speak with her. (In a place where standing on the king's shadow is a crime punishable by death, this is no trivial consideration.)

I expected grudging permission at best, stony refusal at worst. For once I was shown to be a pessimist: the reaction from the woman I questioned appeared to be nothing less than sheer relief. From this I could only surmise that I had confirmed some hidden suspicion, but in a fashion that said the problem would soon be mended.

And so one day, with Jake in tow—leaving Abby to enjoy a well-earned rest—I hiked up the path to Heali'i's hut.

The track that led there was well maintained, relatively clear of vegetation and graveled with chips of stone where a dip made it muddy. Paths like this were to be found all around the islands; larger ones circled the perimeters, while smaller ones marked the boundaries between the districts and penetrated the interior to various locations of note. All around us was forest, as the ground here was too steep for much cultivation, but outcroppings of basalt occasionally served to remind me that we stood on the slope of a volcano—one that was most certainly not dormant. The wisps of steam continually drifting up from its caldera made that *quite* clear.

Heali'i was there, braiding cord into some kind of small shape. She paused in this work as we approached, studying us with unabashed curiosity. I wondered how we appeared to her: a pale woman covered in close-fitting fabric, and a nut-brown boy whose arms and legs were shooting out of his clothing. (Jake had grown nearly ten centimeters since our voyage began.) We certainly did not look Puian, but neither did we look much like the crew of the *Basilisk*.

I gave her a Keongan greeting, then said, "Please pardon my ignorance. I should like to be polite, but I do not know how I ought to address you."

Her eyebrows did a brief dance, from which I interpreted surprise, confusion, and amusement. (Heali'i often seemed to be laughing at me when we spoke, but I never did determine how much of that was her natural demeanor and how much was a reaction to my follies.)

She considered my words for a moment, but not with the wary hostility I had received from so many others. "Who are you?"

"I am Isabella Camherst," I said, and nudged my son forward with one hand. "This is Jake."

Heali'i shook her head. "No. Who are you?"

"We came on the *Basilisk*," I said. "The ship out in the bay." My words came slowly, because it was inconceivable that she could have forgotten that—and yet I could not think what else she might mean.

Body language is not the same in every culture, but I thought the tilt of her head was the equivalent of rolling her eyes heavenward, asking her gods for patience in dealing with so ignorant a visitor. "I cannot say how we should speak unless I know who you are. Your place, your ancestors, your *mana*."

That final term was one I had encountered a few times already—enough to have a tenuous grasp of what it meant—but I lacked the first notion of how to evaluate it in terms she might find useful. Her first two questions I could answer, though, at least in part. "You might call my father a retainer to a chief. My late husband was the younger son of a very minor chief." (These were the best comparisons I could find for "knight" and "second son of a baronet," respectively.) "For my own part, I am not a sailor on the *Basilisk*—I am not a servant of the captain, though of course we respect his authority when on board his ship. My companions and I voyage with him to carry out our work, which is to study and understand many things in the world."

"Your companions," Heali'i said, after a moment's thought. "Who leads you? The red man, or the other?"

In Mouleen Tom's nickname had been Epou, which means "red." The lesser heat of the Broken Sea had not flushed him as badly, but it was still enough for the epithet to return. "The other," then, would be Suhail, whose warm brown skin was much less worthy of remark among the Keongans. "It is not that simple," I said. "I work together with Tom—the red one. He and I are . . ." I used my hands to indicate equal status. (As usual, I am representing our conversations as rather more fluent than they were in reality, eliding most circumlocutions and gaps in my vocabulary—not to mention abject failures of grammar.) "Suhail has recently joined us, but he is pursuing his own goals."

My statement regarding Tom caused her tattooed mouth to purse. I had clearly posed her something of a conundrum, without intending to. Nor were we any closer to answering the question with which we had begun: to wit, how I should address her. We had conversed quite a bit for two individuals between whom such a basic question of etiquette had not yet been settled.

Jake had been listening. I am both embarrassed and proud to admit that his grasp of the language was likely better than mine; children's minds often absorb such things with more ease, and his father had always been better than I with Vystrani. But there were other things of which he had less comprehension, and so he said, "What's *mana*?"

Heali'i regarded him rather as I might regard a child who said, "What's a dragon?" I opened my mouth to explain it to him, but was stopped by a variety of obstacles. I scarcely knew how to describe it myself, having only a partial grasp of the concept, and certainly could not do so in Keongan; yet to explain it in Scirling struck me as deeply rude to our present company (although it would allow any errors on my part to go unremarked for the time being). Furthermore, Jake had addressed his question to Heali'i, who could certainly explain it better than I.

She did not precisely explain. Instead she looked at me and said, "Tell me of your deeds."

I wrote a moment ago that I had at least a preliminary grasp of the concept. I cannot fully explain *mana* to you, though, for I do not fully understand it myself. Heinrich von Kleist has written extensively on the subject, but I have not read the bulk of his work, as I have not had occasion to return to Keonga or any other part of the Puian islands since my time aboard the *Basilisk*.

What I came to understand in Keonga is that it combines aspects of rank, lineage, age, esteem, and spiritual power to create a hierarchy among that people, which must be respected lest one not only give offense but do supernatural harm to another. A direct lineage from the gods bestows a steady flow of *mana*, which raises kings above commoners; elder birth within a family does much the same. But *mana* is no static thing. It may be lost through carelessness and bad behaviour, or the malicious action of others (this being why *tapu* restricts certain aspects of life). It may also be earned—or perhaps it would be better to say demonstrated— through great deeds. A second son who is a mighty war-leader shows greater *mana* than his elder brother who lazes about doing nothing of note.

This, then, was the reason for the entire conversation up until this point: Heali'i did not know where to fit me into that scheme. As a non-Puian, my default position is to be entirely lacking in *mana*, for I am even less connected to the Puian gods than the most degenerate commoner of their people. But they do not write for-eigners out of their system entirely: Aekinitos, for example, was assumed to possess a degree of *mana*, by virtue of being the cap-tain of his ship, and his officers followed in lesser degree.

Had I named myself as the leader of our expedition, Heali'i would have written a small amount of *mana* for me into her men-tal ledger. But I could not do that to Tom; I knew too well the struggles he had endured as a man of plebeian birth. After our years of partnership, I was resolved never to claim any sort of author-ity over him, and certainly not on account of my more prestigious ancestry.

Deeds, however . . . those, I could claim.

"Ah," I said. "I have travelled the world to study dragons."

I meant that only to be my opening volley, the first line of the saga of my life. (Insofar as my limited command of Keongan would permit me anything like a saga.) But upon my words, Heali'i straightened, her tattoo-lined eyes going wide. "It's true, then," she said. "You are *ke'anaka'i*."

I repeated the word silently, my lips shaping the syllables. *Naka'i* was the word I had known as *nataki* elsewhere in the Puian islands.

It referred to different creatures depending on where I was, ranging from the sea-serpents to mere lizards, but in my head I had glossed its core meaning as "dragon." As for the rest . . . "Dragon-spirited?" I murmured in Scirling.

Heali'i could not understand me, but she came forward anyway, three quick steps that brought her close enough to lay one hand over my heart. I only barely controlled the urge to shy back. "In here," she said. "I did not think one could be born in a foreigner."

My first instinct had been to assume that "dragon-spirited" was her way of saying that I had a strong interest in the creatures. This, however, sounded rather more literal. "Do you think I am," I began, and then foundered on my lack of vocabulary. I could not think of a way to say "possessed."

Heali'i nodded, grinning from ear to ear. Because I had not finished my sentence, however, what she was agreeing to was not what I had meant. She took my head in her hands and brought us together so that our foreheads and noses touched, then inhaled deeply, as if taking in my scent. "I felt it in you," she said, still with her head against mine. "I, too, am not human."

"I *beg* your pardon," I said, recoiling at last.

The island woman was not bothered by my reaction. "I have heard that foreigners do not know the true stories. Your spirit comes from Rahuahane. That is why you are fascinated by the fire-lizards and the sea-serpents."

Jake was staring at us both, eyes wide. I looked at my son as if he could somehow explain the strange turn this conversation had taken, but he shook his head. I said, "What, or who, is Rahuahane?"

Heali'i did not answer me immediately. "I am a bad host," she said. "Come and sit in the shade. I will bring cocoanuts to drink and eat."

I was less than entirely minded to accept her hospitality until I knew whether she was a madwoman. I could not quite bring myself to walk back down the mountain, though, not without unraveling the rest of this mystery, and so I sat down where she indicated, with Jake close by my side.

Her answer took quite a while to work through, owing to my imperfect grasp of the language. Often she would get only half a dozen words into her sentence before I had to ask for a word to be explained; the explanation would contain another word I did not know; and by the time we had arrived at a phrase I could understand in its entirety, we had quite lost track of the original sentence. Jake assisted where he could, and often saw Heali'i's meaning before I did, but I could not risk miscommunication on a topic of such apparent import, and so had to confirm his assumptions with her before we could continue. But this, in much more efficient form, is what I learned.

I said before that there are eleven inhabited islands in the Keongan archipelago. That is not the same as eleven *habitable* islands. There is a twelfth, of acceptable size and well capable of supporting life; but a Keongan will throw himself to the mercies of the sea-serpents and the sharks rather than set foot upon it. This twelfth island is Rahuahane.

Heali'i's explanation began with the recounting of a myth. In the early days of the world, Wali, god of the sea, and Apoa, goddess of the land, lay together, and from them were born human beings. Keongans trace their lineages back to these two gods; indeed their entire society, from the lowliest farm laborer up to the king himself, is divided into two great clans (which ethnologists call moieties), one considering itself the heirs to Wali, the other to Apoa. Although Heali'i did not say this at the time, I later learned that each moiety is required to marry out; a man of the sea may not marry a woman of the sea, or land to land. Children, upon reaching the age of majority, choose the moiety to which they will thereafter belong, allying themselves with either their father's people or their mother's.

But human beings were not the only children this divine pair bore. One night Apoa lay atop Wali instead, and what she gave birth to after that were *naka'i*. Again I mentally translated this as *dragon*, but by Heali'i's account *monster* might be the more appropriate word. The *naka'i* were not kindly creatures. They lived on Rahuahane, terrorizing the men and women of the other islands, until a great hero named Lo'alama'oiri went there and turned them to stone. Ever since then, Rahuahane has been seen as cursed: an island of death.

"I was born on an island," I said, "but it lies many days' sail from here—more days than I can count. I do not know this Rahuahane of yours."

"You are *ke'anaka'i*," Heali'i insisted. "Even though you are foreign. Everything about you proclaims it. I have asked questions. You dress like a man of your people; you do a man's work. You stand between land and sea. Just as I do."

This time I understood all her words; her point, however, escaped me. "I thought it was my interest in fire-lizards and sea-serpents that made me *ke'anaka'i*, not my habits of dress. And you claim to be the same sort of person—yet you do not dress or act like a man."

"Of course not," Heali'i said, staring at me as if I were the slowest child in the village. "I dress and act like a woman."

I do not know how long I sat there with my mouth hanging ajar. The tall, strong body. The facial tattoos, exaggerating eyes and mouth like cosmetics. The clothing—bulky by Keongan standards—padding out the bosom, augmenting the hips.

Jake blurted, "You're a man!"

"No," Heali'i said. "I am *ke'anaka'i*."

Had the Keongan language been different, I might have seen it sooner. But in all the Puian tongues, they make no distinction between the masculine and feminine pronouns—only between animate things of the third person, such as people and animals, and inanimate ones such as cocoanuts. Like all those from the *Basilisk*, I had been calling Heali'i "she" . . . simply on the basis of assumption.

It had seemed a perfectly safe assumption. Heali'i had a husband, after all, and Mokoane was unquestionably male. (Keongans swim without clothing.) I knew from one of the participants in the Flying University that the ancient Nichaeans and various other societies valorized the love and intimacy of men, but I had never yet heard of one where they *married* each other.

But of course, as Heali'i said, she—I shall go on using the Scirling pronoun, for lack of a better—was not a man. Not as Keongans reckoned such things. Despite what lay beneath her barkcloth skirt, she was something else: a third gender, standing between male and female, between the moiety of the land and the moiety of the sea.

They are not common, the *ke'anaka'i*. Keongans identify them in their youth, sometimes by physical appearance (as there are infants born with genitalia that do not quite conform to the expected standards of male or female), but more often by their behaviour, which refuses to fit the patterned rituals and *tapu* of Keongan life. Such people are believed to be spirits from dead Rahuahane, born into human flesh . . . and they are dangerous.

"You're scaring people," Heali'i said. "You aren't married. It's necessary, to bind you into human society." She laughed, a hearty sound that carried through the trees. "A foreign *ke'anaka'i*, running around with nothing to restrain her—who would believe it? No wonder your ship wrecked. A Keongan would have thrown you over the side when the storm began, to appease the gods."

She might find it funny, but I did not agree. "I used to be married," I said, and gestured to Jake as proof. "My husband died."

"*Husband?*" Heali'i repeated, appalled. She recoiled from me, staring at Jake. "Tell me he is not your son." Then she waved this away, before I could even comply. "No. No, he cannot be your son. The others have not heard this, or they would have called for the priests. You must say he is someone else's son. The red man, or the woman from the ship."

Jake gave me a frightened look. We both read the same meaning into Heali'i's reference to the priests: their visit would not be a friendly one. *Ke'anaka'i,* it seemed, were not allowed to bear children. "Miss Abby," Jake said, and I nodded. She was already his governess, and therefore spent a great deal of time looking after him; it would be easy to let the islanders believe he was her son. (Half the sailors tended to forget he was not.)

Heali'i sighed in relief. "Good. You already behave as you should, for the most part. You dress and act as a man. Even your hair is short, like a man's." I put one hand self-consciously to my cropped head, which had been revealed when I laid my hat aside in the shade of Heali'i's house. "There is only one thing lacking," she said. "You need a wife."

Jake laughed uproariously at this. Perhaps it was the release of the previous tension; perhaps it was merely the thought of his mother playing gruff husband to some blushing bride that made him so mirthful. The blush, however, was on *my* cheeks. "Don't be absurd."

All amusement faded from Heali'i. "You must be married," she said. "And not to a man. If you are not . . . I don't know what they'll do."

The Keongans. They believed I was a reborn spirit from Rahuahane—a reborn *monster.* I had defused their concerns by coming to Heali'i, but that did not mean the concerns had gone away entirely. Fear made my skin prickle, even in the tropical warmth. "Heali'i, I cannot. I am not of your people! I do not follow your gods, know your ways—do you expect me to live here for the rest of my life? Or take some poor girl with me when I leave?"

She dismissed this with a snort. "I have heard what your home is like; it sounds much too cold. No Keongan girl would be foolish enough to sail there with you. No, you will divorce her before you go. If the gods take offense, that will be your leader's problem, not ours."

"What a charmingly pragmatic attitude," I muttered in Scirling, not at all charmed. Forcing my half-stunned brain back into Keongan, I said, "It is still impossible. My interest is in *men*, Heali'i. I cannot be a husband to a woman, not in—in the physical sense. I would not even know how." Many people over the years have accused me of having no shame, but had they been on the slopes of Homa'apia that day, they would know it to be false. There were some things I could not bring myself to do, not even for dragons.

Heali'i began laughing once more. For a moment I hoped this had all been some great joke—but no. "Do you think I lie with *my* husband? Of course not."

I stopped my tongue before it could point out that there were societies where such things were common. We were not here to debate the sexual mores and behaviours of all peoples; only of hers and my own. "But this would not be fair to the girl. Whoever she might be. To marry her in some kind of sham, and then cast her off when I leave . . . I cannot imagine anyone agreeing to it."

"That," Heali'i said, "is because you have not met her yet."

Messages can travel quite quickly in the islands, so long as there is someone willing to hop in a canoe and paddle over to the recipient's village. My prospective wife arrived at our camp the following afternoon.

I had said nothing of the situation to my companions, and had forbidden Jake to breathe so much as a word of it. Every time I tried to envision explaining this to Tom, my imagination failed me utterly. I kept expecting it to be some kind of grand jest, which I could forget as soon as the joke ended. But when Heali'i showed up with two people in tow, I knew she was serious.

They were both young: a boy and a girl, likely no more than sixteen. Heali'i introduced them as Kapo'ono and Liluakame, both from the neighbouring island of Lahana; I greeted them in my awkward Keongan, wondering if he was her brother, or perhaps a cousin. I saw little resemblance between them, if so.

When the formalities were done, Heali'i said, "Liluakame is perfect for you. She will be your wife until you leave."

I was too flummoxed by the entire situation to be polite. With the sort of bluntness one can only muster in a foreign language one speaks very poorly, I said to the girl, "Do you have any idea what is going on here?"

Liluakame glanced shyly at Kapo'ono. Not quite meeting my eye, she said, "You would be doing us a favour. I want to marry Kapo'ono, you see."

She had to repeat this twice before I was certain I had heard her right the first time. "How on earth could me marrying you help *you* marry *him*?"

"I'm not worthy of her yet," Kapo'ono said. It came out stiffly, and I realized he was at least as embarrassed as I was. "My uncle is going to take me on a trading expedition to Toahanae, and I will make my fortune there. But until then, Liluakame's family will not let me marry her."

"And while he's gone, I fear they'll make me wed someone else,"

Liluakame added. "There is a man on 'Opawai—he wouldn't be a shark, but I do not want to marry him. I want Kapo'ono."

A shark, I presumed, was a term of opprobrium for a bad husband. "But if you were married to me . . . then you would be safe until Kapo'ono returns."

She nodded. I resisted the urge to bury my face in my hands. "You know that Heali'i believes me to be *ke'anaka'i*, yes?"

"That's what you are," Liluakame said, as if confirming that the sky was blue. "Everyone knows it."

I was in no mood to argue about the concept; only about its implications. "Which means my spirit is some kind of inhuman creature from Rahuahane. And you want to be *married* to that?"

"I'm not afraid," she said stoutly. And Kapo'ono, when I looked to him, assured us both—Liluakame more than me—that he did not mind marrying someone who had previously been the wife of a dragon-spirited person. All the while, Heali'i beamed from ear to ear, as if she had just performed a miracle. Now I understood her eagerness: she had found someone who appeared to suit my needs as perfectly as possible.

That was not, however, the same thing as being a perfect match. "What of your parents?" I asked. "We are guests here on Keonga. I cannot afford to risk angering anyone, even if it would help both of us."

You may notice a shift in my speech. Previously I had been pointing out all the factors that made Heali'i's notion impossible . . . but somewhere in the course of things I had instead begun pointing out all the obstacles between us and success. It was my deranged practicality coming to the fore: it might be absurd for me to temporarily contract a marriage with another woman, but if I was going to do such a thing, I would do it *right*.

"I can talk them around," Liluakame said, which did not reassure me.

Between the three of them, however, they persuaded me to at least meet with her parents. I received a flurry of etiquette instruction, so that I might not give offense; I accordingly met them outside the enclosure where our party had originally been greeted, with a bottle of Tom's brandy as a gift and the proper words of respectful greeting on my tongue. This was successful enough that Liluakame's parents regarded me with bemused hilarity—rather the way I might have regarded a spaniel who arrived on my doorstep wearing a top hat and begging my pardon for the disturbance.

It transpired that their reason for marrying Liluakame to the fellow on 'Opawai was that they did not want their daughter to bear the scandal of being a spinster—especially since Kapo'ono's trading expedition was likely to be a lengthy one, which meant Liluakame would be waiting for quite a while. (She assured everyone most vehemently that she did not mind waiting in the slightest.)

"Will there not be any scandal if she marries *me*?" I asked—not quite believing that living in pseudo-wedlock with a half-human foreign transvestite was any improvement over spinsterhood.

The mother cast a dubious eye on Liluakame. "It is not what I would choose for her," she said. "But she would earn great *mana* by taming you."

I can only guess at the translation of that last verb; I did not recognize the word at the time, and did not remember it well enough later to confirm what she had said. The general sense of it, however, was clear enough. *Ke'anaka'i* were dangerous unless constrained by the civilizing institution of human marriage; the challenge of so constraining one was therefore a marker of great courage and strength.

It seemed that everyone was in favour, then—except for myself.

You may think the reason for my reticence was the sheer absurdity of what I was being asked to do. It goes very much against the grain to wed someone knowing it is merely an arrangement of convenience, to be discarded as soon as circumstances allow; that is not what marriage is supposed to be. Furthermore, for me to wed a *woman* was unthinkable in my own society, and scarcely more thinkable while I was temporarily resident in someone else's. Both of these were solid grounds upon which to doubt the wisdom of this course.

Neither of them, however, weighed nearly so heavily in my mind as the personal element. I had envied the two *tê lêng* mating in the mountains of Yelang; I envied the two young Keongans standing before me now. My own husband was dead; I must disavow my son lest we be done in by the islanders; and now, for my own safety as well as that of my companions, I was being told I must undergo a sham reprise of my first marriage, to someone I hardly knew at all.

"I will need time to consider this," I told them, and fled back to camp.

When I told Tom—after first taking the precaution of walking well away from camp with him—he buried his face in his hands.

I alternately watched him and looked away in embarrassment. His shoulders kept shaking with something I thought might be suppressed laughter, probably of a hysterical sort. Finally, when I could bear the silence no longer, I said, "I know it is strange."

"Strange," Tom said, still muffled by his hands, "is flinging yourself off a cliff for the sake of dragons. Strange is what you have done up until now. This . . . is something else."

"Very well—I know it is absurd."

"That comes closer to the mark." He took his hands down, shaking his head. "I needled you in Eriga about attracting marital interest wherever you go, but I admit, I never expected *this*. Must you do it?"

The question dragged at me like the anchor of the *Basilisk*. "I think I must. Otherwise the islanders will think there is nothing binding me to human society."

Tom nodded. A blind man could not have missed the way the Keongans were treating me. Since I climbed the mountain to visit Heali'i, the worst of it had subsided, but it had not gone away; they watched me as if I were a dancing spark that might set a whole village ablaze. I was *ke'anaka'i*; I was unbound by human custom. If I stayed quietly in my hut, they might let the matter pass with a mere shunning. But if I tried to pursue my research, I might frighten them into outright violence.

Laid against that, a sham marriage seemed a small price to pay.

Tom's thoughts trended in a similar direction. "It seems much less hazardous to life and limb than some of the other things you've done."

And less hazardous than remaining in my current state. "Please do not tell anyone," I said, not without a piteous note.

He snorted. "Who would believe me?"

I weighed the matter in my mind: the fear of the islanders, my own fear of following so strange a course. The path before me was peculiar beyond my ability to even imagine, and would drag up any number of memories I was not eager to face . . . but dragons lay at the end of it.

"Then I will speak to Heali'i," I said.

THIRTEEN

My wife—Suhail's concern—Life with Liluakame—Spotting serpents—Into the bell—The underwater world—A ruptured line—To the surface

I have never attempted to hide that I have had two husbands in my life.

I have, however, neglected to mention that in between them, I had a wife.

Liluakame and I wed in a simple ceremony that hardly merited the name. I was grateful for its simplicity and foreignness, which helped to separate my current actions from those which had bound me to Jacob Camherst. My son was not present—not because he disapproved, but because we were pretending he was Abby's son. Indeed, he found the entire thing more amusing than upsetting; it is remarkable what children will accept as normal, especially when their experiences have been sufficiently broad. Tom knew of it, as did the captain and Abby. (She, I suspect, mentally wrote me down as the sort of woman who enjoys the company of other women in more than merely social ways. While not true, it was an understandable conclusion to draw.)

My attempts to keep the entire thing secret from the crew of the *Basilisk*, however, failed to an astounding degree.

It was futile to even try. I could not keep them from knowing that I had temporarily disavowed Jake as my son, for we needed them to perpetuate that façade. Nor could I keep them from knowing that Liluakame was about, for it was her duty as my wife—however nominal that status—to keep house for me. Her father and brother built a more substantial hut for the two of us to reside in, along with Jake and Abby, which drew attention; before long, any number of rumours began to circulate about our precise arrangement. At first I tried to squelch these, but of course the harder I tried, the more I persuaded everyone that something was indeed going on. Jake's approach was much more successful: he began to make up stories about me, each one wilder than the last, burying the truth under a mountain of flamboyant nonsense.

And that, dear reader, is why the tales of my life in Keonga are even more absurd than the normal run of story about me. Under no circumstances was I going to report the truth to the *Winfield Courier*, let alone to my family. In the end I chose to embrace Jake's tactic, inventing outrageous variations when speaking of the matter in person, but glossing over it entirely in print. The result has been a breathtaking mélange of untruths, and as I have already decided that this shall be a volume in which I reveal one secret, I may as well reveal another. (After all, it has been so very long since there was any satisfying scandal about me. I find that respectability grows wearisome after a time, when one is accustomed to being a disgrace.)

The only part which troubled me, once I settled upon Jake's method of dealing with the rumours, was Suhail's reaction.

He had been busy in his own right, diving in the warm, shallow waters of the lagoons that lay between the shore and the surrounding reef. He was, of course, looking for any sign of submerged Draconean ruins. The hunt for these had taken him around the island, a journey of several days—these being the days in which I discovered Heali'i's nature and found myself supplied with a wife. When he returned, he sank neck-deep in the morass of rumours that now filled our camp. Understandably, he came to me for explanation.

To him I told the truth, in as straightforward a fashion as I could. When I was done, he stared at me with an expression I could not read. "Do you think this is right?" he asked.

"It hurts no one that I can see," I said. "Liluakame benefits, along with Kapo'ono. It allows me to conduct my research without offending the local customs. And it is not as if I am going to damage my own future marriage prospects, for I have none." (I had received three proposals in the years following Jacob's death, but none of a sort I would consider for even a moment. At the advanced age of thirty, with little money but a great deal of notoriety to my name, I had no expectation of receiving anything better.)

"But you do not believe in what they tell you," he said.

"In *ke'anaka'i*?" I had given this a great deal of thought since speaking with Heali'i, and had reached some surprising conclusions. "If you mean, do I believe that I am the reincarnation of an inhuman dragon-creature from a Puian myth—then no, of course not. But taking the term in its simpler sense . . . then yes, perhaps I am dragon-spirited."

Suhail's eyebrows went up, and I elaborated. "I have been mad for dragons ever since I was a child, and this, they say, is a sign that marks one as *ke'anaka'i*. Such people also transgress against the norms of society, particularly those which constrain behaviour on the basis of sex; this, too, describes me quite well. And—" I hesitated. "This will sound peculiar, I know. But this love I have for dragons, my compulsion to understand them . . . I have thought of it before as if there were a dragon within me. A part of my spirit. I do not believe it is true in any mystical sense, of course; I am as human as you are. But in the metaphorical sense, yes. 'Dragon-spirited' is as good a term for me as any."

He listened to this in silence, his expression settled into the grave lines it assumed when he was deep in thought. "Do you believe you are neither male nor female?"

I almost gave a malapert answer, but caught myself in time. We had an established habit of intellectual debate, and I valued it; I would not discard it now.

"So long as my society refuses to admit of a concept of femininity that allows for such things," I said, "then one could indeed say that I stand between."

It was not quite the same thing as the Keongan concept of a third gender. But Suhail nodded—less as if he agreed, more as if I had given him a great deal to think about—and there it rested for a time.

I fear I was not a terribly good husband to Liluakame.

In part this was because I found myself almost thinking of her as my servant. I was accustomed to shifting for myself in the field; living in something like a proper house, with someone else arranging my domestic life, tempted my mind into the habits of home. But I think it was more my own troubles than our circumstances that made me fall into such patterns of thought. It was easier to envision her as a servant than as a spouse, for the former did not require any intimacy of spirit from me.

Fortunately, neither did Liluakame. So long as I treated her with respect—which I did, quite scrupulously—she did not ask much more of me, and seemed content to hone her own skills in preparation for her impending marriage to Kapo'ono. She was, on the whole, a very good wife. Thanks to the efforts of her male kin, our ramshackle lean-to was soon replaced with a proper hut, its floor paved with rounded stones, its openings perfectly positioned to admit what cooling breezes were to be had. Had I intended to live there permanently, Liluakame would have started a garden; instead she worked in the garden of a cousin of Heali'i's and brought home plantains, sweet potatoes, cocoanut, and breadfruit, as well as taro from the fields of the men.

The one task that did fall to me, at least in part, was cooking. I mentioned before that this is the purview of men in Keonga; women cook certain things, but men oversee the underground ovens which bake the more substantial dishes. To my chagrin, I found that this became *my* duty, now that I was a *ke'anaka'i* individual living as a man. Like Heali'i, I was not expected to perform all the duties of my apparent sex . . . but if I did not cook such things, my household went without. Jake was old enough that he should have left our side to live among the unmarried young men, but as he had not gone through the appropriate rite of passage, he still belonged to the world of women (which in practice meant the world of Abby).

My odd position did at least afford me one domestic benefit: as *ke'anaka'i*, I could dine with whomever I pleased, without violating *tapu*. I therefore was able to take meals with my son when I chose, or with Tom, or with Aekinitos (once repairs were underway and his mood improved)—the exception, of course, being when research drew me away.

I was eager for that research, not only because of natural inclination, but also because it gave me a reason to avoid the awkward components of my domestic situation. Together with Tom and Heali'i I formed a plan to hike up to the summit of Homa'apia. There, she promised, we could observe fire-lizards to our hearts' content.

The prospect excited me greatly. Before I could pursue it, however, I had matters to attend to in the sea.

We all saw the new storm brewing. The tides were nearly right for Aekinitos and Mr. Dolin to free the *Basilisk* at last; but if she were to have any hope of floating free, the very large weight sitting in her belly had to be removed. "I should throw the damn thing over the side," Aekinitos growled at Suhail. "That lump of steel was dragging us askew all through the storm."

Suhail made a gesture of apology. "The diving bell will take no harm from being in water, if you would be kind enough not to throw it. We could perhaps lower it onto the reef with the boom, and retrieve it once the ship is repaired."

Aekinitos did not look very enthused at the prospect of retrieving it. I intervened, saying, "It would be very beneficial to me to have the diving bell. We have a scheme in mind for using it to study the serpents." To say nothing of its use to Suhail, of course—not that Aekinitos cared a fig for that.

"You will not be able to use it," the captain said. "Even one of their double canoes cannot carry its weight."

Disappointment dragged at me. I had been so very eager to view the sea-serpents. Then Suhail said, "There would not be any ruins on the fore reef, so it is of no use to me there. But Mrs. Camherst might be able to use it to view the serpents before the ship is moved."

"Oh, *might* I?" For a moment I sounded as if I were seven again. Then a twinge of guilt stirred in me. "Though I do not feel right, using your device for my research, when you cannot use it for your own."

Suhail dismissed this with a wave of his hand. "If it will do you good, then by all means. There are some islanders whose job is to keep a watch out for the serpents, so that the fishers do not go into danger. We can ask them."

The islanders in question were a gaggle of boys old enough to take their meals with the men, but too young to undertake adult tasks. They told me with enthusiasm that yes, the serpents were often seen outside the reef, and showed me the drum they beat to warn others when the telltale coils broke the surface. "Are you going to ride one?" they asked Suhail, all eagerness.

"*Ride* one!" I exclaimed.

"Yes," one of them replied, with great enthusiasm. So great, in fact, that I could not follow at all what he said next; his words came out in such a torrent as to utterly defeat my imperfect grasp of his language.

Suhail translated for me, with a slowness I knew did not come from any linguistic difficulty. "He says it is a thing the warriors do. They wait until there is a warning of serpents, then paddle out past the reef and dive into the water. When a serpent comes near, they seize hold of the—" He stopped, gesturing above his eyes.

"The tendrils," I said. "They must be quite sensitive; we believe those are part of how the serpents perceive disturbances in the water."

"Interesting. Yes, the tendrils. He says this keeps the serpent from tossing its head to fling the rider off. Someone who does this displays great *mana*; the longer he remains aboard, the greater the acclaim."

I had not forgotten the circumstances under which I first saw Suhail, back in Namiquitlan. "You want to try this for yourself."

His answering grin split his face. "Can you imagine such a ride?"

"Not for myself," I said firmly. I had begun to enjoy swimming; it was very pleasant to start my day with a paddle in a sheltered cove, away from the sailors' eyes. (A *clothed* paddle, I should note. The locals might swim naked, but I did not. Even Suhail wore a loincloth in the water.) A few days of practice, however, did not make me a champion swimmer. For me to try such a thing would be foolhardy in the extreme.

A little voice in my mind whispered, *As foolhardy as hurling yourself off a waterfall*.

"I will not try it now," Suhail assured me. "If I got myself eaten, you would have no one to manage the diving bell for you. And I would not want an angry serpent to damage the *Basilisk* further."

I laughed. "No, indeed—Aekinitos would raise your ghost in order to vent his spleen upon it."

We were fortunate. Between our conceiving of this notion and the removal of the *Basilisk* from her stony cradle, a serpent was indeed sighted just beyond the reef.

The moment we heard the drums pounding, we sprang into motion. One of the ship's boats and two Keongan canoes pushed out from shore, carrying myself, Suhail, Tom, Heali'i, and an assortment of sailors and islanders. The latter kept watch at a distance while we climbed up onto the ship, where the diving bell had been made ready.

Suhail had made the first preparations before the storm ever drove us to Keonga, welding a metal plate onto the base of the bell, with a collar of oiled leather for a hatch. "It will not withstand any great pressure," Suhail had told me. "Rubber would be better. But we will not be going deep." There was a flattish bit of reef below the outcropping on which the *Basilisk* had grounded herself; it was less than ten meters down, where the pressure ought to be acceptable, and would provide (we hoped) a stable platform for the bell, which ordinarily would hang suspended in the water, allowing Suhail to swim out through the open bottom. Suspension, however, would mean that any swing from the bell—such as that caused by a serpent—might create trouble for the damaged *Basilisk*, shifting it on the reef. Even preparing to lower the bell into the water had been an exercise in physics, taking care we would not tip the vessel over.

I must admit I had second thoughts when I saw the bell awaiting us on deck. It lay on its side, with sacks about to keep it from rolling; the hatch in the base seemed very small indeed. (I have never been claustrophobic, but I defy most of my readers to face the prospect of sealing themselves in a small metal chamber and dropping that chamber into the ocean without at least a moment of apprehension.) I could not allow those thoughts to delay me, though; we did not know how long the serpent would remain.

Suhail was giving final reminders to Tom and the men who would be managing the air pump. Their work was vital; without that umbilical hose and the machine on the other end, Suhail and I would asphyxiate in short order. I looked to Heali'i for my own instructions. "Is there any *tapu* I should know about? Suhail is not dragon-spirited."

"Just don't make them angry," Heali'i said; and with those comforting words, I had to enter the bell.

Suhail followed me a moment later and clamped the hatch shut. There was not much room for either of us to move; the bell was a bit taller than a man's height, but had a bench around the edge, which divers sat upon when the device was used as intended. He and I braced ourselves against this as the men hauled on ropes to bring us upright. The bell thumped against the deck, which I prayed would not collapse beneath us; it did not. Small amounts of light entered through the two windows, but not enough.

He was watching me closely. "You do not have to do this," he said.

I managed a small laugh. "That should be my epitaph when I die. *She did not have to do it.*" Then my words cut off, for with a great creaking of ropes and shouting from the men on deck, we rose into the air and swung out over the sea.

I expected the bell to sway as it entered the water, but its great weight was proof against the force of the surf. I heard the splash of water outside, and felt the bell chill beneath my hand; then the interior dimmed as we went under.

"Breathe," Suhail said with a grin. I had, without realizing it, begun holding my air. I exhaled and gave him an answering smile.

The result undoubtedly looked nervous; there is a fine line between excitement and fear.

I had been in the sea once before, when swimming with the dragon turtles. It was odd now to see that environment through glass: to be underwater, yet perfectly dry. The sunlight slanted down through the sea, beams dancing slightly as the waves shifted. No water came in through our hatch, not even the slightest leak, and Suhail made a satisfied murmur.

The bell settled against the seabed. Suhail rose from the bench and tramped a circle around the interior, making sure our position was secure. Then he nodded, and I went to the porthole to look out.

We had landed where Suhail intended, upon a sturdy shelf overlooking deeper waters. From one side I had a splendidly close view of the reef that had been the downfall of the *Basilisk*, the coloured corals put to shame by the bright fish flitting among them. I could have lingered for an hour simply watching those fish; they have never been of great interest to me before, but their beauty was entrancing.

My time here was limited, though, and so I moved to the other porthole, looking out into the ocean. The reef there rapidly gave way to a more muted landscape. My gaze flicked from place to place, familiarizing myself; I estimated sizes, distances, preparing myself to record what I could about the sea-serpents.

For those, I would not have to wait long. There was not just one serpent in the vicinity; there were several, slipping through the more distant reaches. The question was, would they come closer?

"The water here is *beautifully* clear," Suhail marveled from behind my shoulder. "In most places you would not see them at such a distance—not as anything more than shadows in the murk."

Glass against the tip of my nose told me I had leaned forward instinctively, trying to lessen the gap. "I wish they would come closer," I said. Then I grumbled in annoyance, for my words had fogged the glass. I wiped it clean with my sleeve and returned to my study. The next time I spoke, I took care to turn my head first. "They are unquestionably smaller than the one I saw in the north—less than half the size, I should think. Not juveniles, though; they seem fully formed."

Suhail said nothing, which pleased me. He had a knack for distinguishing between conversation and the audible workings of my brain, and knew not to interrupt the latter. One of the serpents drifted closer, tantalizing me, and I noted its characteristics out loud. "Full complement of facial tendrils—that could be a sign of youth, or of species difference. No evidence of posterior fins. I can almost see vanes on the anterior fins, four of them. Come, my dear; turn this way, so I may see your face."

I do not know how long I stood there, talking to myself like a madwoman, half-conversing with a sea-serpent. When it swam away once more, I turned and found Suhail with one foot on the bench, a notebook braced against his knee. He had been scribbling in the dim light, and held the result up for me to see: a record of all my ramblings.

"Oh, *thank* you," I said. "My memory is good, but—"

The bell went nearly dark. I whirled in time to see a long rush of scales going by the porthole; an instant later I was glued to the side of the bell, but I was too late. The serpent was already swimming off. I could have howled in frustration. "Another one! And this one is larger." I craned my neck, trying to see above, where the serpent circled. "If only I could get a close look at the scales . . ."

The serpent seemed inclined to oblige me, for it bent back upon itself and dove once more. It shot by at speed, and then the bell rang like its namesake as the serpent's tail slapped the side.

I put my hand against the wall, more out of shock than a need to catch myself. The bell weighed a *great* deal; a mere slap scarcely did more than shake it. But Suhail, off-balance with his foot up on the bench, almost staggered against me. He met my gaze and said quietly, "I think you should stop wishing for such things."

The bell rang again. "Oh dear," I said, my nerves returning. "It—cannot break the bell, can it? Or the porthole?"

"Those, no," Suhail answered, looking up with sudden concern.

My heart began beating double-time. "What do you mean by, *those, no?* What else could it—" Then my gaze followed his, and I understood.

At the top of the bell, a small hole gave access to the umbilical which supplied our air. That hollow cable was a sturdy thing, and laced through the chain besides; surely that would be enough to protect it.

I returned my attention to the porthole, trying to see what was transpiring outside. I arrived just in time.

The serpent had circled and come about to face us. I saw its mouth open wide, its flanks ripple peculiarly. I had just enough time to say, "I think it is drawing water in—"

And then the serpent spat it back out.

This time the bell did more than simply ring. It rocked dangerously backward, shifting on the seabed. I caught myself against the far wall, the bench striking the backs of my knees. "Jet of water," I said, and the part of my mind that takes refuge in science made a note to discuss abdominal musculature once more with Tom, who had dissected the serpent up in the arctic. "But this bell weighs a *very* great deal; we should—"

I cannot tell you what happened next, for I was no longer looking out the porthole, and it offered a limited view regardless. I do not know whether the first serpent returned to lend its aid, or whether that jet had been a mere test and now the second, larger serpent mustered its full strength. I know only that the floor of the bell tilted beneath my feet . . . and then the whole thing tipped and rolled, throwing me against the bench, against Suhail, and then there was water spraying all around us, and I was screaming.

He regained his feet before I did. By the time I determined which way was up, Suhail had stripped off his shirt and jammed it against the hole for the umbilical—the hole which had previously supplied us with air, and now, despite his best efforts, was admitting a steady flow of water.

The bell was on its side again; the cable had broken; we were in imminent danger of drowning.

I managed to stand, slipping a little in the accumulated water, and joined Suhail in pressing the fabric against the hole, trying to block the points at which it was leaking. We met each others' gazes, and the panic in his eyes felt much like that in my own heart. "They'll have seen that above," I said. Tom and the others could not possibly have failed to notice the bell being torn from its chain.

"They cannot get to us in time," Suhail said.

My mind had already performed the same calculation. If someone dove in immediately, perhaps—but what good would that do? They could not reconnect the chain, could not haul us from the sea before we drowned.

We turned as one to regard the hatch through which we had entered. Perversely, I blessed the serpent for not merely breaking the umbilical, but knocking us on our side; had it not done so, we would have had no escape, for our jury-rigged hatch was in the base of the bell, and had been pressed firmly against the sand. Now it offered a slender reed of hope.

Suhail's voice was quiet with tension. "We would have to let the water in, then swim out once the force had subsided."

"And hope we can make it to the surface in time," I said.

A heartbeat passed, during which the water continued to leak in.

I did not think of Jake in that heartbeat. Those who claim their thoughts go to loved ones in such moments of crisis are either liars or made of different stuff than I. All my thoughts were bent to the calculus of survival. We were a little less than ten meters down; I was not a fast swimmer. The serpent was still out there, and might come for us once we were free of the bell.

But if we stayed here, we would certainly die.

"Exhale as you go up," Suhail said, and by that I knew he had reached the same conclusion. "Otherwise the air in your lungs will expand and kill you."

I had not thought of that, and nodded. Then he said, "Are you ready?"

Of course not, I wanted to say. But delay would accomplish nothing beneficial, and so I said, "Yes."

Suhail let go of his shirt. The spray of water increased greatly, utterly drenching me. He waded through the growing depth to the hatch. Once there, he wasted no further time, but broke open the seal.

To my horror, the hatch did not open immediately. It had been designed to swing outward, so that the pressure of the sea would assist in keeping it closed; now that worked against us. Suhail kicked it, and that let in a gush of water; then the flood began.

I gulped in the greatest lungful of air I could hold. My body ached with the volume of it, and I remembered what he had said about pressure—but I would need as much oxygen as I could get.

The bell was almost full of water. Suhail had gotten the hatch fully open, and eeled out through it with the ease of a practiced swimmer. I pushed for it, swimming against the inrushing current, and found he had waited for me; he gripped my wrist and helped me out. Then, still holding me, he kicked off from the seabed, and we rose.

Ten meters had not seemed like so very great a depth as we went down, with the water so clear it made distances small. Now, fluttering like mad for the surface, ten meters seemed like ten kilometers. We ascended so slowly—so slowly. Only the growing pressure in my lungs told me we had gone anywhere. I exhaled in little spurts, trying to keep as much air as I could, for soon my body was clamouring for fresh oxygen. Suhail, a better swimmer by far, dragged me up and up and up.

I could not help looking about. The nearest serpent was up at the surface now, but not facing us; it was thrashing away in an unhappy fashion. I saw the underside of a canoe in the water, some distance from the great shadow that was the *Basilisk*'s hull, and knew the Keongans were doing something. But I could not spare any thought for what that might be. I had to swim for the surface.

My lungs were aching. I could no longer tell what was pressure and what was the thirst for air. The surface was still so far away. I tried to exhale again, but there was nothing left in my body. My diaphragm jerked, fighting to draw breath, only my clenched jaw preventing me from inhaling seawater. Suhail's hand was like iron around my wrist, holding fast against my thrashing.

Then my mouth opened, against all my will, and I began to drown.

FOURTEEN

*Return to life—Amowali—Plans for
the peak—The lava tube—Statues at the crater—The barren
zone—Fire-lizards—Unseen peril—A second near miss*

I came to my senses on the deck of the *Basilisk*, coughing out what seemed like half the Broken Sea across its boards. My lungs fought between the need to gasp in air, glorious life-giving air, and the need to expel the remaining water. The conflict between those two impulses racked me for an eternity, until at last my airway was clear and I could breathe.

I lay where I was for quite some time after that, curled on my side, listening distantly to the voices around me. One voice I recognized as Tom's, murmuring an uncharacteristic prayer of thanksgiving. (There is nothing like the near death of a companion to bring religion out in a man.) Others belonged to the sailors and the islanders, barking orders and arguments I lacked the wit to follow just then.

One voice I did not hear: Suhail's.

As that thought came to me, I rolled over and tried to sit up. I hit someone's knees, and fell victim to another coughing fit. When it stilled at last, I found the knees belonged to Suhail, who was gazing down at me in wordless relief.

"Oh, thank God you're alive," I said.

He managed something like a laugh. "Those should be my words. You are the one who nearly drowned."

I remembered his hand around my wrist, dragging me toward life. "I have you to thank for my survival, I think."

Suhail's colour suddenly improved. He had been as sickly as it is possible for a sun-browned Akhian to look; now he appeared much healthier, and I realized he was blushing. "I'm afraid I have to beg your forgiveness again," he said, and edged back a few centimeters, so that I was no longer against his knees.

I noticed, for the first time, how close to me he knelt. Tom was crouching half a pace away, and although there were a few sailors looking on, they were all standing. And I had heard tell of how the victims of drowning were saved, though never seen it firsthand.

My own face must have flooded with colour. All at once I was aware of my state: soaking wet, lying full-length on the deck without so much as a blanket to cover me. Undoubtedly there had been no time for such things when Suhail set about reviving me. The water had plastered his curls to his head; they clung to his cheekbones in damp tendrils. He stared at me with the expression of a man who knows he should look away, but has misplaced the ability to do so.

I do my reputation no favours to admit this, but I stared at him in much the same way. We had just survived a harrowing experience; those among you who have done the same know that it often heightens the senses, giving one a vivid awareness of life and its fragility. I was not so very old yet, and Suhail was naked to the waist, and for a moment I had difficulty thinking of anything else.

Tom broke the stasis, for which I shall eternally be grateful to him. He moved from his crouch, and Suhail retreated, allowing him to help me to my feet. (It may give you some notion of how strongly my near drowning had affected me that I was almost as self-conscious of my wet clothing with Tom—*Tom*, who had seen me naked and covered in mud when I fell victim to yellow fever in Mouleen.)

As usual, I took refuge from embarrassment in my work. "What happened?" I asked, once I was something like steady and had recovered from a new fit of coughing. "Do we know why the serpent attacked?"

"I have an idea." That came from Heali'i, who had been at the railing, calling down to the men in the canoes below. For once there was not the slightest hint of amusement in her expression. She beckoned me to her side, and when she could speak quietly in my ear, she said, "I think the serpent is *amowali*."

I shook my head, not understanding the word. Heali'i sighed in annoyance, turned so that others could not see what she did, and shaped a curve in front of her belly with one hand.

Pregnant. This was enough to drive all thoughts of my recent experience and current state from my mind. I straightened up, looking to the water as if I might see the creature there, but it was gone. A chance—possibly my *only* chance—to examine a bearing sea-serpent, and I had wasted it.

"What did the others do?" I asked, remembering the movement above as Suhail and I broke for the surface.

"A rider," she said, gesturing to where a naked man was hoisting himself into a canoe. I hastily averted my eyes. "He dove in and seized hold as the serpent broke the surface, then turned it away from you."

I was unspeakably grateful to him for it, and told him so as soon as he was clothed once more. He did not seem to mind the risk he had taken on our behalf; his friends were all praising him for his courage and quick thinking, saying he had won great *mana* by that action. Although I do not attribute spiritual significance to the concept, as they do, I could not dispute the general point, which was that he was indeed a man worthy of respect.

Any further questions regarding the serpent itself had to wait until I was on land once more and could speak to Heali'i in greater privacy. Tom, Suhail, and I were loaded into a canoe along with her, while the sailors stayed to prepare the ship for its move to shore. The bell, of course, was left on the outward slope of the reef, to be retrieved when the *Basilisk* was seaworthy once more.

By the time I reached shore, I was shivering badly. The warmth of the islands, which ordinarily I found pleasant, was no longer enough, and I could not catch my breath. Liluakame was familiar with these symptoms (drowning being a hazard the Keongans face regularly), and bundled me into heavy barkcloth blankets to sit by a fire outside our hut. There, Heali'i and I could talk at last.

"Do sea-serpents regularly attack when bearing?" I asked. I did not want to leave the shelter of my blankets enough to take notes, and I was not certain what she would think of it if I did. Keongans distrusted writing in those days; they believed strongly in the power of words, and did not like the notion of those words, along with the knowledge they carried, being left sitting about where anybody could pick them up. But I was accustomed to holding on to such things for later recording.

Heali'i's answering snort was pragmatic. "Wouldn't you?"

I drew the blankets closer about me and forced my thoughts to focus. "Is their breeding seasonal? It must be a very great danger for your people if this could happen any time of year."

She shrugged. "I don't know what they do when they aren't here. Maybe they breed at other times. But we know that when the serpents are around, there's a risk."

Tired and worn as I was, it took some time for the implications of this to come clear for me. "You mean—they aren't always here?"

"Of course not," Heali'i said. "They follow the currents and the storms."

Migration. I did not know the word in Keongan, and had to flounder my way through twenty or thirty words in its stead, but once Heali'i understood my meaning, she nodded. "Yes, like some of the birds. They come and go."

"Do they go as far as the cold?" I asked—this being the only way I could think to refer to the arctic. It necessitated more explanation, this time less successful, for Heali'i had no experience of ice, let alone a region where the sea itself froze solid. (The peak of Aluko'o, which is the highest in the archipelago, sometimes has snow, but Heali'i had never seen it as more than a distant whiteness.) She expressed great doubt that the serpents went so far, but I could not read too much into that, given her lack of familiarity with the world outside her islands.

When I grew frustrated with that line of inquiry, I went back to the matter of breeding. "Where do they lay their eggs?" I asked.

Heali'i shook her head, hands rising as if to ward off the question. "On Rahuahane. That is all I know, and I do not want to know more. For you or I to go there would mean death."

I had not forgotten the story she told about the hero Lo'alama'oiri, who turned all the *naka'i* to stone. Even ordinary Keongans shunned the place. If our spirits were supposed to be those of reborn *naka'i*, of course returning to the island would be very ill-advised.

I was, of course, deeply tempted. I doubt anyone reading this memoir imagines that I was not. Reproduction is a vital part of any species' existence, and we knew precious little about it in most dragon breeds. But I had some experience with the reaction of locals when I trespassed upon a place said to be cursed, and while I did not expect to have a repetition of what happened in Vystrana, I did not want to tempt fate. The islanders might well decide that Liluakame's influence was not enough to keep my dragon spirit safely in check.

Besides, there were other islands in the Broken Sea. All serpent reproduction could not happen on a single forbidden landmass—or more likely in the coastal waters of that landmass, as there was no evidence to suggest sea-serpents were amphibious, although they breathed air. Once the *Basilisk* was afloat once more, I could go in search of other hatching grounds.

But that did not mean my curiosity would lie still and trouble me no more. "Will you show me which island is Rahuahane?" I asked. "If it is not *tapu* for us to even look at it."

Heali'i did not look pleased at the prospect, but she nodded. "We will climb Homa'apia tomorrow. From there you will see where your soul is from."

Repairs had begun on the *Basilisk* almost as soon as she reached shore. With ropes pulling the ship over to starboard, I could see clearly the gash of cracked timbers where the reef had struck. It was a chilling sight; a little more force in the collision and we might have lost the vessel entirely. Some of us would have made it to shore, no doubt—the experienced swimmers, like Suhail—but not all, and those who did would have been stranded.

We would not be leaving anytime soon. Proper timber had to be obtained, and here *tapu* reared its head: the sailors could not cut trees on land belonging to the chief, nor could they take certain kinds of trees anywhere on the island during this season. It seemed to be a combination of land rights and husbandry, but whatever the cause, it drove Aekinitos half-mad with frustration. I was just as glad to be going elsewhere for a few days.

I invited Jake to go with us, but was unsurprised when he chose to stay close to shore. "Some of the other boys are going to teach me *se'egalu*," he said, bouncing with excitement.

I could not help laughing at his enthusiasm. "And what is *se'egalu*, in Scirling?"

"There isn't another word for it. *Se'egalu* is when you take a wooden board out into the water and stand up on it, and then ride the waves in to shore."

We had seen this off the coast of Olo'ea, before the storm blew us to Keonga. I had not known that was the word for it. (Nowadays Scirlings call this "surf-riding.") Nor did I learn until later that in Keonga it is considered a pastime for those of aristocratic lineages; the boys in question were a son and a nephew of the local chief. It was quite a mark of esteem that they invited my son to join them—especially as they believed him to be Abby's son instead.

As for Suhail, he was very nearly as single-minded as Jake, and had no interest in things that lay beyond his purview. "If there are ruins, tell me," he said. "But I don't think it's likely. They didn't build on mountaintops in this part of the world—too much risk of earthquakes and eruptions."

"Thank you for that reminder," I said dryly. Homa'apia was not a terribly active volcano, not compared to its fellow peak on Aluko'o, which is believed to be the youngest of the Keongan Islands. It still had its share of activity, though, with steam vents and the occasional trickles of lava. We would have to exercise care on our journey.

So in the end only three of us went: myself, Heali'i, and Tom, whose strength was at last restored. "It's glad I am to be getting out again," he said. His Niddey accent had faded over the years, but came back strongly now, a testament to his heartfelt sincerity.

I hoped he truly was up to the trek. The summit lay a mere fifteen miles or so inland, but it towered over the shore, and the forest concealed in places a treacherously broken terrain. Heali'i said we would be gone for several days at least.

The first part of our journey was pleasant. Keonga is home to an astounding variety of birds, many of them bright with tropical plumage; I had already made arrangements with local bird-hunters to obtain specimens of several kinds, though the most splendid were reserved for chieftains and the king. Although there are insects aplenty, there are no mosquitos or other unpleasant biters, and poisonous snakes are unknown. Compared with the Green Hell of Mouleen, it truly did seem like the Garden of Paradise.

Soon the terrain grew steeper, though, and my breath came short in my lungs. My near drowning had left me feeling as if I were recovering from a head cold. I coughed frequently, earning me concerned looks from Tom. I was glad when Heali'i stopped and turned to face us.

"I should have asked before," she said. "Do small, dark spaces bother you?"

She directed this question at Tom. (Heali'i had seen me crawl into a small steel bell and let Suhail lock the door behind me. She knew my answer already.) Tom shook his head, looking puzzled. Heali'i smiled broadly. "Good. Then follow me."

Tom and I exchanged mystified looks, but obeyed. Heali'i led us off the path and through an open area that bore touches here and there of maintenance, as if someone wanted it to appear natural, but also to remain uncluttered by too much growth. This brought us to the mouth of what appeared to be a cave.

I mentioned lava tubes before, when speaking of how the chief took shelter from the storm. These volcanic formations are created during an eruption when the hardening lava roofs over its own channel. In the passage thus created, the molten rock retains its heat for longer, and so goes on flowing in a kind of underground river. Eventually this ends, but the hollow remains: a tube boring through the new rock, sometimes for miles at a stretch.

Keonga is honeycombed with these, some of which help account for the arduous terrain, as the collapse of their ceilings leaves the ground broken. This one, however, was almost wholly intact—the exception being where the islanders have deliberately opened vents to the world above, so as to allow the circulation of air.

This, Heali'i said, was our path. It would not take us all the way to the summit; the passage stopped short of that point, near the now-closed vent from which the lava originally issued forth. But it would allow us to bypass the worst of the slope. Quite apart from that practical consideration, this was the route used by the chief and the priests when they journeyed up Homa'apia to perform ceremonies at the top. As such, it was considered the proper way to go.

I felt as if I were journeying into another world—something out of an ancient myth. The tunnel stretched out in near-total darkness, except where a vent allowed in light and falls of flowering vines. Here and there the ceiling was festooned with narrow stalactites, which we all had to duck carefully beneath. Patient hands had carved the sides of the tunnels, mile upon mile of imagery, half of it visible only when you brought a torch close. "Suhail should see this," I murmured to Tom, who nodded. It likely wasn't Draconean, but it would appeal to his archaeological instincts.

Even travelling by that route, the journey was not easy. In places the tunnel became very steep, which made for difficult climbing when the stone beneath our feet was so smooth. The darkness and quiet were oppressive after the light and constant sound of the world above; I found myself missing the rise and fall of the waves, the ever-present wind. It was easy to believe we were making no progress at all, or that there was no end. We would be walking through the darkness forever, stopping occasionally to relight a torch, until we died of thirst—for there was no eating or drinking in the tunnel. "*Tapu*," Heali'i said, and we had no choice but to comply.

There was, of course, an end. I am not writing this memoir from the confines of a Puian cave. Light grew ahead of us, and then we emerged into a different world entirely.

Gone was the lush forest that covered the lower slopes. Here we found ourselves amidst ferns and scrubby bushes, which are all that will grow so close to the volcano's peak. I turned to look back the way we had come, and felt as if I were on top of the world: I could see the ocean stretching out to eternity and the other Keongan islands spreading to either side, with the great bulk of Aluko'o behind my left shoulder and the smaller isles stretching out to my right. From this height I could not see the canoes that plied the waters, except the tiny speck of a sail here and there. A dozen or so of them were passing between Keonga and its neighbour Lahana, in a loose, scattered line.

"Are fire-lizards only found around active peaks?" Tom asked, recalling me to my work.

Heali'i nodded. I took out my notebook and began to jot items down. "Which volcanoes in the archipelago have fire-lizards? And is there *any* chance of us visiting the others? There might be variation between populations."

She laughed, beckoning for us to follow her. "You have not even seen the lizards here yet. One thing at a time."

I closed my notebook and exchanged glances with Tom. That laugh rang false with me, and with him as well, I saw. Heali'i was trying to divert me. Why *had* the Keongans forbidden us to leave this island? It could not be *tapu*; they were not shy about telling us when a spiritual prohibition blocked our way. There was some other reason, and it worried me that they were not willing to share it.

Pressing now did not seem wise, though. Tom extinguished the torch, and then we climbed upward once more, toward the summit some distance above.

The caldera of Homa'apia was a broad crater, barren of all life. Around it stood a ring of enormous statues like none I had ever seen before: great monoliths several meters in height, most of their bulk devoted to the head, with only a small suggestion of a body below. They were abstract and imposing, their strong-featured faces staring with patient intensity across the width of the crater.

Suhail would wish to see these too, I thought. They were not at all Draconean; there was no suggestion of a dragon in those features, much less any of the characteristic elements of their aesthetic style. But something in their stony vigil reminded me of Draconean statues.

"They are the ancestor gods," Heali'i said, in response to a question from Tom I had not attended to. "They keep watch to warn us if Homa'apia wakes fully."

It was a chilling reminder that although the mountain on which we stood was not actively erupting, neither was it quite asleep. "Does the other peak also stir?" I asked, peering toward the other half of Keonga, where the mass of 'Iosale rose.

"Not anymore. Do you know the story?" When we shook our heads, Heali'i recounted the tale.

Homa'apia and 'Iosale were a pair of gods said to have created the whole archipelago—not as a harmonious effort, but as the result of their strife. The stones they hurled at one another broke the earth beneath the sea, raising island after island in fire and steam. "The chaos did not end until the other gods joined the two of them in marriage," Heali'i said, gesturing at the valley of rich farmland where the two slopes met.

"But Homa'apia hasn't entirely quieted down," Tom said, amused.

Heali'i grinned at him. "Not all marriages are peaceful."

We had brought offerings with us: wreaths of flowers, slightly wilted after being carried in our packs for the better part of the day. At Heali'i's instruction, we flung these into the crater, where they made bright spots against the barren earth. She chanted as we did so, and for some time after, lest our activities disturb the volcano's goddess.

It was late enough in the day that Tom and I could not do much research. We retreated from the peak to a spot that was more sheltered, more comfortable, and less hedged about with *tapu*, and there Tom began to lay out our blankets. Heali'i, however, beckoned for me to follow her. "Come. I will show you Rahuahane."

She led me around the summit to the leeward side. At lower elevations this is the drier, less fertile side of the island; most of the rain falls to windward, leaving the other half wanting. This high on the mountain, it was a wasteland.

"Why does nothing grow here?" I asked Heali'i. My voice had sunk to a whisper, for there was something terribly chilling about that lifeless, rocky slope. I had seen rain fall upon the peak; this was no desert, so bereft of water that nothing could grow. And yet I could not see even the slightest hint of green.

Heali'i answered me quietly. "The rain here is poison. It kills the land where it falls. Look—there is your soul's home."

The long scar of dead ground stretched like an arrow toward a small island very near to Keonga's leeward shore. With the tale of the *naka'i* in my mind and this blight before my eyes, I expected Rahuahane to be a blackened rock, advertising its curse to all the world. Instead I saw lush greenery, little different from that which marked the windward side of Keonga. It was perhaps less verdant, owing to its position in Keonga's shadow, and little of its volcanic

peak remained; around the central mass lay a belt of turquoise lagoons and the thick, broken ring of its coral reef, lifted up above
the waves—a formation one sees at times on older islands. From
above, I thought, it would look almost like an eye.

But it was merely an island, like a hundred others in the Broken Sea. I said, "Where are the *naka'i*? The ones that were turned
to stone?"

Heali'i struck my shoulder in an open-handed slap. I staggered
at the blow: she had all the bulk of a Puian man, and meant me to
feel the weight of it. "Do not joke about these things. Be glad they
are hidden; the sight of them might kill you, too."

It occurred to me to wonder whether this legend pointed at a
more prosaic truth. I had found dragon bones in the cavern near
Drustanev; could it be that the *naka'i* were some kind of dragon—
perhaps sea-serpents; perhaps some other breed now extinct—
whose bones yet lingered? Though I was at a loss to explain how
that could have happened, unless Keonga's geology was able to
replicate the natural chemical process which was a precursor to
our more advanced one.

The notion seemed far-fetched, but it gained in strength the
next day, when Tom and I began our work.

There were indeed fire-lizards on the heights. They made their
nests among the ferns and scrub above the tree line and ranged
all through the higher elevations, hunting insects, geckos, rats, and
some of the smaller birds. They are unusual among draconic types
in that they are highly gregarious; a typical flight will contain at
least a dozen members, often more.

Nor do they have any particular fear. Their sole predator is the
eagle, and he will only attack if the fire-lizards appear to threaten
a nest. Because of this, the breed has many traits which would be
detrimental in any other environment, from their ground-nesting

habit to their fiercely coloured hide, which ranges from buttery yellow to ember-red.

I was particularly keen to observe them because their extraordinary breath is an electrical charge—a stronger cousin to the minute sparks that give sparklings their name. When Aluko'o erupted to a serious degree, Heali'i told me, the fire-lizards could be seen dancing in the ash plume, their sparks creating great bolts of lightning in the murk.

Alas, I did not witness that sight. (I hope I may be forgiven my "alas." An eruption on that scale would have meant great destruction and hardship for the inhabitants of Aluko'o, which is not at all a thing to be desired in its own right.) But Heali'i snared a bird from the near edge of the tree line, and I used it as a decoy to entice the fire-lizards into displaying their offensive capabilities. Then she shot one with a poison-tipped dart. "Are they not *tapu* to kill?" I asked. So many things in the islands were hedged about with prohibitions, I found I had assumed, without ever asking, that to kill a fire-lizard would be a great crime.

But that was not the case, and so Tom set to work with his knife, dissecting the carcass for us to study. We discovered that the organ which produces the charge is very similar to that which I had previously discovered in sparklings; and so, once again, I found my taxonomical thoughts quite confounded.

I took a walk to consider this development, while Tom and Heali'i hunted for fire-lizard eggs, which they conceal in volcanic vents—thus explaining why they are only found on active peaks. We were quite close to the edge of the barren zone. Dismissing my sense of foreboding, I set out across the scree.

The air around me smelled unexpectedly sweet, if a little musky. There were signs that Homa'apia was an active volcano, if less so than Aluko'o; here and there the ground was cracked, as if from an earthquake, and I could see steam or stirrings of ash in the air.

FIRE-LIZARD

I stayed clear of these, casting occasional glances toward the distant Rahuahane, but otherwise keeping my gaze on the treacherous gravel beneath my feet.

Not all of the gravel was stone. Two years later, after I had returned to Scirland, I spoke to a geologist with a particular interest in volcanoes; he told me Heali'i was right about the rain in that spot being "poison." The gas rising from the vents creates mild acids, insufficient to damage human skin, but more than strong enough to render the leeward terrain completely inhospitable to plant life. And, as in the great cavern near Drustanev, these acids serve an unexpected purpose.

I must have found the chips of bone amid the scree. My pockets were full of them later, and Heali'i confirmed that she had seen such things there before. They are the bones of fire-lizards, imperfectly preserved and broken quite small, but still identifiable as the epiphyses of long bones. No doubt there were other chips from elsewhere in the skeleton, but it seems I failed to pick them out from the surrounding rock.

I say all of this with speculative caution because I do not remember any of it.

Or rather, I remember *something*, as if through a great haze. I was pondering taxonomy, with occasional drifts toward the tale of Rahuahane. I remember thinking about Heali'i's eagerness to divert our attention away from the other islands. What might the Keongans be concealing there? My thoughts were wandering badly, and I could not chivvy them back on course.

After that, nothing—until I woke up in our camp.

I can fill in some of what is lacking from the reports of my companions.

Tom had found eggs and gone looking for me, on the assumption that I would want to sketch them *in situ* before he disturbed anything. He could not find me, and began calling my name; Heali'i soon joined him and they quartered the ground, increasingly concerned that I had fallen and badly hurt myself.

Fallen I had—but not off a cliff. Tom saw me from a distance, convulsing against the rocky soil. He ran to my side and tried to rouse me from my fit, but was soon distracted by Heali'i, shouting in alarm for him to leave the dead ground. I thank heaven that his strength had indeed returned from his illness; he hoisted me to his shoulder and carried me away, not stopping until he reached camp, where Heali'i pronounced us safe at last.

Many gases can rise from volcanic terrain; some are more insidious in their threat than others. I had avoided the obvious ones, but walked into one I could not see. Heali'i, upon hearing that I had noticed a sweet odor, chastised me for not walking away at once. The name she gave it means something like "the air of poisoned sleep"; it has strange effects on the mind, and could have killed me if Tom had not carried me clear.

"You did not tell me there was any such danger!" I said to her—it may have been more of a shout.

She apologized for this lapse, though with an expression that suggested I should have had the brains to realize that the dead ground was not safe. I was not mollified; the experience had frightened me badly, less for the brush with death than for the blank gap in my memory. It was not like sleep. I had been walking; then I was in camp, and my pockets were full of bones I did not remember collecting. It was as if something else had taken over my body for a time, leaving me none the wiser.

You, my readers, are well aware that I am not a superstitious or even very religious woman. Yet I must admit that for a time, I found myself wondering uneasily if there was truth to the Keongan belief that I was dragon-spirited, in a more literal sense than I had heretofore accepted. Had Heali'i told me this was a common occurrence for *ke'anaka'i*, I would have believed her, and possibly even doubted my own rationality. It was in some ways a relief—and in other ways, decidedly *not*—that she brushed off the question when I asked her. "No, it does not happen to *ke'anaka'i*," she said. "Only to fools."

I had a number of scrapes and bruises to go with my collection of bone fragments, the latter of which I discovered in my pocket soon after. This led to a discussion in Scirling with Tom wherein I related the tale of Rahuahane, and we speculated as to the possibility of fossilized bones there. "You are certain they would not let you go search?" he asked.

"To them, it would look like suicide," I said. "But I imagine the real difficulty would come when I returned, quite visibly not dead. Do you recall how they behaved when they decided I was *ke'anaka'i*?"

"Pitchforks and torches. I remember." Tom sighed. "Well, we might try it when we're ready to leave; then you can sail off and never face their reaction."

On most days it would have been sorely tempting. But I had just experienced in quick succession not one but two near misses with mortality, and was in no mood to contemplate another risk so soon. I would have set out for the lowlands right then if I could have reached the shore before dark. Nightfall would catch me in the lava tube, though, and so I rallied myself enough to go and sketch the fire-lizard nest instead—taking comfort, as I so often do, in my work.

FIFTEEN

*Spiral in the sand—A talk with my son—One creature—
Visitors to Keonga—Hidden concerns—Suhail's proposition—
The chief objects—Riding a dragon*

We made several more excursions to the top of the volcano during the weeks that followed, while Aekinitos and his men labored to repair the *Basilisk*. I did not mean to neglect the sea-serpents, who were of greater interest to me than the fire-lizards (owing to their possible position in the family tree), but it was difficult to study them from our current position. I disliked the notion of attempting to chase them in one of the ship's fragile longboats—quite apart from the fact that any move to take one of those out to sea would likely draw the ire of the chieftain, Pa'oarakiki. Nor were the Keongans willing to hunt them, for which I cannot blame them. The serpents here might be smaller, but their blasts of water were perfectly capable of destroying a canoe. The islanders did supply me with scales and teeth, which I studied with great enthusiasm, and on some days I perched myself in a high spot to observe the serpents out in the water. In the meanwhile, I was confined to land, and therefore confined myself to studying those creatures which could be found there.

The fire-lizards reminded me somewhat of the drakeflies I had seen in the Green Hell of Mouleen. They are both small breeds, and lack forelimbs (though drakeflies make up for the absence by having two pairs of wings). Where some individuals have succeeded in caging drakeflies like birds, however, fire-lizards have proven stubbornly intractable in that regard, either pining to death in captivity, or else burning or melting their way free of the cages with a persistent application of sparks.

I did not attempt to capture one, being content to examine their nests and spy upon their feeding habits. (I took care, of course, not to be ensnared by the volcanic vapors again, having no wish to repeat my previous experience.) Their communication proved to be especially intriguing: they make a variety of clacking noises to one another, which seem to be a method of coordinating their hunts and warning of danger. If anyone reading this memoir has an interest in dragons and a tolerance for carrying finicky equipment around the world and up a volcano, the field of dragon naturalism awaits sound recordings of their calls, which would permit a much more detailed study.

Even shipwrecked on a tropical island, we could not neglect our other obligations. Fortunately, Keonga's isolation provided it with a number of bird species unknown to the Ornithological Society, which Tom undertook to collect for Miriam Farnswood. Most of these he stuffed (dead birds being *vastly* easier to transport than their energetic cousins), but one afternoon he went to negotiate with a bird hunter for live specimens. I did not even notice him returning, despite the fact that the two honeycreepers tied to his stick were whistling madly. When I finally realized he was there, I jumped on my log seat. "What is it?"

"I am trying to identify the expression on your face," he said.

How long had I been sitting there, notebook ignored on the makeshift table before me, pen drying in my hand? I did not know. "It is the expression of a woman who knows there is an idea creeping up on her, but hopes that if she is *very* assiduous in ignoring it, the idea will go away."

Tom dug a hole and planted his stick in it, leaving the birds to settle down, then came to join me. He almost leaned on my table before remembering; he had done that several times, and the table had not borne his weight any of them. Now it was distinctly lopsided. He leaned against a tree instead. "You are not normally the sort to hope an idea will go away. If it is right, why ignore it? And if it is wrong . . . those, you generally beat to death with a stick."

His description turned my sigh into a half laugh. "Why ignore it, indeed. I want to do so because I suspect you were right, Tom. I should not have sent that article to the *Journal of Maritime Studies*."

He frowned. "If it were only a matter of expanding on your previous ideas, you wouldn't look so troubled."

"Just so. The trouble is that I think—no, I am increasingly *certain*—that my previous ideas were wrong." I showed him my notebook, open to my diagrams of sea-serpent scales. "All the islanders assure me they migrate. Heali'i says they lay their eggs on Rahuahane, though of course I have not observed that with my own eyes. The nesting grounds of arctic serpents have never been found. The general assumption has been that they lay their eggs in waters too deep for us to find them . . . but what if they lay them here, instead?"

"It's a long way to migrate," Tom said. "And how do you account for—oh. I see. The difference in size is also a difference in age. We would need a larger sample of scales to confirm that, though."

I nodded. "All of this needs more observation before we can be sure of anything. But here is a new theory for you: sea-serpents hatch here in the tropics. They migrate, but not all the way to the arctic; the young are too small to survive such cold. As they age, however, the center of their movement shifts northward."

Tom was sketching it in the sandy ground, a looping spiral moving steadily toward the pole. "As they get larger, the tropical waters would be less comfortable for them—they would over-heat here. Presumably at some point they become too old to re-produce, or else their home waters are simply too cold for the eggs to be viable."

"Which might be why they lose the tendrils. And they cease to expel water as a weapon, again because of the cold. The shock of drawing it in might kill them."

He brushed the dirt from his fingers. "It's possible. But certainly not confirmed."

"I have to share it, though," I said wretchedly. "No one can test the idea if they are not aware of it. And I cannot bring myself to sit on my hands, waiting for someone else to think of it and *then* test it."

"But that will mean retracting your previous theory." Tom fell silent. He knew as well as I did where that would lead.

A scientist should never be afraid to theorize, publish, receive criticism, re-examine, and revise her thoughts accordingly. For one such as me, however, there was indeed reason to fear. My sci-entific credibility was tenuous to begin with, and to recant my orig-inal ideas would make me a laughing-stock: not because of my theory, but because of who I was. A misstep that would be brushed away from a great eminence in the field was seen as a fatal error on my part.

Even now, the memory of my foolish haste stings. A part of me wishes dearly that I had taken my time, as Tom advised. Another part, however, treasures the heady excitement with which I penned that first draft, talked it over with Tom, edited my words into a more polished state, and sent it off for consideration. The day when I held a copy of the *Journal of Maritime Studies* and saw my own piece in it ranks as one of the proudest moments of my life . . . when I can see through the haze of shame that hangs over it.

The consequences did not come until later, of course. I relate them here because these volumes focus on key expeditions in my career, and so this one will conclude before the aftereffects of that article become fully apparent. But it is common for people to gloss over my errors, as I have become one of those great eminences, and I wish readers to know that not all of my scientific ideas have been sound.

Conscience would not permit me to save face, though. Tom raised a questioning eyebrow at me, and I shook my head. "No. What matters is the advancement of our knowledge, not the advancement of my reputation. And if my original theory was wrong, it will come out sooner or later. At least this way I might be credited with the correction as well as the error." I managed a rueful laugh, holding my hands up to forestall what he might have said. "But I have learned my lesson. I shan't send a retraction right away—not that I could, of course. I will wait until I have more data." The only thing worse than proving myself wrong would be doing so twice in quick succession.

Gathering more data, though, would have to wait until we were off Keonga. There was only so much I could do with the local population of serpents, especially without a dead specimen to dissect.

I grew restless, wishing I were not trapped on a single island. Jake did likewise, which surprised me; a boy of his inclinations ought to have been in paradise. The sea was right there, its waves cool and inviting in the tropical sun. He could collect coral and shells, practice se'egalu and fishing with a spear, and generally shrivel himself into a very brown raisin with long days in the water. And indeed, he did all these things—but occasional outbursts of temper said that all was not right with him. Abby dealt with these as best she could, in her masquerade as his mother, but one evening I discreetly drew my son aside and inquired what was wrong.

He dug one toe into the sand, hands locked behind his back, not meeting my eyes. His shrug was both noncommittal and unconvincing. "Nothing's wrong."

"Have the other boys been troubling you?" I asked. This seemed the most likely source of trouble.

But Jake shook his head. "No. It's just—I'm tired of Miss Abby being my mother."

My first thought was that he chafed at his governess telling him what to do. It had happened before; like all children, he had his rebellious periods. Tension thrummed in his body, though: as if he wanted to step forward, to come under my arm as he had not done in weeks.

I sank to one knee, putting myself below his head. Once, when he was very young and I was both grieving and conflicted, I had kept my distance from him. Here in Keonga, with so many issues to occupy my mind, I had not felt the gap between us returning—until now.

"I miss you, too," I whispered, and it was true.

Jake's will broke. He had been very good about our masquerade, but now he darted forward and flung his arms about my neck. I clasped him briefly to me, heedless of the risk that the Keongans might see us. "The ship will be repaired soon," I promised him, hoping it was true. "Then we shall go back to normal."

We did not stay like that for long. Caution and youthful dignity both took Jake from my side soon after; but there was a spring in his step now that had been missing before. Although he never said this outright, I believe he remembered my absence when I went to Eriga, and feared I wished to be free of him again. Reassured otherwise, he could go about his days with a light and joyful heart.

I took care after that to show my affection in small ways that would not be remarked by the Keongans, and to involve Jake in my daily affairs where his own patience and interest would permit. This was not so often as it might have been, for I passed my time studying fire-lizards, having endless debates about taxonomy with Tom, and drawing up chart after chart, trying to shuffle the sprawling assortment of draconic types into something like a coherent order. It was not enough merely to point at similarities and declare the job done: there had to be a logic behind it. How did lower forms give rise to higher? Which ones *were* the lower forms, if the family included everything from sparklings to swampwyrms, fire-lizards to wolf-drakes? And if it did not include all those things, then where did the boundary belong?

There must, I believed, be some key—some concept I had not yet thought of—that would sort it all into a sensible shape. But no matter how I grasped for it, the resolution kept slipping through my fingers.

Heali'i found me scowling over these charts one afternoon, after we had been stranded in Keonga for nearly two months. "What is this?" she asked. "You spend so much time on it."

She could not read, much less read Scirling, so of course the charts meant nothing to her. I had long since told her the purpose of our voyage in broad terms: I wanted to study dragons. I had not gone into the scientific detail of it, though.

A thought came to me, and I put my pen down. "Heali'i . . . you said you identified me as *ke'anaka'i* because I showed interest in the fire-lizards and the sea-serpents. Yes?" She nodded, and I asked, "Why? That is—it suggests you see fire-lizards and sea-serpents as belonging in a category together."

"They do," she said.

"Indeed, I agree. But I know why *I* think that: I have seen creatures all over the world that share characteristics with those two. You have never left these islands. Fire-lizards are small and gregarious; they live at the tops of volcanic peaks, eat animals of the islands, and spit lightning at things that trouble them. Sea-serpents are large and solitary; they live in the ocean, eat vast quantities of fish, and spit water at the things that trouble them. They both have scales and a slight similarity in the shape of their heads, and that is where the obvious resemblance ends. But many things have scales, fish included—and you would not say they are in the same category, would you?"

Heali'i shook her head. "There is a poem—the *O'etaiwa*—you have never heard it, of course. It tells how the world came into existence, one kind of creature at a time. The fire-lizards and the sea-serpents are together in that poem."

This intrigued me even more, and I jotted down a note to find someone who could recite the poem for me, with Suhail translating. (I did not think to allocate four hours for it, which is the length of time the recitation ultimately took.) "But why?" I asked. "Does the poem say why they belong together?"

"Because they used to be one creature, in the early days of the world," Heali'i said. "Before the *naka'i* changed them."

It was highly unlikely that fire-lizards and sea-serpents shared an immediate common ancestor, no matter which of my charts I favored at any given moment. But allowing for poetic license, the evolutionary point might well be true. "Fascinating," I murmured.

Heali'i studied me with a curious eye. "Why do you care? Even *ke'anaka'i* do not go this far—at least, I have never heard of one that has."

Once again, it was the fundamental question of my life. In one sense, my answer has changed again and again, from year to year and person to person; in another sense, it has not changed at all. Only my fumbling attempts to put it into words have altered.

This time I said, "It is a mystery. And I suppose I cannot look at a mystery without wanting to solve it."

It was a dangerous answer to give, in a land where *tapu* rendered certain things entirely off-limits. Heali'i's expression sharpened.

"Take care you do not offend the gods. Some things are intended to be mysteries."

"I will do my best," I said—which was not the same as saying I would stop.

We were returning from another stint at the top of Homa'apia, emerging from the lava tube and blinking in the sudden brightness, when I saw something new to me: a fleet of canoes approaching from the southeast. These were not the usual small craft of the fishermen, but long canoes rowed by a dozen men or more, and a large double-hulled vessel in their midst. "It seems you have visitors," I said to Heali'i.

She made no reply, but stared intently at the ships as if she could divine their nature from this distance. Perhaps she could: the largest canoe had a distinctive sign painted on its sail that I thought might be an abstract representation of a shark. "Do you recognize it?" I asked. Her expression told me she did, but I hoped to draw her into conversation.

Heali'i shook her head, a smile appearing on her face as if conjured there. "Foreigners," she said—using the word that means islanders from elsewhere in the Broken Sea, rather than non-Puians. She spoke dismissively, and suited action to tone by heading back toward the main path without so much as another glance toward the canoes. I did give them another glance, long enough to fix the image from the sail in my memory; and when I did so, I saw something else. An indistinct shape, much further out to sea, that looked like neither the square rigging of an Anthiopean ship nor the unusual crab-claw sail of the Raengaui island cluster. I could not judge its size, not without any landmark against which to measure it or its distance from shore, but it was a rounded blur in the haze above the water, and it certainly had not been there before.

I could not stay there staring at it, though. It was plain enough that the approaching fleet had Heali'i concerned, and furthermore that she did not wish me to pay any attention to them. I had already lingered for longer than I should. I hastened to catch up, and spoke of fire-lizards all the way back to camp.

No one there said anything about the visitors, who must have come to shore out of sight on the far side of the promontory. I greeted my son, but did not attend to his excited tales of *se'egalu* as closely as I might have, occupied as I was in looking for Aekinitos.

I found him overseeing the men who were replacing planks in the side of the *Basilisk*. "Can you spare a moment?" I asked him.

He waved for me to speak on, but I shook my head. "This is perhaps not something we should speak of in public."

That gained me his full attention. Aekinitos picked up his crutch and followed me across the sand to a rock upon which he could rest, safely distant from anyone who might overhear.

Once there, I told him of the fleet I had seen coming in, the odd shape in the distance, and my growing sense that something was amiss around us—something the Keongans were hiding. "Though I cannot imagine what it might be," I finished. "My knowledge is of dragons and the natural world, not people and their politics. Am I seeing trouble where none lies?"

I wanted him to say "yes." Had the *Basilisk* been intact, I could have faced the prospect of local danger with much more confidence, knowing that if necessary we could flee to safer waters. But until our ship was repaired, we were trapped in the Keongan Islands, with whatever secrets might lurk nearby.

Aekinitos did not oblige me.

"I've had my men asking questions for weeks now," he said, digging the point of his crutch into the sand and overturning a broken piece of conch shell. "Nothing obvious—well, some of them have been more obvious than others. Men say stupid things in the arms of a woman. But the islanders are on a war footing."

"War!" I exclaimed. "Against whom?"

He shook his head. "I don't know. The Yelangese, most likely. The king's wife is the cousin of Waikango, after all. The islanders of Raengaui paint their sails as you described; I would wager my spare anchor that was one of their chiefs paying the Keongans a visit." He scowled. "If I had not lost my anchor in the storm."

"The Keongans would be mad to invade Yelang, though," I said. "They cannot hope to retrieve their war-leader. Outside their own waters, against Yelangese ships—every advantage that protects them here would be lost."

"I know. And they know it, too. More likely they're preparing to defend themselves. This emperor hasn't conquered anything yet; he has to prove himself somehow."

Yelangese history was not my strong suit in those days (nor is it much stronger now), but I could follow Aekinitos' point. The Yelangese Empire was and is a large polity; it reached that size courtesy of the emperors of the Taisên Dynasty, who energetically expanded their territory through the conquest of places like Va Hing. Indeed, it had become *de rigueur* for an emperor to annex new lands and their inhabitant peoples, if he wished to maintain his status in the eyes of his own subjects.

But Yelang had reached the point where further expansion had become difficult. Their neighbours on the Dajin continent— Vidwatha, Tsholar, Hakkoto—were not small states, easily over- run by the Yelangese army; conquering them would be difficult and costly, and by no means assured to succeed. The emperor might well cast a speculative eye toward the Broken Sea instead, for all that his people were not the best sailors. The Raengaui is- land cluster would be a trivial territory in comparison with the size of the empire itself, but at least it was a conquest, and one he could achieve with relative ease— now that Waikango was his captive.

We were on the far side of the cluster from Yelang, though. "I can't imagine this is a useful place to prepare for war," I said. "Not as isolated as it is. Unless the rest of the Raengaui region has been overrun already?"

Aekinitos sighed and slapped the rock upon which he sat—a rare gesture of frustration. "From here, we can do nothing more than guess. The fleet you saw might be refugees, or emissaries come to beg for aid. Or there might be an entire war fleet beached on the far side of Lahana."

I hoped not. Or if there was, I hoped they would wait to launch until after the *Basilisk* was repaired and we were clear of the whole region. "How long will it be before the ship is ready?" I asked.

"Too long," he said grimly.

You might think my two recent brushes with death—three, if you count the dengue fever—would be enough to dissuade me from foolish action for a time. Then again, if you have been reading this series from the first volume, you might not.

In my defense, my next piece of recklessness did not originate with me. The thought had crossed my mind some time before, but I had dismissed it; Suhail was the one who returned to the idea, investigated it, fixed his will upon it . . . and then persuaded me to join him.

He had scoured the waters of Keonga's encircling lagoons in search of archaeological remnants, but had found very little. "If I could use the bell, I might find more," he told me at one point. "If there is anything here, it is likely buried in the silt of the lagoons; I would need to pump the water away to see. But without the bell . . ." He shrugged. The unavailability of the bell was no one's fault. Even if my excursion to view sea-serpents had not left it sunk on the fore reef, it would have done him no good until the *Basilisk* was afloat once more. And possibly not even then, I thought: if the remains were all within the lagoons, our ship could not reach them regardless.

With little to do archaeologically, Suhail had lent his hand where he could in the repairs, but he was neither carpenter nor sailor. And so he had taken to ranging restlessly about the island, going everywhere that was not forbidden to him and taking up every physical challenge he could find.

It was no surprise that this included the sport of *se'egalu*. Suhail loved the water nearly as much as my son did, and surf-riding appealed very well to a spirit that craved adventure. He grasped the principles of it fairly quickly, though his finesse could not match that of the more experienced Keongans, and he was forever trying to coax me into trying it myself.

I always demurred. Our stay on Keonga had greatly improved my swimming skills, but not the point of attempting to conquer the waves. And I did not see the point of teaching myself the practice of *se'egalu* when there was work that could better occupy my time.

The same could not be said for another, more hazardous maritime sport.

I knew something was afoot, because Suhail grew even more restless than usual. He prowled about our camp like a cat trapped inside on a rainy day, unable even to concentrate on his efforts with the Draconean script. I watched him out of the corner of my eye, knowing that he was sidling his way toward a decision, and that I would hear of it when he was done.

Indeed, I saw the moment it occurred. I happened to be taking a break from my sketching of the fire-lizard bone fragments, standing up to ease my back. Suhail had been sitting on the beach, legs drawn up before him and bare feet buried in the sand, arms propped on his knees with a stick of wood in his hands. This he had theoretically been whittling into some kind of useful or aesthetically pleasing shape, but that purpose had faded from his mind, for the knife had for several minutes just been carving strips off the wood, without any apparent direction from above. Then he stopped—stabbed the knife down into the sand—and stood, hurling the stick into the breakers with an easy, side-armed swing.

He turned and saw me watching him. The grin that spread across his face filled me with both excitement and foreboding. "Mrs. Camherst," he said. "Have you ever wanted to ride a dragon?"

My thoughts were full of fire-lizards, who are much too small to ride. I sputtered something less than entirely coherent, not seeing his true meaning.

"The Keongans do it," he said, when it was clear I did not understand. "They have been telling me about it. The sea-serpents, Mrs. Camherst."

Now I recalled. One of the islanders had leapt aboard a serpent to steer it away from us when Suhail and I escaped the diving bell. According to the boys who kept watch for the beasts, it was a thing the younger and, I thought, more brainless island fellows often did.

Unfortunately Suhail asked this question in front of my son, who was quite young and in certain respects entirely brainless. (I do not say this as condemnation. All of us are in certain respects brainless when we are children: witness some of the things I did as a young girl.) Jake had been amusing himself with his collection of marine objects, which had grown to truly stupendous proportions since our arrival on Keonga. Now he leapt to his feet with a whoop. "Oh please! Can we?"

"*You* most certainly cannot," I said. Suhail's eyes had popped at the mere notion; no Keongan who is less than fully grown would ever dream of trying to undertake such a challenge.

My refusal, of course, set off an argument. By the time I was done convincing Jake that he had no business anywhere near sea-serpents, we had gathered Abby and Tom as an audience . . . and Jake had found a new goal to pursue.

"You *have* to, Mama," he said. "It's research! Right? You can't pass it up when it's a dragon! It'll be just like when I rode the dragon turtle, but *better*."

There was much more, all in the same vein; if I did not know it for a physical impossibility, I would have said he did not pause for breath anywhere in the next five minutes. Suhail soon gave up on waiting for Jake to wind down and just spoke over him. "You cannot be certain when the serpents will migrate onward. The opportunity to try this may be passing fast."

"The opportunity to get myself killed, you mean," I said, my voice tart. "I seem to find those often enough on my own."

Suhail laughed. "But always in pursuit of your work, yes? Your talkative son is right about one thing; it *is* research."

"What could I possibly learn about a sea-serpent while dangling from one of its tendrils that I could not learn by watching it from a more sensible vantage point?"

"What it is to *be* one," he said. "The sensation of racing through the water, the movement of its muscles beneath you. Could you understand a horse merely by watching it run?"

I silently damned him for the comparison. In all our wide-ranging conversations, I had said nothing of my girlhood love of horses, which had for a time been my substitute obsession when dragons were forbidden to me. He had lighted upon it by chance. Suhail was right; although I had learned a great deal by observing horses, drawing them, talking to those who knew them, and so forth, there *were* insights that only came from close contact.

And fundamentally, the answer to his question was yes: I wanted to ride a dragon.

Tom shook his head the instant I looked at him. He did not enjoy being in the water, no matter how enthusiastically Jake expounded upon its pleasures. I liked it well enough, but— "I am not that strong of a swimmer," I reminded Suhail.

I was weakening, and he knew it. Had I truly dismissed the notion, I would not have raised so pragmatic an objection. Suhail's grin grew wider. "Your son says you are much better. And I will help you—they tell me it's safer when two go together."

"Help me!" I said. "I seem to recall prohibitions against contact between us."

The wry twist of Suhail's mouth said he had been considering that very question, and had found a questionable way to answer it. "I am told you are neither male or female, but *ke'anaka'i*. I know of no prohibitions against contact with such."

It was a semantic game . . . but one for which I had no good rejoinder. To deny my status as *ke'anaka'i* would be unwise; and I could hardly claim to be a man, or a close relative of his by blood or marriage.

Suhail waited until I met his gaze, then said quietly, "I will not let you drown."

My breath caught in my throat. It was only with effort that I managed to say, "When it comes to being eaten by a sea-serpent, however—then, I suppose, I am on my own."

Let it never be said that I court my own death without proper planning.

The young Keongan men who ride sea-serpents are the kind who take great masculine pride in displaying their courage, strength, and endurance. They go into the water naked, as if for an evening swim, and do not complain about the cuts they suffer from the jagged edges of the serpents' scales.

I felt no need to display anything about myself, and so I advised Suhail to wear more clothing than he was accustomed to when swimming. "It may weigh our limbs down," I said, "but we will reap the benefit in keeping our skin something closer to intact. Sharks may not come near the serpents, but I do not want to test that by shedding any more blood than I have to." We discussed the possibility of gloves as well, but ultimately discarded it: too much would depend upon the security of our grips, which would be compromised by the wet leather.

The greatest amount of serpent activity had been seen on the leeward side of the island, some distance from ill-omened Rahuahane. (This was not surprising. Presuming that Heali'i was correct, I expected that bearing females had gone there to lay their eggs.) A Keongan wishing to ride one of the beasts will go out with several canoes, whereupon the men in them will commence one of their chants, calling a serpent to the surface.

"It's possible that actually works," Tom said, upon hearing of it. "They place a drum on the bottom of the canoe and beat a rhythm; that would carry through the water. Perhaps the serpents have been trained to respond to it."

"Trained how?" I said doubtfully. "They derive no earthly benefit from cooperating; by all accounts, the serpents do not much like being ridden. And I have not heard it said that the Keongans punish them for failing to appear when summoned."

Tom shrugged, granting the point. "Then it is just tradition."

Once a serpent appears—if one does—then the would-be rider waits at the side of his canoe for it to come near. The Keongans assured us the serpents "rarely" attacked canoes, unless provoked; the vessels are too familiar a sight, and moreover stay on the surface of the water, which is a zone the beasts take little interest in. (Most of their prey is to be found at least a meter or two beneath the surface.) As soon as the serpent draws close, the rider dives in and swims like mad toward the creature, aiming to catch hold of two tendrils.

"It is *very* important to catch two," Suhail told me. "If you hold only one, you will be thrown from side to side as the serpent moves, and have no control. With two, you can keep yourself steady—more or less."

I suspected it would be less rather than more, at least in my case, but it was still good advice. The skilled riders, we were told, could even use the tendrils to steer the serpent where they wished it to go—at least in general terms. "Could we not have someone skilled to go with us?" I asked.

Our guide in these matters was a brawny fellow more than two meters tall. He towered over me as he chuckled. "Every man must prove himself first."

"I am not a man," I said, but this made no impression on him. No one was allowed to take the easy road; Suhail and I must face this on our own.

We were not a subtle calvacade, making ready for the endeavour. Nearly every man from the *Basilisk* was there, along with my son and Abby, Heali'i and Liluakame, and a great crowd of Keongans aside. They were eager to see the foreigners test themselves against the serpents of the deep. I thought at first, when I heard the drums and saw the procession wending toward us in the early light of morning, that the chief had come for the same reason.

But his mien was too forbidding for that. Pa'oarakiki stopped some distance away and said—I paraphrase enormously, Keongan oratory being a long-winded thing—"You may not do this."

In suitably polite language, Suhail asked, "Why not?"

"Because you are foreigners," the chief said.

He went on at greater length; it was something to do with lack of respect for the gods, though we had followed all the

instructions given to us beforehand, including prayers and a sacrifice of flowers to the sea. Perhaps he knew my heart was not in
the ritual. Suhail was questioning him with a barrister's patient
logic, attempting to elicit an explanation of why exactly it was
impermissible for us to ride the sea-serpents; but I could soon tell
there *was* no explanation, save that this man did not want us to.

Or perhaps there was more to it than that, after all. He kept glar-
ing at the men who had been teaching Suhail the art of sea-serpent
riding, with a look that promised retribution later. Was it because
they were taking us from Keonga's shores? We would not visit any
other islands, but perhaps going onto the water was transgression
enough. Only . . . I had the distinct impression that his prohibition had been issued to prevent us from learning anything of the
other islands and what might be on them. Why were sea-serpents
now included in his ban?

I could not follow the conversation well enough to guess; it was
flowing too rapidly for me to comprehend. Instead I watched those
around us. Liluakame had assumed a deferential posture, out of
respect for the chief, but she was frowning at the sand as if she did
not understand his objection. Heali'i, on the other hand, was giving me a significant look. Unfortunately, I did not understand what
its significance was.

She widened her eyes at me, eyebrows raised, as if waiting for
something. Then she sighed, clearly asking the gods to give her
patience. In a crass and unsubtle gesture, she dug one hand into
her skirts and took hold of her own groin.

I had settled into the habit of thinking of Heali'i as a woman,
for that was the designation I had first given her, and Scirling is
not well-equipped to speak of people who are neither male nor female. With that gesture, she reminded me that she was *ke'anaka'i* . . .
and that such people occupied a particular role in Keongan society.

"Pardon me," I said, stopping the conversation short. The chief looked at me as if his least favourite oar had suddenly spoken up.

There was no way I could manage the flowery politeness of formal Keongan. I had to make do with what sentences I could cobble together on the spot. "The sea-serpents are the creations of the *naka'i*," I said, "and I am *ke'anaka'i*. It may be so, that it is not allowed for foreigners to try and ride them. But *ke'anaka'i* do many things that are not allowed: for them, it is meant to be."

Had I been the chief's least favourite oar, he would have broken me across the gunwale or flung me into the sea. But I was a person, and for him to argue with me would create a new host of problems for him. Would he deny the intended purpose of *ke'anaka'i*? Heali'i stood only a few paces away, ready to challenge him if he did. Would he deny my status as such? Liluakame stood even closer, married to me under Keongan custom, proof that I was not a woman in their eyes. The elite of their society are hedged about with many restrictions; he could not afford to say anything that might show a lack of respect for the ways of his own people.

Instead he pointed his palm-frond fan at me and spoke in a booming voice. "The gods judge *ke'anaka'i* as well as men and women. They will pass judgment on you."

Which goes to show, I suppose, that the gods have a perverse sense of humour.

Our oarsmen paddled us out of that bay and around the shore of Keonga, heading to leeward. The fresh water spilling out of a stream by the village left an opening in the reef; we pushed our way through the rougher surf there and passed into waters whose deep hue spoke of the rapid descent of the ground below us. I scanned the waves, but saw no hint of serpents.

The islanders were unperturbed. The canoe in which Suhail and

I rode went to what they judged to be a suitable spot, accompanied by two others; the rest had stayed within the reef, their passengers watching us from the lagoon. If I squinted, I could just make out Tom and Abby and Jake, Liluakame and Heali'i. My son gave me a double thumbs-up for encouragement, and despite my nerves, I could not help but smile.

My smile faltered when the drumming began. Keongan drums are relatively small, and they did not resonate well against the base of the canoes, but that did not prevent the beat from seeming as portentous as the ticking of a clock. Despite the warm air, I shivered. Suhail's grin was as bright as ever, but for the first time I wondered if that expression was as much shield against fear as evidence of its absence.

I fortified myself, as always, with my work. I had brought no notebook with me (as it would only be ruined in the water) and had no surety that I would live to set down any observations I might make today, but that was no reason to give up thinking like a naturalist. I kept watch across the waves, thinking about the environment below us, and was therefore the first to see the slick curve of a coil break the surface.

"There," I said, and if it came out low with tension, that was preferable to an undignified squeak.

The drumming changed its beat. Suhail rose from his bench, balancing easily against the canoe's slight rocking. "Yes, I see it. Now if it will just oblige us by coming nearer . . ."

I rose as well, for we would have to move quickly when our moment came. The beast was properly visible now, a sinuous shadow against the blue of the water. Its seemingly aimless wanderings were reassuring to me; I had seen for myself how an angry sea-serpent moves, and knew this one was curious rather than hostile. That, however, would soon change.

It broached the surface just beyond one of our accompanying

canoes, its head appearing briefly before diving below again. I saw the tendrils we must grasp. "Be ready," Suhail said—quite unnecessarily, but the exhortation was as much for himself as for me.

The serpent dove, circled away, came back. I found I was holding my breath: a foolish impulse. The other two canoes had moved apart, their drummers falling silent. We were the only ones remaining. And as it drew close—

"Now!" Suhail and I cried as one, and dove in.

It was a mad dash through the water. In some ways, this is the hardest part of riding a sea-serpent; you must anticipate when its head will rise high enough for you to seize hold, and then launch yourself for it early enough to intercept. Suhail was soon far ahead of me, but I thundered on, arms windmilling through the waves. I saw the serpent's head—a giant eye, staring at me with what I fancy was utter bafflement—and then it was going past, a quick slide of scales, and there was nothing for me to grab—

There! The very end of a tendril brushed across my fingers. I seized it with both hands, then found myself dragged briefly under the surface as the serpent towed me along. I needed a second hold, but there was none nearby. I began to haul myself up the tendril as if climbing a rope. I had drawn heads like this one; I knew the spacing of those extremities, and would have a better chance of seizing a second one closer to the root.

The serpent broke the surface again as I neared my goal; the fresh air came as a relief. My unwilling mount did not like the tug that resulted when my body dragged through the water, and preferred the lesser resistance of air. I slipped against the scales, rolling to the side; then I had another tendril in my left hand, and could plant my knees against the serpent's body and take stock at last of my situation.

I was alone on the serpent's back. The canoes had drawn off; a splashing to one side was Suhail. He had missed his hold, but was gamely trying for another pass.

The tendrils in my hands were fat and slick, and I could not forget that they were parts of a living creature's body, but apart from that, they were not much different from reins. The serpent was not trained as a horse was to respond to the simple laying of the reins along his neck, but I could steer him as an inexperienced rider might: by pulling very hard on one side.

This was not quite as effective as I might have hoped. I felt like a child again, astride a horse much too large for me, who took little notice of my weak efforts. But it was not wholly useless, either. Little by little, the serpent turned toward Suhail.

He got hold of one tendril as we passed. The rest, however, were beneath him in the water. Suhail began a grab for one of these, but aborted it; I found out later that he had made the same calculation as I, which was that for him to take hold that far from my own position would encourage the serpent to roll, toppling me from my perch.

At this point I made a gamble. I dropped my left rein, transferring that hand to the other tendril, and then reached my right hand out to Suhail.

It very nearly landed us both back in the sea. I am not exceptionally strong, and I lacked good traction against the serpent's hide; its scales cut the knees of my trousers to ribbons, and some of my skin beneath. Suhail's weight almost dragged me down. But the serpent inadvertently assisted us, rolling to its left, which brought Suhail upward; and when our scrambling about was done, we held three tendrils between us, sharing the one in the middle.

Whereupon I realized that we were, indeed, riding a dragon.

I cannot honestly recommend the practice to my readers. Apart from the number of Keongans who have been killed attempting this very feat, it is not very comfortable. The ragged cuts on my knees and elbows stung unmercifully. Every time the serpent dove, I was buffeted by the water until it realized the error of its ways and surfaced once more. Again and again it drew in water and expelled it in a blast, for that was its defense against what troubled it, and the beast's mind could not encompass the fact that *this* annoyance could not be disposed of in such fashion; but it came near to working regardless, for the shuddering of the serpent's body whenever this happened threatened to dislodge us. There was no moment of the entire experience that was not a precarious struggle to stay aboard.

And yet for all of that, it was one of the grandest experiences of my life. I lost all awareness of time and distance; I had no idea how long it had been since I dove into the sea, nor where we had gone in the interim. There was only the sun and the water, the serpent beneath my knees and the wind in my face, islands appearing at unpredictable bearings and then vanishing when we turned, and Suhail at my side. He laughed like a madman any moment we were not submerged, and if I did not do likewise, it is only because I was too breathless for laughter. *I was riding a dragon.* In that moment, I felt invincible.

Then the serpent dove once more. I saw a shadow in the water up ahead, a dark and irregular oval. I had just enough time to think, *Oh, it is a cave—*

And then the serpent dragged us inside.

PART FOUR

*In which we uncover secrets
both ancient and modern*

SIXTEEN

In the cave—Ill-omened Rahuahane—Eggs in the water—
A tunnel leading in—Hidden ruins—Firestone—A shadow
outside—The uses of dragonbone

Had my brain worked only a little faster, I would have let
go the instant I realized a cave lay ahead.

Every previous time the serpent dove, I had known
that if I ran short of air, all I had to do was release my grip
and kick for the surface. The beast was reluctant to dive very deeply
while two people had hold of its head, so there was little chance
of a repeat drowning. (My peril would come after, when the serpent was free to turn around and seek me out.) In a cave, however,
there was no such safety: I was trapped, and the serpent was dragging its body along the roof of the cave, attempting (with very near
success) to scrape its burden off.

If the preceding minutes had been one of the most glorious experiences of my life, the next few seconds were among the most
dreadful. I wrestled with an impossible choice: should I relinquish
my hold and hope I could swim free of the cave in time? Or should
I stay where I was, and trust that the serpent would emerge into
open water before it shredded me on the stone above?

In moments of such crisis, the mind becomes oddly focused. I
remember calculating, in a very cold-blooded fashion, the likelihood that even if I escaped the cave, I would not make it to the
surface before my air was depleted. In open water, however, I could
hope that the canoes might find me. I had been revived from near

death once before, after all. If I drowned inside the cave, however, I was surely doomed.

All of this passed through my mind in mere seconds. It could not go on for longer; indecision kept me where I was, and then we were too far into the cave for me to have any hope of escape under my own power. My only remaining chance of survival lay with the serpent, who might yet drag me to safety—if it did not grind me to powder first.

We often speak of hope as a "ray of light." In this instance, that was less metaphorical than usual. The cave was not entirely dark; sun came in where we had entered and was refracted through the murk. But there was more light than a single opening could account for; other beams pierced the water here and there, and up ahead I saw more. The cave was in fact a tunnel.

With a surge of its great body, the serpent shot through into the warm, shallow waters of a lagoon. I did not wait to see where it might be going; the instant I saw light above my head, I kicked hard off the creature's body and shot for the surface. The air that filled my lungs a moment later tasted sweeter than I can possibly describe.

I had lost track of Suhail during all of this, not because he had gone anywhere, but because the situation had so overwhelmed my thoughts, I could spare none for him. (An unlovely admission, but a true one.) When I turned to look, however, I found him floating only a meter or two away, gasping for breath and wild in the eyes at our near miss.

A miss which might yet turn to a hit, if we did not act. "Quick," I cried, "out of the water"—for we still had an angry sea-serpent to contend with.

Land, at least, was not far away. To the left of the tunnel's exit there was a gentle enough slope that we might ascend it. Suhail and I clawed our way out of the water, scraping our palms, for what lay before us was a coral face rather than a kindly beach. Plants had secured a footing on it in places, but this was not the volcanic terrain I was accustomed to, which told me I was not on Keonga. We had, without meaning to, violated the edict restricting us to that island. But which island were we on?

Still breathing hard, I surveyed our place of landing. The coral stretched above the waves to either side of us, a narrow and barren ring enclosing a lagoon scarcely deep enough for the serpent to swim in. (It was still thrashing about, looking for the creatures that had so vexed it.) Within the ring rose the more familiar shape of a volcano's mass, badly gouged where landslides had sent its matter into the sea. It was not a large island, forming a green spot in the midst of its encircling coral—like the pupil of an eye.

The words I said then are not fit to print.

Suhail whirled in alarm. "What? What is it?" He looked about as if expecting the serpent to have climbed up on land after us.

With a laugh that sounded half-hysterical even to my own ears, I said, "We are on Rahuahane."

The island did not look especially ill-omened. The waters of the lagoon were bright and clear where the sea-serpent had not disturbed them. Birds fluttered above the trees. The only ominous note was the total lack of human habitation—that, and the awareness of what our Keongan hosts might do when we returned.

If we returned. Looking the other way, I saw the sprawling mass of Keonga. It did not seem so very far away; we were close enough to make out the canoes, searching for us among the rocks that dotted the sea between the islands. My hand shot out, as if of its own accord, to seize Suhail's shoulder, dragging him down until we both lay flat on the rough coral.

His dark eyes met mine. "What is it?" he whispered.

"The Keongans," I said. "We are not supposed to be off the island; that is bad enough. But this island is *tapu* to everyone. If they see us here . . ."

He did not need me to say more. Suhail closed his eyes and murmured something I think was an Akhian curse. Then he crawled forward until he reached a point where he could study our position.

"Can we swim back to Keonga?" I asked. It was hard to make myself speak in a normal voice, even though I knew my voice would not carry to the men in the canoes. Sound may travel far over water, but they were windward of us.

"Not a chance," Suhail said, without needing to pause for thought. "The current flows against us; that is why the serpent came this way. I am not sure *I* could reach Keonga—certainly not without rest. And we are both bleeding."

My hands and knees were cut from the scales, as was my shoulder from where the serpent had nearly scraped me off on its passage through the coral ring. There were sharks in the waters here; we had both seen them. They did not come near the sea-serpents, but two humans on their own would be easy prey.

My heart was heavy in my chest. "Then we have no choice. We will have to signal the canoes, and hope for the best."

"Perhaps not," Suhail said.

He was looking the other way, toward Keonga's neighbour Lahana. To my eye it lay farther off than Keonga . . . but given what he had said about the current, it might in truth be the easier target. Even so, the distance was daunting.

"Yes," he said, when I mentioned this to him. "We would have to wait until our cuts stop bleeding. And we might fare better if we had something buoyant to cling to—even if it is just a branch." Suhail curved his body on the stone until he could look directly at me. "But we do not know how long they will search for us. If we wait, we may lose any hope of rescue."

I laid my forehead against the warm coral, trying to think. "They will not come here regardless. This reef is considered part of the island; they will not approach it. If we want rescue, we will have to swim out between the islands and hope to be spotted. Then we will have to pray they do not kill us for having been on Rahuahane, or simply for having left Keonga." Not to mention praying that the sharks did not get us, or the serpents.

That thought gave me a new idea, but it was dashed an instant later. The lagoon behind us was quiet once more; the serpent that had brought us here was gone. Even had I been willing to risk mounting one again and steering it back through the underwater tunnel, there was no beast here that might carry us back to safety.

Which left us with only one real option. "We will try for Lahana," Suhail said.

I crawled down the coral until I was concealed enough that I could sit up. This put me facing the central mass of Rahuahane, idyllic in the tropical sun.

Heali'i had said the serpents laid their eggs here.

And, as I had thought before, the possibility of impending death was no reason to cease being a naturalist.

"Before we go," I said to Suhail, "might we look around a bit?"

With no serpent troubling the waters, it was an easy swim across the lagoon to the main body of the island. Even so, my arms were trembling with exhaustion by the time I reached the shore. Suhail knocked down some unripe cocoanuts and broke them open against a stone; we gulped the water inside with no attempt at delicacy. Our wild ride through the sea had left me parched.

After we were sated, he raised a curious eyebrow at me. "What precisely is the story of this island?"

He had heard fragments, but not the full account. I related to him what Heali'i had said, the tale of the ancient *naka'i* monsters and the hero who turned them to stone. "I wonder," I began, and then stopped—for I had not told Suhail about dragonbone preservation. He had seen the fragments I gathered on Homa'apia, but I had taken care not to draw attention to them; likely he thought them in the process of decay. I could not tell him that I wondered whether more preserved skeletons might be found on this island.

Fortunately, Suhail took my aborted sentence in a different direction. "Whether there might be ruins? It does not sound all that different from the Book of Tyrants. And although there are no great cities here, there might be some smaller remains."

Our shared intellectual enthusiasm restored some vitality to my body. I smiled at him and said, "Shall we go look?"

I soon had cause to be glad that I had gone barefoot so often in camp. Without that conditioning, my feet would not have fared well. Suhail and I followed the shore to begin with, but the sand here was littered with small, sharp bits of detritus. Even with calluses to protect me, I was forever stopping to pick something out of my skin or from between my toes.

"They are not amphibian, are they?" Suhail asked.

"Not that we know. They breathe air, but show no adaptation for land, and are likely too large regardless. I expect the eggs are in the water." I shaded my eyes with one hand, trying to see any sign of them below the bright surface. I had removed my hat and kerchief before diving into the water, and my cropped hair was stiff with salt.

Suhail paused and craned his neck. "If I climb a tree, I might have a better view."

He was not so skilled a climber as the locals. They are accustomed from childhood to swarming up palm trees with nothing more than their hands and feet to aid them. Suhail's hands, while strong, were not so callused, and his feet took many splinters in this endeavour. But he made no complaint as he climbed, and after a few minutes he achieved a good vantage. I waited below, trying not to fidget with impatience, to hear his report.

"I think I see something that way," he said at last, sparing one hand to point in the direction we had been circling.

Once back on the sand and relatively clear of splinters, he dusted himself off and followed me around the beach. Mindful of the time, I tried to move quickly; no one would believe we had not been on Rahuahane if we ended up spending the whole day here. I reached the relevant curve of beach before Suhail did and waded out into the water to see.

There were indeed clutches of sea-serpent eggs, in water so shallow I wondered how the creatures avoided fatally beaching themselves. They were half-buried in the sand and almost gelatinous to the touch; the material was partially translucent, so that I could make out the faintest outline of the embryo inside. Had I not assumed that removing an egg from water would abort it, I would have tried to carry one home with me, and never mind the question of how I would bring it along on our intended swim to Lahana.

I dove again and again to study these, while Suhail kept watch from the beach. Finally I surfaced, intending to offer a change of duties; he was not a dragon naturalist, but I thought he might enjoy seeing the eggs.

The words caught in my throat. I had noticed when I came to the beach that a thin stream of water ran through the sand, but had paid little heed to its source. From out here, though, I could see that it poured out of an opening that looked a great deal like a lava tube. The tunnel on Keonga had been beautifully carved;

might the inhabitants of this island, whoever they were, have done the same?

"We should look for something to use for flotation," Suhail called out as I came back to shore.

"You are right," I said. "But there is something we may want to examine first."

He was not difficult to persuade. (In fact, I do not recall applying any persuasion at all, apart from the bare description of what I had seen: that is the kind of man I was stranded with.) We picked our way up from the beach to the mouth of the tunnel, which was indeed a lava tube, though much more clogged with dirt and plant matter than its Keongan counterpart.

Suhail examined the walls closely, even running his hands over them to see if his fingertips might detect patterns that escaped his eyes, but found nothing. I, in the meanwhile, had been peering up the tunnel. We had no torches, nor any means of making fire, but I thought I saw a faint light in the distance. "We might go a little way in," I said to Suhail. "Just to see." And again he agreed.

I once answered a particularly cockle-headed question about how I conducted my research by saying, "I do one thing after another." However malapert that response was at the time, there is truth in it. Many of my discoveries have been made by doing one thing after another. Each step leads to the next, and sometimes there is virtue in not allowing common sense to call you back.

The tunnel was narrow and difficult to navigate in places, for repeated subsidences of the ground had broken the ceiling. The light I had seen proved to come from one such opening, but by the time Suhail and I reached it, we could see more light ahead. So we continued on, and when we emerged from the tunnel at last, we found ourselves in a place of wonder.

It was no natural volcanic formation; a glance was enough to tell me that. A hollow may have existed in the volcano's side, but hands and tools had carved it into more regular shape, creating a chamber walled off from everything around it. Only a collapse in the ceiling above, like the oculus of a dome, permitted a glimpse of the sky. With the sun's light slanting down, the chamber seemed an enchanted place.

There could be no question now as to whether anyone had lived on Rahuahane. The statues around the chamber's edge proclaimed it. Badly weathered as they were, with some of them fallen to stretch in pieces across the ground, the site was unmistakably Draconean.

Suhail sank to his knees, as if he did not want to spare even the smallest fraction of his attention for the task of remaining on his feet. He stared in awe at our discovery, lips moving soundlessly in something that might have been a prayer—or notes on what he observed.

Strange though it may seem, my own reverence was mixed with disappointment. I had, without realizing it, fixed my hopes upon the notion that the "people turned to stone" were preserved draconic skeletons. Instead this discovery was Suhail's: a hitherto unknown Draconean ruin, undoubtedly of great archaeological interest, but holding little relevance for natural history.

I could not remain disappointed for long, though—not in that place. It reminded me of the waterfall island in the Great Cataract of Mouleen, especially where lianas hung in a curtain from the oculus above and dripped the traces of rainwater on the ruins below. Shrouded in shadow, lichen, and vines, the statues seemed to hold terrible power. I was not surprised the Keongans held this place in dread. I cursed the circumstances that had prevented me from bringing a notebook along: any rendering I made of this scene would have to be done after the fact.

With that goal in mind, I set myself to observing every detail and recording it in my memory. So absorbed was I in this task that I jumped when Suhail spoke. "I have never heard of anything like this before," he whispered.

"The statues look much like the others I have seen," I said, gesturing at them.

"To a point, yes—but this chamber? They did not build in caves. And the statues . . ." He leapt atop a block of stone too deeply buried for me to tell whether it was natural or man-made. "I have seen fragments like them, but little that was intact." He whirled, gazing upon me with a look of absolute rapture. "This is the discovery of a lifetime!"

I could not help but laugh at his delight. "I thought your interest was in the smaller things, sir. The lives of the ordinary people, the evidence of day-to-day existence—"

His answering laugh rang off the walls. "Yes, yes. But I would have a heart of *stone* if I were not moved by this!"

Suhail bounded over to study one of the fallen statues, dragging at the plant matter veiling its head to see if he could uncover the face. I picked my way with greater care around the chamber in the other direction, wincing whenever I put my bare foot down atop a hazard. There seemed to be a kind of broad, shallow pit in the floor on the far side, and I wanted to see what it contained.

When I finally saw, I did not care that something was stabbing me quite painfully in the foot. I stood there with a splinter of wood embedded in my sole, unable to believe my eyes.

Earthquakes had shifted them from their places; rain and the accumulation of clutter inside this chamber had choked the gaps between them. But for all of that, the shapes that lay within the pit were unmistakably the rounded forms of eggs.

I staggered forward, unsteady as much because of my shock as because of the splinter in my foot. Now it was my turn to fall to

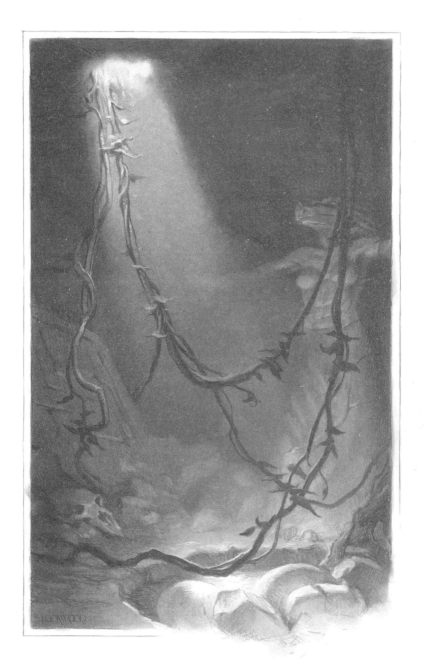

Rahuahane

my knees and dig into the soil, trying to free one of the eggs from its bed.

It was surprisingly heavy and utterly hard to the touch. That was how the eggs had survived: they were fossilized, turned from organic matter to a kind of stone. I wondered what had transmuted them—some process akin to that which preserved dragonbone? And what species of dragon had laid them? They were not sea-serpent eggs; of that much I was sure. Some amphibian or ter-restrial creature had produced these, one much larger than a fire-lizard. A dragon of some kind unknown in the Puian islands today . . . my breath stopped at the very thought.

Suhail was calling my name, but I could not find my tongue to answer. All disappointment had flown. There was enough here to make an academic reputation for both of us.

He came to see what had so entranced me, and fell silent at the sight. "It is proof," I said reverently. "These eggs were not laid here by accident, by some opportunistic creature that found a safe hatching ground. The Draconeans placed them here. They *did* tame dragons—tame them, and breed them." Even domesticate them? I could hardly begin to guess.

"It was a theory," Suhail said, his voice hardly louder than my own. "That the statues we find now, the broken fragments I told you of, depicted fertility gods. Or guardians of the young—we are not sure. Were not."

My gaze drifted across the array of stone eggs, abandoned here by their breeders. What calamity had forced the Draconeans to flee? Even if the seas *had* risen, as Suhail argued, they had not done so over the course of three days. Why did the people of this island not take their incubating dragons with them?

"The eggs must not have been viable," I said out loud. "Other-wise they would have hatched long before they could be fossilized. But why so many? What happened?"

I picked the shard of wood from my foot and rose to search the pit. Many of the eggs were three-quarters buried and hard to dislodge from their places, but after a minute or so of searching, I found what I was looking for: an egg which had been smashed by a falling piece of stone, affording me a view of its interior. I tore my nail pulling it free, turned it over—and froze.

Even crusted with dirt, the inner stone glimmered. A dozen different colours danced beneath my trembling wrist as I used my sleeve to wipe it clean. I had never seen—never *imagined*—a piece even half so large; its light was dimmed by the sheer bulk and the dark backing of the shell behind. But there was no question in my mind as to what I held.

"Suhail," I whispered.

He was at my side in a moment, and stopped dead when I held the broken egg out to him. "Is that—it cannot be—"

"The albumen of the egg," I said. "Petrified. That is what firestone is."

We had known for centuries that firestones were often associated with Draconean ruins . . . but scholars had always assumed that was because the lords of that ancient civilization had prized them. Their rarity and the lack of any natural source for them was explained away by the supposition that there was only one mine, or very few, and that its location had been lost or exhausted in prehistory. The closest thing to a "vein" of firestone anyone had ever found was a cache buried in the dirt, like the one we discovered in Vystrana.

Why had no one ever found one intact before? Time and weathering were not enough to explain it. A great many eggs must have been petrified, to create the world's supply of firestone—petrified, and then smashed. As if by deliberate action.

I cannot recall how many of those thoughts came from my mouth while I stood there in the egg pit, how many came from

Suhail, and how many we pieced together later on. Certainly we did not sort out everything there was to be known. That would require time and further discoveries. But that afternoon, on the cursed island of Rahuahane—the place where the *naka'i* had been turned to stone—I took hold of one end of a thread, and did not stop pulling until years later, when at last I had the whole of it in my grasp.

We dug out the remainder of the broken egg, and I brushed my finger over flaws within the firestone. "The embryonic skeleton," I said. "If we were *very* careful in carving apart one of the intact eggs, we might see what kind of dragons they were breeding."

"It will not be easy to carry back," Suhail warned me.

"Would you have me leave them all here? I cannot be sure of ever visiting this island again." I could not even be sure of surviving my return from it.

Suhail hesitated, torn between pragmatism and his own intellectual curiosity. Then he nodded. "Choose a small one, if you can. We will find a way."

I took the smallest egg I thought had any hope of a recoverable skeleton. Even that would soon be a significant burden: it was fifteen centimeters long, and heavy to match (though firestone, fortunately, is among the lighter gems). Suhail tore his shirt to make a sling and bound the result around his body. I begged his pardon for the encumbrance, but he waved my apology away. We both knew he was by far the stronger swimmer of us two; if I was to have any hope of reaching Lahana, I could not be carrying a millstone around my neck.

We were both lost in thought as we made our way back through the lava tube toward the beach, variously pondering what we had seen, and what we must now face. This saved our lives: had we been chattering as we went, we would have been discovered and very likely killed.

Suhail was ahead of me. He stopped abruptly, and I almost ran into his back. "What—" I began.

I got no further than that one word. Clapping one hand over my mouth, Suhail seized me and pressed me against the side of the tunnel, behind a branch jammed there by some long-ago flood.

Through that imperfect cover, I could still see glimpses of the tunnel's mouth. A shadow was moving out there—something too large to be a bird. And then I heard a voice.

It spoke neither Scirling nor Keongan; that was all the sense my disoriented mind could make of it. Then the tunnel mouth darkened as someone stood in front of it and crouched to look within.

Only the dimness of the tunnel and Suhail's quick thinking kept us from discovery. I did not so much as dare to breathe, and squeezed my eyes shut lest their whiteness give me away. I held myself utterly still against the stone, my mind racing through a useless catalogue of everything that might be visible, about which I could do nothing now. My clothing? Usefully drab, and darkened by the seawater that had soaked it not long ago. My skin? Browned by the sun, though still far paler than Suhail's; I prayed it was *very* dirty from our passage through this tunnel. I wore no jewelry of any kind, and my eyes were shut. It would have to do.

But with my eyes closed, I could not see what the man at the tunnel mouth was doing, and ignorance made the tension worse. I heard a crack as he stepped on a branch, and wished I could melt into the stone. If he entered the lava tube . . .

He did not. He called out to someone else, sounding annoyed, and then moved away. And as he went, I recognized the language, though I did not understand a word.

It was Yelangese.

We remained there until they were gone, and for several minutes afterward. Propriety had long since been flung to the wind, and I took comfort in the solidity of Suhail's body against mine. But we could not stay there forever. Eventually he stepped back, and we stared wide-eyed at one another in the dim light.

"Could you understand them?" I whispered.

He nodded. "They are soldiers. On their way back to camp."

The word jolted me like a fire-lizard's spark. Yelangese soldiers, on Rahuahane. More than two of them, from the sound of it. How on earth had they gotten here without anyone seeing? Fewer people lived on the leeward sides of Keonga and Lahana, but "fewer" was not the same as "none." I did not think even a single Yelangese vessel could have come in secret—not unless they came at night. In which case they were *exceedingly* lucky, for the reefs should have torn the bottom out of their ship.

Oddly, these pragmatic thoughts gave me strength, even as they frightened me. A part of me had been dreading the perilous swim across to Lahana. Having something else to focus on—*anything* else, even so ominous a thing as this—put a bit of steel back in my spine. "We must learn how many there are, and what they are planning."

Suhail stared at me as if I had gone mad. "You want to go spy on soldiers?"

"If they are preparing for an invasion—" I stopped myself, shaking my head. "There cannot be that many of them yet; the Keongans would have seen. So these are scouts, perhaps. They may have a boat we can steal, or at least sabotage. And even if we cannot, the intelligence we might bring back to the islanders could make all the difference in the world."

He had not ceased to stare. "I cannot tell if this is courage or foolhardiness."

"They are not so very far apart," I said dryly. "It is both, I imagine, and experience as well. I have found myself between

an invading army and its target before. This time, at least, I am
not a prisoner." At least I was not yet. I hoped very much to remain that way.

By the look on Suhail's face, someone—certainly not I—had told
him a version of what occurred in Eriga. He tipped his head back,
as if looking through the stone to heaven for aid. "I will go and
look. You must swim for Lahana; that way if I am caught, the islanders at least know the Yelangese are here."

"I will never make that crossing on my own, and we both know
it. If we are to divide our efforts, then *I* will spy on the soldiers,
and you will swim for Lahana."

It was a sensible plan, I thought, but I also knew Suhail would
never accept it. Anyone caught by the Yelangese would likely be
taken prisoner, and he could not abandon a lady to that risk. He
extracted a promise that, if we were seen, I would immediately run
for safety, and swim for Lahana as soon as I could. This I gave;
and so we went after the soldiers.

They were not particularly hard to find. Clearly they had scouted
the island and found it abandoned; perhaps they even knew the reputation of Rahuahane. Knowing themselves to be alone, the men
we followed made little effort to hide their trail, and their com-
patriots practiced no concealment at all.

When we heard voices ahead, Suhail and I sought a vantage
point up the slope. This involved a good deal of belly crawling (I
was extremely glad to be in trousers) and some swallowing of
curses as my scale-cut knees were pressed into the dirt. Ahead of
me Suhail had stopped; by this I knew he could see the camp, and
thought he was so still only to keep the Yelangese from seeing him.

When at last I reached his side, though, I discovered a great deal
more.

The Yelangese ship towered over their camp, stretching the full
length of the curving beach. A net of ropes caged an enormous

balloon that swayed gently in the wind. Below this hung a propeller and a long, narrow craft—and it was the sight of that craft, rather than the ship itself, that stopped my breath in my throat.

Lashings and tarpaulins obscured the shapes, but not enough. The structure beneath the balloon was unmistakably made from bones.

The Yelangese had made a caeliger.

And they had made it out of dragonbone.

SEVENTEEN

The caeliger—Looking for a woman—Flight from Rahuahane—Our reception on Lahana—What and who we found there—Politics of the Broken Sea—A second flight

That is how they got here in secret, without striking the reefs," Suhail whispered to me, not taking his eyes off the camp. "They *flew*."

He sounded impressed. I could only feel sick. There had been attempts to build caeligers before; I knew that from Natalie Oscott, though I did not share her interest and therefore remembered little of the specifics. Most of them had foundered on the problem of weight: the lifting methods available to us at the time were relatively weak, and so the burden of the internal framework, the machinery, and the gondola below had limited their ranges quite sharply.

Dragonbone offered the twin advantages of great strength and minimal weight. With it, caeligers could fly much greater distances. I had always known that society would find uses for dragonbone once they knew it could be preserved—and had myself once used the skeleton of a savannah snake to construct a makeshift glider—but I had not anticipated *this*.

It was to build these caeligers that the dragons of Yelang were being slaughtered.

My eye could not help but try to identify the bones. The long ones had been employed in greatest number, of course, with wires and lashings to hold them together in a framework, but someone had been quite clever in their use of the smaller and more irregular pieces. I saw vertebrae at corners, bone slices forming walls. The caeliger would have looked ominous to me regardless, owing to the circumstances, but the materials of its construction made it outright gruesome. And yet there was a morbid beauty to it; like the great ossuary of Kostratzy, which has been decorated with the bones of deceased villagers, this vessel transformed death into a kind of art.

Suhail's attention had been on the camp and the Yelangese soldiers, who numbered four. When his gaze returned to the caeliger, he frowned. "What is that made of?"

"Bone," I said. "I will explain later."

A resolve had formed in me, as strong as the bones of those slaughtered dragons, that I would turn this discovery against its discoverers. I now knew, or at least guessed, the identity of that shape I had seen out at sea, the day the fleet arrived from Raengaui. And if the caeliger was capable of flying such a distance, I could not leave it in their hands.

I turned my head and regarded Suhail fiercely. "Can we steal that ship?"

His eyes went wide. "Can we get ourselves on board? Very likely. Can we move it once we do? Perhaps. Can we take it where we want to go?" His breath hissed out. "I have flown in a balloon before, but that is no simple balloon."

It was still more experience than I had. My only aerial adventure had been in a glider, and I had crashed. "We must try," I whispered. "It cannot be any more hazardous than attempting to *swim* to Lahana. And if we deprive them of their ship, we may well prevent whatever they are here to do." If we could not steal it, I was determined to sabotage it somehow.

We crept down and around the perimeter of their camp until we were as close as we could get to the ship without revealing ourselves. I blessed the technical considerations that limited the crew to four rather small men, and the cursed reputation of Rahuahane that meant they did not have to post a guard. Otherwise Suhail and I would not have stood a chance.

They were settling in for their meal, cooked over a well-sheltered fire. Suhail's brows knit as he watched them—no, I realized, as he listened. "What are they saying?" I asked, scarcely doing more than mouth the words.

"It sounds as if they are looking for someone," he murmured back.

Waikango, I thought. The king of Raengaui, whom the Yelangese called a pirate, fearing his growing power. Had he escaped captivity? His cousin was married to the king here; he might take refuge with her, thinking the Yelangese would not look for him in the Keongan Islands. Perhaps the foreign canoes I had seen had been carrying an important passenger.

Suhail went on, sounding puzzled. "They are discussing how best to get over to the other islands in secret to search for. . . ."

I waited, but he did not finish the sentence. Finally I nudged him. Suhail looked at me, shaking his head minutely. "Her," he said. "They are looking for a woman."

Only with great effort did I stifle my exclamation of surprise. "Are you *certain*?" I whispered.

He nodded. I tried to think of what woman could possibly merit a Yelangese caeliger looking for her in secret—and then clutched at the palm tree concealing me as one possibility suggested itself.

It was *mad*. They had deported me from Yelang, and I had gone. I knew enough now to speculate that this caeliger was the reason for my deportation; they did not want me investigating where the dragon bones were going and uncovering their new innovation. But why pursue me to Keonga? No, it was even madder than that;

no one knew I was *in* the Keongan Islands. It was sheer chance that the storm had blown us here. The only way anyone could find me was if they went through the Broken Sea with a fine-toothed comb. Why on earth would the Yelangese trouble to do that—and send in pursuit the very thing they wanted to keep secret from me?

That was not a question I could answer while hiding on the edge of a tropical beach, waiting to steal a caeliger. Nor could I explain my suspicions to Suhail. I shook off the matter (or tried to, with limited success) and addressed myself to that task once more. "Should we wait until dark?" I asked him.

Suhail shook his head. "I would not be able to see the controls. The sooner we go, the better."

We did not bother with a diversion. Any such thing would have only roused the Yelangese to alertness, making it likely they would respond with much greater speed once they realized we were stealing the ship. Our plan was quite simple: we went down to the water's edge, out of sight of the men, and swam out into the lagoon. Then we swam around and back in, keeping the ship itself between us and the soldiers at their supper. The rushing of the waves covered what little noise we made. Then it was a quick dash across the sand to the caeliger itself.

The sides of the gondola were high enough to conceal us if we crouched. I stayed low while Suhail oriented himself. At least he could read the Yelangese script on the controls, which I could not. I diverted myself by examining the gondola, noting how the floor was a taut mosaic of scapulae wired together. At least the Yelangese were not squandering carcasses needlessly.

Then Suhail tapped my shoulder. He gave me my instructions in mime: I should flip this lever when he signaled, spin that wheel counter-clockwise, and then man a crank with every ounce of strength in my body. I nodded, my heart beating so loud I was certain the soldiers must hear it. This was madness. Madder than hurling myself off a waterfall. Gravity, at least, had no personal animus against me; it had not travelled through the Broken Sea to find me.

Suhail unwrapped a series of small ropes around the edges of the gondola, leaving them only loosely looped about their cleats. Then he took a deep, steadying breath, and yanked them all free.

The caeliger, freed of its ballast, began to rise.

The Yelangese, laughing around their fire, did not immediately notice. I flipped my lever, spun my wheel, then stood to reach for the crank. Once on my feet, I felt terribly exposed. The soldiers were not so careless as to leave their guns lying about; each man had one alongside him, lying in the sand. I could not take my eyes from those, so certain was I that they were soon to be aimed my way.

One of the men's faces turned upward to the rising caeliger. He stared openmouthed for one long moment; under any other circumstances, it would have been comical. Then he scrambled to his feet, arm outstretched, and began to shout.

Now it was a race. Suhail was doing things behind me; I had no idea what, except that they made an engine grumble to life. I kept labouring over my crank. The propeller began to turn. All of the soldiers were on their feet now, guns in hand. One of them aimed it at me and I flinched, trying to hunch as much of myself as possible behind the dragonbone without stopping my work on the crank.

I could not duck very far, and so I saw one of the other men slap the rifle down, sending its shot cracking well below us. He screamed something at the one who had fired. A third fellow was running down the beach; he took a flying leap off a large stone and tried to seize one of our trailing ropes, but splashed harmlessly into the water. The others were shouting and racing about, but none of them were firing. Why were they not firing?

We were high enough now that they stood little chance of striking us even if they did. "You may stop turning that," Suhail said breathlessly, and I complied. "Come—hold this for me."

The wind had caught us now; we were drifting away from Rahuahane. Unfortunately, that meant we were also drifting away from where we wanted to go. The caeliger had a rudder of sorts, attached beneath the balloon, and it was the control for this that I held. The gondola rocked alarmingly as Suhail darted about, attempting to direct us into the wind, toward the inhabited islands.

He found a way. We came about, passing the bulk of Rahuahane's peak. I drew what felt like my first proper breath in days, and realized that we were flying. It was less personal than my experience in the glider, which had simply been a matter of me and my wings; but it was also more comfortable. In the blazing sunset light, I found myself smiling.

The caeliger settled into its course. Suhail, satisfied with the current state of the engine, untied the egg from around his body and laid it in the bottom of the gondola. Then he stopped, gazing down, not meeting my eyes. "Do you know what they were shouting as we rose?" he asked.

"Of course not," I said. "I do not speak above twenty words of Yelangese."

Suhail turned to face me. "They said, 'It's her.'"

We stood in silence, except for the growl of the engine and the rush of the wind. I could think of nothing to say. Suhail was looking at me as if he had never seen me before. I felt rather as if *I* did not know myself.

He asked, "Why would they be looking for you?"

"I do not know," I said. "I can speculate at bits of it—this ship—when we were in Va Hing, someone arranged to have me deported, I think because they feared I would learn about the caeliger. *Caeligers,* I should say; I doubt there is only one. But why they would trouble themselves to—" I stopped and peered over the side of the gondola, taking care not to shift the rudder. "Should we be dropping like this?"

Suhail swore. We were losing altitude rapidly; I judged we were no more than a hundred feet above the water now. He began to dart once more about the gondola, but even I could tell his efforts were futile, as much from the brief and frustrated movements of his hands as from the fact that we continued to sink. The waves were quite close now—but so, I realized, was the shore of an island. Not Keonga: I could see its familiar mass off to my right, much too far away. The caeliger, fighting against the wind, had brought us to the neighbouring island of Lahana. The only question was whether we would strike land or sea; for my second flight, like my first, was going to end by crashing.

We braced ourselves against the gondola at the last moment, trusting to the dragonbone and its lashings to protect us. The latter failed in places, though not catastrophically. The balloon, sinking down to strike the gondola, knocked us headlong, and my landing drove all the air from my body; but I suffered nothing worse than a few additions to my assortment of bruises.

Lying there on the bony surface of the gondola's floor, I found myself laughing. It was born of hysteria, the sudden release of tension. Whatever else lay ahead—and I knew, even then, that our troubles were not done—I was finally back on safe ground.

Or so I thought, for a few, blessed moments.

Shouting drew us both up from where we had fallen. The people of Lahana had not failed to miss the caeliger drifting toward them from the cursed isle. They had enough warning to assemble a force of warriors, who were even now sprinting across the sand to us; and judging by the weapons they held, they were not coming to make certain we were unharmed.

Suhail attempted to put himself between me and them, but the gondola's open structure doomed him to failure. Large hands reached through and dragged me out, with Suhail following after. "Let us explain," I cried in Keongan, and heard Suhail doing the same. No one had struck me yet, but neither were they showing much willingness to listen.

Then I heard a high, forceful voice crying, "Leave them alone!"—in Scirling.

Abby Carew was the only woman I had heard speaking my tongue in months, but the voice was not hers. I twisted in my captors' grasp and saw, to my utter shock, the crowd parting to allow an Anthiopean woman through.

She was tall, though not in comparison to the islanders, and had the carriage of the well-born. Unlike myself, she wore a dress; I thought it had once been moderately fine, but it had clearly seen hard wearing for quite a few days. She pushed through to me and pried the islanders' hands off me with, as near as I could tell, nothing more than force of will.

This stranger commenced to arguing with the Lahana warriors in their own language, though with an accent that made me suspect she had learned some other dialect first. The thrust of her argument was that Suhail and I had to be questioned, and she was the only one likely to be able to speak with us. From this I guessed that she had not heard us speaking Keongan before she drew near—nor did she have any idea that we had spent nearly two months living on the neighbouring island.

It did not surprise me that she should be ignorant of us. In all that time, I had never imagined a Scirling woman was on Lahana. Now, however, the pieces began to fit together: the injunction against leaving Keonga for the other islands, the Yelangese soldiers looking for a woman. Perhaps it was not me they sought after all, but her. As for why . . . studying her profile, with its strong jaw and full lips, a terrible suspicion began to grow in my heart.

I looked at the ground and saw that the Keongans were taking care neither to stand on her shadow, nor to allow theirs to fall upon her.

"We have heard of these people," one of the warriors said, cutting her argument short. He gestured at me. "This is the *ke'anaka'i* who has been on Keonga—the husband of Liluakame. And this man is one of the other strangers there."

Naturally they had heard of us. Why should there be so many warriors on the sparsely inhabited leeward side of Lahana, unless they were guarding something—*someone*—here? Such guards would certainly be kept apprised of important developments in the Keongan archipelago: for example, the shipwreck of a group of foreigners. *You are not Yelangese*, they had said when we arrived. *Are you Scirling?* Yes, they had reason to look for my people.

"Please," I said, in Keongan. The woman looked at me sharply. "We must give you a warning. The Yelangese are attempting to search your islands in secret; we saw them with our own eyes. They are looking for someone." I carefully did not look at the stranger when I said this, though Suhail was not quite so restrained.

"How do you know this?" one of the warriors demanded.

I chose my words with exquisite care, knowing they might mean the difference between life and death for both Suhail and myself. "We did not leave Keonga intentionally. The warriors there took the two of us out on the water, that we might attempt to ride a sea-serpent. This we succeeded at, but when we finally tumbled from its back, we were in waters far from Keonga, and too far for us to swim home. But we saw the Yelangese on Rahuahane and stole this, their ship, so that we might return and warn you."

My words set off a flurry of discussion among the warriors, much of it too rapid for me to follow. No one asked whether we had set foot on the cursed island, for which I breathed a sigh of relief. That question would come in time, I was sure . . . but in the interim, we might have a chance to think of some way to forestall punishment.

For the time being, they were far more concerned with the Yelangese, and what must be done to address that threat. Even with such incentive, none of them were willing to launch their war canoes for Rahuahane, but they took a variety of other precautions: mounting a search in the area for any other Yelangese; sending word to Keonga that two lambs had strayed; warning someone—that last was quickly silenced, with a glance toward us that said it was not for our ears. And, of course, they had to inform their chief. This was not Pa'oarakiki, the man we had dealt with on Keonga, but the chief of Lahana, to whom these warriors answered.

They also locked us up. Not with literal locks; the only metal the islanders have is that which they trade for, and locks are of little practical use in a society like theirs. Some distance down the beach, however, there was a cluster of several huts, over which other warriors stood guard. Suhail was shoved into the largest of these, and I was escorted, with slightly more dignity, to a smaller one. The Scirling woman accompanied me, saying, "You will have to share this with myself and Hannah, but we have it rather better than the men do."

Unlike the hut in which I had resided since my wedding, this one had closed walls, which made the air within decidedly stuffy. Despite that, the interior was reasonably well appointed by Keongan standards, with soft mats for the floor. Another woman waited there, likewise with a look about her that said she was well-born but somewhat battered by her recent trials. I judged this

Hannah to be perhaps a few years older than her companion—though still younger than I—but when the stranger raised a hand to silence her questions, Hannah complied without hesitation.

Which did not mean I was to be spared questions at all. The stranger faced me and said, "Who are you, and what are you doing here?"

"My name is Isabella Camherst," I said.

Her brow furrowed delicately. "Camherst. Where have I heard that name?"

"I am a dragon naturalist—"

"Ah," she said, her expression clearing. "Yes. You were involved with that business in Bayembe."

The business to which she referred had been bruited about in the gossip-sheets, but I doubted that was where she had heard of me. I wondered: should I speak, or hold my tongue?

I have never been terribly good at holding my tongue.

"Yes, I was," I said. "Your Highness."

Hannah came forward a quick step, but was stopped by the other woman's hand. They both studied me as if I were a new species of insect, which might yet prove to be poisonous. "How did you know?" the princess asked.

"You look rather like your uncle," I said. "And the Keongans avoided your shadow."

Princess Miriam: niece to the king, envoy on a diplomatic journey around the world, following an itinerary that included Yelang. It did not begin to explain what she was doing in the Keongan Islands, living as an honoured prisoner, with Yelangese soldiers hunting her in secret . . . but she, not I, was the one they were searching for. (We did not look so very much alike, but the Yelangese had no reason to expect *two* Scirling women to be running about where there should not even be one. And they had not gotten a terribly good look at me.)

Sighing, she gestured for me to sit. "Forgive me, but I hoped you had been sent by Admiral Longstead. He is no doubt searching for me."

"I'm afraid I do not know the admiral, Your Highness." I spread my hands helplessly. "I truly am a natural historian, travelling the Broken Sea to study dragons. I did not even know you had . . . gone astray." I hesitated, then added, "I fear I may have made quite a hash of things. The Yelangese came in the caeliger you saw on the beach. Without it, I am not certain they have any way to send word that you have been found."

I expected her to chastise me for it, or at best to magnanimously forgive me my error. Instead her jaw set in a firm line. "It is just as well. I should prefer not to be 'rescued' by the Yelangese, if I can possibly avoid it."

The irony scarring that word was unmistakable. "Do you not want their aid?" I asked, astonished. "I know they are not our friends, but if the Keongans are holding you prisoner . . ."

The princess looked to Hannah, who shook her head as if to say, *the choice is yours*. I did not keep abreast of Society's doings; I could not for the life of me remember who Hannah might be, as I knew only people's titles, not their given names. Some peeress, undoubtedly, serving as companion to the princess. (I later learned she was the Countess of Astonby.)

"It has all gone rather sideways," the princess said at last. "We are, as you say, not friends with Yelang, and one of my duties on this voyage was to gather information that would assist my uncle and his ministers in determining how eager we should be to mend that."

"You are a spy!" I exclaimed—which is yet another demonstration of why I have refused all offers of a diplomatic post, no matter where it is the Crown offers to send me.

Her eyebrows rose. "Not a spy, Mrs. Camherst. But I had made arrangements to call at a few ports that were not on my official itinerary. One of these was Lu'aka, on the island of Raengaui."

"To meet with Waikango," I said, beginning to understand. "Are we intending to ally with him? No, that is a foolish question; he has been captured."

"A fact we did not discover until we reached the Broken Sea," the princess said. "After some debate with Captain Emery, I settled on visiting Raengaui regardless. He is by far the strongest candidate in the region for opposing Yelangese expansion, but that does not mean he is the only one. At the very least, it would be worth our while to know who might lead the islanders in his absence—or whether the coalition he has built will collapse, now that he is a prisoner. As for an alliance . . ."

She trailed off, studying me. I did not know what she was looking for; all I could do was sit quietly, attempting to seem intelligent and trustworthy.

"I cannot say whether the Scirling crown will involve itself or not," she said at last. "That decision has not been made."

But it was clearly a possibility. Would we offer diplomatic recognition, I wondered, or military aid? We had tried the latter in Bayembe, and while my actions had inadvertently scuttled our plans there, that did not mean we would not try it elsewhere. An outpost like Point Miriam—named for the very princess now seated across from me—would be a nice foothold for Scirling dominance of trade through the Broken Sea, blocking the Yelangese and potentially even challenging the Heuvaarse.

I had the wit not to say *that* out loud, at least. "So that is why you do not want the Yelangese to rescue you. It would give them a good deal of bargaining power in their dealings with Scirland. But why did the islanders take you prisoner?"

Hannah made a noise that suggested she had not forgiven that outrage, and never would. The princess only sighed. "They saw an opportunity, and seized it. When I said Scirland might consider offering aid, they asked for us to raid Houtiong and free Waikango. I refused, naturally—though I did say that we might eventually be able to bring diplomatic pressure to bear on the matter. Such distant promises were hardly persuasive, I'm afraid . . . and so they took all of us prisoner, in the hopes that they might be able to trade me to the Yelangese in exchange for their captured leader."

A princess in the hand was worth two promises of diplomatic aid in the bush, I supposed. There was no guarantee she could have convinced her uncle and his ministers—let alone the Synedrion—to intervene on Waikango's behalf. And even if she had, it would have taken a year, two years, five. Such things rarely moved quickly, when it was some other land's dignitary languishing in prison. "I suppose they hid you here because they knew the Yelangese would look for you in the Raengaui Islands."

"Yelang and Scirland both," she said. "I cannot imagine that Admiral Longstead sat idly by when Captain Emery's ship failed to return to the fleet as expected."

It was inevitable, then, that the search would eventually reach even the relatively inaccessible waters of Keonga. I supposed the only reason they had not done so sooner was that they did not want to advertise to the world that Princess Miriam had gone missing. But it was a race to see who could find her first, Yelang or Scirland . . . and at the moment, Yelang had the edge.

Her thoughts tended in the same direction as mine. "What of you? Is there any way you could get a message out to the fleet?"

"I fear not, Your Highness," I said glumly, and told her of the *Basilisk*'s injured state. Aekinitos was likely mad enough to steal a Keongan canoe and attempt sailing it back to more familiar waters, but he was not a Scirling subject. I did not think he would be eager to risk himself in that fashion—at least, not without a sizable reward. Before I could decide whether to mention that to the princess, however, another possibility came to me, this one even madder than the last.

She arrived at the same thought even as I did. "The caeliger," we said in unison.

"Suhail and I did not have very much luck with it," I warned her. "Perhaps if he had more time to study the controls . . . but time is not a luxury we are likely to have."

"Who is this Suhail?" she asked me. "An Akhian, clearly—but how did he come to be here?"

I gave her a *précis* of my dealings with Suhail, from our partnership in Namiquitlan to our chance encounter in Seungdal, and all that had followed after. "Do you trust him?" the princess asked when I was done.

"Yes," I said. The word came forth without any need for my brain to approve it first. "I do not know his lineage, but he is a gentleman in every other sense of the word, and very brave. I am certain he will help us if he can."

Hannah looked unconvinced. "Miriam, to reveal your identity to a foreigner . . ."

"The alternative is to remain a prisoner, or to risk the Yelangese using me as political leverage. But it is a moot point if escape is impossible regardless." Miriam focused her attention on me once more. "Tell me what you can of this caeliger."

Under other circumstances—when I was rested, perhaps, or at least had not been subjected to one of the more harrowing days of my life—I might have been able to make a more considered decision as to what I should communicate to the princess, and what might best be retained as a secret. But I was not rested, and my day had been harrowing; and so I sat there in that small, airless room and told her very nearly everything.

The only reason "very nearly" did not become "all" was because the princess remained attentive enough to draw us back to the purpose when I strayed too far into digression. She did not hear the tale of how Jacob and I had discovered the secret of natural dragonbone preservation, nor much of what had transpired in Vystrana. But I told her of Frederick Kemble, the chemist I had hired to continue Gaetano Rossi's research; of the break-in, which I believed to have been orchestrated by the Marquess of Canlan; of the Va Ren Shipping Assocation, which was now profiting from that research. And I told her of the recent interest in the hunting of dragons, which seemed to have military backing.

"Then they likely have more than one of these," she said. I knew from her quiet tone that I had just added another few kilograms to the burden of her worries. "It seems, Mrs. Camherst, that you also have a pressing need to speak with the admiral. He must know of this at once."

I did not contradict her, but neither did I share her enthusiasm for the notion. While it was true that Scirland needed to be apprised of this Yelangese innovation, I did not much relish the prospect of explaining dragonbone preservation to men who were likely to immediately begin planning how to exploit it for their own benefit.

Regardless, it was true that escape needed to happen, for the princess' sake if not my own. And limited although its range must be, the caeliger seemed our best prospect for doing that.

If escape were to happen at all, it must happen soon. The Scirling delegation had been kept in friendly captivity, insofar as such a thing is possible; the Keongans felt no animosity toward the princess or her people. They only held her because she was their best bargaining chip for getting Waikango back. House arrest had been imposed when the warriors saw the caeliger approaching, because they did not know what it portended, and it continued now because of the Yelangese. "They were reluctant to lay hands directly on me," Miriam said, when I asked how she had gotten free earlier.

The rest of the time, the Scirlings were permitted to move about in small groups—albeit under guard to ensure that no one attempted to slip away into the interior of Lahana.

"There has been no need to keep us under closer watch," Hannah said. "What good would it do for the men to overpower the guards? They put us on this side of the island because there are so few settlements here, and what few are nearby have had their canoes taken away. We could escape this location, but we would still have no way off the island. They would find and stop us well before we could steal long-distance vessels from anywhere else."

The caeliger, of course, changed that. Our bad landing would not have inspired the Keongans to believe it was capable of travelling very far, but even if they did not think that craft a danger, the Yelangese most certainly were. Messengers had been sent; soon additional warriors would come and take the princess to a more secure location.

It could not spirit us all to safety, though. Only a few could go; the question was which few those should be.

From the start of her captivity, the princess had insisted upon sharing meals with the rest of her crew. This violated the *tapu* which said men and women should eat separately, but Miriam had thought it wise to preserve opportunities for conversation with Captain Emery, precisely for eventualities such as this one. The Keongans permitted no fire that evening, but did allow us out of our huts to share a cold meal of cocoanut meat, bananas, and taro paste, which gave us a chance to speak.

The men had spent their time questioning Suhail, much as Miriam had questioned me, and had unsurprisingly lit upon a very similar notion. Under the guise of asking one another to pass platters of food, Hannah and the captain arranged the plan. Four would go in the caeliger: Suhail, for his previous experience and knowledge of hot air balloons; one Lieutenant Handeson, who knew balloons and engines both; the princess; and myself.

I would have argued this last point if I could have. The full range of the caeliger was unknown, but would certainly be improved the less weight it carried. My presence might mean the difference between Princess Miriam reaching Kapa Hoa (which was the closest island outside the archipelago) and Her Highness drowning in the sea. But she considered it vital that my knowledge of the Yelangese caeligers be shared as soon as possible; and so I must go. I could not dispute it too strenuously, not without the Keongans noticing something amiss. They did not speak Scirling, but they could recognize the sound of an argument.

"They are good people," the princess said to me quietly, as we waited for the moment to strike. It must come soon; the island was falling into dusk, and soon there would not be enough light to see the caeliger's controls. "I do not applaud their actions, of course— they should not have taken me prisoner. But I have a good deal of sympathy for their position. By all accounts, Waikango is not only a gifted war-leader—a gifted *king*—but a just and decent man. I would rather have him for an ally than the Yelangese emperor."

I looked at her sidelong. "Do you intend to speak on their behalf, once you have returned? Despite what they have done?"

She gave it due thought. Unlike myself, the princess was a woman who considered everything before she committed to it. "I do," she said at last. "There must be repercussions for the ones who kidnapped me; we cannot let that go unanswered. But I think the men responsible knew that they would ultimately be punished for what they have done. I am not held in the same esteem as a princess of their own people, but they have violated proper behaviour nonetheless. Such actions have consequences. They accepted those consequences, for the sake of their people."

Her tone was one of quiet respect. In her shoes, I do not know that I could have been as forgiving. The Labane who took me prisoner in Mouleen were loyal soldiers of their inkosi, and they knew that by venturing into the Green Hell they risked death, but that did not make me any more charitable toward them. Then again, the Labane had not treated me half so kindly as the Keongans had treated Miriam.

The princess caught my gaze and held it. "Remember that," she said.

Before I could ask her precisely what it was I should remember, the men sprang into action.

It was not an easy fight. The Keongan guards were all large men, and armed; the Scirlings and Suhail were unarmed, and moreover were attempting to avoid killing anyone, on Miriam's orders. But they also outnumbered the islanders, with so many having been sent away on various tasks. Nor did they have to achieve permanent victory: they only had to occupy the guards sufficiently that we four could run for the caeliger.

We pounded across the sand toward that distant craft, tipped askew on the beach high above the breaking surf. Lieutenant Handeson took quick stock of the machinery and then all but threw two containers at me. "Quick! Fill those. Salt water is not the best, but—" I did not hear the end of his sentence, for Miriam had taken one of the containers, and we were already moving toward the sea.

While the two of us worked, the lieutenant and Suhail banged about the caeliger, cursing steadily. It seemed that something had broken, and must be wedged. "A branch!" Suhail shouted as we returned with water. "About this long—no thicker than my thumb—"

The beach was a bad place to look for branches; every tree in the vicinity was a palm. But Miriam and I ran up the slope and began rooting around in the fallen leaves, trying to find one whose stem was of a suitable size. In the middle distance, the knot of men was still deep in their scuffle around the huts. Someone had begun running toward us—a Keongan, by his size—but the engine of the caeliger was going; as soon as we found a wedge, we might take off and leave him behind. My hand closed on one at last, and I sprinted for the caeliger, calling for the princess to follow me.

From behind me, I heard a cry.

The messengers had gone for reinforcements; now the reinforcements had arrived. Two had come out of the trees, and they must have overcome their reluctance to lay hands on royalty, for they had Miriam in their grasp. I stopped dead in the sand, palm leaf clutched in my hand. I could not possibly free her from them, and if Suhail and the lieutenant came to my aid, the Keongan running toward us would stop the caeliger from taking off.

"Go!" Princess Miriam called, her voice more steady than I would have believed possible. Steady, and commanding. "Go! Find the admiral, and tell him where I am!"

To this day, I do not know if it was obedience or cowardice that turned my feet toward the caeliger. Suhail helped me over the edge; I tumbled to the floor, and a moment later that floor swayed beneath me as we left the beach behind.

EIGHTEEN

Over the sea—Something in the gondola—Sails on the horizon—We flee—More sails—The wishes of the senior envoy—The Battle of Keonga

She expected that to happen," I said dully, staring up at the web of ropes that held the caeliger's balloon. "She did not think she would get away with us."

"I think it would be better to say, she planned for the possibility." Suhail took the palm leaf from me, stripped it, and jammed it in among the recalcitrant machinery.

Lieutenant Handeson helped me to my feet. "She gave the orders ages ago, not long after we were taken. If anybody had a chance to escape, they should go. The Keongans won't hurt her, and this way, we can send a rescue."

Whereas if she came with us, they would move heaven and earth to retrieve her. I wondered suddenly if she had ever intended to get on board the caeliger. It would fly farther and faster with only three passengers—and if we were lost at sea, she would not be lost with us. No, I thought, not that last; she had shown no fear of drowning. But our chances were indeed better without her, even if Hannah and Captain Emery would have preferred to have her away from the Keongans at once.

Of course, any rescue would depend upon our speed. The Yelangese did not yet know that the missing princess was on Lahana, but no doubt they would wonder at the failure of their caeliger to return. Furthermore, the Keongans must assume that we

The Caeliger

would reach other territory and pass word along to our people. They would move Miriam, and soon.

I rose to my feet, moving carefully in the gondola. Dragonbone might be highly resistant to impact, but its light weight made the whole structure feel alarmingly flimsy. "What can I do to help?"

The answer was, very little. Between the two of them, Suhail and Lieutenant Handeson had sorted out the controls; the caeliger did not need three people to operate it. "Ordinarily I would say that flying at night is very hazardous," the lieutenant said dryly. "But there is nothing out here for us to hit except the sea, and perhaps the occasional gull. So long as we keep a reasonable altitude, we should be fine. You should get some rest, Mrs. . . ." He trailed off, plainly realizing he had no idea who I was and why I had been included in the escape group.

"Camherst," I said. We had a brief discussion of our plans; they amounted to "fly toward Kapa Hoa and hope we do not crash before we get there," which did not leave much to discuss. Then I attempted to bed down, for I was indeed very tired.

There was a straw mat in one end of the gondola that I thought was intended as a place for crewmen to catch naps. When I settled into it, however, I found something else occupying the corner: the petrified egg from Rahuahane. Suhail had untied it from his body while we flew across to Lahana, and it had been overlooked in the crash.

I angled myself to hide the egg from Handeson's eyes. This, too, was a secret, and one I could yet protect. If the Scirling navy learned there was an enormous cache of firestone on Rahuahane, the princess would not be the only thing they brought home from Keonga. I did not want the island raided for its treasure, and *especially* not before it could be properly studied.

Fortunately Handeson was busy with Suhail. They seemed quite impressed with the engine, which was, I gathered, a substantial improvement in smallness over the ones to which Handeson was accustomed. I wondered if that, too, had dragonbone components in it. (I later discovered that it did.) I tucked the egg into a coil of rope and then lay before it, hoping I could smuggle it off the caeliger without anyone else seeing. It did not look like firestone—the outer shell was dull rock—but I did not want it to attract any curiosity.

My thoughts would not permit me to rest. It was all too much, and too rapid; our discoveries on Rahuahane had been knocked clean out of my head by the encounter with the princess, let alone my breathless experience riding the sea-serpent. I wanted a moment somewhere quiet to ponder what I had seen, and paper on which to sketch it before the details slipped from my memory. But the gondola of the world's first truly effective caeliger was not the place for such things, and our flight to obtain a rescue for the king's niece was not the moment. I lay in the darkness, looking at Suhail's profile against the brilliant background of the stars, listening to him murmur belated prayers in Akhian. I could not remember the last time I had prayed. I hoped Tom, Jake, and Abby were not too worried for me. Had anyone told them we had been found on Lahana?

And so the hours passed, until dawn came, and with it, sails on the horizon.

I had risen as soon as the light began to grow, having slept only in the most fitful snatches. Suhail had not slept at all, and looked as drawn and weary as I had ever seen him. He and the lieutenant were growing concerned about fuel; the wind was not entirely cooperating in our efforts to reach Kapa Hoa, and their best guess at reading the Yelangese navigational instruments said we were at risk of falling short. It was a pity, I reflected, that no one had thought to make the gondola watertight, for dragonbone floats quite well. Cut away the balloon, and we might have had ourselves a perfectly serviceable canoe—albeit one without a sail or paddles.

Because they were occupied with the caeliger's machinery, I was the one who first spotted the sails. "Come look," I said, breaking into their low-voiced discussion. "Are those not ships in the distance?"

They were both at my side in an instant. "They are," Handeson said, bright with relief. "We'll have to fly into the wind to get at them, but that's better than hoping to make Kapa Hoa. Let's come about."

The hope of rescue put new life into our limbs. We brought the caeliger about, its propeller beating against the wind, and made our way toward the sails. Now, with the wind in our faces, I felt our speed at last, as I had not when we flew over the featureless nighttime sea. The engine truly was a remarkable achievement, and although the Yelangese had been partly responsible for putting us into our current predicament, I must own that without their engineering, we would not have come out of it alive.

Even with that speed, the sails drew closer but slowly. I went into the prow of the gondola and peered toward them, as if squinting would lessen the distance between us. There seemed to be quite a lot of them—three ships? No, five. Quite a fleet, to be in this part of the Broken Sea. And the shape of their sails was odd, to my Anthiopean eye . . .

"Suhail," I said, loudly enough for him to hear. "Lieutenant. I am not a sailor, nor terribly familiar with this part of the world— but I believe that style of sail is common on Yelangese ships, is it not?"

Once again they rushed to my side, studying the ships in tense silence. Then Handeson swore (proving that a man may be both a gentleman and a sailor, but when the spurs bite home, he is more

sailor than gentleman). "Those are junk sails, all right. The Yelangese aren't the only ones who use them, though. Those might be
from Seungdal, or—"

Something was bobbing alongside one of the vessels in that
little fleet. A large, ellipsoid shape, which did not seem to touch
water. At this distance we could not see the gondola below, but it
was impossible to mistake for anything but another caeliger.

"It's the Yelangese," Suhail said, in that remarkably calm-
sounding voice I had come to recognize as a sign of great tension
in him. "And they are coming this way."

The three of us looked at each other. No one had to put the question into words: would we allow ourselves to be taken by the
Yelangese, or would we risk death in the open sea?

"Regardless of the princess' situation," I said, "they will be *exceedingly* displeased to know that we have discovered the secret of
their caeligers."

"Discovered, and stolen," Suhail added.

Handeson swore once more and lunged for the caeliger's controls.

To this day, I wonder what the Yelangese thought when they
saw one of their own caeligers first approach, then turn tail and
run. Whatever discussions took place on their decks at the time,
however, it did not take them long to correctly interpret the significance of our behaviour. As we put the wind to our backs and
began to fly away with all haste, the second caeliger rose majestically into the air and gave chase.

Our lead on them was substantial, but that only benefits the fleeing party if there is somewhere to lose the pursuer. We had only
the open sea—not even any cloud cover in which to hide. Moreover, the Yelangese had both fresh supplies of fuel and a vastly superior knowledge of how to operate their craft. It would take them

some time to catch us . . . but catch us they would. It was inevitable, and all three of us knew it.

Our caeliger fled across the waves, with the second one following. We soon lost the Yelangese fleet; it evened the odds, at least, and I had wild visions of a boarding engagement fought high above the sea. (Surely, I reasoned, the Yelangese would not fire guns at us, not when they might puncture the caeliger's bag and send us crashing into the waves.) An hour passed, perhaps more, with the second craft slowly gaining on us. But before they drew close enough to take action, Suhail cried, "Ahead! Look!"

Once more, there were masts upon the horizon. "More Yelangese?" I said under my breath. They were searching the Broken Sea for the princess, and might well have divided their efforts. If we had indeed found more ships from the empire, it would no longer be a choice between capture and the risk of death: we would have to choose between capture and the *certainty* of death. Provided, of course, that the former did not lead inevitably to the latter.

Handeson crowed. "No! Square rigs! They're Anthiopean! And—" He stopped, and seemed to be quite literally holding his breath.

The sails grew larger. There were three ships, grouped in a loose formation, and the men aboard them were scrambling about, clearly alarmed by the two approaching caeligers. I could see them quite well, because our own craft was losing altitude rapidly. Even I could tell that the sounds emerging from its machinery were not encouraging. The sailors appeared to be racing to aim their cannon in our general direction, but they would not need them; we would be coming down even without interference from artillery.

The gunshots I heard, though, came from behind us. It was the Yelangese, firing their rifles at the three of us. We took cover behind the dragonbone walls of the gondola, which began to drop even more precipitously; they had pierced the bag (which may have been their target to begin with), and we were losing air. Then, without warning, their caeliger sheered off, turning back into the wind and heading once more toward their own distant fleet.

Perhaps they hoped we would sink into the sea, leaving no example of a caeliger in foreign hands. As I have said, though, dragonbone floats quite well. "Quick," I cried, "throw everything overboard that you can"—for if we lightened the gondola by enough, it might stay afloat long enough for that remarkable engine to be retrieved.

We splashed into the waves before we could get very far in shedding ballast, however. The falling bag dragged the gondola onto its side; Suhail and Handeson both leapt clear rather than burden it with their weight. I clung to the bones, because tucked into my arm I had a bundle of fabric that concealed the petrified egg.

"Ahoy the—the wreck," a voice called from above, in the blessedly familiar accents of the Estershire coast. "Just who the bleeding hell *are* you?"

We had found the Scirling navy.

They fished us out of the sea, and the caeliger along with us, balloon and all. The latter had not sunk; it proved to have a framework inside it, likewise built of dragonbone, which kept it afloat. I looked grimly at all the bones and half-wished they had all gone to the bottom of the sea. But I had already told the princess about dragonbone, and she had sent me here to tell the admiral; the only way that cat could be stuffed back into its bag was if Miriam were to die. (And I hope I need not say I wished very much for that *not* to happen.)

Lieutenant Handeson took over in the first instance, saluting with proper naval precision despite looking like a drowned and unshaven rat. His bedraggled state, not to mention the shirtless Akhian and the woman in man's dress who accompanied him, meant it took a moment for the sailors around us to recognize him; Captain Emery's ship had been part of this very fleet. Once they realized what they had caught, they immediately began signaling the next closest vessel, which was the *Conborough*, the admiral's flagship.

It was no coincidence that we found them where we did. I soon understood that the Scirling officers knew the Yelangese were searching for Miriam, and were attempting to beat those men to their shared quarry. Both groups had gotten far enough in searching the Broken Sea that their thoughts bent to Kapa Hoa, and if they did not find her there, they intended to continue on to Keonga. Given but a little while longer, then, it seemed that rescue might have come to us, without any need to fetch it.

Such a rescue, however, would have arrived ill-informed. And so I soon found myself standing in front of the admiral, still clad in male garments, but these at least dry and in one piece.

Most of Admiral Longstead's attention was on Lieutenant Handeson, the only member of our little crew who seemed at all reliable. I was after all a woman, and a mildly notorious one at that—yes, he recognized my name—and Suhail was Akhian. But the princess had sent me because I knew about the caeligers, and given that he had just seen a second one fly away with all speed, he needed an explanation. Moreover, I now suspected that Miriam's words just before the escape had not been mere idle musing. She wanted to be certain I understood her views.

When we had finished telling him our tale, I added, "You may wish to make haste, sir. Not that you would tarry, of course—but I suspect the Yelangese may be making their way to Keonga as we speak."

He frowned at me. "They were headed for Kapa Hoa, the last we heard."

"Indeed. But if the caeliger we . . . commandeered—" Handeson had used that word; it had a better ring than *stole*. "If it originated with that group of ships, they will know where it had been sent. They will also know, by our decision to flee from them, that there was no longer a Yelangese crew aboard; the fact that we fled toward you, however accidental it was in truth, will suggest that the caeliger was in Scirling hands. They may think the princess was with us. But regardless, they will want to investigate Keonga, and retrieve their men if they can."

Longstead mulled this over, then shook his head. "You may be right, Mrs. Camherst. It hardly matters, though. We will want to reach Keonga before those island devils move Her Highness elsewhere. I do not fancy starting our hunt anew. The Broken Sea is far too large of a haystack for that."

His choice of term for the Keongans made me apprehensive. "Sir—I do beg your pardon. But before I left, Her Highness spoke quite a bit about her feelings toward the islanders. She acknowledged that those directly involved in her capture and imprisonment must be punished, but did not want to see retribution visited on all their people. She is quite sympathetic to their cause, even if she deplores their most recent method of fighting for it."

"I don't give a damn about their cause, Mrs. Camherst," the admiral snapped. "I will do whatever it takes to bring Her Highness back to safety."

"Your pardon, sir, but I am not speaking on my own behalf in saying this—though for my own part, I will add that I have found the Keongans generally to be friendly hosts, and certainly I have more cause to consider them my friends than I do the Yelangese. But I am conveying the *princess'* wishes. She would be very displeased if you initiated hostilities with the Keongans."

Admiral Longstead's neck reddened. "This is *my ship*, madam—"

"I do not dispute that. But I believe Her Highness was appointed the senior envoy of this embassy, was she not? Was the secret detour to Raengaui excluded from her brief, or included?"

When the admiral did not answer right away, Handeson murmured, "It was included, ma'am."

"There you have it," I said. "If you are attacked, then by all means defend yourselves—though I should hope you would, out of common decency, attempt to limit the carnage to a minimum and move toward peace at the first opportunity. But to strike against the Keongans, without first attempting diplomacy, would be in direct contravention of the wishes of your senior envoy."

This account of my speech makes me sound quite levelheaded, but the truth is that however moderate my choice of words, my temper was hanging by a rather thin thread. I had sympathy for the admiral's frustration; he had misplaced his most valuable charge for an extended period of time, and wanted to expunge that failure, along with everyone who knew of it. But I had family and friends on those islands, and I counted some of the local inhabitants among the latter. Nor did I want to fail at the task I believed Miriam had set me.

"We sail for Keonga," the admiral snarled. "What happens when we get there . . . we shall see."

The winds were not fair for Keonga; they seemed to fight us, as if defending the islands. Or so I was told: I was awake for very little of it, exhaustion having vanquished me at last. The admiral was gentleman enough to cede his cabin to me for the time being, and there I collapsed, regaining my strength while I could.

I woke long enough to eat supper and to be told that we would not reach Keonga until the following morning. We were not that far, but as I have mentioned before, a number of reefs surrounded the archipelago, adorning the tops of islands either unborn or long deceased. However impatient Longstead was, he would not risk his ships by charging blindly ahead when it was too dark to see the warning surf.

Suhail also spoke to me during this time. "What happened to our find from Rahuahane?" he asked. His tone was casual, as if speaking of nothing terribly important, but he had chosen a moment when no sailors were near, and he avoided naming the thing directly.

"It is here," I said. "The lieutenant who helped me stow it did not see why I place such importance on a superstitious trinket—a mere carving of an egg—but, well, he is not a naturalist. I could hardly expect him to understand."

"Indeed," Suhail said. He did not grin, but his eyes were merry at my explanation. So long as no one broke the egg, the nonsense I had spun would stand.

I slept again after that and woke a while before dawn. On deck, I discovered our little fleet of three was proceeding cautiously, men standing at the rails with log-lines to constantly monitor the depth. We had entered the treacherous waters girding the Keongan Islands; all about us were patches of troubled surf, the easy swell of the waves sent into turmoil by the changing terrain below. I found myself holding my breath, and made myself exhale.

One of the ways sailors find islands—particularly if they do not have the benefit of modern navigational equipment—is by looking to the sky. Clouds often form above land, and these can be seen on the horizon long before the land itself is near enough to make out. So it was with our approach to Keonga . . . but as we drew near, it seemed to me there was something peculiar about the clouds I saw. Over the rush of the waves, I could hear an odd sound, almost like a drumbeat.

From behind me Suhail murmured, "Smoke."

I gripped the railing until my knuckles ached. He was right: smoke was casting a pall over the island. It might have been ash from a volcanic eruption; a part of me almost hoped it was. But I heard one of the lieutenants bellow, "Cannon fire!" and knew that it was not.

The Yelangese had indeed made sail for Keonga, and they had arrived before us.

They must have rendezvoused with allies along the way. Seven of their ships were arrayed off the coast; an eighth had run aground on a reef and was now burning. Smoke also rose from Rahuahane—a signal fire, lit on the beach by the stranded men of the caeliger when they saw their countrymen approaching. But the Keongans had been keeping watch as well, and by the time the Yelangese ships drew near, they were ready.

Princess Miriam was not the only thing they had been hiding from us. Aekinitos had said, mostly in jest, that there might be an entire war fleet on the far side of Lahana. He was wrong only in his choice of location. They had been arrayed throughout the archipelago, a great mustering of Puian canoes from many parts of the Broken Sea, in preparation for the possibility—the likelihood—that their attempts to trade Her Highness for Waikango would not succeed before the Yelangese found her. They had paddled out as the Yelangese approached, forming a defensive line a little distance from shore, and there they had waited.

The Yelangese, taking this as proof of Miriam's presence, had not hesitated to fire, and so the battle was joined.

Battles are not pretty things, but this one was especially ugly. The Puian war fleet had but few guns and no artillery. Aekinitos had ordered his men to drag their cannon up to the promontory, from which they offered what supporting fire they could, but it was very scant. Many of those engaged in the battle had only spears and shark-tooth clubs with which to fight. The agility and speed of their canoes gave them a certain advantage in shallow coastal waters over the Yelangese ships, and their small size and great number meant that although a cannonball might strike one craft, five others would continue onward—but the shots *did* strike, crushing many warriors and sending them into the sea. Where the canoe fleet reached a ship, men swarmed up on too many sides to repel them all at once, but the casualties were great.

Such was the fruit of the ordinary elements. Both sides, however, had unexpected weapons, and did not hesitate to deploy them.

I have recounted my own ride upon the back of a sea-serpent, and said that the more experienced Keongans are capable of steering the beasts to a limited extent. On that day, in the waters around the archipelago, I saw the truth of it with my own eyes. They do not ride the serpents merely for entertainment, or to prove their virility and strength: they had also been practicing for war.

Half a dozen serpents raged in the waters around the fleet. Two of the seven ships were sinking, I realized, their hulls cracked by the terrible force of the serpents' water blasts. These had destroyed some canoes as well, for a serpent lashes out when and where it will; the rider can only attempt to direct its head toward the enemy or else into open water. As weapons and as mounts, they are nearly as dangerous to their own side as they are to the opponent. But the psychological effect of them that day cannot be understated. The Yelangese came to the islands expecting to brush past a few dozen canoes, but found themselves facing hundreds, with the great beasts of the sea fighting on their side.

They had a weapon of their own, however, and it rained death from the sky. The other caeliger swooped across the bloodstained waters again and again, too high for even the strongest island warrior to hurl a spear, but low enough for the men in its gondola to shoot accurately into the fracas below. They had begun by picking men off from the canoes, but when the serpents entered the fray, they shifted their efforts to those beasts and the men who controlled them. There had been more serpents before; now two floated dead in the water, and a third rampaged freely, attacking anything in its path.

I had not forgotten Admiral Longstead's declaration of his resolve to rescue the princess. If she had not been moved, she was on Lahana, and the Battle of Keonga stood in his path. I ran to the quarterdeck, hoping against hope to persuade him not to add his cannon to the weapons aimed at the islanders.

To my surprise, I found him standing quietly, watching the battle with close attention, but giving no orders to join it. "You will not fight?" I asked.

"Let them carve one another up," he said. "I suspect the Yelangese will win, with that thing in the air, but they will be badly bloodied. Then we will move into range and hail them. They will give way, or if they do not, we will take appropriate steps."

As little as I wanted him to fire on the Keongans, I found myself almost equally dismayed to hear him say he would stand aside. "You will just sit here and watch men die?"

"Should I risk my own men on their behalf, Mrs. Camherst? I was not sent here to involve myself in a local war. If I could sail past them to reach the princess, I would do so. If they fire upon us, I will answer in kind. But otherwise, I will wait."

The most infuriating part of it all, then and now, was that Admiral Longstead was right. He could easily have routed the Yelangese if he moved in; they were already beleaguered, and the Scirling ships were both larger and superior in firepower. But why should he do so? We were not so much at odds with Yelang as to risk starting a war with them in this fashion.

And yet it tore my heart to stand there while the battle raged, watching the caeliger slaughter helpless men and beasts from above, and do nothing.

I hate above all else to do nothing.

People have accused me of lying on this point, but I truly do not remember making a decision. I remember thinking only that I must *do something*. Then I was over the railing and plummeting toward the sea, with Suhail shouting after me.

I hit the water with a great splash and sank deep, but soon kicked back up to the surface. A second splash inundated me; when it receded, Suhail was nearby, dashing the water from his face with a quick shake of his head. "What are you *doing*?" he demanded.

"The admiral will not go closer to the battle," I said breathlessly. "I must find my own conveyance."

The creature was almost to us. I had seen it approaching before I went over the rail: a sea-serpent, one of those which lost its rider in the battle, perhaps, or else a curious visitor. I struck out for it before Suhail could get more than two words into his description of exactly how mad I was. He was not wrong; but he must claim a share of madness for himself, along with a good helping of chivalric honour—for when he saw what I intended, he did not abandon me to do it alone.

We had learned some lessons from our previous ride. I felt almost competent as we caught our holds with a minimum of trouble; soon we were atop the serpent as before, and together encouraged it to swim in the direction of the battle. This was not difficult, as the blood in the water had attracted its attention. But once there, we faced two challenges, each one alone far greater than the simple task of riding: we must figure out something of value to do, and then find a way to do it.

I thought at first to go for the Yelangese ships, as the other riders were doing. But there were any number of difficulties in doing that: a churning sea of chaos lay between us and those targets; we should have to steer through the canoes, which I did not at all trust our ability to achieve; the Yelangese would be shooting at us the whole way, both from the ships and from the caeliger; and we might do more damage to the side I intended to support. The sea was simply too crowded for me to have any certainty of directing the serpent's blast in a safe direction—given that I had not practiced for it at all.

Suhail was shouting something at me, but I did not hear it. My gaze had fallen upon the caeliger.

Had ours been functional, we might have used it in the battle, but the puncturing of its bag had released whatever gas the Yelangese were using to create lift, and the engine had taken a wetting besides. I had no way to get at the enemy caeliger, and would not have been much use with a rifle even had I thought to take one from our ship.

But it was possible that someone else—some *thing* else, I should say—might be able to strike that high.

The caeliger was approaching, completing one pass across the battle and preparing to make a turn. I saw one of the men above notice us. He was too distant to have a good shot, but held his rifle and waited. That, I realized might be my death—or Suhail's.

"Pull!" I cried to him, and suited action to words, hauling with all my might upon the tendrils we held.

Even our combined strength could not have moved the serpent's great head. I did not expect it to: I sought instead to vex the creature enough that it would lift its head of its own accord. And so it did, flanks rippling with the motion I knew meant it had drawn in water, preparatory to expelling it. But its head barely crested the waves, which would not be enough at all.

Half a dozen thoughts and more flashed through my head at once: serpent cranial anatomy, the tendrils we held, rings in bulls' noses. The strength of dragonbone. The likelihood that I would fall into the water before I could even test my theory. The bullets now piercing the water around us as the caeliger drew near—and above all, an internal voice crying, *What are you doing?*

What I was doing was releasing my grip upon the tendrils behind the head and hurling myself forward, down the serpent's long snout. There were tendrils there, too, much smaller, fringing the serpent's nose . . . and it was these I now seized hold of and pulled.

I thought to bring the serpent's head up to an angle where it would expel its blast of water at the caeliger, hopefully damaging it as the other serpents had damaged the ships. The dragonbone components would likely survive unbroken, but if I could break the machinery, or knock the men from their perch, or rupture the caeliger's bag, I might yet save some of those below.

It shames me as a natural historian to admit this, but: I had not stopped to consider that I was riding a younger cousin of the beast we had killed in the arctic.

The serpent did not merely lift its head. The entire front of its body rose snakelike into the air, just as its cousin had done in attacking the *Basilisk*. I found myself dangling from its snout by a desperate grip on the edge of one of its nostrils. It did indeed release its water—I could not see where it aimed—but a moment later it struck something hard, as its head collided with the passing caeliger.

We all crashed into the water together, serpent, riders, and flying machine. They had swooped too low in approaching us, believing that we had no way of striking back at them. No one else had been foolish enough to try what I had done (for the Keongan riders know that the anatomy of the snout is exceedingly tender, and that interfering with it is a good way to send the beast out of control). It would not even have worked had we not been at the edge of the battle, in waters quiet enough that the caeliger felt safe in descending for a better shot.

But descended they had, and I was too ignorant to know how unwise it was to try and take a serpent by the nose. In my recklessness, I had succeeded in removing the caeliger from the sky.

I saw quite a few engravings of that moment in subsequent months and years; some of them are still to be found today. All of them depict me standing proudly atop the serpent, feet planted firm on its scales, hair blowing majestically in the wind (conveniently ignoring that it was less than ten centimeters long at the time), and often in a dress. (Skirts, I suppose, blow more majestically than trousers.) None of them show me dangling for dear life from the serpent's nostril. However prosaic the reality of my act, though, it made for very good storytelling later on, and I am not surprised it became so widely known. The crew of the Scirling ships had seen it; the Yelangese had seen it; the islanders had seen it. My son had not, and I thank heaven for that, as it was bad enough once he heard the tale of what his mother had done. But I made myself well and truly famous with that act, which many say ended the Battle of Keonga.

NINETEEN

Reality, again, is somewhat less dramatic. The fighting continued; the Yelangese were not vanquished for some time, and then only because it occurred to Admiral Longstead that he could gain a degree of goodwill from both sides by moving in to halt what would otherwise have been a long grind to the finish. The Scirlings ended up playing peacemaker between the two sides, at first militarily, then diplomatically, once the princess stepped in.

The process by which that occurred was a marvel of misdirection, and even now I am not sure how it was arranged. No one wanted to say out loud where Her Highness had been; there were too many onlookers, ranging from some of the Yelangese sailors to the men of the *Basilisk* to a surprising percentage of the islanders, both local and visiting with the war fleet, who did not know she had been on Lahana. Admitting the truth would not have made anyone look terribly good. So everyone pretended she had come in with the fleet; that Suhail and I had never flown away on a stolen caeliger; and that when I rode into battle on the back of a seaserpent, I did so from the shores of Lahana, where I had been recuperating after my harrowing first ride. There were rumours, of course—there are always rumours—but it has never, until now, been public knowledge that Her Majesty was once a political hostage in the Broken Sea. (I would not reveal it here, save that I have royal permission to do so.)

All of that, however, came later. In the immediate aftermath of my deed, Suhail and I floundered in the water, putting as much distance as possible between us and the downed caeliger. The sea-serpent had decided that vehicle was the cause of its suffering, and set about destroying the thing with all dispatch. The Yelangese crewmen floundered with us, and one seemed to have a notion of setting upon us as the sea-serpent had upon the caeliger; but fortunately he was forestalled by the arrival of a longboat. Men aboard the *Boyne*, one of the other ships in Admiral Longstead's little fleet, had seen me go over the side and, not having any notion of what was going on, had set out to rescue me.

The sailors pulled us in, then took on the Yelangese, who judged that captivity in Scirling hands was preferable to remaining in the water with an angry sea-serpent that might soon go looking for new prey. It had done quite a good job on the caeliger, considering all the dragonbone; the bones themselves had survived its bite, but the lashings had not, and so the waves were now littered with a motley osteological assortment.

When the battle was done, we came ashore on Keonga, escorted by a dozen war canoes. There the chief greeted Admiral Longstead, but I saw very little of that meeting: Liluakame wormed her way through the crowd to my side, the first friendly face I had seen, and beckoned for me to follow her. "Where are we going?" I asked. Fear sprang up in my heart. I could think of no reason that my wife should be there, but not my companions or my son, save that something dreadful had happened to them.

"To the temple," Liluakame said. "Quickly."

This was the platform I had seen when we first came to Keonga, high upon the promontory that divided the *Basilisk*'s cove from the place where the chief dwelt. There were still a few sailors up there,

watching over the cannon Aekinitos had brought up for the battle, but I did not pause to speak with them. Apart from reassuring me that the others were safe and well, Liluakame had
discouraged any conversation. This was a side to my wife I had not
seen before, in our brief cohabitation: focused and urgent, taking
me in hand as if I were a child she could not spare the time to
educate. Weary and confused as I was, I found myself happy to
follow her lead.

The temple itself was a modest structure by Scirling standards,
but an impressive feat of engineering for the islanders, being a series of stone platforms and low walls constructed entirely without mortar. The walls demarcate a system of enclosures, the inner
ones being more *tapu* than the outer, and ceremonies of different
sorts are performed at different locations depending on their nature. Liluakame took me only within the outermost enclosure, that
being the only one I was considered fit to enter. There I found
Heali'i waiting.

She led me through a process of purification and repentance,
which, she said, might earn me a degree of mercy from Pa'oarakiki
when he was done with Admiral Longstead. (Suhail, I later learned,
had been taken to a temple the warriors use.) She spoke as if the
transgression for which I repented was departing from Keonga
against orders, and that indeed was part of it; I did not ask whether
she knew my crime was greater still. *Ke'anaka'i* were believed to
die if they set foot upon Rahuahane, yet I had gone and lived. I
suspect Heali'i knew, but to this day I cannot tell you what she
made of that: whether she questioned my identity as dragon-
spirited, or the reality of the curse upon that island, or merely
chalked me up as a very fortunate exception.

My Scirling companions were waiting outside the temple when
I emerged. Jake flung his arms around my middle hard enough to
squeeze all the breath from me; Abby did much the same. Tom,

looking more haggard than usual, tried to offer me his hand; I flung my arms around him instead, and damned what the gossips might say if they heard. The last few days had been distressing enough that I could not be content with a mere handshake.

Fortunately, dealing with two errant birds was not particularly high on the Keongan agenda, not with the aftermath of the battle to address. Four of the Yelangese ships had fled, but that still left the islanders with a great many prisoners to sort out, agreements to settle, and other matters to arrange. All of us from the *Basilisk* were told to remain in the area of our cove, where the sailors alternately worked on repairs or stood around and gossiped about recent events, depending on how closely Aekinitos was watching them. I fear I may have doomed them to a lot of profane shouting, for I was not free to tell the captain where I had been and what I had done, and the lack made him as grumpy as he had been when he broke his leg.

There I remained for three days, until Heali'i came to us once more.

"You are lucky," she said. "Because you made sacrifices at the temple"—sacrifices of flowers, I should say; I do not want anyone thinking I cut a pig's throat—"you are only to be sent away."

"Sent away?" I repeated, as if I had not understood her. I had spent those three days planning another excursion to the peak of Homa'apia, so as to give the sea-serpents time to calm themselves. My research had scarcely begun. How could I leave?

Heali'i gave me a look which said I should be grateful for my good fortune. "Yes. You earned great *mana* with your deeds, but you also violated *tapu*. Even *ke'anaka'i* can only go so far, and this one does not have that protection." She nodded at Suhail. "You must leave, and not return."

I had been exiled from Bayembe, but by my own government; I had been deported from Yelang, but as a result of political machinations I deplored in any case. This was the first time I had been sent away by the people whose goodwill I had hoped to earn, and it stung me deeply. Telling myself that I *had* earned their goodwill—that was why I was not being threatened with execution—did little to assuage the hurt.

But I could not argue, for Admiral Longstead had no intention of leaving me on Keonga in any case. The diplomatic arrangements the princess had made were delicate things; he could not risk me trampling all over them. And trample I would, even if I did not mean to, simply by the nature of my involvement with preceding events. I had stolen a caeliger from the Yelangese navy; I had violated *tapu* in Keonga; I knew far more than was good for anybody about what had really transpired with Her Highness. He wanted me well away from this place before I made anything worse.

The *Basilisk*, unfortunately, was not yet seaworthy, though supplies from the little Scirling fleet meant she was close to it. So it was that we found ourselves bundled onto the *Boyne*, the smallest of the admiral's three ships, and bound for the port of Phetayong: myself and Suhail, of course, for we had been exiled, but also Tom, Jake, and Abby, for they would not be separated from us.

It was a bitter leave-taking. I divorced Liluakame before I went, breaking the promise of marriage in order to fulfill my promise of freedom. She thanked me with a brilliant smile, no doubt already dreaming of her sweetheart. I would not have wanted to take her to Scirland regardless, nor would she have wanted to go; and yet it was peculiar to bid farewell to someone who, for however short a time and under whatever strange pretenses, had been my wife. But I was lucky even to have that farewell: I had no opportunity to speak with the other islanders we had come to know, such as the men who took us to ride the sea-serpent. Furthermore, I could not stop thinking of the work I was leaving undone. I had hoped to make a stealthy visit to Rahuahane when the *Basilisk* departed; that was now barred to me. I could not return to the peak of Homa'apia and continue observing the fire-lizards there. I could not question Heali'i about the stories her people told of the creatures that had dwelt on the cursed island, to see what nuggets of truth might have survived the intervening centuries of narrative embroidery. I had only my notes, my memories, and the petrified egg, which I had retrieved from the admiral's flagship.

Heali'i's final words to me before I departed were, "Do not be so sad. You are dragon-spirited. Your soul will return here when you die." I suppose she meant it to be comforting.

In Phetayong we sorted out our affairs and waited for the *Basilisk* to rejoin us. The admiral had at least been kind enough to send us with a letter of credit, so we could afford a respectable hotel; if that was the princess' idea (and I think it may have been), then I am grateful to her for it.

I struggled with the question of what to report to the *Winfield Courier*. I had been out of contact since before the *Basilisk* was wrecked; how could I resume the thread of my narrative now? I must account for more than two months of silence and explain what had transpired during my absence, but the full story could not possibly fit into a single missive. Furthermore, some parts of it must be omitted—Rahuahane, the caeliger, Her Royal Highness— but I could not pretend nothing had occurred, for stories would soon be reaching home by other routes, and what I said must not look like a falsehood.

You may see the result in *Around the World in Search of Dragons*, and entertain yourself by comparing that text with this one to find the points of divergence. It is a brief account, which sufficed for the moment, if not very well; by the time I returned to Scirland, word of the battle had reached audiences there, and I was pressed into telling a much more detailed story. But by then I was prepared to do so.

The *Basilisk* rejoined us a little over a week later, bearing in its hold the diving bell we had abandoned on the reef of Keonga. It was a gesture of friendship from Aekinitos to Suhail, and did much to make us feel as if the proper order of our expedition had been restored. We made energetic plans to sail to Ala'ase'ama, where (as many of you know) I resumed my study of fire-lizards.

Before we could depart, however, our arrangements underwent a sudden and unexpected change.

A packet of mail found us in Phetayong, having in some cases chased us from port to port for months. It was like receiving letters from another lifetime, so far had the world of my correspondents faded from my thoughts. I learned that the *Journal of Maritime Studies* would be publishing my article with its incorrect theory of sea-serpent evolution, and dashed off a note begging them to withhold it until I could write a new version; this, alas, did not arrive in time. I read and answered a great many other letters . . . and, in so doing, discovered at last what rumours had grown from my supposedly innocuous reports.

My first instinct was to burn the letters and pretend I had never read them. After all, the rumours merited no better treatment. But it was not fair to hide something that involved another person, and so, after much pacing (and more cursing than I should admit to), I went in search of Suhail.

I found him on the shore near the docks, slumped against the algae-covered stump of a post, a letter fluttering in his hands. It was covered in flowing lines of Akhian script; that much I saw before he noticed me and put it away, though he knew I could not have read it regardless. "Is everything all right?" I asked him. Surely, I thought, rumours from Scirland had not reached his own people—not so quickly, at least.

My question was a foolish one. I knew by his expression that everything was not all right. Before he saw me and put the letter away, he was as grim as I had ever seen him, though now he looked resigned. "A message from home," he said. "My father has died."

"Oh," I said. Words seemed to have escaped me entirely. Here I had been fretting over scurrilous gossip, as if the tattered state of my reputation were the most important thing in the world. I felt ashamed of myself. "My condolences."

Suhail shook his head. He seemed to be dismissing my unspoken imputation of grief. I still knew nothing of his family, save that he was estranged from them to a sufficient degree that he did not even use their names. Whatever had lain between him and his father, it meant he did not weep now.

"Thank you," he said, as if realizing that a shake of the head was not a proper response to condolences. "But I'm afraid it means I must return to Akhia."

I blinked. "What—now?"

"Yes."

The grimness was there again, a stony layer beneath the resignation. "Yes, of course; how foolish of me. Your family will want you with them at a time like this."

"It is not that—not precisely. Rather—" Suhail caught himself, stopped, and shook his head again. "It does not matter. But I will not be able to go with you to Ala'ase'ama."

My heart sank. I had, without realizing it, begun thinking of him as a member of our expedition, fully as much a part of my work as Tom was. But chance had brought him to me, and now chance would take him away again.

I have written before about the regret I feel upon parting from the individuals I come to know in my travels. This parting, I confess, struck deeper than any other. Suhail had weathered more trials at my side than anyone save Tom; with him I shared secrets I could not even permit Tom to know. My association with him was not respectable—and I would bear the consequences of that for some time—but I had come to treasure it. Only a determination not to end our partnership by embarrassing myself kept me from showing the depths of that loss.

To conceal it, I reached into my pocket and took out my little notebook, then tore a page from it and scribbled a few brief lines. "Here," I said, giving it to Suhail. "That is my direction in Falchester. I hope you will at least write to me, as occasion permits."

He accepted it with a smile that was a mere ghost of its usual brightness. I noticed that he took care not to brush my fingers as he did so: we had returned once more to propriety. "Thank you," he said. "And I wish you the best of luck in the rest of your journey. Peace be upon you, *sadiqati*"—which means "my friend" in the Akhian tongue.

By the next evening he was gone, having taken passage on a ship bound for Elerqa. That quickly, he was lost to me, and the melancholy of it stayed with me for a long time after.

There is little I can say about the remainder of the expedition that would hold a tenth so much interest as what has come before. I will instead speak of what happened after I returned to Scirland, which was not documented in my reports to the *Winfield Courier*, nor collected in my travelogue afterward.

Part of it is widespread knowledge regardless. As I had predicted, Tom became a Fellow of the Colloquium, because of the work he had done during our expedition. It both pleased and

Thomas Wilker

saddened him: acceptance from that body was a goal we both pursued, but his Fellowship did not magically transform the world around him into one where his birth did not matter. He had not expected it, but the disappointment was there nonetheless.

The Colloquium did not unbend so far as to admit me to their ranks, but the following Acinis, in a grand ceremony of the Synedrion, the king inducted me into the Order of the White Horn, making me Dame Isabella Camherst. Officially, this honour was given in gratitude for my courage and quick action in saving the fort at Point Miriam from attack by the Ikwunde army. The Crown had reviewed those events and concluded that, accusations of treason notwithstanding, I had indeed acted in the best interests of Scirland, and so they wished to reward me. (This did not, however, prevent the aforementioned unnamed member of the Synedrion from drawing me aside and reminding me that I was still under no circumstances permitted to return to Bayembe.)

That story, of course, was cover for the truth, which is that I was knighted for my part in the rescue of Her Highness: the woman who now rules as our queen. This, again, was Her Highness' doing, but naturally none of us could speak of it directly. Admiral Longstead had told me before I left Keonga that any whisper of that matter would see me put on trial and likely imprisoned, and so I held my tongue.

It is often said that the poor are insane, while the rich are merely eccentric. So it is with knighthood, I discovered: as Mrs. Camherst I was disreputable, but as Dame Isabella Camherst, I was just scandalous enough to be worth inviting places. The more frivolously social invitations I declined, but the Nyland Brothers approached me about publishing my travelogue as *Around the World in Search of Dragons*, which sold through its first edition in less than two months, and I soon embarked upon a lecture tour throughout the kingdom. If my audiences at times asked more questions about my personal life than my professional work, and if I suffered the occasional heckler who chose to mock my retraction of my sea-serpent theory, I took care not to complain where any but my closest friends could hear.

As pleasing as these developments were (not to mention a welcome improvement to my financial situation), I found myself wishing for the peace and quiet of my Hart Square townhouse, where I might work on the material I had gathered during my expedition.

Much of this work concerned my taxonomical questions. I had learned my lesson from the premature publication of that article in the *Journal of Maritime Studies*; I would not publish this theory until I was certain of its strength, and moreover could prove it with an abundance of supporting evidence. As it transpired, that evidence would not come into my hands for some years yet, but in the interim I accomplished a great deal that laid the groundwork for the discoveries that would follow.

I also took up a hobby that puzzled many around me. I told everyone I was interested in the fossils then being uncovered in several parts of the world, and in pursuit of that, I studied with both a sculptor and a lapidary, learning to cut and carve stone.

My true aim, of course, was the dissection of the petrified egg. It sat for the better part of a year on one of my bookshelves, seeming like nothing more than a stone carving of an egg (which is what I told everyone it was). Given the wealth of firestone concealed inside, I could not trust its dissection to an outsider; I must learn to do the work myself. When at last I deemed myself ready, I made a plaster cast of the egg, weighted the cast with lead (so the housekeeper would not notice a change in its mass), and began the process of extracting the embryo within.

First I chipped away the rocky exterior, which had formerly been the shell. The mass of firestone glowed with muted light, its usual brilliance dimmed by sheer thickness. I held an inconceivable fortune in my hands, and was about to cut it to pieces. (Somewhere, I fancied, the lapidary who had taught me gem-carving was weeping inconsolably, and did not know why.)

I was more concerned with what the firestone held. When I held it up to a lamp, I could see the outline of the embryo within, and nearly melted with relief. For a year I had worried that the egg we carried away from Rahuahane would prove to be sterile, or that its contents would have been destroyed by the petrification.

With the greatest of care, I carved my way toward the nearest extension of the embryo. When I broke through, however, my disappointment was intense: instead of a bone, I found only a dust-filled hollow. I had hoped the petrification process was like that which preserved dragonbone, and that I might extract the skeleton entire. To find nothing but dust so discouraged me that I gave up for the day, hiding the egg where the maid would not find it.

I woke up in the middle of the night with a fresh idea. Natalie, woken by the noise of me banging about, found me carefully pouring plaster into that hollow. "What on earth are you doing?" she asked.

"Taking a cast of where the skeleton was," I said. (She and Tom both knew of my inadvertent visit to Rahuahane, and what Suhail and I had found there.) "If I am very careful, I may yet be able to learn something."

"Could you not learn it during daylight hours?" Natalie asked, yawning. But by then I had enough money that I need not worry at all about the expense of candles or lamp oil, and I went on working.

The entire process took weeks. I would carve until I neared a hollow, then drill through and fill it with plaster. When I had done this with all the easily accessible portions, I removed them and began the procedure anew with the deeper portions. The vacuoles did not quite form a continuous whole, and so I had to take my casts in stages, pausing each time to draw the current appearance of the mass, in order to be certain I could reassemble the plaster in the correct configuration afterward.

But at last it was done, and I could see what manner of dragon the ancients of Draconean civilization had been breeding.

"It's like nothing I've ever seen," Tom said when I showed it to him.

"Indeed," I said. "I have already ordered several books on embryology; they should be delivered soon." (We knew virtually nothing of draconic embryology in those days, and do not know nearly enough about it now, though our understanding has at least advanced from the total disgrace it once was.)

Tom bent to peer at the lumpy, imperfect casts, which I had wired together in my best approximation of their original posture. "The tail and wings are clearly not well-developed yet—the tail in particular," he said.

"Perhaps full development of the tail came after hatching. Human children, after all, are born with strikingly different proportions than they attain as adults." I turned the casts around so he might view them from another angle. "Underdeveloped wings are certainly to be expected; it is a common feature of birds. But the jointing of the legs—well, it is difficult to make out, given the state of the casts. But it seems peculiar. I cannot tell whether this is an ordinary stage in draconic embryo development, or whether it indicates an extinct species."

"Or one not yet discovered—though that seems less likely, especially nowadays." Tom straightened and grinned at me. "Admit it. You are already planning how to gather specimens of dragon eggs so that you can dissect them and sketch out the sequence of development."

I could not help returning his smile. "You only guess that because your thoughts tended in the same direction. But yes, I need comparative materials. It might go quite some way toward reconciling the stories of the Draconeans with the reality of modern dragons if the ones they tamed were in fact a species that has since gone extinct."

Tom gestured at the casts. "Will you be publishing this?"

The question made me hesitate. It is a scientist's obligation to share what she learns; only then may others examine her work and find where it is wanting. Nor can a single person discover everything there is to know, which makes it imperative that those investigating a topic build on each other's efforts. But my error with the sea-serpent theory had left me shy of publishing anything I was not certain of—and besides, there was the matter of where and how I had acquired this specimen. I did not want to send treasure-hunters flocking to Rahuahane.

"Not yet," I said slowly. "It must be known eventually, yes—and I will write it up, though not send the paper to anyone, so that if something happens to me the information will not be lost. But I do not feel that I am ready to share this with others until I know more."

In hindsight, I am more glad than ever that I made that choice. Ordinarily I believe secrecy to be anathema in scientific endeavours; in this case, however, it allowed subsequent events to fall out in a fashion rather more controlled than it might otherwise have been.

But as I so often do, I get ahead of myself. The answers I sought lay some years in my future still; they would have to wait upon news from Bayembe and fresh work in other parts of the world. The treasure I had retrieved from Rahuahane, though, was not the pile of poorly carved firestone stuffed in a hatbox at the top of my wardrobe. It was that plaster cast, and all of the questions it created.